LOVE IS STRANGE

by the same author

fiction

POOR SOULS

THIS IS IT

STUFF

SUMMER THINGS

WINTER BREAKS

IT CAN'T GO ON

S.O.S.

THE WORKS

non-fiction

COLLECTING MODERN FIRST EDITIONS

P. G. WODEHOUSE

JEROME K. JEROME: A CRITICAL BIOGRAPHY

MODERN FIRST EDITIONS: THEIR VALUE TO COLLECTORS

THE PENGUIN BOOK QUIZ BOOK

CHILDREN'S MODERN FIRST EDITIONS

BESIDE THE SEASIDE

ALL SHOOK UP: A FLASH OF THE FIFTIES

CHRISTMAS

WODEHOUSE

JOSEPH CONNOLLY

Love is Strange

faber and faber

First published in 2005
by Faber and Faber Limited
3 Queen Square London WC1N 3AU
This paperback edition published in 2006

Photoset by RefineCatch Ltd, Bungay, Suffolk
Printed in England by Mackays of Chatham plc, Chatham, Kent

A CIP record for this book
is available from the British Library

ISBN 978-0-571-22709-9
ISBN 0-571-22709-0

2 4 6 8 10 9 7 5 3 1

To the memory of
Giles Gordon
and
Alexander Walker

People don't understand
They think lovin'
Is having money in the hand.

'Love Is Strange', Smith/Baker, 1965

THE END

This then, I know it, just has to be the closing: the very last moments of my life. And although I clutch at them keenly, still I am failing to hold on to even any small part of the matter in hand: this business of my teasingly gentle but inevitable passing. The only concerns that storm now into what, I suppose, is still this mind of mine, assume the form of shadowy and puny, suddenly stuttering and then quite gorgeous highlights from it has to be, yes, a truly terrible past. Sex: the sweet and rank hit of it (of course there must be that) – but more, the thrill of the struggle, the ripping out of the darkness during all those fantastic and midnight abductions . . . and now seeping into me (of course, but naturally – for how could I escape it?) the insinuation of a spreading stain (its slick and wicked glimmer).

And now – as I lie here quite uselessly – I recall when Melissa, she smiled and then she said to me: You do know Clifford, that I have no limit? For love – for you – I would happily do anything. But, my Clifford, Clifford of mine, you must know too I won't ever do that. And nor did she. But before, my life had been shaken asunder by the runaway train that was, shall we call her for now, the only other woman who ever truly mattered. And the love and all my good intentions went at first just sour and then so very wrong, and quickly after, oh – quite bad, before a black enough sin came then to be so deep drenched in crime, and this pulsing locomotive that I had so eagerly boarded, it roared and was shrieking as it just jackknifed up and away into Hell, booming and gleeful as it took us all on down (I becalmed, and she – clinging so hard on to what I suppose she still and most sincerely imagined to be something a bit close to my soul and centre – screaming . . . and then, yes – oh yes then: screaming wildly). She would, I am sure, laugh away hideously – my blackly glittering lady – any such mad suggestion that here was truly the way things had gone. Should she deign to acknowledge at all the awful chain of events. And just this is to assume, of course – in the glare of, oh . . . everything she has inflicted upon, God, so very many – that she, so newly fastidious, would choose to remember even any tiny atom. And now – as I lie here quite uselessly – I must be content with a sort of cold refuge in the narrow truth that she has now no longer the power to reach me.

There are people, you know: seemingly looking down upon me from here and there and all around (as I continue to lie here, quite uselessly). I do not appear able to recognise, however, who any single one of them might possibly be – and nor, if I am wholly honest, can I be sure of their comportment, the very nature and essence of the gathering (not even – and now I am straining my hardest – their collective or separate genders). *Known* to me, presumably – why else, goodness, would they all be milling about me, here? Wherever here might be. It seems quite white and charged: I feel enveloped by a hostile welcome.

Speech would appear to be out of the question – and even were it not, what is it, exactly, that you would have me utter into the face of this distorted and coagulant mass of unimagined features (swooping down, and fading back)? This, it occurs to me now, is maybe all a baby can ever be aware of, marooned and pinioned in a pram, when all around are gurning and gesturing wildly in their blank determination to vie for the little creature's exclusive attention, regardless of not just its supreme impassivity, but even its palpable terror.

So I think, you know, all I can do now is simply latch on to and settle down deeply into the folds of just one and no more from among this boisterous and jostling tumult within me – just a single raucous upstart amid the crowd of all these jagged and glancing memories of mine. But not. I really don't think, the kidnaps or the slaying. I feel too weak to face that, frankly. Maybe soon, but no – not now: not at all *yet*. So possibly . . . mmm, it just has to be, really, my wedding day, yes. Yes – the day of my wedding: that will do nicely. The day of my marriage to the heaven of Melissa and a touchstone, truly, to the start of all this: everything I am brought to (just lying here, quite uselessly). The start of when it became so twisted and all began to go so very badly wrong (though well before the uncut purity of the evil, before it had come close to just killing me).

So for now, then – let us hear those wedding bells ring out, their clamorous pealing summoning me back with a fresh and candid urgency to that distant sunlit morning, filled and sweet with love and hope, all those years and years ago.

♠

The suite at the Savoy – oh yes, I well recall all that, the tracts of its mirrored and comfortingly creamy, so near powder-soft opulence – made me feel, mmm – it very nearly suffused me with . . . well what, now? Safety, I think, comes as close as I feel I can approach – a sort of safety, yes, as I just dumbly stood there, rigid at its centre. It was the only thing that day that fed me – and yet I was excited (though hardly nurtured) by just the possibility (and there was one, wasn't there?) of justified hope and maybe even an illuminated future looming – one so bright, indeed, that it would in the merest of flashes strike down blind all the past and render it no more now than a dazzle of doubt, too instant and fragmented, maybe, to have even existed; or possibly it would just take light and burn and smoulder and crumble down to only ashes. And the love – the love would triumph, surely, as love is always said to. If love was what we had here – if love was the stuff we were dealing with now, and not just something strange.

Oh and Melissa, I might add – and should anyone be passingly interested, then they might as well hear it from me – was not my first and only wife. There had been, in fact, one more before her. Well *two*, if we are seeking the strictest accuracy – but the very first, whose name will come to me, I have no doubt, as I continue to dwell upon details and other things entirely (as is, I find, so often the way), was – as, indeed, I was myself – no more than sixteen years of age. We were married on a ferry boat by a rank and grizzled oaf who, if memory serves, had styled himself Captain. On the isle of Jersey, she had seemed thrilled while imagining us to be consummating our blessed and beloved union; in truth – and even as she continued to preen and twitter – I unsmilingly raped her, which felt quite wonderful, I can tell you that. I made the return crossing on my own (I just walked out and left her) and more I cannot tell you: more I do not know.

And then there had been Sonya – who was not, as one could easily suppose, a Russian, remotely exotic, or even very interesting in any way at all. I married her when she asked me to do so. She was just a good woman, my Sonya – she looked after me devotedly for more than three or five years as I continued to do no more than just about passably well in my chosen profession. Which is – did I mention? – that of tailoring. I know – fairly bizarre: not at all what you might expect. It wasn't, of course, the path for which I was initially destined. Disinter my father and

4

quiz him on the matter, if you've a mind to: he will doubtless still be both purple and raving (into the fungus, into the ether). But simple goodness, I can only suppose, came to disagree with me. I left Sonya. I just left her. She wailed and clawed at me as I walked through the door. Sent her some money – not too much. She wrote to say she could not bear a divorce (she loved me too much!) and I, for my part, was perfectly content to let things so remain.

Melissa, then – she was later. Her I came to marry in the face of the cold and very dangerous fury of the blackly glittering lady – because her I had known for just ever and ever: always she was there. She had not at all objected to my marriage to Sonya: it pleased her, I think, to have someone close by whom she could upon a whim subject to bitter ridicule, or else a more serious torrent and pitiless damage. Melissa, however, she minded a great deal. *Me*, she kept on intoning: it should be *me* – it was meant to be *me* . . .! And her eyes at times like that: they made you sick and hot with stripped-raw fear.

Mary. Yes Mary – that is the name of the child, the little girl thing I married the very first time around. There: I knew it would come to me. It always does, if you just remain patient. Though as to all this apparently serial bigamy (trigamy, I suppose it is now – all rather hard to keep track) I cannot altogether make plain to you (I can't quite see it myself) why or how it has come to pass. Why I failed to instigate the business of divorce before blithely entering into yet another of my marriages. And consequences. I am all too aware, are always lurking: they are always just waiting to pounce.

A thought now occurs to me: it could be quite amusing, should you feel open to the very idea (should the mood just happen to have you), if my only real and licit wife after all these decades have tumbled by is still the little girl thing, the ferryboat child, my sweet and dear rapee. Mary: there – I hadn't forgotten.

5

Oh and did you happen to get that, did you? Just that moment as I said it? The heavy and immutable word that I didn't truly imagine I had just dropped in, oh so gently? *Decades*. Yes – that one. Tens of years, tens of years, the rolling on and forward of all those tens of years. And then to find myself on the verge of one more marriage. Which is, I quite see, a fairly foolish situation, on the face of it. And yet . . . experience, that is the key. When a man is my age (and I don't seem able at the moment to quite know what that is) he should not shrink from pointing with pride to the wealth of his various achievements. The generation of tens of millions of pounds and several directorships while still a relatively young man. One of the faster times recorded on the Cresta Run. A rather major literary prize and a decent sort of honour from the Queen. The giddily joyful deflowering of twin blonde beauties on subsequent afternoons. Stealing – at dead of night and from close to the Ritz – a deep indigo Bugatti and then kissing it goodbye, filled with flowers and not much short of the brow of Primrose Hill. To have devoured with slurping and red-cheeked relish thirteen dozen Colchester natives at a single sitting! And swilled them well down with a magnum of Krug, sucked with glee through a crystal straw. That subtle approach at Heathrow one time from a representative of a leading model agency, and declining politely (one hopes with polished grace). Membership of not just White's and Pratt's and Boodle's, but also the Athenaeum, the Garrick and . . . what's that other one? Beefsteak. A newspaper column, twice weekly and internationally syndicated. An open invitation to a position in the Cabinet . . . diving down to the wreck of the *Titanic* for romantic plunder . . . a guaranteed place on the first British shuttle to outer space . . .! Oh yes. Oh yes indeed. All of this – and so much more – has eluded me utterly. All I have done is bad for me, and so much worse for others. But as to marriage . . . oh good Lord. Why would I? Why would I do it again? 'A bit of company'? But

I had company, didn't I? The blackly glittering lady, we are extant partners in each other's company, and have been during the course of every breath we have ever drawn. Oh well. It is becoming clear I have no answer.

And I can't, I think, any longer refer to her (can I?) as the blackly glittering lady. I enjoy the phrase, as well might have been gathered – and it surely does pick up on this quite recent polish of hers (her excitement and her danger); nonetheless, it is signally unwieldy. What I call her to her face (and now we are here, let me ask you: do you imagine it, this face of hers, to be broad and high-cheekboned, the wide and insistent eyes – they that glitter – as dark a brown as brown can be before it becomes lost to sight in the deadness of onyx, just two flecks of white to flag up the life beyond? Is that at all how you see her, the blackly glittering lady? Well if so then no, I'm afraid: she's really not at all like that). But to this face – the skin is sometimes shockingly pale, though a flush of rouge is never far away from the heart of the thing – I address her as Emerald. Which isn't really right. But this is what I do. For myself (when we spent that day, sorting out stones) I adjudged Ruby to be good and clearer – but no, she said: oh no no no. Ruby has quite the wrong connotations, as she patiently explained to me. One thinks of cheap port and even cheaper barmaids who might sloppingly dispense it (although I hadn't, until she put it to me, thought of that at all: all I saw was a blood-deep and glistening jewel). Emerald, she said, is what it has to be. And then she started to call me Diamond – and it's always best not, on the whole, to enquire. I mean to say (and I've thought of it a bit – not too much or often), did she hastily decide that here to hand was a pretty and simple pairing? Two treasured gemstones, and please let's just leave it like that? Or did she perceive in me notable properties? An acknowledged value, this hardness (if not durability) and a bright white light within? I doubt. Could the facets, maybe, have come into play? What on earth can I tell you? It's not for me to say. But neither name is right for us, although they continued to be mutually bandied right on up to this, my wedding day. No – Emerald and Diamond, and I have always thought this, they are each of them – in any sense you care for – far too pure and precious. Jet, is what I should have called her. Jet is what she is. And me? Well how the Devil do you expect me to know? I simply couldn't tell you; but if you came to press me . . . well in that case, maybe Jade?

Well right, then: very well. Enough of all that. It is time to find out now whether even such a hope as this might ever be justified – time for the gates and my arms to be both swung wide so as to welcome and enable this love for Melissa to triumph (as love is always said to). If . . . love is what we have here. If . . . love is the stuff we're dealing with, now . . . and not just something strange. So what I must do is . . . What I must do . . . What I must . . . What I . . . What. *What* . . .?

But wait: hold. The cord of my memory is tugging me elsewhere. There is an obstacle now that I am very aware of – some big reason why I can no longer pursue this. All my face is throbbing to the bone, and now I am conscious (as conscious as I can be, now and for the last time, as I continue to lie here quite uselessly) of a man now hovering above me who I have seen here before – a man who long ago I had decided was a doctor (there is something about his grimness, his quick and quite unflinching insolence). Just look at him now: he has done with plucking at what sad flesh there is left to my cheek and is pulling quite roughly at I am unsure quite which of the watery pouches slung beneath these eyes. His slack-lipped mouth would appear to be moving – he might be just chewing, or maybe saying something wise, or else grotesque. And from just behind the bulk of him there rises now a general sort of stirring – the shadows, they slant and shift, as dust and light are stark and jostling briefly, settling down soon into a gross rearrangement. I think I know I can give no sign, but what I feel sure I have just been party to is a further and maybe quite signal transition: one more strut has been rudely kicked from under my remains. They say – and I know you have heard it – that when one is aware that life and oneself are scudding away from you and yet just gently fading, when light and dark become oddly indecipherable, when any unspent muscle from somewhere deep within the general shambles is as near to clenched as it can be and flexing weakly on the rim of the final flight or tumble, that a fast-spliced and clattering cascade, momentarily agleam with each of life's exalted moments, will rattle across those dear searing eyeballs and leave one just able to gasp with fear and yet somehow sated, with no more left now save a final whimper before the last hurrah . . .

But no. Oh no no no. I scream in defiance at all of that. I am fighting hard and it will not happen; this doctor – if doctor he be – can pinch the other cheek, for now it is turned. If I am to go – and this is a given, we just have to accept it – then I intend to go my way, and in my own sweet Devil-given time. I want to go back to remembering. I do, I do – and for the life of me I fail to understand death's rush (for it has me anyway). And so now I am determined to go back further and further – all the way back to the very beginning. To where the colonnade of one's endeavours and all those milestones along the way recede into the dagger-point of a whiter sort of distant invisibility. The beginning, then: let's go there, while I still feel able to barely withstand this terrible thing. The beginning, yes – for where else (at the end) can I run to for shelter?

MORNING

I was young, so young – oh dearest God, I was just a little child. But how young, though, do I think I can have been? Must it really be all those tens of years ago if I still can recall it all so clearly (so clear it is) and yes, so utterly? Not just the simple words and sniffled noises of this single exchange from among millions with my mother, but the rise, rise and gentle falling of each and every cadence, the sometimes throaty and the very much more nasal sighings as she looked away, or downwards; the creases at her eyes as she did so, and those sharper ones too at the corners of her mouth, the puckering and stylised striations ranked up like powdered needles above her chin that gave her still-sweet lips just the faintest air of having been coaxingly poached in buttermilk, and left now to cool. The smell of her fingers – quite old grease from the knobs on the cooker and then just a feather's breath of lavender (that touch of hardness in the fingertips, not at all like the plump and fleshy pillows of her palm when it fondly cupped my cheek, a warm thumb idly stroking the down there, once). I smelt then the sticky slap of that powder, as it clung to the rouge: I sometimes touched with the pad of a finger this peachy and motherly dusting. I knew that face, and loved it; for years I needed it so much more than my heart, my limbs and eyes, for its presence alone could make me function, make me see – that face, and the dear sad woman who showed it to me . . . here were not just the boundaries of my being but much more so, its palpitating core.

'Here, Clifford – here. Do you want to open the packet of tea?'

'Oh gosh yes, Mummy – give it to me. Didn't know we got a new one. Oh I really hope it's the Bird of Paradise – I jolly do, I jolly do. I'm only missing four now.'

'I think I know that, Clifford my sweet. You've told and told me for days on end. Don't do it like that – you're tearing it all down the side, look.'

'Well you're going to put it in the tin thing anyway, aren't you? Just four more cards to get and then the whole album's complete. Ooh – here it is – got it. What is it? What is it?'

'What is it, Clifford? Let me see. Is it the—?'

'It's the Barn Owl. It's the Barn Owl.'

'Oh dear. Never mind. Maybe next time.'

'No no, Mummy – the Barn Owl's *good*. Haven't got the Barn Owl. Only *three* to go now. Just three more. Oh great. I'll just get the album and then I can stick it in.'

'Oh you *are* lucky, Clifford. Aren't you, my pet? You haven't really had very many duplicates at all, have you?'

'Well I kept on getting the Egret for ages – but Brian and Anthony, they didn't have the Egret at all and so I brought in two of mine and then I swapped them for, um – Harry, old Dismal, he gave me the Grebe, and then I got the Kittiwake off of Anthony.'

'Is this Anthony Parsfield? Not "off of", Clifford. From. You got the card *from* Anthony. Not "off of".'

'Oh *crumbs* no! Not Anthony *Parsfield*. He's never got anything decent to swap *ever*, old Parsfield. Old parson's nose *Parsfield*.'

'That's not a very nice thing to call him. I thought he was a friend of yours?'

'Oh *crumbs* no! He's not my friend. He sort of used to be *kind* of my friend, but that was last term. I'm talking about Anthony *Hirsch*. It was Anthony *Hirsch* I got the Kittiwake off of.'

'Clifford . . .!'

'From, then. I got it *from* him. All right? I'm going to get the album.'

'Remember you've got your prep to get done, won't you? We're not doing the jigsaw till you've done all your prep.'

'I know, I know. Maths and Jog tonight. I really hate old man Meakins. He always gives us twice as much rotten prep as all the other masters. He's rotten, Meakins is. Mmmm – they always smell so great, these teacards. Smell! Here – smell it!'

'But you don't like tea, do you Clifford? You never drink tea. Mm – 'tis nice.'

'I know, I know – but I just love the smell of the *cards*. Hate tea. Horrid. I love *Tizer*! Tizer for ever!'

'Yes well – too much of that stuff and you'll have no teeth left.'

'It's just so yummy, Tizer. Can I have some now?'

'*Prep*, young man. Maybe if you're good – later. When we're jigsawing. Come here. Is that a mark on your pullover, there? Oh it's *not*, is it? How did you manage to do that? I hope it's not ink.'

'Where? Where's there a mark?'

'There – on the – come here and let me . . . oh it *is* ink, it *is*. Oh *Clifford* – how on earth did you manage to get it on your—?'

'Oh gosh that must have been when Pearson came round and did all the inkwells after break and he said there was no room in mine because of all the squidged-up blotch and he made me dig it all out and I had to use my dividers and they're bent now and I thought I'd been really good, actually, because I didn't get even a bit, not any, on my hands and fingers and everything. I didn't see that. Sorry.'

'Oh . . . I suppose it'll wash out. Now come on, you grubby little ragamuffin: *prep*.'

'I will. I'll just stick this card in. And then I will. I'm starving. Is there anything to eat? Absolutely *starving* . . .'

'Supper after *prep*, Clifford. The sooner you get it done, the sooner the four of us can all sit down and have supper. I'll give you some digestives on a plate. Would you like some Nesquik?'

'Oh. Daddy – he's in tonight then, is he? Not one of his out nights.'

'No – he's in. Daddy's in tonight. Do you want a glass of Nesquik or not?'

'It's just that he never likes it, does he? When we're doing the jigsaw and everything and he wants to listen to his music and he says it's *distracting*. He always says it's *distracting* and it's crazy you know, really, because we're ever so quiet. Are there any – have you got any choccy fingers?'

'Loves his music – it's Daddy's way of relaxing, isn't it? He works jolly hard, your Daddy, you know. We'll just have to try and be a little bit quieter. Now off you *go*, Clifford, or there'll be no time for supper or jigsaw or anything else before bedtime, will there? Nesquik: yes or no?'

'Mm, yes – Nesquik. I said yes. I said so.'

'You most certainly did *not*, young man. I've asked you twenty times. Look – you go off and I'll bring it to you on a tray, my lord and master. Off you go.'

'And choccy fingers . . .?'

'*Ooh* . . . you're a little rascal, aren't you Clifford? Mm? You really are a little rascal. I'll see what I can find. But only if you go off this *minute* and get that prep done. Clear?'

'Thanks, Mummy. I will. I'll just stick this card in. And then I will. Barn Owl – isn't it great? Just three more to get now. Where's the glue?'

'You had it last. Weren't you covering your exercise books at the weekend?'

'Oh yes. Didn't work. The covers kept on coming up again all over the place. Sticky tape's what I need and Daddy says it's too expensive. Anthony's got some on a *dispenser*. It's lousy, that glue. Doesn't stick anything. Hopeless.'

'Oh Clifford never *mind* about the glue! Just get your *prep* done, will you? *Now*, Clifford. This minute.'

'But I've got to stick the *card* in, haven't I? So I've got to find the glue first, haven't I? How can I stick it in if I haven't got the *glue* . . .?'

'Look for the glue *afterwards*, Clifford. Hoooo . . .! You go off and *I'll* find the blessed glue, all right? And I'll bring it in with your milk and biscuits. All right?'

'OK, then. I think it might be in the box room, actually. Thanks, Mummy. Hey – do you think we'll finish it tonight? I think we could. I think we could actually finish it tonight.'

'Finish *what*, now? Hm? What are you talking about *now*, Clifford?'

'Jigsaw. There's only the centre bit left. And that one edgy piece – which I don't actually think can be *there*, you know, because I've looked through the box about ten million times and it just doesn't exist, that edgy piece.'

'Never mind the – *Clifford*, if you don't get moving right this second there'll be no time for *anything*. Now I mean it: march, young man. Straight into that room and get it all done. If you're not hard at work when I come in with your tray . . . well then woe betide you, Clifford. There'll be wigs on the green, I can promise you that.'

'All right – I'll do it now. Rotten old Meakins . . . *No* other master gives half as much prep as Meakins, rotten old Meakins. Oh and Mummy . . .?'

'Oh what is it *now*, Clifford? You really are trying my patience.'

'It's just that . . . you won't forget the choccy fingers . . .?'

'Hoooo . . .! What am I going to do with you? Hm? What am I supposed to do with you, you naughty little scamp? Hm? Now *go*, Clifford, or there'll be no biscuits and no supper either. Scoot! Vamoose! Oh and remember to put a bar of the fire on. I don't want you catching cold. Ah – I think I heard the door. Was that the door, sweetheart? Did you hear it? That'll be your father.'

'Yes it was. I'm going now.'

♠

All the bedrooms are just upstairs – over that, there's only the dusty old loft. Mummy and Daddy's is at the front with a big it's called a bay window, if you want to know, which is just like the one in the sitting room downstairs, and it's got that sort of curvy wooden thing going all around it at the top, the one in Mummy and Daddy's room, and this is called a pelmet. There's this really huge wardrobe in there too with creepy creaky doors which is really dark and scary inside and it smells of lots of old stuff and of Daddy more than Mummy – his pipes, which remind me when you sniff at them of when there's a squishy old fruit at the bottom of the bowl and it's all gone sour and brown and yucky. Also his vests which are stringy ones and Aertex ones (and these are like Shreddies, only white) when he takes them off and puts them in the box in the bathroom with the cork on top. His shoes are all right, though – really really shiny when you slide your stockinged feet all over the smooth bit at the front and a smell that's a bit like wine gums, which I like a lot – a lot more than fruit gums anyway, and green is my favourite.

My room, that's at the end of the passage and just between Annette's and the box room. The box room isn't where people go and do boxing or anything, but it's got Mummy's sewing machine in it, which is called Singer (and I said but it never sings, does it? So why's it called Singer, then?) and it's black and the thing under the table that works it is called the treadle, which everyone knows, and also in there is the bureau with the flap that doesn't flap any more as well as piles of all different stuff that's far too good to throw away. Annette's room is bigger than mine because I measured it, and the window's bigger too, but that's because she's two years older than I am which is really unfair because she's the girl and I'm the boy and I think I should have the biggest room but Daddy said I could have it when I was just one year older than Annette and I said well when will that be because it could be ages and ages and he just said wait and see (which he does say quite a lot, actually – that and things are *distracting*) and I did wait, I waited, and then Anthony Hirsch at school, he just laughed at me and told me to stop being so thick and to just grow up because it wasn't ever going to happen no matter how long I waited because it was a simple law of basic mathematics. I know he's right now, and I feel like a bit of a twit. And talking of rotten old mathematics, I'd better get started, I suppose. The Jog – that won't take me five minutes; all we've got to do is trace a relief map from our textbook of Dogger Bank and colour it in. But the maths I don't really get because it's all about x's and y's as well as numbers and you've got to work out what they all equal and they've all got to equal the same, I'm pretty sure, so it's all a bit complicated. And there's just heaps and heaps of it because of rotten old Meakins – the whole of page 92 and nearly three-quarters of page 93 and he even goes mad if you blotch the line you've got to draw under your work with a ruler but he won't let us use a pencil for it and it's really hard with your Osmiroid because the nib goes all sort of cross-eyed when you press on it and then when you take the ruler away it goes all blotchy and then Meakins, he just goes mad. And I've got a biro, which is great. It is called Bic and you can see right

19

through it like glass and it's got a sort of tube of ink which goes right down the middle that you never have to fill up, which is really great. Anthony Hirsch has got them in blue (like mine, mine is blue) and also red and green and black and he wears them on the front of his blazer and they look great, really great. But Meakins – he won't even let us use them because he says they will ruin our handwriting which is totally mad, really, because in his class all we're doing is numbers and equals signs and pluses and stuff and rotten little x's and y's . . . which I suppose I'd better get going on, now. But Meakins, I think he is diabolical – that's what Anthony Hirsch is always saying he is, and I think that's completely spot-on.

But I like my room, really – I like it better than Annette's because I can see out to the garden when I stand on the bed and when a pigeon comes along and lands on the pointy bit of the shed I can guess what number I will count up to before it flies away again – which is actually jolly difficult, as a matter of fact, because if you guess say eleven, well you never know if the pigeon is just going to shoot right off again the second it sort of touches down, or if it's going to sit about for just years and years and years and sticking its nose into its arms, and things. Also Mummy, she hangs the washing out there on Mondays if it's decent, and so you know what shirt and stuff you'll get at the weekend. Daddy wears white shirts all the time like all men do. Once, Mummy did something wrong or funny with the washing and one of his shirts came out all pinky and Daddy, he just went diabolical. Mummy said she thought the colour was nice and why didn't he try it because it would bring out his eyes and he said there are laws in this country and do you want me to be arrested? I didn't know that policemen could not let you wear things, but I was hoping that he would wear it you know, because if he was arrested then I wouldn't really mind all that much because when he is here I am always distracting him. Anyway he didn't.

I've got this table in my room which I do my prep on, and also kits. It's all brown wood, like my bed and the cupboard and everything here, really. Anthony Hirsch's room is all colourful; he's got a thing called a window seat which is in the window which you'd have to be thick not to know, and it's got red cushions with white bits on the edge and they all fit really well. All his furniture fits right against itself and is the same size as the room and he's got a drum kit and a plug-in guitar which is also red with this handle on the side that makes it make this wah-wooey sound like in the Shadows who I like a lot, but most of all Cliff. I keep trying to get everyone to call me Cliff instead of Clifford, but nobody will. The boys at school, they just say *you're* not Cliff: Cliff is a cool cat, *you're* not a pop singer. And Dismal, he keeps calling me Cliffy, which I hate. He won't stop – so I go to him Harry Wing *isn't* Harry Wing – he's Dismal Dismal *Dismal*. And Mummy and Daddy, they say Cliff is common. Annette, she mostly calls me Dopey, but that's sisters. I got 'Living Doll' for my birthday but I can only play it on the radiogram in the sitting room when Daddy is out because he says it's all wailing like in the jungle. The music he likes is all the stuff they play when people have died at church. Anthony Hirsch can't really play the guitar, but he hits the drums and cymbals which are really loud. Also his mother always smells like really expensive flowers or something and she has these dangly earrings in her ears (obviously). His father's car is called Jaguar. Mummy and Daddy said to me that this is because they are jooish, so what I've decided is when I'm grown up to work and work really really hard so I get jooish too. I wanted to paint my table and stuff red in Valspar Two-To-Four-Hour Lacquer which they've got in the window at Stammers but Mummy said think of the mess and Daddy said it would be a crime to cover the beauty of the grains. Which is a bit like why I'm not allowed to put anything on the walls in my room except this picture of a

21

sort of horse and cart in the middle of a river which has been there since before I was born and probably the Battle of Hastings. The walls are like school semolina but Daddy says if I pin up my picture of Cliff and the Shadows then I'll only ruin them. What I've done though is I swapped with Dismal a Matchbox Vauxhall Victor with a wonky back wheel that he was too thick to even notice for an orange light bulb which is Mazda because his father is electric. It's great and makes the whole room look like a spaceship in Dan Dare or something. Mummy says not to let Daddy ever see it which isn't very hard because he never even comes here but I don't know what can be wrong with it unless I am ruining the electric. Then he'd just go diabolical.

I heard the stair go creak, and that means that any moment now Mummy'll be coming in with my tray, so what I've got to do now, and really really quickly, is get all these rotten maths books out of my satchel and spread them out all over the table and now I'm going to chew up the top of my Osmiroid and look like I'm thinking hard and working all this stuff out.

'Here we are, Clifford. I'll just leave it over here. How's it going?'

'Hm? Oh – it's jolly difficult. Old Meakins. Did you bring the glue?'

'The glue's there – but don't break off to do that now, Clifford my pet. You'll spoil your concentration. Oh it's *cold* in here, Clifford. You didn't put the fire on.'

'Forgot. I'll be ages doing this. All night, probably. Rotten old Meakins.'

'Don't work *too* hard, my sweet. There – that's the fire on, now. All nice and cosy.'

'I won't. Thanks, Mummy. Got to get on . . .'

She's gone now, and I've just eaten the two choccy fingers all at the same time. What you do is, you hold one in each hand and you stick them in both sides of your mouth like rich people with cigars only twice, and then you go nyanyanyanyanyanyanyanya as you crunch them all up like logs in a sawmill or Chip 'n Dale in the cartoon, which I like. Then you drink the Nesquik all in one go and if you don't lick your mouth what you get is this brown moustache which then goes hard and feels all stiff on your lip. I've wiped my fingers on my shorts, which I hate, because of not just biscuit crumbs but also some glue because I've stuck in the Barn Owl now (which is great – only three more to get) and this glue bottle, it's completely hopeless you know, because it doesn't matter how carefully you squidge up the little rubber bit at the top because it still just splurges out everywhere and just gets all over the place. What I want is a red dispenser with Sellotape in it, but Daddy just says stuff about it soon being Christmas. Anthony Hirsch didn't have to wait till Christmas: he just *got* it.

But I do hate my shorts, you know – always hated shorts, and you're not allowed to wear proper long trousers till you get to senior school and then you don't have to wear your cap in town either, but that won't be for about a hundred trillion years. I'm going to be excused now. We keep our lavatory in the bathroom which is always completely freezing but you mustn't say you're going to the bathroom because bathroom isn't English and toilet is terrible. There's this thing near Kenton Road that says Public Toilets and I said to Mummy is toilet the same as lavatory and she said no Clifford it is not, but once I went in and it *looked* the same, honestly. Jolly smelly, though – and there weren't any murderers in it like Annette said there'd be, but she's just a cowardy-custard little girly.

In my room there's a carpet in the middle with leaves and zigzags and lino at the sides which looks like all the brown wooden furniture but the pieces of wood aren't real or anything, more like a photo in a book. In the bathroom there's just lino, though, which is blue like my soccer shirt but not as dark as my soccer shirt and at the edges by the window it's all sort of cracked up and what's underneath, that looks even more like

Shreddies than Daddy's Aertex vest because it's brown, and everything. I like Shreddies a lot. I used to like Sugar Ricicles the best and on the packet it used to say Ricicles Are Twicicles As Nicicles which I think is really clever if you think about it (I thought about it a lot) but then I told Mummy to stop buying those because they had Noddy on the packet and it's just so childish. What I've got at the moment is Puffed Wheat which is shot from guns which is amazing, really – and it must be true because inside the packet you used to get one of the Lone Ranger's real silver bullets and I asked Mummy to make me a belt with all those little slots in so I could have it full of silver bullets like the real Lone Ranger and I'd already got a mask which was free with the *Dandy* and then I could go Hi Ho Silver, which is his horse, and the Indian gentleman Tonto could call me Kim O'Sabby and stuff – although of course I don't really own a horse, or even an Indian. Trouble is, I really hate Puffed Wheat and Mummy says well you got me to buy them so you'll just have to eat them all up but I really hate them and so Mummy, she's eating them all up now, and she hates them too. She made me the belt and it's great – but it'll only ever have one silver bullet in it now which is hopeless, really. So she got me more Shreddies which I didn't really want her to because there was nothing free inside, but at least they're decent.

The curtain in the bathroom is called a net curtain, and if you suck it it tastes of fog. There's not much else in there except for the bath, which you'd have to be thick not to know. It's huge and hard to get into and there's a meter you put pennies in and even if you put in five you only get about a puddle of hot water and I think it's a complete waste of money because with 5d you can get ten flying saucers, or else a sherbet dip and two piccaninnies. The water comes out of Ascot which goes boom like when they throw a hand grenade and it's filled with blue and yellow fires. I hate it all. The only good baths were when Corn Flakes were doling out submarines and Mummy had to get some baking powder and you put it in and the submarines, they went up and down except one night they didn't and they sank and the bath just got filled up with baking powder and I thought I might bake and I cried a bit and Mummy said not to be so silly but it's just that I didn't want to turn into a cake. This was childish.

There's a mirror on a shelf in there, and after I've been excused I sometimes put it on the floor and then I sort of hang my shorts down so the bottom bits are just touching my shoes and I think that's what my long trousers would look like (except your pants wouldn't be showing, obviously) and I'd really like to have some. Nobody real wears short trousers. All the people in *Wagon Train* and *Maverick* all wear long trousers – but I don't like what they wear in *Robin Hood* which looks like ladies' stockings and no trousers at all. But people were old-fashioned then. We don't actually have a television, but we're getting one next week and I jolly can't wait. I watch quite a lot at Anthony Hirsch's house; they've got two – one for someone called Nanny, but there aren't any babies or anything.

That's Mummy on the landing. She's calling me down for supper. What I'll do, I'll do the relief map thing before breakfast, and then if I'm just a bit early for school I can crib all the algebra stuff off of Dismal. Oh gosh OK then: *from*. All right?

The four of them now were sitting around the walnut, square and gate-legged dining table, one of Clifford's ankles banging at the barleytwist stretcher. Soon his father would lower his cutlery and tell him in no uncertain terms to cease his infernal racket, young man – but this evening he had yet to do so, and therefore Clifford, for now, continued to make it. The dining room was as cold as the garden beyond. Clifford and Annette were always aware of the curtains either side of the single French window puffing out languidly, and shifting with the draughts; you could even hear them sigh and murmur. There was a black pot-bellied Aladdin paraffin heater standing over there in the corner, look, but both Clifford and Annette could never bear its being lit because oh yuck, it made them sick – and anyway the warmth was weedy. One of the fund of reasons why Clifford so yearned for his father to be out was that then just the three of them – he and his Mummy and Annette – would always have their supper in the front room next door, Clifford and Annette with plywood trays on bare and polished knees that glared with a fierce and chapping redness, the shins below them glowing and sheeny in the light of the anthracite, warming in the hearth. But Clifford's father, he said that such slack behaviour was wrong, quite wrong, not at all the way to do things. If the good Lord has seen fit in his beneficence to bestow upon this family the considerable advantage of a separate dining room in which to partake of the bounty He has granted us, then it surely behoves us to gratefully avail ourselves of our singular privilege. Clifford's mother had recently taken to stuffing odd and laddered nylons with old school vests and undarnable socks and then ramming these unspeakable cylinders (just to look at them, it made Clifford squirm: he never could have touched) into the whistling crevices beneath the single French window to snugly abut the strips and then slivers of corrugated cardboard wedged into the length of the jambs and transom – but still the room was gelid and cheerless. Annette used to say that it was her nose that got the coldest, and she would hold it gingerly as if its very presence was a total surprise to her – or maybe she was about to squeeze down on a bright red bulb there (honk it like a clown) – but her father then would instruct her to cease that tomfoolery and to pick up both fork *and* knife, young madam, and not to be shovelling at her cabbage as if she were no more than a navvy on a road gang, clearing clinker.

'I wonder, Gillian, if you might be so good as to pass to me the sauce.'

Clifford's mother's hand was already outstretched, two fingers hovering and now twinkling above the pair of screw-topped chunky glass bottles.

'Tomato or brown, dear?'

Clifford's father now lowered his cutlery and dabbed at his small moustache with the pad of a finger.

'Will you *please*, young man, this instant cease your infernal racket. I am indebted to you. Why *brown* of course, my dear. I would only ever want brown with bubble-and-squeak. If you pull at your nose any longer, Annette, it is more than liable to come away in your hand.'

Gillian passed to her husband the bottle of Daddies – which was, it just barely occurred to her, completely within his reach.

'Sit up, Clifford . . .' she said quite idly, for want of something better. 'Is it all right, everyone?'

Clifford just tightened his mouth while Annette set to combing her hand through her thick and auburn shock-loose hair, scrutinising the ends before they fell from her fingers.

'Very adequate,' said Clifford's father, with nearly gusto. 'More than acceptable. As ever, my dear.'

'Thank you, Arthur . . .' whispered his wife.

'Maybe,' he adjudged, 'a drop more Adam's Ale. Possibly, Clifford, you might see fit to bestir yourself and hie away to the kitchen for replenishments?'

'Oh – I'll do it,' said Gillian, making a lunge at the water jug.

Arthur reached out to gently stay her hand.

'Let the boy do it, Gillian. Valuable training for later life. He has young legs. Off you go then, Clifford – there's a good lad.'

'Yes, Dopey,' put in Annette. '*You* do it.'

'Oh no look,' objected Gillian. 'He'll be for ever, Arthur, and his food'll get cold. I'll do it – it'll only take a jiffy.'

She took up the jug and bustled away, leaving her husband to conjecture aloud that she was spoiling those children of hers, did she but know it, and they wouldn't – you mark his words – one day thank her for it.

'So, young feller-me-lad – eat up that cabbage, Clifford . . . plenty starving would be grateful of that. What did we learn at school today then, hey? Ah Gillian – yes indeed, pour on: pour away. Thank you, my dear. I was just enquiring of our young scholar here what new knowledge the powers that be have succeeded in dinning into that head of his. Well lad? Speak up.'

Annette was plainly quite delighted by this emphatic new focus (she rammed an index finger into each corner of her mouth and tugged her lips away into a teeth-baring grin). Clifford for his part set his two bare and frozen legs to scissoring madly beneath the table as if he were desperate to entrap between them something wrigglingly elusive, and eager to be gone. He closed tight his eyes and jammed a finger down the back of his collar.

'Answer your father, Clifford . . .' prompted his mother – both of her eyes alive with solicitude.

'Oh – you know . . .' forced out Clifford. 'This and that. Usual. Bit of, you know – maths, and everything. We did adverbs a bit with old Collywobbles. Anthony Hirsch says there's this pro-gramme on the television tonight and it's called *Double Your Money*.'

Two of Clifford's father's fingers quickly confirmed that the moustache lay still in its customary position.

'I quite fail to see . . .'

'And it's really good, Anthony says. They ask you questions, like in school, only if you get the right answer they give you all this money and then if you get them right again they give you *twice* as much money and it all goes on and on until you get just masses – trillions and trillions – and me and Anthony, we both think that it would be really great if at school you got money for answering questions and stuff because then it would help you *remember*.'

'I rather think,' Clifford's father was soberly cautioning, 'that when we do – against my better judgement, as I think, Gillian, I have on more than one occasion made perfectly plain to you . . . when we do, in fact, very soon take delivery of our own television set—'

'Can't *wait*!' put in Clifford excitedly, flipping his fingers and rolling his eyes.

'I rather do believe I was *talking*, Clifford. Do pray tell me when you give me leave to continue . . .?'

'Say sorry to your father,' said Gillian, as automatically as the last time.

'Sorry . . .' Clifford supplied, from low in his throat and with the due degree of reluctance.

'*Obliged* to you . . .' allowed Arthur, with a withering indulgence. 'So as I believe I was saying, before a certain rather ill-mannered young man saw fit to interject . . . when finally we do welcome into our household this new and, I have to say, extremely expensive item . . . we might, as I say Gillian, have been better off by a very long chalk in lagging that loft of ours, once and for all, and concreting over the brambles. Anyhow, that aside, I might tell you here and now that we most certainly shall not be watching any programmes of the sort you describe, Master Clifford Coyle.'

Clifford just gaped at him. And so did his mother and Annette.

'No indeed,' Arthur went on – enjoying very much this frisson of despair, all of his making. 'I see this machine as very much a tool of communication. The international world situation, as it is happening all around us. Wildlife documentaries. Concerts, I understand, are broadcast quite regularly. I do not see the television as some extension of these rubbishy little comic-cuts that your mother sees fit to squander her housekeeping upon, on your behalf, Clifford. We shall not be watching the televisual equivalent of the *Deano*, young man. I do hope that is understood by all. Er . . . something *amusing* you, young lady?'

'Stop that sniggering, Annette,' put in her mother. 'And you, Clifford. Don't be so rude.'

'Possibly,' opined Arthur, his eyebrows reaching up high to his hairline, 'I have inadvertently perpetrated an extremely comical *joke* . . . quite the most comical joke of the *century*. I see that young Clifford has now eagerly joined in the general merriment of this happy little throng. May your mother and myself, pray, be permitted to be apprised of the source of all your evident *hilarity* . . .?'

'Well, Clifford,' sighed Gillian. 'Answer your father.'

'It's *Beano*,' smirked Clifford. 'And *Dandy*. But not . . . *Deano* . . .!'

Whereupon he and Annette dissolved into the sort of fit of giggling that would soon have them weeping and take minutes to subside.

'Be that as it *may* . . .' said Arthur, quite sharply – not at all caring for this descent into flippancy. 'Whatever the silly little rag in question is or is not *called*, the television set will, I assure you, be devoted exclusively to a higher purpose.'

Clifford wasn't laughing any more: his face was slapped dry. These words of his father were slowly seeping into him. He saw so hopelessly just how things were shaping: he and his mother would be busy on a jigsaw and his father now would be not just listening to his drab and rotten music but looking too at a black-and-white vision of all these ancient boring men who would be plucking at strings and blowing into trumpets and then each and every time Clifford would eagerly whisper Oh look *there*,

Mummy, *there* – that bit – do you see it? Is part of the pillar box and I'm pretty jolly sure it just fits in *there*, look . . . then his father would frown and set to clicking his teeth and tell him quite tetchily that he is being *distracting*. And all the cowboy shows and the dopey cartoons – all the things like *Double Your Money* . . . they just would not *be* . . .!

'But surely, Arthur . . .' tried Gillian, gently '. . . once in a while, that wouldn't hurt . . .? I mean I well understand what you're saying, of course, but surely, well – once in a *while* . . .?'

Arthur sat back in his chair and spread his fingers wide on the table before him. He smiled quite broadly – this pricking Gillian with a spasm of uncertainty; a more or less amazed Annette just goggled at Clifford, and Clifford felt colder than before.

'It is, I regret, quite impossible. All the programmes of this nature are of course on this wretched commercial station. Channel *nine*, I believe I have seen it referred to in the *Telegraph*. American rubbish and quiz shows liberally interspersed, if my source is correct, with advertisements for such as *detergent*. Our apparatus will receive only the BBC. No one should wish for more. How else do you imagine I should have agreed to such a thing? Good. I am pleased we all understand one another. And now, my dear – do I recall that earlier you mentioned the possibility of a rhubarb crumble?'

Clifford was staring now, hard at the wall behind his mother's head. He did not take in the detail of the life-sappingly bloodless and bleary lithograph that hung there in its dull gold-painted plaster frame, suspended from a rail by a couple of chains. There were two such pictures in the dining room, each very largely the colour of tea; in one there was a cow, in this one there was not. Clifford's gauzy sight of it was beginning to go liquid beneath the gelatin of tears that soon would roll up and blurt outwards and spatter his cheeks.

'May I . . .' he said quite steadily, 'please be excused from table?'

'I'll be in in a minute,' said his mother, as she watched him step down. Her heart was still being eased through a mangle and her eyes, they were hot in their throbbing with not just the ache of love, but an age-old and worn-out powerlessness. 'I'll be in in a minute and I'll give you some Smarties . . .'

'*Baby* . . .!' rasped out Annette, as Clifford made to go. 'Dopey's such a *baby* . . .!'

'See!' crowed Arthur. 'You do see, Clifford, don't you, what your sister now thinks of you? Ought to be *ashamed* of yourself, boy of your age. All my years I've never *seen* such a display . . .!'

'Arthur . . .' said Gillian, so terribly softly. 'Please. Enough.' She sighed and stood. 'Crumble . . .' she whispered, quite abstractedly.

♠

Mummy'll be in soon to see I've done my teeth and said my prayers and tuck me in. I think I've got to go to bed miles and miles too early but Daddy says that when I am a full-grown man in a house of my own and earning a living I am free to go to bed at whatever hour that pleaseth me (I don't know why he says pleaseth because he hasn't got a lisp, and anyway it doesn't really help).

He was even worse than usual, this evening. It's just rotten, what he said about the television. There's another programme – two, there's two other programmes on that Anthony Hirsch has told me about, and I just bet you anything that they're on the decent channel as well. One is called *Take Your Pick* and it's a bit like *Double Your Money* only you get to open boxes with presents in, or else they give you loads and loads of money when you answer peasy questions. Then they ask you some more questions and you mustn't ever say yes or no. You can say anything else you jolly well want but you're not allowed ever to say yes or no and because if you do they clonk a gong – and I said to Anthony Hirsch that I'd be really really good at that because if you can say anything else that you want then I would just keep on saying to them Clifford Coyle Clifford Coyle Clifford Coyle (which is my name) and they'd have to let me open up all the boxes and get all the presents and give me all the money and stuff because that's the *rules*. There is also a booby prize which is a jolly funny sort of word but what it means is it's no good, not like all the other ones which are really whizz. Last week, Anthony Hirsch said, it was a bag of marshmallows and a toasting fork, which I think is actually a pretty decent present because they're jolly yummy, marshmallows are, and I like the pink ones best but Mummy says they're the same as the white ones only pink, which I don't get. They get gloopy though if you stick them right in the fire and then Mummy says think of the mess. Sometimes – and I think Anthony Hirsch is making it up because they just *can't* – but sometimes, he says, they dole out a *car*. Not a toy or anything, not a Dinky or a Corgi or a Matchbox but a real big proper one, which must be in a pretty big box if you ask me. This, as rotten old Meakins keeps on saying, stands to reason. And you'd know you'd got a car just by looking at the box because they wouldn't put marshmallows and a toasting fork in a socking great box like that, would they? Sometimes it's a Ford Angular, Anthony says, and once they had a Sunbeam. I jolly wish we had a car. Anthony's father's car is dark blue like our blazers and it's got a silver lion thing that shoots out of the front and he says it's Jaguar, the lion thing, which I don't quite get because that's the name of the whole car and not just the lion thing on the front. It's maybe a nickname, like Dismal. Anyway, sometimes when me and Mummy are walking to school, Anthony and his father shoot up in Jaguar and give me a lift and whenever it's raining my Mummy, she says it's a blessed relief. I ask her a lot why we haven't got a car like loads of my friends have – and even some people's *mummies* have cars, but not real grown-up ones like Jaguar – and she says, Mummy says it's because money doesn't grow on trees (like when you want proper cavalry to put in your fort because you can't have a fort without soldiers) and have I any idea what my school fees are costing poor Daddy every term and anyway he's just bought a Hoover. And I said well you can't go to school on a *Hoover*, can you? Well you *could* but it would take just ages and someone would have to push it and the whole thing is childish. And if it really does cost all these oodles of dosh to send me to rotten old school, then why don't I just stop going to the school which is hopeless anyway and then we can get a car like Anthony Hirsch's father's and maybe even Mummy could have her own Sunbeam. Mummy just says I'll be grateful in later life which I suppose means when I'm about a hundred years old like the ancient old ruin in Stammers in the Lane which sells the red Valspar Two-To-Four-Hour Lacquer I can't have and looks like he's been there since the time of Baby Jesus in Bethlehem and Poncho's Pilot, or something – and then I'll be able to go to bed at whatever hour that pleaseth me. I think when I'm grown up I won't go to bed at all *ever* and then I'll buy Jaguar. Daddy says cars are I think he says a lugjerry, which I don't get and he wouldn't tell me, and then he said that there's nothing wrong with Shanks's Pony and I said to Mummy what's he talking about a pony for and has he gone screwy and she said it's an eggs-something and not to say screwy about my father. Pression. An eggs-pression. Which is daft. It's like when he says Adam's Ale and ale is beer like in A Double Diamond Works Wonders So Drink One Today sort of beer, which you would be thick not to know, and all it is really is water from the tap in the kitchen so why on earth doesn't he ever just say so? When I'm grown up I won't ever say eggs-pressions, I'll just say what it is.

Anyway, it's been a pretty crummy evening, and not just because of what Daddy was saying about the television. I don't see the point of even *getting* one if you can't see anything good on it. Oh yes and the other thing, the other programme that Anthony Hirsch, he says is really really great is called *Sunday Night At The London Pa-Something-Or-Other* and it's got singers and comedians and people like Mister Pastry who I really like when he gets all in a mess with custard pies and Arthur Askey who says Hello Playmates which I got from a comic I once got called *Film Fun* and there's this bit on it called Beat The Clock where a clock is ticking and then sometimes they have people who aren't so ancient and once they even had on it Cliff Richard! I'd really like my hair to go up at the front like Cliff Richard's does but Daddy says it makes him look like something out of the jungle and Mummy says he only has it like that because he is a pop star and on anyone else it's common and if he was normal he'd have it cut nicely, which I don't get. I think that being young, it takes just ages. At least I know I won't ever be old and doddery and pongy and dead and stuff – it just won't happen. Anyway, all *we're* going to get to see is old men in moustaches and suits like my father and all just sitting around and moaning and talking junk like they do and boring old geography lessons about stuff like Dogger Bank (which I mustn't forget I've got to do a relief map of and colour it in).

We did do quite a lot of jigsaw, but we didn't finish. Found the edgy piece, though, which was great – and when I shouted out Here! Here! It's here, Mummy, it's here – Daddy said Right That's It – I'm fed up with you being so distracting, so just pack it all up this instant, young man. Well *I* was fed up with all his rotten music but you can't tell *him* to pack it all up, oh no. He's got all these LPs and he polishes them like they're furniture or something and it takes him ages and ages just to get them out and put them on. It's all dull and slow stuff and goes at about nought miles per hour and it's plonky and screechy and it's all by dead men called Showpang and Bark and Gilberty Sullybum and he's a little bit better because all these people sing a lot of silly words which I never quite get.

Annette spent most of the evening cutting out pictures from Mummy's old *Woman's Own*s and her *Girl*s and *Radio Times* and stuff because she's got to stick them all together for Free Activity. Well jolly good luck with the glue, that's all I can say: it splodges just all over the place, that rotten old glue. I got Smarties, and I saved the three orange ones till last and sucked them and they go white. Daddy lit his pipe with three nuns and it was stinky as per usual. Mummy says she likes a man with a pipe and I always say well you're not going to see a *woman* with one, are you? I think the liquorice pipes that you get in the penny tray are good, with all the red sprinkles on, but real ones that you blow into are horrid. I think when I'm grown up I might smoke those huge cigars that toffs in the *Beano* do, also top hats that look like LPs and fur on their collars and a pair of glasses that isn't a proper pair because they've only got one bit of glass on a string thing. They get out of Rolls-Royces which are really big and expensive cars that belong to the Queen, and then they go into the Hotel de Posh, which I don't know where it is (it may be made up because it's not round here) and then they treat all the Bash Street Kids to a slap-up feed with bangers and mash and chicken and loads of fizzy pop and also jam tarts. I don't know anyone like that, but Anthony Hirsch's father, he took us once to a proper restaurant called Wimpy and we had wimpy and chips which was the best food I've ever eaten in all my life since I was born, but Mummy says that sort of food is not good for you and Daddy says it's the Yanks over here, like it was in the War. Every day, every single day, Mummy and Daddy say about twenty million times 'during the War' and 'since the War' and 'before the War' – on and on and on. I don't know why they do, but they do. And I say but all the battles have been over for ages and we beat the stinky Germans and we're top country so why do you talk about it all the time? Daddy says I say this because I don't know I'm born, which is silly because I do, but I don't say that to him. Mister Churchill, he smokes cigars like the ones I mean. I bet he goes to the Hotel de Posh all the time because he won the War. I wish he'd ask me, but I don't think he will. I also wish that money did grow on trees because we've got heaps of them in the garden and then you could just sail about picking off ten-shilling notes and maybe even quids and then you could probably just *live* in the Hotel de Posh with servants and stuff and they would put on 'Living Doll' at whatever hour you pleaseth. Mister Churchill isn't the Prime Minister any more. Mister Macmillan is, though – and he talks about Sue's crisis non-stop (they're maybe related) and he also says, because we did it in Current Affairs, that we've never had it so good, but he doesn't live here with my father. He looks a lot like the prehistoric old ruin in Stammers in the Lane, actually – not my father, but Mister Macmillan, but my father will soon look like that I suppose because he's already jolly old – not like Anthony Hirsch's father who's much younger and smiles – so by my next birthday he could be really really ancient or even dead, like Grandad.

Which reminds me: we've got to go and see Grandma on Sunday because she's in a home. We're in a home too – Mummy and Daddy and Annette and me – but Grandma, she's in a special big home where they keep all the people who are chronic and old like the man in Stammers and Mister Macmillan who are maybe in the same home, but I don't know for sure. She's always got sherbet lemons in a scrunched-up paper bag and I think that's why her teeth are all yellow like that and on her lip there's this moustache which ladies don't have, like pipes. Anthony Hirsch, he's got these three hamsters in a cage which are called Rag, Tag and Bobtail and they all whizz around on this wheel and whoosh up and down chutes and everything, and Grandma, she smells like that. She keeps metal things in her hair and her hands are all covered in blue and nobbly lines and brown bits like the Ordnance Survey maps you get in Cubs. I hate it most of all when she goes Come here Clifford and give your old Grandma a nice big hug and then you just have to, and Mummy keeps on pushing at you from the back and then Grandma, who also smells of the old pillows in the box room as well as Anthony's hamsters, she asks me if I know that she could eat me all up, which is revolting. Mummy says she won't be here for long, but no one will say where she's going. She's maybe going to marry the man from Stammers and make babies.

Mummy'll be up soon to tuck me in and everything, so I've got to sort things out. My toothpaste is called Pepsodent and on the box it says You'll Wonder Where The Yellow Went When You Brush Your Teeth With Pepsodent. Grandma would need about twenty tons of it. I don't brush my teeth because I hate it. What I do is I squeeze some Pepsodent on my finger and rub it at the front of my mouth a bit and then I suck my finger and dry it on my flannel and then I squeeze out another dollop down the sink because if you don't do this then Mummy says are you sure you are brushing your teeth young man because I never have to buy another tube. It's really really cold in the bathroom and the light is really rotten which is scary when it's night-time. I have to listen to be sure that Annette isn't outside before I go back to my room because sometimes she barges in and wants to do funny things in here with me which I don't really like because she'll lift up her nightie and say do you want to watch me when I'm being excused and look at my bottom and my hole in front and then she wants to touch my tuppence because she hasn't got one, you see, and I think it's because she's a girl, or something. I like it when *I* touch it, which I do when I'm in bed, but it's funny when she does it because it feels all sort of different and it's tingly like when you climb up the ropes in P.E. I think she's just annoyed because she hasn't got one like when she didn't have any Smarties and I did because she ate all of hers up the night before.

It was OK this time in the bathroom, and I got back safely. Now I've just got to stash all this stuff underneath my two pillows. What you need is this transistor radio (Daddy says wireless!) which I got last Christmas. On Anthony Hirsch's you can get I think he says his name is Ray Joe Luck Sam Berg, probably a pop star, but I haven't heard of him before – and anyway I bet he's not nearly as good as Cliff. On mine what you get is it sounds like the sea did on the beach at Bournemouth, and then it just squeaks a bit and so you go twiddling like mad at the dial thing and then it goes like when Mummy's frying eggs for Sunday breakfast and bits of voices and then some rotten old music that Daddy would like. It is really brilliant, my transistor radio, and I listen to it every night after I promise to Mummy that I won't – only you've got to be careful because if you go to sleep and leave it on then in the morning it doesn't work at all and I thought when I did that that it was broken but Anthony Hirsch told me that what it needs is a new battery and I said to Daddy that what it needs is a new battery and you can get them at Stammers and he just told me that money doesn't grow on trees, which you would have to be thick not to know. Also under the pillows you need a torch, and this has to have a battery as well. The man in Stammers must be awfully rich because he gets to sell everyone all of these batteries. He maybe doesn't live in Grandma's home after all but in the Hotel de Posh instead, so it could be they won't be getting married at all which is maybe a good thing for the man in Stammers, really, because if they both made babies then Grandma, she would only want to eat them all up. The last thing you need is a new slice of Hovis which you have taken from the bread bin in the larder with the sliding sort of concertina-ey lid on top. It's really great when you put it on your face in the dark and then you press it in and you really breathe in deeply before you bite a big hole out of the middle and then you eat up all the rest. It's great, but if you wake up later, you feel all crumby.

'All right, Clifford? Brushed your teeth?'

'Yes, Mummy.'

'Let me smell. All right. Good boy. Let's just tuck you up tightly for the night. Have you said your prayers?'

'Yes, Mummy.'

'What did you ask God to do?'

'I asked him to please God bless my Mummy and my Daddy and my sister Annette and to please God make me a good boy.'

'And you *are* a good boy, aren't you my sweet? Nighty-night then, Clifford. Sleep well. Happy dreams. See you in the morning.'

'And I also said to God that he should only do all that, only if it pleaseth him.'

'Pleaseth him?'

'Yes.'

'Why did you say that to Him, Clifford?'

'Oh I don't know. It just seemed polite.'

'You're a funny one, aren't you my sweet? What am I to do with you? What am I to do with you?'

'I don't know. Nothing much.'

'Nighty-night, Clifford. Give me a kiss.'

'Night night, Mummy.'

She's gone away now, and she's turned off the light. What I'm going to do next – before the Hovis and before the transistor –

is to shine the torch up to the sort of crusty big round thing in the centre of the ceiling and it lights up my aeroplanes which are hanging there on fishing line and the shadows on the walls make them look like real ones. They're Airfix kits and one is a Hurricane and the other is a Wellington and I painted them all myself except for the transfers which you get given and you wet and you put on. There used to be a light up there with a shade with a fringe on but it was taken away and Daddy said it was all right to hang up my planes there because there was a hook but I couldn't hang them anywhere else because if I did, then I'd ruin the ceiling. Also up there is a sort of porridgey mark next to the round thing with little lines coming off of it and it looks like somewhere called Tasmania in the atlas. Lines coming *from* it, I mean. I take ages to get warm in my bed so what I do is I curl up really small and my feet are all tucked up behind me, and then it's really cosy. In winter I get a hot water bottle wrapped up in a towel, but I don't now because Daddy says it's not nearly cold enough. We've got cheese pie for school lunch tomorrow and it always makes me feel sick, even the smell. It is the worst food I have ever eaten in my whole life, since I was born. Wouldn't it be good if they doled out wimpy and chips instead? Or bangers and mash and chicken and loads of fizzy pop and also jam tarts. But they won't.

Sometimes I forget to be excused before I go to bed, and I hate it when that happens because when I get up and it's really late I have to go past Mummy and Daddy's room to get to the bathroom and you sometimes hear things in there. Last time it happened, Daddy was going *Do* it, just *do* it Gillian – don't argue, just *do* it. And after, when I'd been excused, I heard my Mummy crying – and Daddy, he kept on telling her to stop being stupid. I came back to bed and I tried to get warm again and then I started crying too because it made me sad if my Mummy was sad. And in the morning, all the crying had gone into all this crusty sort of stuff around my eyes and before my Mummy came in to wake me I picked it all off, so she wouldn't see. Because if she knew I'd been crying, it would make her very sad.

♠

'Oh look, Mummy – look! It's Anthony Hirsch's father's Jaguar with Anthony Hirsch and his father inside it.'

'I do hope they see us,' said Clifford's mother – and by golly this morning of all mornings she truly did mean it. The day was chill and drizzly, barely light, and there was a mountain to see to at home. A twenty-minute walk all the way up to Clifford's school (then twenty minutes back) – it always ate up such a chunk of the morning; it was bad enough at the best of times, but when the weather was like *this* . . .

'They've seen us! They've seen us! They're stopping.'

'Oh what a blessed relief. Good morning, Mr Hirsch. Hello there, Anthony. Thank you so much. In you get, Clifford. In you get.'

'Always a pleasure, Mrs Coyle,' smiled Anthony's father, leaning across to pull shut the door. 'Clifford's a good lad, aren't you Clifford?'

Clifford looked down as he gamely clambered over the back seat (Anthony cuffed him round the head with an exercise book and Clifford grinningly punched his arm) really warm and glad that Mr Hirsch had just said that, glad that his mother had been there to hear it. And Clifford's mother, as she waved away the car, she was nearly beaming now – because he *was* a good lad, her little Clifford, a good sweet lad; and even now as she turned away, adjusting the ribbon on the pleated sheet of plastic that covered her head, already she was feeling the dullness of that ache, the tug of his departure.

It's just as well that none of us is late to bed in our house, because I really do need, you know, to get an early start. I've trained myself over the years to wake up on the dot of six-thirty: second nature to me, now. I could, I suppose, get away with leaving it for just a little while longer, but I was never one for cutting it fine – rush rush rush, not me at all: far more comfy with plenty of time in hand. I used to set the big old Westclox alarm with the bells on top (wake the dead, that thing would) but I hated being woken so suddenly. And Arthur, he'd . . . well sometimes he'd put his arm over or turn around or something and start up his grunting and it wasn't very pleasant, if I'm honest, first thing in the morning. I've never ceased to be amazed at how terribly bristly he gets, Arthur, just between the time he comes home from work and first thing the next morning. It must be horrid, I think, being a man. I do often think that. All the big feet and heavy bony arms and the, well – perspiration that always, I don't know, seems to just sort of linger. Or maybe that's just Arthur, I really wouldn't know: not the sort of thing you talk about, is it? It's the hair, though, mainly: it grows in his nose and in his ears, these days – beastly little forests of it. Didn't used to. But the shiny pink spot at the back of his head, that's getting wider day by day. Of course you don't mention these things. There was a letter the other week – just last week's issue, I think it could have been – to Evelyn Home in my *Woman's Own*, could have been *Woman*, about how awfully sensitive men can be about this sort of thing – well most things, really; men can, as we all know, be terrible babies. Anyway, it certainly doesn't do to go stirring things up. I can't think that my Clifford will be like that – no, not ever. I mean I hope I'm not being just a silly old mother hen here – I do know that he will grow older and I'll not

43

hold on to him for ever (this is what a mother must do – bravely wave goodbye as they fly the nest, cope with as best you can the tug of their departure) but somehow, I don't know . . . I don't ever feel that he will be coarse and ungainly . . . is as close as I can come to expressing it. And Clifford, he hardly ever perspires. All his singlets and school shirts and things – they come up just beautifully with only a warm rinse and a little bit of Dreft. Arthur's vests and unmentionables, goodness – I have to boil and steep them in Omo, and still they don't come up as bright and as white as I'd like; I sometimes add just a touch of peroxide.

And the minute I'm up, I don't yet wake anyone, but I quickly get ready for the day. I suppose it's silly, but I rather pride myself on the fact that Clifford and Annette, they've never seen me in the mornings until I'm quite presentable. I don't think it's right, somehow, for the lady of the house to ever be unkempt. Men are different, but for the lady – I just don't think it's right. And children, they need a constancy in their lives – a constancy, yes, which I think it is one's duty to provide. I could be wrong, but that's just me. Oh I'm not saying that it's any sort of a great palaver to get myself ready in the mornings because I always wear grips and a hairnet to bed – which was awful, just awful in the beginning when I did it because you could wake up feeling as if something was biting into your head, but I'm used to it now. And it's such a godsend, first thing: off with the net, out with the grips and just a bit of fluffing out with this special little comb I've got – proper little hairdressing comb, it is, with a tapered handle – the ones the professionals use; I bought it in the sale last January in Marshall & Snelgrove. I also treated myself to that little dark green costume that everyone always says makes me look so trim. It was eight-and-a-half guineas, but it's beautifully made and will last me for ever. Which it well might have to do . . . but no, I'm not going to be worried about all the money business again: I can't devote another morning to worrying about money. Economy, now – it's second nature to me, really. I'm very proud, though, of this little perm of mine, because it's the first one I've ever dared to tackle all on my own, at home. I always used to go every eight weeks to the salon in the Lane called Aimée (I think because the woman who ran it, she might be called Amy: nice woman, but a bit of a gossip, so it's as well to mind your p's and q's) but when she put up her prices to thirteen-and-eleven I felt I could no longer justify it (what with everything else). That awful Mrs Farlow above the bakery has always sworn by a Toni home perm, and so I thought to myself well, Gillian, if Mrs *Farlow* can manage it without looking like a dog's dinner then surely it's not beyond you. Three-and-eleven-pence-halfpenny, it cost – and I must say it was no trouble at all and I'm ever so pleased with the way it turned out. Clifford, he said I looked beautiful (oh he's such a sweet, such a sweet). Annette, she just thinks it's old-fashioned, but Annette, she thinks everything's old-fashioned – but there, it's a phase, isn't it? It's what girls go through. She'll see there's more to life than fashion when she's got responsibilities of her own (and just what sort of a wife and mother she'll make, I do not know). Arthur, I don't think that he's noticed the perm – or at least he hasn't said; but that's men for you, isn't it? That's men all over.

And getting up early, at least you've got the bathroom to yourself. I always like a spot of rouge – a little help to Mother Nature! I used to buy Coty, but it got so expensive. Outdoor Girl is what I use now (Woolies, but ssh! Don't tell anyone) and then a dab of powder. I've had the same big tub of Max Factor Peach Blush for, ooh – just ages, now. I don't know what I'm going to do when it's finished. Maybe they do something similar in the Outdoor Girl range. What a name, though: Outdoor *Girl*. Heaven knows I'm no longer a girl – and the only time I go out is to get in a bit of shopping, or to take Clifford up to school. Annette's convent, that's more or less just round the corner, St Ursula's – but Clifford, oh goodness, that prep school of his, it's really quite a trek. Such a blessed relief if Anthony Hirsch can give him a lift. Lovely car his father's got, I must say; I don't know what it is he does, exactly, but he's clearly well-to-do. Jewish, of course, but he seems a very nice man. Rag trade, Arthur says – and I say well so what if he is? Nothing wrong with that, making nice clothes. After all those years of mending and making do we've all come through, all the rationing of fabrics, we could all do with a little colour back in our lives. I make nearly all my own clothes, now (the Marshall & Snelgrove costume was a naughty indulgence). I get Butterick patterns from John Lewis, and they also do some lovely remnants. I even got a *Vogue* pattern once (going up in the world!) but it was a bit too advanced for me, if I'm perfectly honest. I'm no expert – I've only had the Singer for just under a year (I pay the Hire Purchase weekly from the housekeeping – five-and-six, which is a bit of a stretch, but there: it's a necessity, these days. I do dresses for Annette, and the prettiest little coatee which she refuses to wear; she says she wants jeans – well she can want. Don't tell Arthur – about the Hire Purchase, I mean: he'd be furious if he knew. Dead against anything like that. Well I am too, really – I hate to think of us in debt, but . . . no no no. I'm not going to worry. I'm not: let's just get on with things).

It's just that . . . well . . . standing here now by the sink in the kitchen – the only blessed moment I can ever call my own (once Arthur's at work and I've got the children off to school), just stirring my tea and dipping in a digestive – it's hard, really, not to dwell: not to let your mind wander. Which is why it's so good that I keep myself busy all the time: too much thinking, it can't be healthy. But Arthur, you see – I know he's worried, you can tell he's concerned, but he won't ever *talk* about anything, you see. I simply can't remember the last time the two of us actually sat down together and talked about, oh – anything at all, really. Any single subject under the sun. He'll just say something like oh, by the by – I shan't be in tomorrow evening, and I'll say to him oh, all right then, Arthur dear. Or I'll suddenly chip in with Oh – Annette, She did ever so well in her English today, eighteen out of twenty, and he'll say Oh – that's nice to hear: good for her. Sometimes – not often – I'll say (shouldn't, really) Are you all right, Arthur? Everything all right with you, is it Arthur? And he'll say, Me? I'm all right – can't complain, you know. Why – is there anything ailing you then, Gillian? Not got a cold coming on or anything, have you? And I'll say No no, nothing like that, I'm as right as ninepence. And then there'll be a bit of silence – Arthur, he likes his crossword of an evening – and then suddenly he'll be saying to me Because if you *do*, Gillian . . . you know, if you feel you might be getting just a touch of the sniffles, I can very much swear by a dose of Beechams Powders: they're Trojan, they are – sort you out in no time flat. And I'll smile, maybe set down my sewing (I used to like to knit in the evenings, but Arthur, he found the needles too distracting) and then I'll quietly assure him that I'm really quite fine, right as rain, fit as a fiddle. Next thing you know, he's tapping out his pipe and giving that growling yawn he always does – arms right up above his head, and a not too savoury view of all the doings at the back of his mouth (he won't ever go to a dentist, you know – even made an appointment for him one time, and still he wouldn't go: I was that embarrassed) and then he stands up and folds his paper and says that it's him for Bedfordshire and he'll just see to the fire or shall he leave it to me?

So I get to imagining . . . oh, all sorts, really, which can't be healthy. I mean it's not as if Arthur doesn't hold a good position, or anything. He's a solicitor's clerk in a very respected firm of partners whose head office is quite near Baker Street, quite near Regent's Park (he took us all once to have a look at the building:

I did feel proud). We both agreed, oh very early on, that Annette should go to a nice private convent. Arthur's C of E and not too bothered either way: I was baptised a Catholic, but I don't go to church as often as I should – I always try to make sure that Clifford and Annette do, though. No, so it wasn't the religious side (and you should just hear Annette! You should just hear what she says about the nuns!). No, it was more the fact that the nice little girls around here, they all seemed to go there, and the uniform, it's ever so fetching – white and green peppermint stripes, smart brown blazer and the sweetest straw boater. Arthur and I, we wanted better for Annette than we'd had for ourselves – we're both of us quite ordinary, really. I've never worked, not like Arthur – but it would be nice if Annette could one day qualify as a secretary, or something; meet a well-to-do businessman, and have a lovely life.

But I don't think either one of us quite realised that the fees, well . . . every couple of terms Arthur seems to receive this letter, and they regret very much, the powers that be, that owing to, oh – this and that, the fees are set to rise again (that's all well and good, Arthur says, but my *salary* isn't set to rise though, is it? Oh no – oh no). It wouldn't be so bad, but then there's Clifford. Neither of us really said anything when I found I had fallen pregnant with my dear little Clifford; I only went to the doctor's because of just a little trouble in the waterworks (I'd left it for ages, because you don't like to trouble them). You could have knocked me down with a feather when he told me. I was immediately, oh – so terribly happy. I well remember that – but I felt that I shouldn't appear so, not straight away, and certainly not until I'd listened to what Arthur had to say about it. I got a nice bit of cod that night and I did him a parsley sauce. It's funny the things you remember: apple pie and Carnation for afters. For dessert. Arthur said: What are we celebrating? I told him, then – said I'd been to the doctor's, told him what he'd said. Arthur, at first, he just kept sitting there, and I got quite frightened. And then he looked down and he said 'I see.' And I think I maybe know what he was thinking: How on earth did that come about, then? Because Arthur, in those days, he was ever so careful. After a bit, he sort of folded his arms and then he said: 'Well. Well. We'll just have to soldier on.' But are you *happy* about it, Arthur? I remember leaning across the table and asking him that, I think because I really had to know. He was attempting to be brave, it seemed to me; he patted my hand, sort of smiled, and then said 'Shoulders to the grindstone.' Well it wasn't at all what I needed to hear but I think that all men, you know, they're probably all that way. They think it's not somehow manly, don't they? To express what they're feeling.

Poor Arthur. He's kept so very many things bottled up inside him, even during the years I've known him. For instance, he was never in the Services, you know, during the War, and a lot of people, I think he thought, used to talk about that. I didn't meet Arthur till soon after VE Day – it was at a party in Camden Town put on by the local Conservatives in honour of Winston Churchill. My father – dead now, died some years ago, can't say I miss him overmuch – he was a fully paid-up member, very staunch ('Winnie will save the day!' – the number of times he said that), and he wanted me to go in his place because by that time his arthritis, it was just so bad he could barely get himself from one room to another. My mother (dear old soul – still going strong), she was dead against my going (I wonder if she still remembers?) and the two of them ended up having quite a good old ding-dong. Nothing to do with the Conservatives or Churchill (she's as true blue as the rest of us) – it was the thought of Camden Town she couldn't bear: a low and dangerous place is what she called it, and she wasn't very wide of the mark – it still is a very terrible place, and I'd never go there again. Anyway – long story short, that's where I first met Arthur; he did stand out – all the other young men were in uniform, and there was Arthur in his brown serge suit (he'd still wear it if I let him) and a celluloid collar. We got to talking – well, I say talking, but of course I said nothing. Not just about the suit – I didn't open my mouth! Heaven knows what he must have thought of me. I was hopeless around boys – got all tongue-tied, didn't know what to say, felt all fingers and thumbs. It had been the same with the chaps I'd met at the munitions factory in Middlesex. I'd spent the last eighteen months of the War inspecting twenty-five-pounders and mortar shells. Sometimes their talk got just a little bit ripe for my taste, but they were good lads, really. Went to the pub with one or two of them – Dicky I remember, so terribly young and always wearing a Fair Isle pullover. I was terrified, quite frankly. They must have thought me a very dull sort of a thing, and they were probably right: I certainly *felt* rather dull. Anyway – Arthur, he told me he was working towards becoming an articled clerk, and I said oh well I'm sure that must be nice for you, not having a clue, of course, what on earth he was talking about. He asked me to the Gaumont the following Saturday and I said well maybe – what's on? And he said he wasn't quite sure, but he knew it would be good. It was like that in those days – no one really had the first idea. Anyway, the following week – it was on the Thursday, as it turned out – we went to the Gaumont and it was a re-what-do-you-call-them, re-release, another showing of an old film – *The Hunchback of Notre Dame* it was, with Charles Laughton and Maureen O'Hara – such a sad picture, so very very sad, I thought. I don't suppose for a minute that Arthur would remember that that was the film we went to see, but you wouldn't really expect it, would you? Men to remember things. Well – not things like that, anyway. It was after, in the Kardomah, that I asked him – why it was he was never in the Army or the Navy or anything. I asked him nicely, though – I was a bit more easy in his company by this time, and I just sort of slipped it in quite casually. Feet, he said: it was his feet that did for him. At first they thought he would be all right – 'Excused Boots', but otherwise fit – but then apparently some other more senior medical officer came and had a look at him and decided alas no, he wouldn't do at all. Oh – how sad, I said: poor Arthur. But I remember not being at all able to tell whether *he* was sad about it: he gave nothing away, quite like my Arthur. 'One of those things', is all he said. And then we gave our order for a selection of fancies and another pot of tea. We were courting – if you can call it courting, what we did – for two years and more. It was my mother who said it was time I settled down and I put this to Arthur and we more or less agreed that we could, the both of us, do a whole lot worse, and so he bought for me just the next week this lovely little ring from Bravingtons. It's real nine-carat gold with these twinkling zirconias all set into a cameo shape. And I wear it with my wedding ring every single day. I'd feel awful without that ring; only take it off to do the washing-up.

And still he keeps everything all bottled up inside him, that's really the point of what I'm saying: never talks, you see. And his feet, poor old thing, they're still pretty chronic – fallen arches, is what it comes down to, and more corns than you could shake a stick at: he has these special insoles. Clifford, little scamp, he once whispered to me that whenever Arthur was coming down the stairs, it made him think of Donald Duck; I had to be quite sharp with him – but it can look quite funny, I suppose (but don't, for goodness sake, ever let on about any of this to Arthur: he wouldn't at all be best pleased, as well you might imagine). A car would help him a lot, of course, because he finds it hard to walk very far. Up to the Lane, that's all right – and of course he can hop on the 47 to work, drops him just outside the door. And still he'll never hear a word against Shanks's Pony – so you see he is brave really, soldiering on: quite the infantryman, in his own little way.

Oh my goodness – just look at the time. You see that's the *trouble*: you make yourself a nice cup of tea to have with a digestive, and then because you're not active you let yourself think about all sorts of nonsense – off you go, reminiscing away, and before you know it half the morning's run away with you. Well that's quite enough of your daydreaming, thank you very much, Gillian: let's get down to business. Just look at the time! And I've got a mountain to see to. I'll just rinse out this cup and saucer, and then I'll get on to the sitting room. I always do the breakfast dishes the minute I get back from taking Clifford up to school, I just can't bear to leave them. We never have much on weekdays – the children, they have cereal, whichever one Clifford has pestered me to buy this time (and it's muggins here who ends up eating it, mostly) and then a bit of toast and Marmite. Arthur, he likes his porridge in the winter, and maybe a boiled egg. Saturdays and Sundays I do the thing properly – goodness, the rashers I get through – and Arthur, he says he'll help me dry; when it comes to it, though, he'll be tinkering in his shed, as per. What he gets up to in there I really couldn't tell you.

Jean Beery, her next door, she was telling me how she swears these days by the latest washing-up liquids in a funny sort of squeezy plastic bottle – gets it done in half the time, she says, if you buy a little Spontex mop: Addis, she says, they do them too. Well yes I daresay, but it's all so expensive; I'll stick with my trusty old crystals and cloth – it's what I'm used to and it gets the job done. Mind you, I used to say all that sort of thing before we got the Hotpoint ('It's such an extravagance . . .!') and I don't know where I'd be without it, these days. I used to do all the sheets and everyone's clothes in the sink right here, you know – I did, and I was as red as a beetroot, and my arms like hams. And the mangle, my goodness that was hard work. But with the

Hotpoint, you just drop it all in – keeping the coloureds quite separate, of course (golly – once I left a pair of Annette's red socks in the white wash and one of Arthur's work shirts came out all sort of pinky. I said it was nice and he should give it a go: thought I'd never hear the end of it – you would have thought I'd asked him to wear a tutu and a leotard, the way he went on). Now what was I on about . . .? Oh yes – the Hotpoint. So then all you have to do is just pop in the powder, press the button and hey presto! We haven't got a drier though, so I still peg out if the afternoon's fine – else I take it down to the Launderette (what will they think of next!) and give it all a jolly good spin; it's quite a weight, but I've a wicker basket on wheels. Everything is so much easier for us housewives, these days; when I think of what my poor old mother had to go through – fetching and carrying, lighting the range, boiling all the water, seeing we all had clean clothes and plenty to eat . . . seven of us, there were, including my Grandad and Great Auntie Florrie, always wheezing like a bellows, poor love, God rest her. But look at me! I've got my Hotpoint, I've got my Hoover, I've got my Singer – and best of all, my little Kelvinator refrigerator: no more off milk (what a waste that was) and no worry any more about buying for the two days, over the weekend. We're all of us just so spoilt, housewives today, did we but know it. Just you compare our life now with the terrible War years: all those blackouts and bombs and hiding in the cellar. Jean Beery's husband – he's taking them both off to Spain for a week, this year. Spain! I said to Jean, I says to her Goodness, Jean – you're living like film stars! And they've got a little ornamental pond and a brand-new Humber Snipe; I don't exactly know what it is Mr Beery does – Evelyn, his name is; funny name that, for a man, I think – but clearly they're quite well-to-do. Never blessed with any children, of course – a bit why I think I feel so perfectly at ease with her, rather strangely. I don't seem to get on with any of the mothers I see while I stand about and wait for Clifford, or when Annette's got a Prize Day, or something. All they ever do is go on and on and on about how terribly clever their own children are – never let you get a word in edgewise – and anyway they're all part of a set, you've only got to look at them. They don't eye me in at all a kindly manner. (With poor Jean, though, I think it's her tubes.)

Very well, then – first let's get the house all to rights, and then I'll just quickly pop out and do the shopping. I don't at all mind, you know, polishing and cleaning – especially in the sitting room because . . . well, I expect everybody's the same, it's there we keep all our better little bits and bobs: the more quality items. When you're cleaning, it sort of lets you see them again as if it's for the very first time, appreciate them more. Oh now look, goodness, I'm not saying we've got treasures – it's not quite Buckingham Palace, no Ming vases or anything of that sort – but there are one or two little pieces I'm very fond of. It's not a large room – the centre carpet's twelve by nine, I do know that because we had to measure it up when we got it in the sale at Gamages – a fifteen per cent saving, and they delivered the following morning. I was really looking for something beige, but I don't know – this one, the one we ended up with, it just sort of caught my eye, stood out a bit. It is beige really, I suppose, but it's got a border in maroon, and this sets off very well, I think, the curtains I'd run up for the bay, look – sort of winey-coloured rep, quite smart with the nets behind – and my goodness are they a devil to keep clean, let me tell you. I put them on a very hot wash, but sometimes within just a few days they're all dingy again. It's because of the window frames – we've got gaps all over. It's just like the French window in the dining room – I'm forever trying to keep out the draughts. Arthur, he says he'll fix it, fix them all, but I wonder. Anyway – the sitting room: the ceiling and the upper parts of the wall are magnolia, and under the picture rail we've got a creamy sort of floral paper that I wouldn't mind changing, if I'm frank, but it's hardly a priority. Along with the centre lampshade; it's parchment with saddle stitching at the edges and every time I look at it it reminds me of skin, which is horrid. There's not a lot of furniture – the moquette three-piece, which is beige – but I made these covers for the back and arms with more of the winey rep from the curtain material. A boon, I'm telling you, when sticky-fingered children and your husband's Brylcreem are the order of the day. On the cabinet we've got a Doulton vase that belonged to my mother. Royal Doulton. She said to me – *you* have it, she says to me, Gillian: what good's it to me now? I'm old. I've always loved that vase – it's sort of quite curvy and old-fashioned and it's covered with leaves and flowers. It reminds me of when I was a girl because my mother always used to keep her balls of darning wool inside it, and I was the only one whose hand was small enough to reach in and pull them out. It's funny – there was never a question of my mother putting the wool into a drawer, or something: the vase, that's where it was kept, and that was the end of the matter, really.

The radiogram – that's Arthur's pride and joy. Just give him his music, his pipe and a crossword, and he's as happy as Larry. It's made by Ferguson, which is a very good firm, and the cabinet is lovely, truly lovely – walnut veneer, Arthur tells me, and all matched up like the dashboard on a Rolls-Royce, no less, is what Arthur says. I use proper beeswax on the radiogram because it's nice, isn't it? To look after something if it's good. I'm rubbing it in now, and the smell of it alone is a total joy. Jean Beery was telling me about this new sort of polish you can get now that you spray on, like a fly killer, or something; gets up a shine in no time flat, is what Jean says about it – but I'm happy with the beeswax; a bit of elbow grease, it never hurt anyone (and anyway, with all of these new things, you're only paying for the can). Of course with Jean, it's all this Channel Nine, that's where she gets it all from. The advertisements. They really do work, you know – they're no fools, are they? These people. Jean, it sometimes seems to me, she rushes out and buys just everything she's told to. I do understand what Arthur means about it, the commercial station, but I do feel sorry for little Clifford – you should have just seen his face when Arthur told him we'd only be having the BBC. Oh well – he can always go round to Anthony Hirsch's house; I always tell Arthur they're busy doing their prep – it's our little secret, Clifford's and mine. I've cleared a space over by the window where we used to keep the magazine rack. That's where the new television will go – Thursday, it's coming. Between ten and eleven, I think he said. It's a fairly large affair, according to Arthur (I've not seen the brochure), but the cabinetwork, he says, is very much the pukka thing. It's all really quite exciting, Channel Nine or no.

I'm dusting around now the brown tiled fireplace (lifting up the clock and the candlesticks) which I think must have been put in when the house was first built – before the War, probably about 1930, is what Arthur thinks. It's just as well I've got Jean next door, though, because the party walls, well – sometimes if the two of them are having a good old ding-dong you can hear just everything, so it's good we're all friendly. It makes me careful, late at night, knowing that every little sound is going to travel. One of the reasons, between you and me, why I don't like Arthur messing me about – that's one of the reasons I really don't care for it.

I have to sweep around the floorboards at the edges of the room with a dustpan and brush. Arthur, he gave the wood two good coats of Darkaline over the Easter holidays, so they're ever so shiny and it's no trouble at all. The Hoover makes easy work of the carpet – there's a light at the front of it and the suction is really quite impressive: I'm ever so proud of my Hoover. It's awful when you empty the bag, though – I mean to say, all that dirt, where *can* it come from? Because we're all of us very careful not to drag it into the house – everyone knows to wipe their feet. Oh my goodness! I've just seen the time! I'd better get my coat on or else all the bread'll be gone. I don't dress up, not to go to the shops – not like some I know, mentioning no names: are you hearing me, Mrs Farlow? No – I mustn't be beastly: she does make such a lot of effort, Mrs Farlow. But still I'll put my face on – bit of lipstick, touch of powder – and then it's just off with the pinny and on with my coat. And hasn't it served me well, this old coat of mine? I like it because it's a colour that goes with anything, and it's ever so warm – I don't think the ones you get these days are made nearly so well. I put on a scarf, bit of colour at the throat, and my brooch in the shape of a basket of flowers – it's only paste, Arthur got it in a jumble sale that time we took the Underground out to Amersham – that's been pinned on to the collar since I don't know when. I still do like a hat, only a plain thing, because sometimes the wind, it can blow at you from all directions and I don't endure a hairnet and grips all night just to have my Toni destroyed in Kenton Road, thank you very much. Then it's on with the gloves and I pick up my basket and I'm away out the door.

Oh my goodness – that gave me the shock of my life! It's the telephone in the hall – I'll never get used to that ringing, it's just so loud, always makes me jump out of my skin. Now who on earth can that be? And just as I was about to go out. I bet it's Mother.

'Primrose 5056 . . .?'

'Gillian?'

'Oh hello, Mother. What is it? What's wrong?'

'At my age, Gillian, everything's wrong. As one day you'll find out. It's all very well for you – you're young.'

'Not that young any more. What is it, Mother? What do you want?'

'Have you been to the shops yet?'

'I'm just about to go. Why? Do you want something?'

'I wanted to remind you to get my sherbet lemons. You always forget.'

'I don't forget, Mother. When have I ever forgotten? They're on my list. Look: bread, tea, apples, oranges, Golden Syrup, paraffin, Mother's sherbet lemons. See?'

'Well just make sure you don't forget.'

'Everything else all right with you, Mother? We'll see you on Sunday.'

'If I last that long. I have to go now. I'm busy.'

Ho hum. Still – it's not her fault, is it? It can't be much fun being old – she didn't *ask* to be old, did she? Poor thing. Just as well she telephoned, though, because I had – I had completely forgotten about her blessed sherbet lemons. I'll put them on my list. And while I'm in Lawrence's I'll get just a few of those cachoux for Annette that she suddenly says she loves so much. But goodness they're expensive – eightpence an ounce. An *ounce*, mind you – not a quarter. Still, if she loves them so much . . . I do hope she's getting on all right, Annette. I mean to say she gets very good marks in all her tests, but her reports, I don't know . . . the nuns don't ever seem to be quite, well – *pleased* with her, somehow. They don't *say* anything – they're never particular – but that's just the feeling I have about it. And at home, more and more, she never really speaks, you know – doesn't seem to have anything to say. Not to me. It's not a bit like Clifford – we're forever, the two of us, nattering on and on. But Annette, I don't know . . . she just sort of looks at me – she *looks* at me in that way she does, and heaven only knows what's going through her mind. Oh well. I just hope she's all right. That's all. Now for goodness sake let me get out of here else before I know what's happened it'll be time to collect Clifford from school and Arthur'll be wanting his tea and goodness knows there's still a mountain to see to.

♠

Every morning the second part of the English lesson was ritually punctuated by the sonorous tolling of the Angelus bell. Sister Joanna would stand as if programmed at the very first and distant sound of it, her colourless lips often still slung ajar from whatever enunciation she had immediately abandoned. The whole class rose and joined their hands before them; all would lower their heads, and most would screw up tight their eyes, although no one had expressly instructed them to do so. The following through of the rest of the ritual – the murmuring of prayer, the synchronised forming of the sign of the cross made perfect by the stylised and accusatory steeling of Sister Joanna's eyes – was as mandatory as it was now automatic.

As all the girls noisily hauled and scraped back their chairs and wriggled themselves into their places again – teasing out the seconds the whole kerfuffle took them for exactly as long as they accurately gauged Sister Joanna would tolerate – each of them was utterly aware that in nineteen more minutes the bell for the end of the lesson would be sounded and then, following on from a short intermission always set aside for what was optimistically referred to as a period of reflection, they would all walk in silence to the stark and joyless refectory and stand around in further yawning and ache-making silence for however long it took for the Reverend Mother to be pleased to enter and take up her place at the centre of the top table on the dais beneath the vast and shadowy crucifix (whose outstretched figure was said, at Easter, to ooze real blood from between those holy bones) and then say Grace in that gruff and rather bear-like, Annette had decided it must be, growling low and indecipherable intonation. It was usually Sister Andalucia who would then lift and tinkle the little golden bell, at the dying sound of which all the muted girls would set themselves to sitting up straight on their backless settles before the long and broad-planked tables while resignedly awaiting the plonking before them of a niggardly meal for which they had all, out loud and in advance, offered up their collective and mighty gratitude to not just God Almighty but the Virgin Mary (and the fruit of her womb, Jesus). Annette had long ago identified the ponderous aromas in the forlorn and echoing chamber as those of steamy boiling, the same as when her mother would be lost to sight in the hot fog of steeping her father's unmentionables – and then there was the pervasion of a sickly sweet and sticky beeswax – the very one, Annette would swear, with which her mother for some reason would devotedly anoint with almost love and a truly fastidious caring the Ferguson radiogram in the sitting-room corner.

A thin and reluctant sun was filtering now through the high and coloured window depicting a young and bald and bearded man who clutched in his right hand a big black book and he looked up to heaven while seemingly unaware of the bonfire that totally engulfed the better part of his nether regions and which was even licking up towards his belt. Annette – during the endless ages it always took for Sister Andalucia to tinklingly signal the end of the meal (a further round of Grace) – had been staring up at this fool for what seemed like just years, and had ages ago decided that in those days God in his omniscience must have made all of the best people completely fireproof, which he doesn't do now. Or maybe he does, I got to thinking – so I asked Sister Agnes who takes us for R.I. because I thought that she just must be one of the best people in God's kingdom, ever so pious, and so I asked her – Sister Agnes, I said, has God made you fireproof? Sister Agnes, she got quite red and she said rather crossly to Annette that talk of that sort could lead the child to her excommunication, rapidly followed by eternal burning in the Devil's inferno. This sounded horrid – because Annette now knew full well that God, he doesn't any more make anyone fireproof, and even if He did, she doubted she would qualify because she's not that pious. And so now, as she smarmed her tapioca around the creamware bowl with the back of a spoon so they wouldn't come round and tell her to finish it, she tried her hardest not to raise up her eyes to the coloured window, because she couldn't ever look at it now without just seeing there one of the last of the fireproof fools – and it just simply wasn't worth it, was it? Going to Hell for. And certainly not having to queue up and see the Pope in the Vatican and he just turns round and says to you OK, right, that's it: you're excommunicated. Mummy would hate it if that ever happened to me. More if it happened to Clifford, of course, because she likes him much more than she's ever liked me. And Daddy – Daddy too, he'd be pretty cheesed off because this convent, 'this convent of yours', is what he always calls it, it costs him a ruddy fortune. He did! He actually did say ruddy when I was actually in the room. Ruddy ruddy ruddy! Mummy would've gone all quiet, but she didn't happen to be there, that time. But then Daddy, he's not very pious. I think, though – about that man in the window – that what it must be is that they just had loads and loads of asbestos hanging around in those days, like you stand the teapot on, and all God's best friends got first bagsies of it, and pretty much scooped up the lot. I'm not going

61

to ask Sister Agnes, though, because she'll just go mad and start hitting my legs with that ruddy big rosary she's got hanging down from her waist and it really stings and of *course* you're not allowed to hit back – you're not even allowed to *say* anything because God is always looking down and listening, which you know from the Catechism. 'Who made you? God made me. Why did God make you? God made me to know him, love him . . .' – well, *you* know. It goes on and on like that for a whole long book, but the point is you don't ever take chances because He never sort of takes time off, *ever* – He's always looking down and listening – even on the Sabbath, which you're not supposed to. Which is really rather odd – but I suppose it's all right for him to break the rules because they're all his rules, aren't they? I know I would if they were my rules. And He's *obviously* very pious – so although it's a puzzle, you've got to have Faith. Faith, Sister Agnes says, is what you've got to have when something seems to be totally nutty or even not true but in fact is all right and a sign of God because He understands and we don't because God obviously got the top brain because it was him who was doling them out in the Garden of Eden and all we can do is have bags and bags of Faith and pray to his doings, a wonder to behold.

After what they call lunch here – half a boiled potato and a slice of Spam (which looks like the flannel Mummy says Clifford's school shorts are made of, only it's pink) and a dollop of weed from the pond next to the playground with the fish in it, that's what they gave us today, that and rotten tapioca which is just like sick – whenever our so-called lunch is over, we're all meant to do Rest. In the summer, they have all these bunks out on the lawn and we're supposed to lie in them and not bang our feet on the end or anything and take these moments for quiet reflection, which nobody knows what it means. Anyway, it's pretty jolly freezing today, so what we do is we all just mooch about and do stuff. Helen, she always goes to buy another pile of holy pictures off of Sister Jessica. From Sister Jessica. They cost thruppence each, and fivepence for the coloured ones and Helen, she's just got millions of them – she's got so many rotten holy pictures that there are three rubber bands around her missal just to keep it shut, and even then it's all bulgy and bursting. You're crazy, you are – that's what I've just told her. You could've bought piles of sweets or probably even some *jeans* with all the dosh you've spent on holy pictures. Just because you think you'll go to *Heaven* . . .! I *will* go to heaven, Helen went then (nearly crying – *baby*) – I'll go to Heaven a jolly sight faster than *you* anyway, Annette, because you, you're just not pious at *all*. I *am*, I said – I'm jolly pious. I just don't have to *prove* it by carrying round millions and millions of holy pictures and that stupid bottle of holy water you're always showing everybody and dipping your finger in.

'Right that's *it*, Annette! You'll go to Hell now. Annette's going to Hell everybody! Did you hear what she said?!'

'Oh shut up, Helen . . .'

'I won't shut up, Annette, because you are a tool of the Devil! You called holy water *stupid* and that means you're going straight to Hell.'

'Well that's just where you're *wrong*, little Miss Smartypants Helen Bradshaw – because I am *not* going to Hell I'm going to *Heaven*. So nya nya nya with *knobs* on.'

'*And* I saw you sucking the crucifix on your rosary in benediction and that's a mortal sin, getting Jesus wet when it's not with holy water.'

'Well it's not a sin to get *you* wet, is it Helen?'

'Don't! Give me that – give me that bottle back, Annette, or I promise you I'm going to tell Reverend Mother. Don't, Annette – I'm warning you! Ow! Oh – you're *horrid* – you're really *horrid*, Annette – I'm *soaked* – you've soaked my hair and I'll probably catch a cold now and *then* you'll be in trouble. And look! You've got holy water on the floor and that means you've made God cry and you'll burn in eternal damnation and I'm going to tell on you to Sister Joanna and she'll tell your mother and *then* you'll be sorry!'

Annette then, she lowered her eyelids into an expression of contempt and then she just wheeled away – disgusted with Helen, and rather alarmed by the consequences of all these sins. She didn't *mean* to spill the holy water on the floor – it's just that Helen, she was always just so *annoying*, thinking she was just so pious, with that whiny little voice of hers and her stupid bunches with the stupid bows.

There's still a bit of Rest left, so what I'm going to do is, I'm going to suck my last cachou – Elizabeth Taylor, I read in *Girl* that she sucks them too, and she's really beautiful – she's beautiful like I'm going to be when I'm as old as she is. And now I'm going off to find Margery. She'll tell me I'm not going to Hell and that Sister Joanna won't talk to my mother. Sometimes, you know (my eyes are getting hot now, but I mustn't let it show), I really just hate this place; sometimes I do – I really really hate it, this ruddy old convent of mine. Clifford, he doesn't have any of all this at his prep school – it's just normal, his school, and they're not always praying and doing the rosary and the stations of the cross and everything and they don't have all these mad and really scary nuns all over the place – and holy water, I don't even think that Clifford would know what holy water was! He probably won't go to heaven or anything – he's not going to get to sit on the right hand of the Lord because he's not even a little bit pious, but on the other hand – not the Lord's other hand – he *is* beyond the age of reason so he can't just go round getting away with everything and saying he knoweth not what he doth.

I wish I could go to a school like Clifford's; then I could talk to my Mummy, and I wouldn't have to be so afraid of God all the time.

♠

If Gillian was honest, it was the steaming breath and the wet and bristly snuffle of the horse's muzzle as it truffled in the cradle of her hand, that's what she loved. Every morning she'd bring him sugar lumps – it was almost, now, as if old Hercules had come to expect it. I won't be seeing him for very much longer, though, because Dave the milkman told me only last week that in just over a month or so, United Dairies are giving him one of these electric floats, and Hercules, he'll be taken to a farm or a field or something just to frolic about for the rest of his life. Heaven knows he's earned it, dear old thing. It's such a familiar sight, though, the bright orange milk cart, and Hercules' head bobbing up and down between the shafts. Dave was telling me that he doesn't have to guide him, or anything – he just instinctively knows which front gates he should stop at. The clip-clop of horses – it's all set to become another thing of the past. There's still the coalman, of course (a cheery man, if ever there was: never did know his name. You don't want to get too close to him, though), and then there's the rag-and-bone man with that very funny noise he always shouts out: Jean Beery says that what he's actually saying is 'Any Old Iron or Lumber!' and well yes, I'm sure she's right (take her word for it) but for the life of me I can't ever make sense of a single word. I suppose it doesn't matter, really – you hear the cry, and you know he's there. I gave him an old tin bath not too long ago (it's been in the shed for donkey's years; Arthur said we could use it to grow tomatoes in and I had to say to him as kindly as I could, Arthur dear – we must face facts: that day will never dawn. If it wasn't for my little packets of seeds and the spring bulbs and my lovely big hollyhocks on the farthest wall, the garden would be nothing more than a wilderness). And I also gave him, the rag-and-bone man, these rather nasty old grey blankets that my mother ages ago left with me, for some reason or other: she does the strangest things, some- times. I think they were War Issue, or something; anyway – not nice. What surprised me, though, was that the rag-and-bone man, instead of just piling them up in his cart, the blankets and the old bath, he said to me 'One and a tanner suit you, lady?' You know – in that cockney way they've got. And I said oh goodness – I thought you'd take them away for nothing! It turned out he was offering *me* the one-and-six, and I tell you I was so bowled over I told him to keep the money but to use it to buy some little treat for the horse: sugar lumps, or something. I doubt he did, but still.

Anyway, I've given Hercules his daily little treat (lovely brown eyes and great big teeth, but he never ever bites) and Dave has just put our two pints of red top on the doorstep. They'll be all right there till I get back from the shops. Normally I leave going to Mr Levy's till last, because the fruit and veg, it really weighs you down. Dear old Mr Levy – been in that greengrocer since he was a boy, he was telling me, and he must be now well into his sixties. Always gives Clifford a lovely big strawberry, whenever they're in season: they leak right through those brown paper bags if you don't get them home quickly, though – terrible mess. He's got this awful big growth on the side of his neck, and Jean Beery, she was saying there's nothing they can do. But I've got paraffin to get today, worse luck (I used to get two gallons, but I can't, I just can't carry it, so I just get the half-size, these days, but still it's very unwieldy). Also from Mr Levy I want to get

66

an orange box. You know the quite large type, with a central division. Clifford's comics (he won't ever throw them away – he keeps hold of every single one), well they're just getting ridiculous, now – you can barely move for them in his room – so I had this idea of standing the orange box on its end to make a sort of a quite deep set of shelves and then I can fix that bit of winey-coloured rep I've got over from the sitting-room curtains all around the top with some drawing pins. That'll form a sort of cover, you see, so you won't see the wood and the labels – it'll be a bit like those kidney-shaped dressing tables that Annette fell in love with in John Lewis that time, and she wanted so much. Quite out of the question, I'm afraid – they're just so expensive, for what they are. Oh but look – I've just had an idea: I could, couldn't I, get two more orange boxes some other day and maybe if Willis's would do me an offcut of plywood to make a sort of a table top across them, and then I could get hold of a remnant of something quite pretty and make some little curtains for it. And I'm fairly sure there's still that mirror of Mother's in the box room. I think I will: give Annette a little surprise – maybe make her smile, for once. She's at that age, you see – she still quite likes all the little-girly things (although less and less, I have to say – all her dolls she put up into the loft) but then she'll be going on about all sorts of modern things like, well – it's those jeans, most recently. I don't think they're ladylike – the fabric, it's terribly coarse. But if she's still so mad for them when her birthday comes round . . . But goodness, by that time it could well be some other fad altogether. That's the age she's at, you see.

Oh my goodness – and talking of modern, will you just take one look at those two! I'm on my way out now from Rumbold the baker's (the usual farmhouse, and two small tins) and I'm on my way over to Lawrence's next because if I don't get Mother's blessed sherbet lemons I'm sure to forget again (it's annoying, actually, because I'll have to break a note) and I've fairly been stopped in my tracks. There's this young lad, look, and his girl-friend, I suppose she must be, and the way they're decked out, it just defies all belief. I mean I've seen pictures of all these young people's fashions in the *Daily Sketch* and on advertisements and the rest of it, but I didn't really think that ordinary people would be seen in the street like that. The young man – and why isn't he at work, by the way? Earning his keep. Instead of just wandering about in the middle of the day. I daresay he might be a delinquent (you just wait till he has to do his National Service – that'll sort him out) . . . he's got his hair all piled up high in the front like that Richard pop star that Clifford's always talking about, and he's grown these, what do they call them . . .? Some sort of silly name, I'm fairly sure – sideboards, I think they call them – they're practically halfway down his face, and then he's got these extremely tight trousers and gaudy socks and a very long jacket in a pastel colour, believe it or not – lilac, it is really: my Arthur, he'd have a fit. And as for the girl, well – we had a name during the War for young madams who went around looking like that: the hair I've seen in *Woman's Own* – it's called a beehive. And she's made up to the nines, the little minx, and showing so much leg you'd think she was on the stage. Well if that's the look of today, you can keep it, quite frankly. What *do* they think they look like? I despair, you know, sometimes – I mean to say whatever happened to elegance, a bit of refinement? If my Clifford and Annette ever got themselves up like that I just wouldn't know where to put myself. You sometimes do wonder if all we went through during the War was worth the hardship and the effort if this is how the young people thank you. They're cocking a snook, aren't they, at their elders and betters. What must their parents be thinking? I don't know what the world is coming to, to be perfectly frank with you. It's like all this so-called 'contemporary' furniture, I don't know if you've seen it at all. There was something about it in *Woman's Own*, not too long ago. Everything's so spindly – it's not like real furniture at all – and these little black legs stick out at all sorts of funny angles and the colours, well – they're like you'd expect to see in Bertram Mills, or something. You couldn't really live with it, could you? You couldn't ever feel restful: I can't see it ever catching on. And the shapes of some of the chairs, it's really quite comical – like a big sort of a dog basket on legs, is what some of them look like. You'd have to be a very funny-looking person indeed to get comfy in a chair like that, that's all I can say about it. You'd have to be like someone out of a picture by that foreign so-called artist Picasso they're all making such a song and dance about – with both your eyes on the same side of your face and your arms and legs in all the wrong places. How they can call it art I simply fail to understand: my Clifford's done better in his first year at prep school. And as for what passes as 'architecture' these days . . . it's no more than a cigar box: where's the architecture in that? I don't know – all this modern this and modern that: I sometimes think the world's gone mad. Ooh – and I must just pop into Menzies' and get a new pair of nylons; I'm going for forty-denier this time because otherwise no sooner have you put the blessed things on than you've got a ladder. I do resent the money – they're just so expensive and they don't last you two minutes, but there's nothing to be done about it. Oh dear – I think I'll leave the ice cream and the cupcakes (Clifford will create) and I'm rather afraid that Annette's cachoux will have to wait too. So much expense, and we're still only in the middle of the week: it's going to be a little bit of a stretch.

Oh no: all I need. It's Mrs Farlow, gossiping away with Mary Jessop, thirteen to the dozen. All dressed up as if she's off to the Palace to have tea with the Queen, as per usual – I just don't know what it is with Mrs Farlow. They've stopped their chattering now, and oh fiddlesticks, they're looking across. Mary Jessop – big-boned woman, a face you'd never trust in a million years, martyr to her knees, as she keeps on telling you – her hand, look, it's just gone up to her mouth as if to silence an outburst and she's peering at me closely and now those two heads of theirs are both back together again and they're whispering intensely. Mrs Farlow, she's eyeing me now, and I'm not at all comfortable: I don't feel easy with it. I just know they've been talking about me and I feel they've got something they're determined to say and it's far too late now to pretend I haven't seen them but I really would love it if I could just get out of here but how can I simply turn round and walk away from them now? But I really think I have to – but oh look, it *is* too late because here comes that smile now, that horrible smile that Mrs Farlow puts on that always seems to me to be downright cruel.

'Oh *hello*, Mrs Coyle. Look who it is, Mary. Look who's here. It's Mrs Coyle.'

'Oh so it is. Mrs Coyle. How are you, dear? Doing your shopping?'

'Hello. I – yes. I'm quite well, thank you. And yourself?'

'Oh – much the same, much the same. Mustn't grumble, must we? My knees, course – they're giving me gyp, but when are they not. How is, um – *Mister* Coyle? Mrs Coyle?'

'Oh *yes*, Mrs Coyle. How *is* Mr Coyle? All right, is he? Keeping well?'

'He's, um. Yes. Quite well, thanks for asking.'

'Oh good. I'm very pleased to hear that. I says, Mary, I'm very pleased to hear that. I must say he *looks* very well, doesn't he Mary? Looks, I would say – well *contented*, is how I'd put it. Whenever I see him out and about – quite late in the evenings isn't it sometimes, Mary? Yes – really getting on it is, sometimes. I expect he works very long hours. But I always says to you – don't I Mary dear? I says oh look – there goes Mr Coyle – and my, doesn't he look well within himself? Doesn't he look *pleased* . . .?'

'She does say that. You do. And she's right, of course, isn't she Mrs Coyle? I mean to say I've seen him myself with my own two eyes and he certainly does – at those times, anyway, when it's getting on a bit – look very very pleased with life in general. You must be so happy for him . . .'

As Mrs Farlow and Mary Jessop locked eyes in complicity, the blood continued to pound within Gillian's eardrums, and she could no longer continue her scrutiny of the kerbstone.

'I must just . . .' she said – and then she turned away abruptly and walked down the street with a gathering deliberation, her head chock-full of such things now as had no right at all to so much as be there.

♠

'I feel sick . . .' said Clifford, quietly. 'I felt sick even before we came in and I just *smelt* it. I can't eat this – I'll just be sick.'

Anthony Hirsch slapped him playfully across the shoulders.

'You should do it like I do it. Just cram the whole rotten bit of pie into your mouth all in one go and then you chuck down about twenty gallons of water and you just imagine you're eating something really really yum like raspberry ripple or roast Sunday chicken or something.'

Clifford looked around him. The clanking of cutlery was now quite sporadic, and the muted rumble of dining-room chatter was sharply pointed up now by the clack of the stacking of plates as they were passed from hand to hand to the trolleys at the heads of the tables.

'Everyone's finished . . .' he said, so miserably. 'Everyone's finished and I've only started. And that means rotten Mrs Chadwick will come over and I just hate her, I just hate her. She really hates me, Mrs Chadwick does.'

'I quite like cheese pie,' Harry Wing said then. 'It's not as good as Friday mince, but I don't think it's too bad.'

'Yeh well that's just because you're *dismal*, Dismal,' Clifford shot at him with anger. 'And anyway – if you jolly well like it so much then why don't you eat *mine*?'

'Because, Cliffy, we're not *allowed* to. Mrs Chadwick, she's looking over here right now with her beady eyes and I'm jolly well not going to get into trouble just because of *you*.'

'Oh no she's not, is she? Is she, Anthony? Oh . . . I just *can't* eat this. I can't. I just feel so sick . . .'

'Pass a chunk over under the table, Clifford,' Anthony urged him. 'I'll break it up and chuck it around the floor.'

'Oh gosh *thanks*, Anthony. Here – got it? I've still got loads left, though.'

And he was aware, just then, of a hush all around him, spiked only by the odd whoop and tail-end of laughter of those who had still to catch up with it. The voice that now cut through the hush – it sounded to Clifford, he always said to his mother, sort of like the Queen, except it was really really strict and he felt just stiff with fear and really very queasy (like when in P.E. with Mad Man Mallison he had no choice but to take that terrible run-up to the springboard and Mad Man Mallison was on the other side of the brown and huge and hulking horse, slapping at its rump, hard and repeatedly and blowing his whistle and roaring out to Clifford now to come on, come on and *clear* it, you pathetic little article).

'Do you appear to have *dropped* something, Hirsch?'

Anthony looked up at the woman who loomed above him. He saw just the fine powdered hairs faintly glistening on her lip, a double row of pearls slung around her jowls; he could raise his gaze no further. His mouth was quite dry, and his eyes as wide open as they ever would go.

'Me, Mrs Chadwick? I don't think so, thank you Mrs Chadwick.'

'Ah but I *do* think so, Hirsch. Pick it up.'

'Pick what up, Mrs Chadwick?'

'You will report to the Headmaster's study directly after lunch, Hirsch. Is that clear? Now pick it up *immediately*.'

The silence in the dining room was total, now – more than a hundred boys were craning their necks, all of them quite shiveringly pleased to be so safely remote from the centre of whatever it was they were aching to witness. Anthony slid down from his chair to the floor beneath the table and quickly resurfaced with his hands cupped around a mound of crumbled and sticky cheese pie, together with a fair bit of fluff; his thumb was smeared with orange from the Mansion polish.

'So you see, Hirsch – your memory was defective, was it not? What was it, Hirsch? Your memory – what was it?'

'Defective, Mrs Chadwick.'

'Indeed, Hirsch, indeed. In common with your brain. Now kindly return what it is in your hand to its rightful owner.'

'Um – I don't quite understand what you, um . . .'

'Hirsch! If you do not this instant place all of that food onto Coyle's plate where it belongs you will be in such serious trouble that it will have you *reeling*, boy. Is that clear? You are already seeing the Headmaster – do you wish to make it worse for yourself?'

Anthony lowered his head and let the bits of broken pie tumble from his fingers and on to Clifford's plate. Clifford's face was taut and whitening with shock and fear, and his cheekbones were aching (the stomach coping badly with this new and alarming fluttering of panic).

'Please, Mrs Chadwick,' he said. 'It wasn't Hirsch's fault, and—'

'Did I ask you to speak, Coyle?'

'No – it's just that—'

'No *what*? No *what*, Coyle?'

'No Mrs *Chadwick*. It's just that—'

'Well then cease, boy: *cease*. If I did not ask you to speak – then you do not speak. Is that clear? I should have thought that that would be perfectly clear even to the dullest of boys such as yourself, Coyle. Hirsch, go and instruct the servants to bring in the pudding. We're running extremely late because of your appalling behaviour. Coyle – eat your lunch.'

Clifford looked up at her.

'Did you hear me, Coyle? It's perfectly good food, for which I believe you offered up thanks to God at the outset of the meal along with all the rest of us. You did *say* Grace, didn't you, Coyle?'

'I – I, yes. Yes, Mrs Chadwick.'

'You were not *lying*, were you? You would not *offend* God, would you?'

Clifford's eyes were hard and beginning to glaze, and the sulphurous smell that arose from his plate was making him swallow and making him heave; so too was his physical terror. His eyes now were alive with injury as he opened his mouth to maybe say something – but then he closed it again, and slowly shook his head. Pale green Bakelite sideplates with a brown and shiny mass briskly ladled on to the centre of each of them were now being clatteringly dispensed around the tables. A florid woman's hand was angrily stayed as she went to collect up Clifford's plate. Mrs Chadwick glared at her with warning, and although Clifford caught fleetingly in the eye of the florid woman a languid blinking and the dying note of sympathy, he knew it couldn't help him. Mrs Chadwick now clanged a large and white-enamelled jugful of water next to Clifford's short and stubby Duralex glass.

'You may drink as much as you please, Coyle. The other boys will now enjoy their chocolate puddings – and you, Coyle, will eat up every single morsel of your pie as I stand over you and watch you do it. Do I make myself perfectly clear? Coyle? I believe I asked you a question?'

'Yes. Yes, Mrs Chadwick.'

'I make myself clear?'

The first of the hot and heavy tears fell away from Clifford, and splattered the white of his hand as it gripped on hard to the table's edge.

'Yes. Mrs Chadwick.'

'*Perfectly* clear?'

'Yes, Mrs Chadwick.'

'Say it.'

'Perfectly clear, Mrs Chadwick.'

'Excellent. Then you may commence. The rest of you boys will stack up your plates on the trolleys when you have finished your puddings. At what time we say Grace is completely dependent upon when Coyle here decides to stop being a very spoilt and faddy little *baby* and eat up his lunch. This may well erode into your break time and even make you late for afternoon classes, for which the punishment will stand. This will be Coyle's fault, and you may wish to discuss it with him at some later hour.'

Here was the signal for the drone of resentment and the hissed-out threatening undertones: '*Coyle* . . .!' and '. . . *get* you for this, Coyle!' and '. . . *eat* it Coyle, you *baby* . . .!' Anthony's eyes made it clear he was sorry and there was nothing he could do. Dismal, with the tip of his spoon, was scoring tramlines into the scant remains of his chocolate pudding; he now smarmed away the design with the back of his spoon and with the edge of his tongue protruding from his mouth, he straight away set himself to creating an elaborate trellis.

Clifford, now – despite all the gnashing at his lower lip – was openly crying, and the misery of it embittered him; he was

75

engulfed in a bursting heat, and so terribly ashamed. Such was the gall within him that he barely even registered the sour and corrosive mess of pie that he rammed into his mouth with a hard-eyed resolve, swilling in water and ballooning his cheeks, coughing hard and turning red as he grimly did his best to swallow it all whole – then coughing out more as he tried not to choke. He hated her, he so much hated her, Mrs Chadwick – he hated and hated her with all his heart. Mr Chadwick – the Head – he was all right, bit scary, but I think Mrs Chadwick is actually in real life the proper Devil from hell that you get in R. I. and I bet she has a long and red and pointy tail to prove it. When I am grown up and a really jooish toff and everything and I've got a top hat and cigars and a fur-collared coat, then I'm going to come back to this rotten school and she's going to kneel down and go Ah, Sir Lord Clifford Coyle, what an honour, have you brought the Queen with you, as luck would have it? And I'm going to get my men to hold her on her arms and then I'm going to fill up all her mouth with sacks and sacks of this rotten cheese pie that I've got specially from Sickland and then I'm going to get my men to chuck millions of custard pies at her and then I'm going to get in my Rolls-Royce and shoot off to the Hotel de Posh and have seconds and thirds and fourths of chocolate splosh because that's my favourite pudding in this rotten old school, if it didn't have a skin on, and I've only just finished stuffing in this stinking rotten pie and she's said like I jolly well knew she would, rotten rotten Mrs Chadwick, that I may step down now, Coyle, and there – you see? It wasn't so bad now, was it Coyle? After all that fuss – what a *baby*. And *no*, Coyle – you may *not* have chocolate pudding because only boys who behave and eat up their lunches without having to be *told* are deserving of pudding as well you know – so you just take out your plate to the kitchens, Coyle, and see if you can't *learn* from this lesson and be grateful you're not booked to see the

Headmaster along with that extremely badly behaved *friend* of yours, Master Anthony Hirsch.

'Now what do you say, Coyle? I can't hear you.'

'Thank you, Mrs Chadwick.'

'Very well. Now cut along, else you'll be late for class.'

And then what I'll do is stick safety pins in all over her and I'll boil her in oil like they used to do in the old-fashioned days and then I'll get all these cannibals round and they can have her for their tea – except they'd all be really *sick* because even with stacks of Daddies sauce she'd be just like cheese pie only with knobs on. Plus now I've got a loose tooth – it wiggles all sideways when you push it with your tongue. They might all drop out now, all my teeth, because of Mrs Chadwick and then I'll only be able to have Lucozade and I'll wind up looking like my Grandma. If I can make it looser and it comes out before bedtime, though, I'll get sixpence from the angels, if I can scrounge a bit of silver paper – which is really super, actually, because I've already got one-and-nine saved up and if I get another sixpence that makes, um – hang on, another three makes two bob and three carried over, or remaindering, so that's two-and-thruppence which is great because in Moores in the Lane they got this Airfix Spitfire which they won the Battle of Britain and they cost half-a-crown in places like Smith's and Woolworth's but it's in the window at two-and-a-penny so that means I can get it and then I've got enough remaindered over for four piccaninnies from the ha'penny tray in Lawrence's.

I feel rotten about Anthony, though. There's just time if I step on it to whizz down and hang around old Chadder's study a bit and then say something decent to him when he comes out. Maybe he'll just dole out lines and not give him the slipper. I'll give him a present, or something – but I think all I've got on me is the Poodle from Dogs of the World in Rice Krispies but I'm sure he's got the Poodle because there's just so many masses of them, and it's a stupid dog anyway. He hasn't got the Scottie but I can't really give him the Scottie because I've only got one Scottie and it's rare. I only need the Golden Retriever and then I've got the set. No one's got that one, though, because it's the rarest. I don't suppose I'll get it anyway because Mummy, she says she won't buy Rice Krispies any more because she says it was muggins here who ended up eating all the last lot. I liked them at first, but then I got sick of them. I still like Shreddies the best, but it's mouldy now because there's nothing inside. I like the Greyhound best because they go at about a hundred miles an hour and they're really really thin and bony, like a skeleton or something; Mummy, she likes the Long-Haired Dachshund, but she would like that because it's all a lickle-ickle sweetums and girls and mummies and ladies, they always like all that, which actually you would have to be quite thick not to know. And talking of thick, it was stupid when Mrs Chadwick said that me and Anthony, we were both thickos or something because I jolly tell you this: we're both a jolly sight cleverer than *she* is, any jolly day of the week.

Anthony, then, came out of the Headmaster's study, and he carefully closed the door behind him. His cheeks were pink and his eyes were quite glassy; his hands he now thrust tight into his armpits.

'Oh gosh,' said Clifford, with real regret. 'How many?'

Anthony tried on a sort of grin, but it didn't quite fit.

'Two on each. Not too bad.'

Anthony, he's being an awful lot braver than I'd be being, is what Clifford was thinking now. This slipper, it's not actually a slipper, if you want to know – it's a zonking great gym shoe, and it jolly well stings like billy-o, everyone says.

'It's just *so* unfair. That rotten Mrs Chadwick. I wish somebody would just go and kill her, or something. I'm really sorry,

Anthony, about . . . I mean I didn't mean to . . . you know. Or anything.'

'Sokay. She's just mental, that's all. We'd better get up to old moaning Meakins or he'll only go mad.'

'I hate Meakins. He's completely mental. Have you got the Poodle?'

'*Course* I've got the Poodle. Everybody's got the Poodle. I'm going to put hot water on my hands. Don't think I'll be able to write, though, for a bit. I'm only missing the Scottie and the Golden Retriever.'

'Well everyone's missing the Golden Retriever. Oh gosh – oh great! I've just remembered. I've got money! I can give you that.'

Clifford unbuttoned the back pocket of his shorts and he tugged out impatiently his Davy Crockett wallet. Inside was a wad of blue and white notes with swirling calligraphy and ovals and a portrait of somebody or other. 'Nix' was bold upon each one of them: 'This note is not worth the paper it is printed on'. Clifford pressed the bundle into Anthony's hand (feeling quite jooish, and like a toff) and Anthony said Oh *ow*, Clifford, ow my *hand*, you total and utter platypus. And then he said Oh great – are you sure? I love this stuff: did you send off for it from Ellisdon's? Yup, said Clifford – ninepence, but you get twenty-five, so it's well worth the money. And Anthony said they used to be sevenpence-ha 'penny so they must've gone up. Hey look, Clifford – why don't you come over tonight because there's *Popeye* on and then *Maverick*. And Clifford said Oh wow – *Maverick*, I really love Maverick when he's in his fancy waistcoat and his hat at the card game in the saloon and then he goes 'Waaaal, gennulmen . . .' and he bungs down all this dosh, all these dollars . . . oh hang on, though – that's not fair because I've just given you all of my Nixes and I'll have nothing to chuck on the table when Maverick goes and does it. Anthony said that was

OK because he'd give half of them back to him and anyway he had piles of Monopoly stuff, which wasn't nearly so good because it wasn't nearly so floppy, but still. And after they could have tubs. Tubs! Oh my goodness: tubs! Only, marvelled Clifford, only at Anthony's house would you ever get tubs because tubs are what you got when you went to the Odeon when the lights came up after *Look At Life* and you're told that salesgirls would now be visiting all parts of the theatre – and they did, with this tray thing all round their necks and their little red torches and the lit-up sign that says Kia-Ora which is an orange drink in a carton that you press holes in and the straw makes rude noises when you get to the bottom. You don't want to be last in the queue or anything, though, because sometimes the lights go off again and it's beastly if you've got to find your way back again in the dark – but Mummy always waves this scarf thing at me. Oh yes and when you *do* get a tub you always keep and suck on the wooden spoon thing after; sometimes you got a Frutie or a Choc-Ice which are really good but in the dark and everything they can go all icky in the middle and then when you come out of the cinema you've got it smeared all over your face and someone spastic like Dismal'll say Oh look – somebody give the little baby a little baby's *bib*. I really do like Anthony Hirsch, you know – he's my friend and I think he's great. When I'm old and a toff and everything, there's no real point going to live at the Hotel de Posh; I'll just move into Anthony's house – I don't think his father would mind because he's really nice for a grown-up, and he smiles. I think I will now, actually – give Anthony my Scottie. I think I will. Meanwhile we've got to face moaning old Meakins. Just as well I cribbed all his tragic algebra from Dismal before break, otherwise he'd just completely go mad. That Dogger Bank thing too – I just traced Dismal's. I can colour it in when Samways is collecting up the books because he's so completely ancient he just takes years.

Actually, I don't really know, now – about the Scottie, I mean. Because I've got only one of them, see, and it's really really rare. And maybe Mummy or Annette or someone will get to really like Rice Krispies and then we'll start getting them again and maybe then I'll get the Golden Retriever and I'd look pretty thicko, wouldn't I, if I'd doled out to Anthony my one and only Scottie. My tooth, it's getting really really loose. If the angels stump up, I'll be able to go to Moores in the Lane and get the Spitfire, tomorrow.

♠

It was only when I got back and had hung up my coat that I felt such a fool. What a time Mrs Farlow and Mary Jessop must have had as they both stood and watched me just scuttle away like a startled rabbit. How they must have hooted. I do so wish I were more the sort of woman who could, oh – I don't know, the sort of woman who can *face* things, really. Face up to situations. Someone with a bit of standing like, well – Mrs Goodchild, she's the perfect example. She wouldn't have stood any nonsense of that sort from the likes of Mrs Farlow and Mary Jessop. But with her, of course, they would have been kowtowing thirteen to the dozen, wouldn't they? Bowing and scraping. Oh yes – wife of the manager of the Kenton Road Westminster Bank and a magistrate, I think I heard from somewhere: could have been Jean – I think it was Jean who told me. Her eldest is at Oxford University and Jean says they get their turkey at Christmas from Selfridges. But then what would Mrs Goodchild have been doing in the Lane with a wicker shopping basket over her arm and worrying about the weight of a paraffin can and whether she could or couldn't afford an ounce or two of cachoux? Which I didn't ever get, you know – Annette, she'll be crotchety. Oh gosh – and Mother's sherbet lemons: have to remember them before next Sunday or there'll be the Devil to pay. And I didn't get the paraffin either, come to that – and nor did I go to the Library to change Clifford's book: it's still in my basket. I don't know what it is about those two women – they just make everything fly right out of my head and all I wanted to do was to get back home as quickly as I could and get a bit of a fire up and going for when the children come in. Get it all cosy for the children, and Arthur. Arthur, tonight – he won't be stopping. Just popping in for a change and a bit of a wash and brush-up, he told me this morning before he went off. Well. I don't know. Frankly. Quite what is going on. But whatever it is, I don't feel it's really my place to, you know – ask, or anything. Arthur, he is after all the master of the house – the founder of the feast. Me, I've never worked, you see, never had a job – and if it weren't for Arthur, well . . . what would we all do? And none of this *certainly* has anything to do with Mrs Farlow and Mary Jessop: how could they have the *gall*, talking like that to me, the way they did? And in the middle of the *street*. I just wish I'd said something – I just wish I'd said something, anything at all, instead of just turning tail, like I did. It's not as if *their* men are anything to write home about; Mr Farlow – tall, he is, a rather sallow-looking man, doesn't look at all well to my eye, never once spoken to him – all his money was inherited, everyone knows that much. Little chain of drapers in the Home Counties, according to Jean Beery: very nice I'm sure, just sitting back and watching the money roll in. And as for Mr Jessop, well: he calls himself a Building Contractor. He's even got it painted on the side of that rusty old Morris Traveller of his – and secondhand, Arthur says, they're no more than two a penny, not nowadays they're not. Building *contractor* . . .! Navvy, more like. His boots are a disgrace and you wouldn't want to shake him by the hand, you can take that from me: I'll leave it there. Wouldn't give either of them house-room, if I'm honest. Anyway, next time I bump into those two and they start up with all their talk, *ooh* – I'll give them such a look.

Oh. Was that the door? Can't have been, can it? It can't be that late already, can it really? I'm all at sixes and sevens today – not really thinking straight.

'Is that you, Annette . . .?'

'Well yes. Expecting somebody else?'

'Well no – it's just that you're rather early, aren't you?'

'Bit. Not really. What's for tea? Did you get my cachoux because I've completely run out.'

Gillian had known that it would be the first thing that Annette would have to say to her, and she had made up her mind to be quite firm. She just doesn't seem to realise, this girl – and Clifford's just the same, Clifford's no better – that money simply doesn't grow on trees. We all have to scrimp and scrape to make ends meet. We can't all be Mrs Goodchild. What would they have been like when there was a War on, these children? Arthur's quite right: they really *don't* know they're born.

'I'll get them tomorrow,' said Gillian. 'I've been just a bit busy.'

'Oh *Mummy*—!'

'Tomorrow, Annette. Don't make such a fuss. Have you got prep to do?'

'Homework. I keep telling you, Mummy – in my school they call it homework, in Clifford's school they call it prep.'

'Well anyway. Have you got any? Because it would be as well to get it over before supper, nicely out of the way, and then you can get the full benefit of the evening. Your father, he's out tonight.'

'Good. Least we won't freeze to death. I'll be in my room.'

Yes, I'll actually be in my room, if you really want to know, all evening and all night and right up until I've got to get back to my horrid and stupid old convent again in the morning and I won't get any sleep at all and then I'll get these old-man bags under my eyes and everyone will go Oh look here comes Boris Karloff like they did last time and I don't even know who this Boris Karloff is but I bet he's on Channel Nine, because all the girls have got it. It's been a really beastly day and it's going to be a really beastly night because *yes*, Mummy – I do have homework, or prep as you call it: I do, yes – heaps and heaps and heaps of it, actually, because not only have we got to write an essay on springtime and what it means to us, not only do we have to construct an isosceles triangle, do an equation and show workings, not only do we have to decide whether Joseph was top saint and if so why, but also *I*, just me – *I've* got to write out the whole of the Our Father twenty rotten times. Twenty *times* – and all just because that weedy pathetic little Alice went and sneaked about me and Margery to Sister Joanna.

I did eventually find her, Margery – she's kind of my sort of friend, but she's not yet my best friend because I've never been to her house and we haven't swapped special presents. My ex-best friend is Clodagh because in break on Wednesday she went off with Susan and all that lot which I think was an act of spurning and very disloyal, and I turned the other cheek. So I don't actually have a really proper best friend at the moment, but it might soon be Margery because her best friend is Olivia but she's away with ringworm and may not be back till next term and Margery says it's like leprosy that the Africans get and even worse than polio that Emily's got with her callipers and you can even die from it and then go up to Heaven. So she might be my best friend, Margery, but I don't want to ask first until she asks first.

But I found her, anyway, after Helen said she was going to tell on me to Reverend Mother and Sister Joanna and probably Cardinal Redmond as well, if she's got his telephone number, who came to talk to us before half-term about transubstantiation and also about how you mustn't let the Communion host ever touch your teeth even if it's just a little bit because here is the body of Christ and if you go and bite him well then you're obviously going to go to Hell, no doubt about it at all. Margery, she'd been doing cat's cradle with her rosary in the boot room and she'd got it all in the most awful tangle, and so I helped her unpick all the knots. I said hallo and she said hallo and then we got talking about how Sister Joanna is really a man, which everyone knows, but she got special dispensation from the Pope and she shaves her face every day and Clodagh said that she'd definitely got tattoos. The thing they all wear around their face, the nuns, this is called a wimple (because it hides all the pimples, hee hee) and it's kept on with these pins which they stick in their head. They're not allowed any make-up like Outdoor Girl or Coty or anything but their cheeks are sometimes red anyway because wimples are very tight and I once asked Sister Geraldine, who's about the only nice nun, the only not mad and loony one, I once asked her how come she didn't explode or something when it got hot in the summer – because they wear these long thick black dresses and white cuffs and long sleeves and shoes like Daddy's and everything as well as wimples, you know – and what Sister Geraldine said was she offers it up, which, when you think about it, is really jolly pious. I think Sister Geraldine, actually, must be one of the not quite proper sorts of nuns – a bit like in Guides, which I did for about two months and I hated and I wanted to leave and Mummy said well why in heaven's name couldn't you have told me before I got you all the blessed uniform and I said because I didn't know, then. Anyway – you know like when in Guides and you don't have many badges and there's this older girl and she's just covered in them and she's sort of really top Guide and everything? Well I think it must be a bit like that with nuns, except if they get badges they have to keep them on their vests and pants which are also black, otherwise it's a sin. Not a mortal sin, but jolly venial. Sister Geraldine probably I think doesn't have too many badges because whenever I see her she's on her hands and knees in the main hall of Big School and slopping around this huge grey rag on the black-and-white floor they've got there. She's got this metal bucket which is always steaming and she wears a rubbery sort of apron and she's even got her sleeves rolled up, which I thought was a sin for nuns. Maybe that's how she got to be second class – because she exposed her naked flesh for all to feast upon, a bit like Mary Magdalen who (a) was not fit to touch the hem of a garment and (b) then washed feet for a living. But she's always scrubbing that floor, poor old Sister Geraldine (not enough feet to go round, I expect) – and it's crazy really if you think about it because that floor, that black-and-white floor that they keep in Big School is the main one you're not allowed to even go on. Which is just typical, actually, because all these nuns they're all just mad and loony.

'Let's find Alice,' said Annette quite suddenly. 'Come on, Margery – there's still a bit of time before English. Let's go and find Alice.'

'Alice? What on earth do you want Alice for? She's only in 2A. She's pathetic.'

'I *know* she's pathetic. She's pathetic and weedy and that's just the point. We can hurt her badly.'

'How . . . how do you mean? Hurt her badly. Say she's got a guilty conscience, do you mean? And no matter how much she prays she'll never get an indulgence?'

'No – not that. I mean, you know – hurt her. I often do – hurt Alice. I like it. She just stands there while you do it. Come on!'

Alice was sitting on the bench at the door of the chapel (just by the font of holy water) seemingly intent upon extending the worm of multicoloured knitting that trailed away from the little gadget in her hands unto, who knew, maybe infinity. She had just been telling Sister Jessica all about how her father had made her this French knitting gizmo because the proper ones, they cost seven-and-eleven in the shops and her father, he said that that was daylight robbery no more and no less, you see, and so what he did was he just bashed in these sort of carpet tacks, I think is what he said they were, bashed them into one of my Mummy's old Silko wooden spools of thread and look – it works just brilliantly: do you want to see? And Sister Jessica, she'd been really nice about it – said it was very neat work – and Alice was pleased and what she wanted to do now was just to get this French knitting to be really really long so that she could wrap a million miles of it round and round her waist and it would become really fashionable and be in all the magazines and everything and maybe even someone like Alma Cogan would want to wear it or something, and then I could sell them at five guineas an ounce. Except I'm really unhappy now – I'm scared, and I'm really very unhappy now because I've just looked up and seen that Annette girl standing right next to me, and some other girl too, I think she's called Margery, and I really don't like this, I really don't like this, and there's nobody else around and I really don't like this and I wish Sister Jessica hadn't left me when she did and I wish it was going home time and the bell would go and my Mummy would come and get me.

'Hallo, Alice. This is Margery. Say hallo to Margery.'

'Hallo . . . Margery.'

'And me. Say hallo to me as well, Alice. Got to be polite.'

'Hallo. Annette.'

'Hallo, Alice. What are you doing?'

'I'm – it's knitting. I'm trying to get it really long.'

'Well where are the needles then, Alice? If you're supposed to be knitting.'

'It's not that sort of knitting. Look – why don't you just go away?'

'I said, Alice, you've got to be polite. And that's not polite. Is it Margery? Not polite at all. What sort of knitting is it then, Alice?'

'It's French. It's called French knitting.'

'But you're not French, are you?'

'No. Of course I'm not French.'

'Well then you're *lying* then, aren't you? Alice is telling *lies* to us, Margery – and right outside the chapel. I should think Jesus, he must be weeping now, because of what you've just done.'

'Don't! Don't – *say* that . . .!'

'Well it's true. I think the only thing that can save you now if you don't want to burn for ever in eternal damnation is the blessed Sacraments. Close your eyes, Alice. Stand up straight and close your eyes.'

'I – I don't want to. Close my eyes. Just go *away*, can't you . . .?'

'I said close your *eyes*. Now, Alice – do it *now*. Got them closed? Right, then. Smell this – smell what I'm going to put under your nose – close your *eyes*, Alice, and stay *still*. I'm not going to tell you again. Now you smell this and tell me what it is.'

'I – I don't know what it is. It's horrid. Oh golly, Annette – it's just horrid, Annette – what is it? What is it?'

'Shall I tell you? Do you really want to know, weedy Alice? It's my *bottom*. I stuck my finger in my *bottom*! And now it's in your *nose*!'

'Oh – *urrrrgh*, Annette – you're disgusting! You're just *disgusting*, Annette – and you're disgusting too, you are too, Margery. Why are you both *laughing* like that? It's not funny – it's *disgusting*. Now you just get your hands off me, Annette, because I'm going to tell on you and then you'll be *expelled*.'

'Oh you need to cool down, Alice. Hold her, Margery. Yes – just get her by the arms, that's it. Oh stop squirming – you can't get away. Here, Alice – lots of water to cool you down.'

'Oh *stop* it, Annette – you're a *sinner*. You're a disgusting *sinner*. You've soaked me! That's *holy* water and the Lord God is watching down on you. Ow. Ow. *Owww*! Oh *please* stop it, Annette – that really really hurt me . . .!'

'It's meant to hurt you, Alice. That's what Chinese burns are *for*, stupid. Here's another one to keep you going.'

'Aa – *owww*! Oh you're *beastly*, Annette – I just hate you. And it *doesn't* hurt, so there! It *doesn't* hurt because I have God's protection and you've just got the *Devil* . . .!'

'Then why are you crying, Alice, if it doesn't hurt? Why are you crying, then? Oh listen – aren't you lucky? That's the bell. Oh well – we've got to go now, Alice – haven't we Margery? Or else we'll be late for English. I tell you what – just to show we're all good friends again and everything, I'll lend you my nail scissors.'

'You're just *beastly*, Annette . . . and I'm going to tell Sister Joanna of you. I don't *want* your rotten nail scissors – just *go*!'

'Not polite. OK – I'll do it for you, then.'

'Oh . . . *no*, Annette – oh no *please*, Annette, don't do – oh you *have*! Oh you're just . . . oh why did you have to *cut* it, you beast! You beast! I'm just . . .'

'Crying again. Pathetic. Bye bye then, weedy little Alice. Bye bye. Come on, Margery. Let's leave the little baby – she's probably going wee-wees in her panties. Let's just leave her.'

Yes. And just because of that, just because Alice had to tell on me I got my hair all twisted round and my ear pinched really hard by that rotten ruddy Sister Joanna and then she started hitting at my legs with her rosary beads and screamed at me to get down on my knees and beg the Lord to take away my violent tendencies. And then she told me to write out the Our

Father twenty whole times and have it on her desk first thing tomorrow morning and that if I didn't then I go to see Reverend Mother and that when Father Doobey comes over on Friday I should beg the Lord's forgiveness in Confession. Well I'll write out the rotten Our Fathers because I don't have a choice but I'll never have time for springtime and what it means to me and St Joseph and all that muck about isosceles triangles – I'll never do all that as well . . . but I'm jolly well not going to Confession with Father Doobey, I can tell you that for certain. Last time I went I started making up all sorts of stuff just to have something to say to him, really. You can't always just go 'telling lies' and 'not thinking enough about other people'. I mean I wasn't going to tell him about all the things that I really think about, which some of them could be the work of a serpent trying to get into my bosom, because then he might think there was something wrong with me and he'd probably tell and I might go to Borstal. I know they say they won't, but they probably do. Tell, I mean. So I confessed to 'plotting', which I thought was good. He said well what do you mean? Plotting? And I hadn't a clue so I pretended I was crying and then he asked me through this grille thing in the box (it's echoey and quite dark and spooky in there) if I had any other sins to confess to him and I said oh yes: robbery, and having these accessories after the fact, which I know burglars do because I heard it on the wireless. I would've said murder, but then he definitely would've told, no doubt about it at all. What he said then was instead of the usual three Our Fathers and three Hail Marys he said come in to the vestry, my child, and we will talk further on the matter. Well I really didn't want to because I wanted to go home because *Girl* came out that day and I hadn't seen it and I had nothing else to say anyway and couldn't even remember most of what I'd told him already. Anyway, you can't say no because he's a priest and they sit on

I think it's the right hand of God – anyway, I'm fairly sure that in R.I. they say they sit on one of his hands, God's, and if I did say no he'd be bound to report me to Sister Joanna or even Reverend Mother and she could tell the government about these accessories I'd blabbed about and Mister Macmillan, he could hang me by the neck until dead. So I followed him into the vestry and it smells of old things and polish and something else I couldn't get and then I did get because it was a bottle of whisky which he opened called Haig, and Daddy – he keeps one just like it in the shed. Father Doobey, he came and sat next to me and said what I was was deeply troubled, but I wasn't really, not the way he thought, anyway. And then he said I must be cold in here and started rubbing my knees up and down and then all over my legs and things and his face was all red and right in front of mine and I thought he might start long-range spitting and the whole thing was horrid. Really ancient old men, they smell really bad, you know. All like tweed jackets and pipes and that whisky. Boys are nice because they're more like girls – like Clodagh's older brother who once – I've never told anyone, not even Clodagh – kissed the front of my mouth behind Woolworth's. Clifford too is nice to touch, except he never ever lets you: he just likes touching Mummy. But Father Doobey was really horrible and I stood up and I said I had to go now and his hands they were really big and all rubbery a bit like Sister Geraldine's apron and he was getting all over my knickers and under the elastic and everything and maybe that's allowed if you are a priest like it's allowed when you are a doctor but there was nothing wrong with me, was there? No aches and pains. So I said I had to go and he said he won't talk to anyone about it, this, which was good: I thought he might have told on me.

Anyway. I'd better get started on these stupid prayers because I just heard the front door go slam and that means Mummy's gone up to collect Clifford from Anthony's and so there'll be supper in about half an hour so I better get something done, I suppose. It's so freezing up here, though, I might take it all down to the sitting room and do it on a tray. But about Father Doobey, I just think it's what old men do, I don't know why. It can't be strange because Mr Levy in the greengrocers, if ever I go up there on my own and he gives me a plum or something, he does a bit of it with his hands – and even Daddy, you know, he does it to me too. Twenty rotten times I've got to write this stupid prayer. Our Father . . . who art in Heaven . . . hallowed be thy name . . . thy kingdom come . . . thy will be done: over and over, again and again . . .

'I swear it only rains whenever I'm either taking you up to school, or else when I'm fetching you back from somewhere. It's been fine for the rest of the day. Oh here, Clifford – don't just go leaving your coat on the banister like that, it's dripping all over. Go and hang it on the hook over the bath, there's a good boy. Put on your slippers and change your socks if they're damp. And tell Annette that supper'll be soon. Are they damp, Clifford, your socks? Are they? Let me feel. Oh they are – you're soaked right through. It's those blessed shoes – those new soles, they haven't lasted two minutes.'

Not that it matters, I suppose, because his toes are already touching the ends (you've only got to press and you can feel it) – and Annette too, she's due for new sandals and indoor shoes for school. They're just so expensive, children's shoes nowadays, and no sooner you've bought them than they've grown out of them again – happens in no time. And it's not like with the uniform which you can get a few sizes larger so there's ample room to grow into it. Last summer holidays when we all went to John Lewis and Clifford and Annette kept on putting their feet in the X-ray machine there (it's amazing what they can do now – you can see all the little bones in their toes. Clifford, I can never tear him away from the thing, silly little boy: he must've used it about twenty times. Still, can't do any harm). The sales-girl there, she said he was into a one, and I said let's have a size two, then – get a bit of wear out of them, at least. And she says to me, the salesgirl (couldn't have been more than twenty years old, no more than a little chit of a thing) – Well madam, she says to me – quite on her high horse – of course you may purchase whatever you will, but please let me first ask you this: do you *want* your son's feet to be deformed? Do you *want* him to have the most severe foot troubles in later life? Well I ask you – what on earth are you supposed to answer to questions of that sort? Well *no*, I said: of course not. Well in that case, madam, she went on to me – quite as if she were the Queen of Sheba and I was something the cat dragged in – well then, she says, I wholeheartedly recommend that you take the size one. So I did, of course – we got the size one and in no time at all there was a hole in the welting and the water was getting in and I just couldn't face traipsing all the way back to John Lewis and so I had to take them up to Dudgen's on Kenton Road and the old boy there, he put on them these new Stick-a-Soles, I think they're called (they're made by Phillips, which is a good firm), because he said it would be cheaper and would last just as long as the more conventional sort of repair. Yes well – two minutes later and they're leaking again, aren't they? Why don't they make things to last, like in the old days? But as I say, it hardly matters because he's completely grown

93

out of them, now. We should've got a size two, like I said in the first place; but then they still would've let in water, wouldn't they? And then on top of that maybe Clifford would be, I don't know – deformed in later life, though I can hardly believe it. Oh well – it's back to John Lewis on Saturday, I suppose. I know I should stick to Start-Rite and Clarks, but they're just so expensive. Maybe I could find something cheaper on Kenton Road? Freeman, Hardy and Willis are a possibility – although Jean Beery, she says that all their shoes are made from cardboard and come from Hong Kong, which can be no good to man nor beast, can it really? And Clifford's hair – it's all over his collar: it gets these spurts. So that's another three-and-six to be budgeted for. I tried to cut it myself, one time, bit of a trim, but it's harder than it looks, if you want the truth, and he told me all the boys were ragging him about it because of the way it was all up on one side. And talking of Clifford . . . he's just been into the kitchen to ask me for some tinfoil now because he's got another tooth out; not just sixpence to find – I know, I know it's only sixpence, but it all mounts up, you know. And as I say, it's not just the sixpence, it's the remembering to slip into his room just before I go to bed and trying to get the tooth out from under his pillow without waking him up. Last time he wanted to put it under the mattress, if you please, because the angels, he said, the angels could do anything. Silly little boy. *Ooh* I do love him . . .

'And don't stand directly in front of the fire. You're not, are you Clifford?'

'Why not? I'm cold.'

'You know why not. Because you'll get *chilblains*, won't you? Told you a hundred times. Annette—?! Annette – can you hear me?! Annette! Come down for your supper. Annette?! Oh Clifford – I don't think Annette can be hearing me. Run up and tell her it's time for supper. Tell her I'm just serving up. There's a good little boy.'

'Oh it's *freezing* up there – why can't she come down on her own?'

'Oh Clifford just do what you're told or there'll be no jigsaw after supper and no sweeties. Oh she's here – it's all right, she's coming down. All right Annette, yes? Did you not hear me? I'm just serving up.'

'I'm starving. What is it? Don't hog all the fire, Clifford. I'm freezing.'

'You'll get chilblains. And stop *pushing*, Annette, actually. What's all that stuff?'

'Oh . . . homework. Piles of it. What's for supper, Mummy?'

'Ha ha – Annette's got *homework* . . .'

'Shepherd's pie – I've just to get the top nice and brown. Be quiet, Clifford. Get the trays out, Annette, there's a dear. And the forks, and everything. Then we can all snuggle in cosily and you can tell me all about your doings and what you learnt at school.'

'Don't want to talk about school . . .'

'Me neither. Can I have Tizer, Mummy? Daddy's not here.'

'Oh . . . I suppose so. What are you having, Annette? Do you want some Tizer?'

'I'll just have Sunfresh. Tizer's too fizzy.'

'You're mad. Tizer's great, Tizer is. Tizer for ever!'

'*Childish* . . .!'

'*I'm* not childish – *you're* childish. So nyah.'

'Stop it the pair of you. Have you done what I asked you to, Annette? Because I'm just serving now.'

As far as Clifford was concerned, the rest of the evening was totally super – completely great, until you-know-who had to come along and spoil it. The shepherd's pie was really yum because it always is and there was tinned peaches and Carnation for afters which is never on an ordinary day, just when it's Easter or something, and Mummy told us that it was a secret and not to tell our father. What we always do when it's sitting-room suppers is we draw the curtains – I can do that – and then I push up Mummy's chair really close to the fire because that's where she likes it (she never seems worried *she* might get chilblains) and then Annette goes and gets two of the chairs from round the table next door in the freezing room and what she does is she sits on one and she puts her tray on top of the other one and I go on the poofy right in front of the fire guard and I balance my tray on my knees which you have to be good at and your face gets all warm and it feels it's gone orange and we don't have the light on that hangs from the circle in the middle of the ceiling but we do have the little lamp thing on the mantelpiece which is a china kookaburra on a branch of a tree which is an Australian bird which nobody knows – Anthony Hirsch, he didn't know when he came over that that's what it was – and on its head is a lampshade but I always say it's his hat he's got on and I think it must be the only kookaburra in the whole wide world with a hat on, and that includes Australia which is miles away. This is cosy, and you get shadows on the ceiling and on the walls and every-thing and Mummy's and Annette's faces, they go all glowing and the fire it goes snap crackle pop sometimes like Rice Krispies with Dogs of the World in but also like when you break up the icy puddles on the crazy paving in the morning before school with the heel of your wellingtons. One rotten thing, though – Mummy didn't go to the Library to get me another Jennings. I don't like books because they're boring like the books in school – but I really like Jennings. I also like the *Beano* and the *Dandy* and I used to like the *Beezer* and the *Topper* as well but Mummy said that I can't have all four of them because they're just so expensive but I can have two of them and so what is it to be, young man – and I said well then I want the *Beano* and the *Dandy* because they're the best which everybody knows but I did like a lot Pop, Dick and Harry in the *Beezer* which is a father and his two sons who look the same except one's got black hair and one's got yellow hair but they both have black shirts, which I would really like. There was a gangster film on television at Anthony Hirsch's and there was this gangster in it, which is someone who breaks the law in a gang and he's against all the policemen, and the gangster had a black shirt and he had a white tie and I'd like that too because the only tie I've got is my school tie and that's just blue and green with stripes and not nice at all, ask anyone at school. Anthony said you don't know it's a black shirt and a white tie because it could be a brown shirt and a yellow tie because of the television makes everything black and white and we'll never ever know until we get a colour television if it's really a black shirt and a white tie but colour televisions don't even exist on Mars, which you would have to be quite thick not to know. So I liked *them* in the *Beezer* and I liked Ginger in the *Topper* and he has red hair and you can tell because the *Topper*'s got colour. But Anthony Hirsch, he lent me *Jennings Goes to School* and I didn't like it because it only had three pictures in and then I did like it because it's really good but I don't get all of it because Mummy says I'm a bit too young. It's just like real school, except that they live there all the time, which we don't. Except it's not really like real school because the worst teacher they've got there is called Mr Wilkins and he just goes I – I – cor – *wumph* and blows his top and stuff – he doesn't actually go round chucking those big wooden board rubbers at people and not chalk either like all the loonies do in my school. And the headmaster is Mr Pemberton-Oakes (MA Oxon) – which I thought at first meant that his mummy was a cattle in the Nativity, but it doesn't. But he doesn't hit anyone with a gym shoe like Chadwick does and makes them cry, and Mrs Pemberton-Oakes, I don't think she exists but if she did she wouldn't really be the Devil and I bet the only reason why rotten Mrs Chadwick has got all this stupid hair all puffed up like that is because otherwise all her horns would poke out. And the decent master in Linbury Court School – that's the name of it, Jennings's school that he goes to – is Mr Carter, and we don't have any decent masters at all, they're all just mad like moaning Meakins who is maddest of all and really moany. Jennings is really called John Christopher Timothy Jennings and his friend has blondy hair and spectacles and he is called Charles Edwin Jeremy Darbishire and they call each other Darbi and Jen which Mummy says is old people but she's wrong because they're not and they say stuff like Oh wizzo, Jen, and oh fishhooks how ozard, Darbi, which isn't really real but I still think it's jolly good. Anyway, I've read four of them now and I wanted Mummy to swap *According to Jennings* for *Take Jennings for Instance* which is new, but she didn't because she said the rotten old Library was closed, but she will do it tomorrow when she gets some more of Annette's stinky sweeties which she likes because she's a girl and more of those sherbet lemons for Grandma so her teeth can go on looking like a load of Fyffes bananas all stuck inside her mouth. Bananas are great, by the way, except every time you go and peel one someone says you couldn't get them in the War because they were a lugjerry and you had to be rich and go to the black market. I expect Anthony Hirsch's father was jooish enough to buy bananas and he would've gone in Jaguar and the lights in front would've lit up all of the black market and you could see what you were doing. I stick all the Fyffes labels in the backs of my exercise books.

And earlier was good too because I did go over to Anthony's and Anthony's father, he telephoned Mummy so she knew to come and get me from there but then he also said that he'd take me back in Jaguar if she liked and I heard Mummy go on the other end that she wouldn't hear of it, which I don't get because she did hear of it because he was talking it into her ear. Anyway, we watched two *Popeyes* and he is a cartoon and speaks like a duck with a pipe in his mouth and he eats all this spinach which shoots up in the air when he presses on the tin and he catches it in his mouth which is really clever except I wouldn't want to even if it did make me super muscly like Popeye is because spinach is like wet stuff from the pile of muck at the end of the garden and it's not nearly as good as Bird's Eye peas which are a million times better and also as fresh as the moment when the pod went *pop*! It said so in an advertisement in *Maverick*, which was great because of his waistcoat and his hat and he won all this money with a poker and then he had to get out of town pronto. I didn't tell Mummy I had a tub which was raspberry ripple or she wouldn't of given me tinned peaches and Carnation which was yum. In *Popeye* there's a fat man called Wimpy who eats wimpys non-stop which are also yum.

After our supper, Mummy took the plates out and Annette kept writing stuff out in the corner and kept on saying out loud things like Give us this day our daily bread and she'd only just had supper. Actually, this is a joke, did you get it? Because I know it's from a prayer, that bit about bread, and it goes on we must forgive our truss puss gain stuss, which I don't know what it means, and ends up Deliver us from evil, which maybe if I'd said to God when Mrs Chadwick was jamming all the cheese pie in me with a garden spade he would of come down and smote her, but I doubt it. And then I got to put 'Living Doll' on the radiogram and I played it five times because Mummy and Annette, they really like it because Cliff is great but they still won't call me it, Cliff I mean, and then Annette had on Alma Cogan and the Everly Brothers which she got with her First Holy Communion Record Token and Mummy and me, we'd nearly finished the whole of the jigsaw – there was just a bit of roof left – when the door of the room, it suddenly opened and Daddy was there and he switched the switch at the wall and it all got bright and we all went blinky and he said Let's all shed some light on the matter, hey? And then he said what is all that row? It sounds like monkeys in the jungle. Everyone just didn't say anything and Mummy, she got up and turned off the radiogram, worse luck, and then she said Arthur, I thought this was going to be one of your out nights . . .?

'It is. It is indeed. I'm only just calling in briefly. That's a fair old blaze you've got going there. I only hope there's enough coal for the weekend . . . Well well – confectionery and the hit parade, how the rich and idle do disport themselves. How nice to see how the other half lives. Well – must depart. Everyone attended to their homework, I trust. Don't get under your mother's feet now, either of you – I expect she has various duties to attend to. Approaching your bedtimes, I should have thought. Is that not the case, Gillian? Good night Clifford, then.'

'Good night, Daddy.'

'Good lad. Don't do the latch up, will you Gillian. Else we've got ourselves into a state of affairs. Shouldn't be over-late. Well good night then, Annette. I said good night then, Annette. Do you hear your father speaking to you, girl? Gone deaf have you, all of a sudden?'

'Answer your father, Annette . . .'

'Good night, Daddy.'

'Very good. Right then. I'll be off.'

And as the door closed behind him, Clifford and Annette, they just looked at one another and their eyes near audibly locked and although it didn't really happen very often, they both of them knew just exactly what they meant. Then they slid over their glances in unison to their mother who still just stood there, two stiff fingers of one hand idly stroking at a bangle on her wrist.

'Turn off the centre light now, will you Clifford? There's a good boy. Don't go on working too late, Annette – you'll strain your eyes. Now then – why don't we have on the Everly Brothers again? And then hands up who's having the last of the Smarties!'

♥

See that, did you? Heard it all? Couldn't really have failed to – the look, that look on everyone's faces as I walked into the room. And good God, the worst of it is that that was meant to have been one of my rather better, less intimidating, entrances, believe it or no. I'd actually rehearsed it – gone over and over it on the top deck of the bus over a couple of pipefuls. This time, Arthur, I'd kept on telling myself, make a bit of an effort – try not to come over as the ogre at the feast, or however that . . . what is it? Saying, is it? Goes or doesn't go. Because it was old Geoff in the office, you know, who first observed it in me. Came as a total bombshell. Said to me, he said Arthur old man – hope you won't think I'm, you know, sticking my oar in where it doesn't belong and all the rest of it, but um . . . And me, I said back to him Well come on then, Geoff, out with it – we've been friends for how long? And Geoff (nice chap, you know – gentle sort. Wouldn't hurt a fly – you know the sort, I'm sure you've met them – thin on the ground these days, though: not like before the War). Anyway, Geoff, he says to me Well it's just that I've been noticing, Arthur – like when I bumped into you in Kenton Road that time. Member? I was just coming out of the Post Office, Saturday it was, three, four weeks back, and there you were with Gillian and the nippers. Yes? Member? Think you'd been to the Electricity Showroom. It's not the first time I've noticed it and I vowed then and there to make a mental note and next time we were, you know – having a chin-wag, sort of style, I swore to myself I'd, um, bring it up, as it were. I mean to say it's no skin off my nose either way, if you know what I'm saying to you Arthur – it's just that I thought, well, maybe he doesn't know, just maybe he isn't, well – aware of what he does and the general sort of effect it has on all parties concerned, if you get my drift. Sorry if I'm talking out of turn, old man – I mean I'll shut up right now if you want me to: you've only got to say the word, Arthur old boy.

Well – that's Geoff for you: takes an absolute eternity to get anything said, and even then there's precious little to get your teeth into. But it's his nature, you see – he's kind-hearted by nature, old Geoff is. Cut off his own right hand before he'd offend a single soul, old Geoff would. Single man, he is – and more than likely to stay that way, if I'm any judge: I used to take pity.

'Oh heaven's sake *out* with it, Geoff – there's a good lad. Told you – won't be offended. Too much water's gone under the bridge.'

'Well, Arthur – it's just that I've noticed that when you're with your, you know – family, sort of thing, well . . . you're really quite different, you know. Not the same, when you're around them . . . not at all like when it's, say, tea break at work, or something. Not the same at all.'

'Really? Well how do you mean, Geoff? How do you mean, not the same . . .?'

'Well it's – hard to put a finger on, really. Sounds a bit daft, in the cold light of day. But just take the way the two of us are talking now, as a for instance. Just chatting away, aren't we? The two of us. Normal sort of thing. But if your boy were here, say, or Gillian or someone, well then you'd sort of be, I don't know – pontificating. Now don't go taking offence, will you Arthur?'

'Pontificating? What exactly, um . . .?'

'Well you see like now – you just batted it back to me, didn't you? Which is absolutely spot-on, no problems there. I've just got the feeling that if you were, you know – en famille as 'twere, you might have gone something like, oh – I don't know, something like: "*Pontificating*, you say? There's a mighty word from so humble a mouth." Something on those lines. See? What I mean? A sort of a put-down all the time – but not just a put-down, a put-down's not so bad – but you use all this sort of language that, I don't know – you don't seem to, normally. Not on a day-to-day basis. Not in my earshot, anyway. Not around the office. Well: that's more or less what I mean. That's pretty much the long and short of it. Make any sort of sense to you, does it old man?'

Well I think my first reaction was probably bluster – I'm fairly sure that would've been my way of dealing with it all. You don't know what you're *talking* about, Geoff, I very likely was going to him: all in your imagination – watching too much of that Channel Nine, too many plays, that's your problem, Geoff. But then I got to thinking, turning over a few recent little scenes in my head, if you know what I mean – and do you know by jingo, I thought, I think that man's hit the nail on the head: give him a cigar. Because I *do* do that – I *do* do all of what Geoff was going on about, and I never realised – never heard it. Never really saw it till now. It's just – what I *do*, is all I can tell you: never ever gave it a second thought. I mean it must've started, ooh – way, way back, is all I can imagine, and then over the years it must just have become second nature, natural to me, somehow. It's born of two things, is the nearest I can come. When Gillian and me, when we were both first married, it was a gay old time, what with one thing and another: we had a whale of a time, first off. She was a bit of a corker in those days, I don't mind telling you, and we fairly got up to all sorts. She looked up to me, Gillian did – a very fair little wife, she was: no complaints on that score.

Always calling me the 'Master of the House', that sort of thing – and not just when there were people about, either. I think I must have grown into the role, as the years flew by. You know – if there was any little question, any niggling little quandary, I used to feel that I was being called upon to, well – *pontificate*, if you like (want of a better word). And once I had pronounced, as it were – well, all was right with the world once more and we could all carry on in our merry little way.

I suppose it all became more, what shall I say – intense, when Annette came along; and then Clifford, of course (now there was a surprise: knocked my budget squarely into a cocked hat, did Master Clifford. He was the beginning of the other worry, the biggest worry; it all got going with Clifford). Because now, you see, I was not just the master of the house, I was *father* of the house as well, and didn't she let me know it, Gillian, at every given opportunity. And it changed for me, you see. Instead of seeing it as, oh I don't know – some sort of an accolade, a badge, a bit of status or something, I came to feel it was all becoming rather a burden, something I had to carry around with me night and day, something I could never put down and let someone else take a turn. I'm not saying it was Gillian's fault – or the young 'uns, not their fault either. How could it be? They're only nippers – how could they be to blame for anything, really? But I couldn't . . . how can I say this? I, couldn't accept it was *my* fault either, this pressure, this growing pressure on me to shine, to perform, to always be right, always have the answer. Because if the truth be told, I didn't have the answer, I never had the answers to anything at all – I was out of my depth, had hardly a clue; and half the time these days I'm not at all sure I even understand the nature of the *questions*, and never mind the ruddy answers.

So that, I'm sure, is how it all came about – and then I think I must have entered into the second sort of phase, the second part of this where I came to positively need it: I *required* this sanctimonious and I suppose it must be oh God so dreary, so very dreary and predictable, all this nonsense I come out with, the language, this air I have about me – I came to need it, you see, in order to hide behind. To conceal what little there is left of me. So that when someone asked me a perfectly straightforward question, instead of coming right out and answering it, and there's an end to the matter, I would instead comment in a suitably arch and deprecating manner upon the oddness or stupidity or inappropriateness of the question, whatever ruddy question it happened to be. And it's all got muddled now – here's the pity. Because some of the things I say I do genuinely believe, you see. Like take that pop record of Clifford's by that yahoo with the nancy haircut, can't remember the little idiot's name – Richard someone, is it? Can't stand it, terrible row, ought to be banned along with all the rest of the hit parade, I believe they call it. But other things I say – like when the two of them, he and Gillian, are working on their latest jigsaw, well I really don't mind that at all, you see – quite like it, as a matter of fact: a peaceful scene, isn't it, of an evening, let's face it. Perfectly fine in anyone's book. But at some point and for some reason or other that completely eludes me I must have said, mustn't I, that it was distracting – distracting! – and so whenever in the evening these days a jigsaw is mooted, well then either Clifford or Gillian will say Oh dear me no we can't do it in here because it's one of Daddy's 'in' evenings and you know how he finds it so *distracting*. Same with Gillian's knitting – used to find the gentle and rhythmical click-clacking of it really rather soothing (made me feel, and please try not to laugh, that I was Master of the House, or something), but in some idle moment in between knocking out my pipe and pretending to grapple with 17 across or 20 down, I must in my infinite wisdom have pronounced that it too was 'distracting', the knitting, and so of course it would never again happen, not in my sainted presence.

So what I'm trying to say, I suppose, in this rather lumbering and roundabout way is that I am *aware* – I do now *know* about this, thanks to not just Geoff but a good deal of thought on the matter, though still it doesn't seem to *help* me at all, this knowledge. I don't seem to – no matter how hard I try, and I do, I do try hard, believe it if you will – I just don't seem to be able to stop it. It's all out of my mouth and hanging in the air and causing this miasma of despair to descend upon all and sundry before I'm even aware that my brain had so much as even formulated the words. During the fairly early days of all this, quite a number of my so-called 'out' evenings were in all honesty for *their* sake. I had nowhere to be, nothing to see to – I just removed myself and my terrible manner from their blameless presence: gave them a chance to just breathe again. And I know, I just know they came to look forward to such evenings – I am wholly aware (and I'm not saying it doesn't pain me), that when I am out, it can only be seen to be good news, and who, pray, could fail to understand? That, though, was as I say in the early days. It's different now. I go out now because I need to, pure and simple – not that it can, in truth, be either thing. Because you see, if you find yourself ambling about aimlessly, evening after evening, eventually – it is the nature of the beast – something will find you. The gods will discern and plumb the murky nature of your need and sooner or later it will find a place to lodge. Did I say gods? I don't really think it was the gods, you know, who were at the bottom of the plotting that has brought me to this. Gods had nothing whatever to do with it. I honestly do not believe it to be overstretching the truth, you know, when I say that if only I could have found it within myself to be a more loving and demonstrative husband and father, then I would not now find myself reduced to what little I have become. If only Gillian had maybe once or twice just answered me back (a thing, of course, she never would do); if only my old pal Geoff had been a bit less of the white man and had told me, made me aware of all this just so much sooner; if only I myself could just have seen and heard what was all around me, and all of it of my own sorry making. Well there – they didn't, I didn't, and here I now find myself.

Tonight, tonight I made an effort; I know it doesn't seem so, but I did. I stayed on the bus for two extra stops because I hadn't yet got it all satisfactorily worked out in my head, not just yet: I'm so very unused to all this. And then, when I thought it was as good as I could make it, I walked back to the house quite slowly (saw the glowing of the fire against the curtains) and let myself in as quietly as I could. I'd bought a box of, what are they . . .? Half a pound of Dairy Box, from Lawrence's in the Lane. My idea was this: they all would have had their supper – in the sitting room, of course, with the blazing fire, not around the table next door watching icicles form, as I always had deemed simply had to be the way – and they would be chattering away thirteen to the dozen, doing a bit of jigsaw, maybe, and then I would come in with a smile on my face (do you hear that, Arthur? With a *smile* on your face) and say something on the lines of Oh, I decided I wouldn't go out after all – it's bitter out, terrible night – and look everyone! Dairy Box – I know how you like them. Mm – let me get a bit of a warm by the fire. Oh I say – you have done well with that jigsaw, haven't you? It *has* come on – you'll be done with it in no more than two shakes of a lamb's tail. (Annette, of course, I would endeavour to include in the general bonhomie – couldn't decently address her directly, the way things are currently standing.) And the idea was that I would be welcomed – welcomed by my family, and then I was going to say to Gillian (I'd worked it all out, you see – I'd worked it all out on the top of the bus), I was going to suggest to her that she knit me, why didn't she, a nice new scarf that I could wrap around my face when the next peasouper descends upon us all – and I tell you what, Gillian, if you're agreeable, why not get started on it right here and now? And she'd say – she'd be smiling, of course, smiling and laughing in the way that she used to – she'd say oh *what* a lovely idea, Arthur – and have you eaten? Because I've got a bit of ham, I could do you a sandwich with a couple of gherkins. And I'd say no no – I had a pie in the pub. You just see to all your wool and needles and so on and I'll just slip into the kitchen and make us all a nice cup of tea – or would you prefer Tizer, Clifford? Eh? I know you like it.

Yes well. You heard what happened: you saw what went on. I can't really explain. It was just the sight of the Smarties, really (sounds so terribly stupid) – what did they want with my Dairy Box if they were already gorging themselves on a packet of Smarties? And Clifford, he already had some Tizer, look – and that terrible song was on the radiogram, that really did make me sour, and then Gillian jumped up and she turned it off and suddenly all was silent and they were all just looking at me, all of them just giving me that look that they did, and so I . . . well, I said what I said and I left them to it and now I am here. Here I am. In this place: again. I seem to have, I believe the technical term for it is an addictive personality (it's a sort of a disorder) – which I must say came as a total surprise to me. You know – when I realised that that is what I was. I can only suppose that the reason my addictions had never previously made themselves known to me is that, well – never before had I been subject to their teasing, been at the mercy of their pitiless guile. Before, in my life, I'd never really *done* anything, you see – never ever been anywhere to speak of. When I was a lad, money was so very painfully tight that I never seemed to have anything at all that I wanted. Made a few toys out of sticks, and things: bits of old wood, coils of string. Once my father and mother took me to the Peak District for what turned out to be my first and last holiday, as a child. Instead of sitting at home in our Clerkenwell basement watching the rain cascading into the drains, we all went to the Peak District for a week and watched it happening up there. I left school, if you can call it school, and – still a child – got a job at the haberdasher's, Cole's it was called, on the High Street, lifting and carrying. My father, he died of exhaustion at the age of forty-three – never really knew the man – and my mother, she said to me I should go out and strive to make something of myself; I didn't want, she said, to be working with my hands all the hours God sent me: look at what happened to your poor old father. I was an only child: I don't think that either of them could have faced it a second time. So I read in the Library that even if you hadn't the education to be something so mighty as a solicitor at bar, still you could study to be articled as a clerk. Which I did do – all the while heaving boxes and bales, though, to keep myself only just barely alive. I failed the exams, and I'd worked so hard. I never told my mother that I failed my exams – I've never told Gillian either, come to that. She fondly imagines me to be a solicitor's clerk, but I'm not, not really. Oh I'm a *clerk* – oh God yes I'm a clerk, but all I do is filing, really. Filing and making appointments for other people and lifting and carrying, is basically what it is. I'll do any sorts of overtime. I thought when the War came, the Army would rescue me – take me away – but it was my feet that did for me. And that's been my life, I'm afraid to say – not like the kids of today, is it really? Kids of today – they didn't have to go through the War (my mother, she died in a raid – direct hit, it was: a direct hit on our hole in Clerkenwell. Had she not urged me to get out and earn myself a living, I'd have still been with her, the moment it struck). And money – they think it grows on trees; money, they think it's like water from a tap – they really don't know they're born. So I suppose what I'm saying, what I'm trying to get across here, is that before, oh – just a few years ago, really, no more than a couple of years, it can't be, I'd never been exposed to just anything at all. I am now, though – these days I'm exposed to all sorts, and each of them has got me by the throat.

And how, one might wonder (and it's a reasonable question – I could well understand it), can I possibly afford to live even as modestly as I do, if that is the nature of my work (and always has been, and always will be)? After all, I have a mortgage to service, do I not? Two children – yes two, it was one, but then it became two – both attending private schools. Have you any idea, any idea at all, the level of money they charge you, these places? I almost quite literally just simply fail to believe it can be true, to be perfectly frank with you. But there – I'm caught. Completely caught, aren't I? And then there's Gillian's housekeeping to see about, isn't there? To take care of. And lately there's also been the Hoover, the little fridge – that Hotpoint, that was a pretty penny, I can assure you of that. And the children, Clifford and Annette, they constantly seem to be in need of, oh – something or other; if it's not one ruddy thing, then it's another – shoes, pencils and pens, oh God I just can't go listing it all: you know what kids are like. Well, as to the household appliances, I really had to get them. Gillian, she was working herself into an early grave, you only had to look at her. I just had to get her those because, well, just look at it: what else have I brought her? What else? She got herself a little Singer (she doesn't say it's because we can't afford new clothes); said she saved up for it out of the housekeeping – which is really quite funny in itself, poor Gillian, were it not so very shame-makingly sad; it is a miracle to me how she makes it stretch at all, the money I give her. And if I could give her more I would. If she'd got a ha'penny over come pay day it would be cause for a celebration. I know she's got it on the H. P., the Singer, but I've said nothing about it – not brought it up with her. Well I can't, can I? She knows I'm dead against any sort of debt – how many times have I bored the woman into the ground going on and on and on about it, the iniquity of debt? The awful truth is, though (and this is just the sort of thing I mean: the sort of thing that's happening to me now, and I can barely stand it), I believe every word of what I'm saying – I do think that debt is a killer, and a shaming road down which to wander. But how on earth do you imagine I managed to get for her the Hoover and the Hotpoint and the Kelvinator? The lowest sum possible I pay to them every week; even if I die when I'm a hundred (so very unlikely) I doubt we'll yet own the things. And, um – the school fees? Ah yes – the school fees. I started by borrowing at the bank. The bank, though – being a bank – was quite quick to see that there was no possibility of my meagre and seemingly forever frozen wages ever keeping pace with the constantly rising school fees; they politely suggested I set about making alternative arrangements. I asked for a raise at work. They said no. They politely suggested that if I was unhappy in their employ, I maybe ought to set about making alternative arrangements. So I went to a money lender, and with him I remain. No matter how much you pay, the debt is always rising: the relationship can never be fleeting: it would send you insane, if you saw it on paper. And don't think they are at all hard to find, these loan sharks (is what I am told they are called). In fact it would not be stretching the truth over-far to suggest that it is they who do the finding; they sense the desperation, you see. No matter how distant, they track the hum and follow the whiff, baying as the pungency rises, and trace it right back to the stench of source: me, in this case. And so then I discovered whisky, which costs me more than two pounds a bottle (money I should be giving to Gillian; and I would if I could). I consider it a necessity. At first, here was just a little something for myself, a small and solitary comfort, just a wee thing clawed back from the ravages of all this expenditure. But I got to like the taste of it remarkably quickly; at first it was just for the warmth, more than anything – a hot little pull at it, made me feel cherished, made me feel there was somewhere I could go. But soon, a bottle was lasting me no time at all.

So. I am deeply in debt to all the wrong people and I hate, I loathe, I just detest any so-called man who could get himself into so hopeless a situation. My need for whisky is absolute – and I really can't stand that, you know: reliance on a substance, any substance at all, I utterly despise it. The other thing I have long held in the most total contempt (just ask Gillian) is gambling, of course, and so that is what I next turned my hand to. That is, in part, why I find myself here. In this place. For here I am. Again. Because all it comes down to, you see, is simply survival, the meanest and most precarious form, now, of just about survival. The spluttering aeroplane with a punctured heart which must constantly strive to keep up, keep up, keep on up just a little while longer: the lift – the lift it must always be beating the drag. The lift, it must vanquish the drag, or else we must surely go down, and then we go under.

That Hortense, she's just walked in now. You know straight away – never mind all the thick air and the gloom and the heavy smoke that hangs in a veil down here, you always know if some-one with hope in their eyes is squeezing themselves in or else if some wild and devastated blighter is barging his way out again because the room, this room, well, it's really no bigger than your average parlour, largely I suppose because that's exactly once what it must have been. Yes – in another time, this rather damp, it always seems, and nondescript but oddly and chillingly warming little basement flat in what must be a, well what now, Victorian, almost certainly a Victorian sort of tenement house, I think that's what it is . . . some years ago, maybe – before the War for sure – this will have been a modest little family home, I expect: enough space for two or three people, four at a pinch, and a bit of a garden out at the back. Before that, though – I mean round about the time they built it, this house – here were probably just the kitchens and the scullery and the larders and so on, to service all the rooms above. And whoever lived upstairs, well-to-do tradespeople conceivably, they're all dead now, aren't they? Long gone. Along with all the poor skivvies and wretches who in return for a crust and a roof over their heads worked themselves to death on behalf of their so-called betters – like my forty-three-year-old father, for one. Dead – all dead. Everyone who was alive just a hundred years ago – Queen Victoria, the old Queen, her Prime Minister, whoever he may have been, and the butchers and newsvendors and shoeshines and ladies of quality and schoolchildren and soldiers and the people who used to shovel up the buckets of horse manure from the streets of London – all of them are gone, all gone, every single last man jack of them. Even the undertakers – the final leeches, excepting the government: gone, all gone. The buildings, though – that's where London really comes into its own, isn't it? Well all cities really, I suppose – it's true of all cities, that – but I've never been to any other: London is all I know. The buildings, they soldier on, don't they? Grim and impassive, through thick and thin. Even with all the bomb sites we've still got strewn all over, the city, it seems so remarkably unchanged. Because we adapt, you see – like the colonies of ants. You step down hard slap bang in the middle of this drilled and dedicated army and there's a little bit of a to-do for a second or so while they briefly break ranks and pick up their dead and then on they go, thinking the Lord knows what – off they go, scurrying away with this single-minded urgency to eagerly attend to nothing at all. And that's just what we've been doing, I suppose, since the end of the War. Just getting on with it, whatever 'it' is (because no one ever tells you) – just making do and mending: soldiering on.

So now, this old building – or this little part of it – has evolved into what it is now, because it somehow must justify its continued existence. Rosie's, they call it – but I've never seen a Rosie down here. And it attracts the sort of people who are faced with a similar dilemma; but it isn't one really, is it? A dilemma. Adapt or die? For the moment I should be pleased that I unhesitatingly plump for the former option: let us hope it remains so stark and clear. So this room, now – it's all just badly mismatched bits of bedroom carpet and shaded light bulbs that are barely worth it. There's a fizzy sort of music, just about audible – could be that nigger jazz, but it needn't be. Then there's a mish-mash of sofas and chairs and the little bar there, tucked into the corner, and Saul, he's the man who runs it – walks with a limp and one of his eyes is glass (blue – unlike the real one, which is brown: we don't ask why or how) – he always has one hand raised up to a ribbed steel shutter just above the optics, ready to haul it down should someone come in who isn't altogether welcome. Anyway it's Hortense who's come in now – never seems to take a night off, Hortense doesn't; it's an odd name, Hortense (the leaden jokes, they're all made nightly). I doubt it's her own. And anyway, she's making a beeline right for me, which doesn't, I have to say, surprise me even a bit. She knows that I am an all-or-nothing sort of a person – and so if I'm here at all, it's got to be worth everyone's while. All these people who are slumped around me whom I barely know and hardly care for, tonight they'll all end up winners in one way or another; only myself and the people I love – we are the only poor souls who are slated to lose. Except that tonight, of course – tonight could maybe be the night I strike it lucky: let's just keep our fingers crossed.

'Freshen that up for you, will I sweetie?'

I looked down at my glass of whisky and I laughed. I laughed in one convulsion – more like an unstoppable sneeze, but far more guttural. Bit like, maybe, when they do that, what is it – when you're choking and they do a manoeuvre on you; here was a bitter gobbet of mirth, just forced out of me. It was simply those words of hers – and hearing them down here. The single thought that anything could be freshened; the very idea of me as a sweetie . . .

'What's so funny, dear? Something tickling your fancy, is it? You look tired, you do Arthur. You know that? You maybe want to slip next door, do you? Have a bit of a lie-down? Nurse Hortense come in and soothe your fevered brow? How's that sound?'

My first thought was Oh God *please* – I've only got about eight quid on me and that I've got to save for the game because if I don't walk out of here tonight with a minimum of fifty (hundred I'd be laughing) then I am in very big trouble all round – and with Mickey in particular; you don't know Mickey, and believe me, you don't at all want to. And you, Hortense – even for a brisk rub-down and that thing you do with those so great udders you've got, you still are expecting thirty bob from me, aren't you honey? Not that I blame you – we've all got to get by somehow, the best way we know. And then I was charged with it – lust, it was all over me. Wasn't even thinking about it before – wasn't the way my mind was going. But then she said it, didn't she? Said what she said and I remembered the last time and I looked at her hands with the blood-red talons and then she was licking her lips at me like that and I was stroking her hip as it curved away in that green and showy cocktail frock and *Yes*, I said: *Yes*, Hortense, let's do that now because if I wait until after the game there may not be the one-pound-ten that is all you ask for lifting me out of all this, if only for just a few brief and squirming, joyful moments.

So we went next door, Hortense and me, into a partitioned-off section of what was once half a room, before they subdivided it. From beyond the stud and plasterboard walling you could hear this poor old devil going Lick! Lick me, lick me! And a gravelly-voiced strumpet, she came back with Get off, grandad – you ain't paid for no licking. Did it put me off? make me feel sad or grubby or even disgusted? No: I simply wanted it more than ever – and Hortense, she's a good girl really because I think she sensed this and she set about me soon and quite thoroughly. All over in no time flat – barely had time to disengage that one engorged nipple from among my gums. I was momentarily exhausted, and then I was no longer.

'Your moustache,' Hortense was giggling, as she hitched up and tugged together all her pink and black elasticated under-things, criss-crossing straps and galumphing back her breasts into a virtual pair of underwired windsocks (because she's a big girl, Hortense, no bones about it). 'It's ever so bristly, your little moustache. All right are you, Arthur? You OK my love? Yeh? Nice. That's thirty bob then, sweetie.' She brought her lips down on mine as she thrust the notes rustlingly into her cleavage, and I closed my eyes and I kissed the gin inside her.

The game, it was well under way by the time I chalked up another Scotch and got myself in there, but there's never a prob-lem with cutting me a hand: well look at it – why on earth would there be? Jimmy was dealing – they say he's Maltese; I don't mind what he is, quite frankly. Big man though, Jimmy – meaty hands, the cards when he's holding them, they look like minia-tures: you wouldn't want to get on the wrong side of him. The other faces were sort of familiar to me – I once, maybe, knew one or two of their names. I nodded to each of them briefly, lit up my pipe and took a good pull of whisky and then I tossed a pound into the centre of the table, quite as if it didn't at all matter to me – as if it were litter I was eager to be rid of (this is how it's done: I've watched them and I've learned. This is how it's done). The game itself . . . well it isn't a game, not in any sense a normal person would readily understand. What I mean to say is it's not poker or rummy or anything you'd know, and nor is it a game in the sense that you might actually enjoy it. It's all down to num-bers, fundamentally – cards are dealt and the highest number to be twisted wins the pot: ace is the lowest card, some reason, and Kings are top of the pile. It's tedious, it reminds me of filing – but then, when you start to win (when you start to lose) there's an urgency that comes and smothers you, and then you're sitting forward – something jerks you and you're hunched there, we all are – and your pipe, that's gone out and your drink is lying abandoned. I like that – well I sort of like that, but it scares me too: I sometimes clutch my heart, the fear can be that great.

Like take now – that quid I bunged down? Gone. Scooped up: like it never existed. So I've put down another – and it's a Jack I've drawn, and this is good. Bald man next to me – how he can see through those glasses of his I do not know, they're like mullions on a church door, or something – he's turned up a three, so that's him out. Next person's got a nine, and the bloke next to him, he's only drawn a six. I put down my Jack and the fat man at the end, he's got a Queen, so that's the end of that, then. And now I'm doing sums. Eight quid I had; thirty bob to Gypsy Rose Lee and I'm down to six-pound-ten. Two more I've just dropped now, so there's the arithmetic. But that's the way, isn't it? The way it goes. If I'd just thought I'd save my thirty bob – go back later and wake up Gillian, tell her to stop being stupid and just do what she's told ... and say I'd just been the winner of the last two rounds – well then I'd be on eighteen quid and well on a roll and towards my goal of fifty (hundred I'd be laughing). As it is – four-pound-ten and I've got a bar bill too, that must be up to about fourteen, fifteen shillings, the prices they charge – and once I worked it out: what you pay for a bottle here, nip by nip, you'd get the best part of a case at Victoria Wine: licensed robbery. Except they're not licensed. Anyway look – I've got to go careful. Not that you can – you can't, can you? Go careful. The cards are what they are. The only careful thing to do is to not ever come down here, and it's far too late to think like that. So anyway, another quid's gone in – and the bald man, I think he smells blood because he's upped it now (you can do that – you can up the bet in ten-bob increments, and people either follow or fold). Well I've got to follow because *I've* got a Queen this time and that means there are only four cards in the whole pack that can beat me – so what are the odds against him having a King, the bald man? There's a ten to my left and then a two is chucked in, with a disgusted sigh. I put down my Queen, the bald man hisses and throws down a Jack. It's all up to the fat man now – I'll soon know what he's got because he's arching back the card, look, and now he's going to flick it: and damn me – oh God – if it isn't a Queen. All I hear is a collective gasp, and I know I've been a part of it. What happens now is, the two of us we each draw again. He goes first – and it's a seven! A seven, a seven – he's only got a seven! There are six cards now that'll beat a measly seven, and there's quite a pile of crumpled money to be scooped. So I gesture with impatience over to Jimmy and he scoots across a card and I flip it over quickly and I'm staring down now – and what I feel is anything you say I feel – at the ruddy Ace of Diamonds. I fall back in my chair as if I've been kicked there. A muted roar is rising around me, and the fat man he's grinning like a child and he keeps on saying Luck of the draw, luck of the draw, as he shuffles all the money towards him. If I'm going to pay for my drinks (and I will, I must – they have ways of dealing with people who don't) and if I'm going to allow enough for at least one more large one and then the bus fare home, then I'm talking two quid max as my remaining float. Which is a far cry from the fifty I was needing, God help me (and it won't be a hundred: I won't be laughing).

And then I get the feeling that everybody's looking. My eyes come up from my drink and I glance around me and it's true, they are. What's wrong, I say: something up, is there? And Jimmy, he takes the cheroot from the corner of his mouth and he says to me You in or what? And I say yes, course – I'm in, I'm in. And then he says Well? Well then? And then I twig to what's been going on – I was so preoccupied that I must have, I don't know, just drifted away for a couple of seconds, could barely have been more. The new cards have already been dealt and everyone's stake is on the table, bar mine. Sorry, I say – sorry about that, everyone – here we are, here's my quid. Sorry. Sorry. And now I sneak a look at the card in my hand, and oh God, oh joy, I can barely believe it! This is the moment, here is the instant that goes so far to making all the pain worth while. I'm holding in my hand the King of Spades – the sternness of his profile, it makes me want to kiss him. It's the fat man speaking again: he wants to double the stake if no one objects because soon, he says, he's got to be getting himself off. Fine with me, I say – and I drop down another pound note (my last, as it happens, but he's not to know that, no one is – and anyway it's only temporary, it's only for now). One chap drops out ('too rich for my blood') but the others are game. Then an eight (why did he follow? If all he had was an eight?) and now there's a Queen and God I do feel good, as I quietly place next to her my noble King of Spades. I'm nearly on to the money – I'd forgotten the fat man, but I remembered him now because he's just slapped down the King of Hearts. I can barely believe it! Exactly the same thing has just happened again. Even Jimmy – even Jimmy's just said something, and Jimmy – this is known – Jimmy, he just never speaks at all, unless it's a threat. But he has now, spoken – I heard him. What he said was Hm: don't happen often. And he's right, he's right – it don't, doesn't – it doesn't happen often – it happens *never* – it *never* happens, this, because in just the last two rounds now, the fat man has drawn the very same high card that I got, and now we've got to draw again, just like last time, and I'm not sure I can bear it again, the sensation of not knowing if soon I will soar, or soon I will crumple. Jimmy, now – he's slipped over the cards: one to me, and one to the fat man. All I can do is just tease away the corner from the table . . . it's . . . it's looking good. I scoop up the card and I cradle it with care within the palm of my hand as if it is a precious thing – which, of course, it is (to me – very). I have a Jack. A red Jack.

119

I look over at the fat man. And in his eyes, I see nothing. He doesn't look unhappy, though, that much I can take in. He couldn't, could he, have a Jack? I mean it couldn't be, could it, that we have to draw *again* . . .? The tension, then, I think it could break me. As it is, I'll never know – whether it would or wouldn't have broken me, the tension – because now he throws down a Queen and my face. I think my face must have said everything he needed to know. I haven't even put down my card, and already his hands are all over the heap of crinkled notes and now as he rakes them towards him, they make that rushing noise – it is the noise that along with the coughing clank from a one-armed bandit that penniless people, they know so well and pine for. Well, says the fat man, pushing back in his chair as he struggles to his feet – and my eyes now, they're right on a level with this ruddy great backside of his, and my God is he getting his moneysworth from the seams on those trousers: he's got to be twenty stone, this man. Well, he says – and he's actually ramming now all these pound notes into the side pockets of this blazer he's got with brass buttons all down it and some sort of RAF badge, looks like: both hands grabbing at the loot and crushing it into these gaping pockets. Well, the fat man says – and I don't want to think about just how much he's won, to be perfectly honest with you; I mean the bald man, he won a fair bit, but it's the fat man who's the cat that's got the cream – he was coining it in even before I sat down at the table. He could easily have fifty – he might even have a hundred because look at him: he's laughing. Well, he says – thank you, gentlemen, no doubt we will encounter one another again at some future date I trust not too long distant: but until such time, adieu! I was indifferent to his total existence until he upped and came out with that little lot: I hate him now, and I always will. But just look at the weight on him, will you? God's punishment, that could well be. It's a judgement on him, that's what that is. Could have a heart attack and keel over like a big dead horse just any moment at all. Shame it couldn't have been about ten minutes ago, but there it is. And me? Well I'm off too now, I suppose. Make a bit of a show of looking at my watch – shoot up the eyebrows in a display of mild surprise – and then shuffle over to Saul and settle up the bar bill (eighteen and nine – how can they begin to justify it?) and now I'm in the narrow little hall with all the flaking plaster just above the wainscot and there's a bit of a smell of urine, and maybe of cats – and oh look, it's Hortense, Hortense is here and she's pulling back the bolts and as she takes a quick shufti into the black outside, right and left, a flurry of icy air is all round my ankles and now she's holding just open the door and she's saying to me OK, dearie – off you go, then – had a good evening, have you sweetie? Now don't be a stranger, will you Albert? And I say goodnight, Hortense. See you soon – but until such time, adieu! And I don't say – what would be the point? – oh and actually, Hortense, it's Arthur, not Albert, my name. I don't say that to her, no. Because how could it matter? It's not, is it, as if we were lovers.

It's cold, damn cold out here – and all around me now, it seems so utterly dark. I'm in good time for at least two more buses, though. I think I've got to get myself out of this little front garden now, because it really is as black as the pit round here and my foot, it's just been sucked sideways into something quite marshy. I don't wonder what it is – I don't think of anything now because I'm aware, you know, quite suddenly of someone beside me. I go hallo? Hallo? Who's that there? Help you, can I? And he strikes a match and lights up his cigarette and then I get to see who it is, this person just standing beside me.

'Oh. Oh it's you, Mickey. Hallo. How are you getting on? All right?'

'More to the point, how are *you* getting on, Arthur? Done well in there, did you? Bit of a tickle? Made a few bob? I hope you didn't go blowing it on booze and floozies.'

'No – course not. Yeh – did all right, did OK. Little touch.'

'I am very pleased to hear that, Arthur. Very pleased indeed. Because it won't have slipped your mind, will it? Arthur. Our little appointment for tomorrow evening? It wouldn't do to forget it.'

'Course I remember, Mickey. Course I do. Be there on the dot.'

'Pleased, Arthur. I'm pleased. Because as I say, it wouldn't do to forget it. You see, Arthur, we haven't been doing business for too long, have we? Now I don't know what you heard about me, but do know this: you cross on a deal with me, Arthur, and listen – I *will* do you harm. You hear me? You will be the subject of definite harm. All right? But no offence, Arthur. I'm sure it'll never come to that.'

'Ha ha. No. Course not.'

'Well goodnight then, Arthur. Until tomorrow evening, then.'

He threw down his cigarette and the darkness was once again total. He was gone, then – didn't see him go, I just knew that he was gone. I was shaking; I put one hand on top of the other, and I felt them both shaking. I can't think about it, though – what Mickey just said to me. What I'm going to do is I'm going to walk quite slowly out of this blessed little garden and on up to the bus stop and while I'm doing that I'm going to go over in my head what paltry little plans I have left to me. And how I'm going to put them across to Gillian. I have thought in the past (it has occurred to me) about her getting some sort of a job, but face it – what is it she could do? And anyway – fair do's – she's got her hands full, hasn't she? What with the kids and the house and all. So it's down to me, as per usual – and all I've got is this: I'm going to ask the boss around for supper. I know, I know – it's not a masterstroke, is it? It's hardly a brainstorm. But I figured that if I could get him, you know, in a nice and cosy domestic sort of an atmosphere – see the wife, see the kids, see the little home I've got there . . . well then after a very decent little supper (and I've no complaints on that score – she's all right in the kitchen,

Gillian is, she's pretty all right), then he might, you know, the following morning, say, see his way to maybe upping my salary. For the first time since God knows when. Well there's a chance, isn't there? Slim, yes – but it's a chance, and I've just got to take it. And then there's the lodger idea – there's good money to be made out of a lodger, Geoff at work was telling me that time: he does it, on and off. And it's cash in hand, which can only be all to the good. So that's another little scheme. And of course I could be giving up the whisky and the tobacco and losing to the four winds whatever is remaining down at Rosie's but I'm not, of course, going to. Because I just can't, it's as simple as that.

Well I'm at the bus stop now, but there's no sign yet of a bus in the distance. And oh God – who comes up to me now but that ruddy Mrs Farlow from above the baker's and that frump of a friend of hers, can't remember her name – something Jessop, it might well be. I think it's the housey-housey, the lotto, they go to, most evenings – squandering their housekeeping. The number of times I seem to run into them . . .

'Oh hello, Mr Coyle. Well this *is* a coincidence. I say this *is* a coincidence, isn't it Mary? We were only this very afternoon having a little natter in the Lane with *Mrs* Coyle, weren't we Mary?'

'We were. Only this very afternoon. It's quite a coincidence. And she *did* seem well, didn't she? Very well within herself.'

'Very well *indeed*, is what I'd say Mary. Very well *indeed*.'

I sort of smiled, I think, and then I hitched up the collar on my coat and quite swiftly moved away. I'll maybe walk, I thought – it's not that far, I'll maybe walk. And Gillian – she's up there in my mind, now. That Farlow woman, she's made me think of Gillian, just by that mention of her. So I think I'll have to wake her – I don't like to do it but I have to have a bit of a tumble now because I've got the taste for it, you see, from Hortense. Addictive – it's addictive, in the way that most things are. I mean I know she's got an early start in the morning and everything,

Gillian, but I won't take up much of her time: all she has to do is just tug at me a bit – I'll be doing the bulk of the work for her. Once – just one time – she really wasn't having it no matter how much I went on at her and I got into a little bit of a state that night, I recall. Had to go in and see how little Annette was doing – just for a bit of a stroke, mind – nothing at all nasty. I don't think she even woke up – because I wouldn't, you know, ever want to harm her, or anything. It's just the balance I have to keep because once, you see, once, it isn't ever enough: not to me. But I love them, you know – I really do love them, all of my family – I love them dearly. It's just that the way I do it, well . . . it often comes out a bit strange. It's really just a question of the lift forever having to beat the drag: the lift must beat the drag.

I sometimes do hope, you know, that this – all of this, my life as it is – that it's really no more than only a phase. And all I'm doing is just going through it.

♥

Annette had just taken down the small mirror from the bathroom shelf and now she was placing it on the floor of her room just a bit to the side of the tallboy – wedged it from behind with a couple of Malory Towers, so as to keep it vertical and from falling right over. Next she slipped her feet into her mother's two-tone cream and navy court shoes and squinted downwards to see how they looked. They're miles too big, of course, because I only take a $2\frac{1}{2}$, but I actually think the general sort of look of them is really pretty good. It's true what Margery said, I've proved it now – even a little and dumpy heel like this, it does make your legs look longer like a woman in that magazine called *Vogue* which Mummy never gets but you see it in the newsagent – and a bit more curvy, which is why women wear them: I'm not stupid, thank you very much – I do know that. This slip of Mummy's I've got on – it does, it feels really really nice on me. All sort of slippery and really really nice. When you slide your hands all over and close your eyes you can sort of think how it would feel if a boy in the Fifth Form of a boys' school was doing it to you and you were going to later abandon yourself to the rapture of love and lots of proper kissing. If you lick some red liquorice comfits you can rub the stuff all over your mouth and it looks quite real. Elizabeth Taylor, she always has these really red lips and they're shiny too so I think she must lacquer them – but not obviously with the lacquer that you use on floorboards because that would taste foul. Every time you see a picture of her, she's got a new dress on – and she's also got fur coats and jewellery and just everything, really. I wish Mummy would dress like that, but she doesn't; I would if I was grown up. The dresses that Mummy wears, she's been wearing since probably before the War, I should think. She sometimes makes a new one but it looks just like all the old ones, so I can't see the point. And she makes things for me that are like for a little girl – all frilly and spotty and the sort of thing weedy and pathetic Alice would wear. I want some jeans but all Mummy says is that Daddy would have a fit. Clodagh's got some that she said were called Levy, but I don't think this can mean Mr Levy in the Lane because he only sells things like plums and greens. It is probably a coincidence.

There's baggy bits at the top of the slip, though, because I have yet to flower into the something of womanhood – that's what it said in a book that Clodagh had she said was by Milzum Boom. Deirdre in 4A, she's got all these bosoms that are nearly as big as Elizabeth Taylor's – her gymslip, it goes all gapey at the armholes because of all these bosoms that she's got at the front. Margery's are coming along quite nicely. She let me touch them in the boot room and I said that they felt nice and a bit like plums and she said that it felt nice when my fingers were on them and she said that she went a bit tingly. If we had been caught doing all of this, the Pope would have to have made us martyrs. I keep pulling at mine on the pink bits that are called nipples to try to bring them out, but they never come. Margery asked me if I ever touched myself in my legs at the front of my bottom where you go wee and I said that I did, all the time, and although it felt of something, I still just don't know what it is it feels of. It was better when I got Clifford to do it, but he only did it once and he pulled out his hand and he got all silly and probably embarrassed and he looked like he was going to burst out blubbing or something, or like it had hurt him, or something. I'm going to go into his room, later on. Got to make sure that Daddy's asleep, though, because otherwise he might come into my room like he sometimes does and go all grunty which I don't like at all. I expect he just wished he was married to Elizabeth Taylor and just abandon himself to the rapture of love, which I don't suppose Mummy does, much. I'd like to marry Elizabeth Taylor, and I'm a girl. All her house is pink and she's got this huge long car with no roof and that's pink too, which is my new favourite colour. I saw it in *Girl*. Also in *Girl* I cut out this picture of this boy who is called Fabian who I hadn't heard of and underneath it said he was dreamy, which I'm pretty sure means really really nice – but it could mean too that you dream of him when you are asleep which I would quite like to do, but no luck so far. He's got a really nice smile with dozens of teeth and piled-up hair like Elvis the Pelvis, only it's pale. I wanted to pin this picture of Fabian up on the wall (it says he is an American pop singer but I haven't heard any of his records) because everyone I know at school has pictures of things pinned up on their wall which is why they are called pin-ups, which is obvious. Clodagh – I don't go round to Clodagh's house any more because she's not my best friend any more since she went off with Susan and all those lot, but when she was my best friend and I used to go over I saw all these pictures pinned up above her bed of Cliff Richard (who Clifford really likes so I try not to say I like him too much or he'll keep going on and on and on about how he was right all the time; I'll never call him Cliff, though – not ever, no matter how much he begs and begs me, because he's just a little boy and Dopey suits him better). And as well as pictures of Cliff Richard, Clodagh she had up the Queen and these ponies and Snow White and the Seven Dwarfs, which are really sweet and I really like Dopey, but don't tell Clifford I do, and also her cat and Sir Laurence Olivier who is terribly old, not old like Grandma but pretty old anyway, and I think he must be a relation. Anyway, none of them's as good as Fabian – but Mummy, she went all crazy when I asked her if I could borrow four drawing pins because she said that Daddy would have a fit because I'd go and ruin the walls. Which is really unfair because just everyone else has pictures up and I jolly can't which I think is just so unfair. So I keep the picture of Fabian who I have decided is my boyfriend at the moment, I keep it just under my bed and inside my diary – which actually I've just got to write in before I go off and see Clifford (I heard Daddy come in so he must be asleep by now).

I finished all the rotten prayers and I did write a bit about springtime and what it meant to me (zero, actually) with bunnies and Easter eggs and stuff, but St Joseph and the isosceles triangles I just couldn't do any of because I got so tired and so there'll be trouble for that and I won't be allowed to blame Sister Joanna which I jolly well should be able to do because of it's all her fault. And in R.I., Sister Agnes will think I haven't written about St Joseph because I'm not very pious and it's not fair to say that because I am quite pious – not as pious as Helen is or thinks she is with her millions and millions of holy pictures, but still more pious than say *Clifford* because he just isn't pious at all, but then he's a boy. I bet that book of Clodagh's by Milzum Boom is on the Index, by the way, with all the good stuff which is wicked and bad for you. There's this huge library of books probably in the Vatican which is the house the Pope stays in in Italy with his priests and things and it's all full of these thousands and thousands of books that nobody's allowed to read. Well *he* is, obviously, because they're his books with his name in and he's Pope and also inedible. It may be not that word, but it means when you can't ever make any mistakes ever because you're top of the holy people and as pious as even someone like St Joseph, who was baby Jesus's father as everybody knows and he was in swaddling clothes and lay in a manger and you see him in the Nativity with oxen and wise men and Mary, obviously, because they had to have a mummy. Except she wasn't – not really. And St Joseph, he wasn't really the father either because God was and what Mary and Joseph had was Immaculate Conception which means you have a baby as usual and everything, but it's all done so that it's really really clean and spotless, so they didn't have to think of the mess. It's quite complicated, but you can sort of understand if you've got just buckets of Faith and you offer it up.

My diary, it's quite big and it's made of leatherette which is the same as on the chairs in the dining room except that my diary is bright green and the seats on the chairs are boring old brown, like everything else in this house. It had a lock on it but it broke really easily. I try to write in it every day but I never do. It's really private, my most private thing, and I wish I had a dressing table like the one I saw in John Lewis with curtains and things because then I could keep it in there instead of just under the bed with my perfume and my feathery scarves and powder puffs and jewellery which I also haven't got. Mummy said at supper that she was going to make me a dressing table out of orange boxes and remnants, which is just typical of my luck. I write in my diary in inedible ink, which may not be the right word but it means that no one can go rubbing it out or anything and so it will endure for ever like this sceptre'd isle which is set in a something sea. I always start off with 'Dear Diary' which is a bit pathetic because it's obvious really and anyway the only person who reads it is me and so what is the point? Actually, I don't really read it ever because it's pretty boring and there's loads of smudges and everything and it would be better if I used my biro but this wouldn't be as romantic as a proper pen. Anyway, here goes:

'Dear Diary – it is the end of the day now and what I have done is this: (1) Got into trouble because of Helen's holy pictures and Sister Joanna. (2) Made new best friends with M*A*R*G*E*R*Y who is really good because she does things you say and you can touch her bosoms if you want. Other girls call her Marge but I won't because then they say you can't tell stalk from butter which I don't understand because you can. (3) Hurt Alice really badly, which was very nice and I want to do it again. (4) Wrote out twenty Our Fathers because of see above.'

I'm really tired now: it's got quite late. I'm just going to open my door and really quietly go down the passage to the lavatory and then I can listen at Mummy and Daddy's door and see if it's OK to go in and see Clifford who will be sleeping like a baby. When I'm grown up and I've got my own house somewhere really nice like Hollywood or next to Selfridges and with this huge pink sofa and everything, I'm going to have my own room because I'll be able to afford it. I'd hate to share a room with someone like Daddy – it must be horrid. Mummy said once that I was just like my father and that Clifford, he took after her, she said, and I think she really must have hated me that day, I really must have done something really really bad or something, because she's never before said anything to me so nasty and unkind and normally she's not like that at all, not ever, so it must have been me. I knelt in my bare knees on the lino of the bathroom that night and I kept on saying Mayor Cooper, Mayor Cooper, like you're supposed to when you're to blame, and then the next day I did penance by giving away my Milky Way to someone completely pathetic like Alice except it wasn't Alice and then I really did suffer like a sinner because it says on the wrapper that it is the sweet you can eat between meals without spoiling your appetite and I don't know if that is true because I didn't eat it obviously but by supper my appetite was having a fit. They also say that the gooey bit in the middle of Milky Ways, that it's whipped and whipped a thousand times and that's what I should have been when I was going Mayor Cooper – and I tried it once with an elasticated belt but it's hard to reach and it jolly well hurt.

It's quite spooky, actually, when the house is all dark. It seems much bigger and you bump into things that you know where they are and it's even colder than it is when all the lights are on. It's completely quiet in Mummy and Daddy's room, which is good – at least he's not being beastly to her like he is, sometimes. So I'm just going to turn the handle on Clifford's door and then slip in there ever so quietly and I'm going to do it jolly quickly too because I forgot my slippers and my feet are completely f-f-f-f-freezing.

'Clifford . . .? Clifford – are you awake? It's me. Budge over.'

'Hmmm . . .? What . . .? Is it school time?'

'Oh don't be so stupid, Clifford. And *whisper*, because it's jolly late.'

'Oh what are you *doing*, Annette . . .? Why don't you get into your own bed?'

'Oh do shut *up* Clifford, can't you? Just shift over. There. Now just let me . . . oh take your *hands* away, Clifford, and just don't be so pathetic. Like a baby. Look – give me your hand . . . there. That's nice, isn't it? And I'll do yours. There. That's nice . . . isn't it? Isn't it?'

He's not saying anything, Clifford. Anyway – *I* think it all feels nice. I don't know what's wrong with Clifford. If *I* had a little tuppence like his sticking out and if I had bosoms like Deirdre's in 4A I'd just stay in bed or go to the boot room and keep fiddling about with them all the time. I don't have anything boys *or* girls have – just my wee and parcel holes, which is just so unfair.

'It – it is nice,' said Clifford – and Annette, she only just caught it because it sounded so muffled through the pillow he was biting. 'But it's *rude*, Annette. What if we get caught?'

'Sh. We won't get caught. Is it tingly?'

'It is quite tingly . . .'

'Margery said it was tingly. Not that bit. Another bit. Why don't you put your finger in, Clifford? See how far it will go.'

'Are you sure you won't be wounded? What if you start bleeding?'

'Oh don't be so stupid, Clifford. You don't get wounded when you pick your nose, do you? I'm not going to bleed out of my wee hole, am I?'

But Deirdre did, because Clodagh told me – and she even saw the red on her knickers. Clodagh thinks that it's because Deirdre must be really very pious because the only other person who does all this bleeding is called Padre Pio which sounds just like pious except without the S on – and he just bleeds all over the place but only from his hands and feet like Jesus on the cross because he's got stigmartyr and not out of his wee hole because he obviously hasn't got one because he's a boy and so he must have this tuppence sticking out like Clifford. Except the saints and priests and the Pope probably don't have anything at all,

131

because God wouldn't like it. It must be very difficult if you're as pious as that and you want to be excused – but God, he works in mysterious ways a wonder to behold and if you've got Faith he can lay his hand on you and bring you balm, even if you're completely bursting.

What I want to do now is practise proper kissing for if I ever meet Fabian, but Clifford, he just jams his lips together really tightly and if you tell him to be romantic and try to pull his rotten mouth open it gets all wet with his dribbling like a baby and once he even bit me, but I don't think he did it on purpose. Proper boys are older than Clifford, of course, but I still don't know how Elizabeth Taylor ever manages it – but she's got piles of husbands it said in Mummy's *Woman's Own* which is quite a good idea I suppose because if one's no good, you can get another, and also she can afford it; she maybe has these trees that money grows on that we can't get. Anyway, what I'm doing now is stroking Clifford's tuppence, ever so gently, and it moves a bit sometimes like it's a little baby hamster, or something. And he's got his finger right in, now – and that's nice too in a funny sort of way but it feels a bit like I want to go to the lavatory which I will do, after.

When the door handle turned, Clifford whimpered once and Annette, her eyes were struck wide and her limbs were frozen. All senses strung tight and alert now, as she awaited confirmation. At the first chink of light as the door inched inwards, she jackknifed up and rolled away and out of the bed at the far side and she crouched there, trembling, pulling some bedspread down over her head. She squeezed Clifford's arm in warning and she thought he might be crying so she squeezed him even harder because he had to see that he had to stop. She knew now that her mother was somewhere in the room because all around was that certain sense of her, and Annette bit down quite hard into her lower lip in order to stop it just quivering wildly and she offered up to Jesus the pain it was causing like a good sinner would and she did not know what she would say if she were hauled out and caught. Her mother now was hovering on the other side of the bed and she appeared to be rummaging around just a bit and then she bent over and very softly she kissed Clifford's forehead and smoothed back the tangle of his hair with the gentlest of touches and Annette ground down her teeth even harder because she knew that her mother had done this because Clifford, he takes after her, and me, Annette – I'm just like my father. She did not dare move until the door closed noiselessly behind her mother, and the room again was still, and thick with a held and breathless silence.

Gillian let go now of her held and breathless silence and exhaled with relief as she padded down the passage and on into the bathroom: she had thought at first that oh my golly I'm not going to be able to find it, am I? That blessed little tooth of Clifford's – and I'm certainly not about to go pulling up his mattress if he's been silly and that's where he's gone and put it. And then suddenly I felt it with one and then two more of my fingers and I eased it out carefully from under his pillows (which were all tossed about, along with the sheets – I hope he's not got a fever, or anything). So I pocketed this little silver pellet and replaced it with another – a rather more bulky one, I'm afraid it is, because I searched my purse for a sixpence and I even went to the Black Magic casket with the little red tassel that I keep all my treasures in because I've got in there this little suedette pouch with a drawstring that my watch came back in one time when I sent it off to be repaired, and now I keep it filled with any change I think I might just be able to spare from one day to the next. Not a single sixpence, though – would you believe it? There was half-a-crown there, which rather surprised me (I must have been flush that week, I honestly can't imagine how), and various ha'pennies and other bits of copper but not a single sixpence to be found. So I had to settle in the end for two thruppenny bits all twisted tightly in a torn-off corner of kitchen foil. Not very angel-like, I suppose, but well – there it is. He looked so sweet, my little Clifford – all gone to dreamland, my little baby boy. When I felt his head, he seemed all right – no hint of a temperature or anything like that. So maybe he just had a bit of a bad dream – because normally, you know, he barely moves at all when he's asleep at night. In the morning, his bed – it hardly needs making.

Ooh, I'm tired – and it'll be half six before I know it; the night, it'll simply run away with me. But I just want to have a little bit of a wash, before I get myself back into bed – or maybe I'll go downstairs and just nap on the couch. Arthur, he was in an awful state when he finally got in. He could barely manage to get himself up the stairs – I had to go and help him because he was making that much noise I thought now at any minute he's going to wake up the children. It wasn't that he was the worse for drink – although there was that smell of it off him, of course; that whisky smell that's just all over him whenever he's been out. I wonder at how we can afford it, whisky, because it's just so expensive – but there, it's his money isn't it, I suppose. He is the master of the house, after all – because me, I've never had a job, never worked, so it's different. No – it was his feet, you see. He'd walked all the way from goodness only knows where and I said to him but listen to me, why on earth didn't you get the bus home, Arthur? What did you want to be walking for with it being this late and you with your feet, and everything? And he said that he had felt like a bit of a stroll and he'd missed the last bus, and I was left to take my pick out of those two, whichever I chose. And then I'd got him into bed all right and he started getting funny. I told him: Arthur, I told him – it's really late and you'll wake up the children and you know I've got to be up in the morning. But no, no luck – he wasn't having it. Not having it at all. So I did a bit of what he said, but I didn't do the other thing because I think it's just plain dirty, if you want me to be perfectly honest – and how would *he* care for it, I would very much like to know. If women kept on wanting all sorts of grubby things doing to them oh well then we'd soon hear about it – the men would be up in arms, wouldn't they? Not that any woman ever would, of course, so they're perfectly safe, aren't they? I sometimes think I should have been a nun – but then, of course, I never would have had my little baby Clifford, would I? And what would be the point of me then? And Annette – I wouldn't have had Annette. Anyway, I got it all, the Arthur business, done and dusted in a couple of twirls – not too much mess at all – and now he's in there, snoring his head off. So I'll just have a bit of a rinse.

He was so very sweet, though – my little Clifford. So sweet and innocent. I hope he's always like that, my little boy. Because it doesn't last for ever, does it? This stage. How much longer will I be swapping his little toothypegs for sixpences? How many more Christmases will I fill up his stocking with all those little surprises from Santa? You make sure you just stay all sweet and safe and innocent, little Clifford, my little boy. Don't you be in a hurry to grow up, like a lot of the young people nowadays. Because childhood, you know – it's only a fleeting thing. And then look what happens.

The most mouldy thing about P.E. class these days is that I just can't get out of doing it any more. For the first three weeks of term what I did was I just turned up to the gym in these stupid white shorts and singlets we've got to wear which my arms look really thin in, but I kept on having my clonking outdoor shoes on, and the new P.E. master Rawlings – who is just mental like Mad Man Mallison and every other P.E. teacher we've ever had and ought to be in a cage at Bertram Mills and you chuck him bananas – he just came up to me and he said Well well well Coyle – forgot your gym shoes, eh? Well in that case you will be unable to take part, you stupid boy: retire to the wall bars and observe. He's just so thick that it took him three whole lessons to twig that I wasn't stupid but *he* jolly was – and so now he goes Well well well we'll all just have to wait around now for young Master Coyle to go all the way back to his locker and get his gym shoes – *move*, you horrible little specimen, Coyle – *move* yourself lad: I'll time you – if you're not back here in two minutes flat I'll have you down on the floor and giving me twenty press-ups. He's a pig, and hair pokes all out from under his arms and that hopeless vest and his neck is as fat as his head. So anyway I had to shoot off and I drove my Formula I Vanwall all down the corridors and made all the squealy tyre noises and the brakes and everything and did this really great three-point turn in the locker room and the engine and all the gears and everything were really screeching loudly all the way down on the home stretch and I just got in under the chequered flag and beat all the Ferraris and BRMs and Alfa-Somethings and I just knew he *hadn't* timed me or any-thing because grown-ups never ever do time you like they say they will, they just say it – but I knew if I hadn't been super-sonic quick he would've got me to do these beastly press-ups which I can't do anyway and he puts a foot on your bottom, Mad Man Rawlings, and shouts out *chin*, lad – get that chin up and back straight and everyone's looking and laughing and every-thing. When I'm older I'm going to kill him – him and Mrs Chadwick.

And the other rotten thing about P.E. as well as having to do it is that we have to share this term with 4A who are all big and they think they're all like Maverick or something and they push you about if old Monkey Rawlings isn't looking and one of them who everyone calls Skimpy because he's about the size of the Science Wing (but you don't when you're talking to him), he always prods his finger in me and says things like Watch it sonny, and it's really sore. He's actually Dismal's older brother, Skimpy is, and I'm always going to Dismal look Dismal why is your brother so foul and why don't you tell him to stop being such a bully and picking on me all the time and Dismal just says well he bullies and picks on me more than he does on you so just stop moaning. I'm glad I don't have an older brother. He'll be a P.E. teacher when he grows up, Skimpy will, because he's all just shouting and he goes Feel my muscles all the time and he's diabolical and mental like Rawlings is. And it's his fault last term I got nits because Dismal says he got them off of Skimpy, that he got them from Skimpy, and I must have got them from Dismal and then loads of other people did as well and I don't actually know what nits is except Dismal, he's a nit as everyone knows – but when I got home and said to Mummy I've got this nits she said she didn't know where to put her face, which I didn't get because you can't ever move it because it's kept on the front of your head. And she washed my hair with this stuff that smelled like the heap of muck at the end of the garden and it really stinged my eyes and she rubbed and rubbed and rubbed and it wasn't like when she does my hair on Sundays with Vosene, it was really hard and my ears were all red. So all that was because of Skimpy – but if I was a nit I wouldn't want to go on him with a bargepole.

'Right, you miserable shower! Now listen up all of you very carefully because I'll only be saying it the once. As you will observe, I have laid out the equipment just so – never let it be said that I do not have your best interests at heart, gentlemen. Don't groan – just listen. Now then – you run to the far wall, double back and touch the wall bars. A forward roll on the mats there and – stop that scratching, Simpson, you're not in a zoo – a forward roll on the mats and then up and over the box. Springboard leap, nice and clean, over the horse and stand to attention and then you – Gibson! Do you want to see the Headmaster? You don't? Well then stop your shuffling, boy. You go over the horse and then up to the top of the rope. Down the rope, straight back here and touch the wall bars. I'll be timing you. Clear? Right, everybody. On your marks . . . set . . .'

And then that really loud silver whistle he's got like a necklace and you've got to close your eyes when he blows it and then everyone shoots off and they're bumping into each other and saying push off and barging and they're all falling off the mats because there's only two of them and everyone except me is all at the same time because I'm going quite slowly because they're really jolly rough in 4A and it's bad enough doing all this which I can't remember what he said anyway but if you get bashed as well then it's even more rotten. I hate P.E. It's stupid. You do all this and get hot and the floor mat makes your arms go all burny and just because Mad Man Rawlings says you've got to. He was probably a General in the War and ordered all the Germans around except we're not Germans which, as moany old Meakins says, stands to reason. I think someone should plug him plum full of lead, Mad Man Rawlings, with both sixguns blazing. I would – if my Cisco Kid gun and holster was real and not just caps, I would any day. Then you could just blow on it like in *Maverick* and then it would be End Of Part One and next is Daz and Fabulous Pink Camay and Bird's Eye Peas – fresh as the moment when the pod went *pop*, which is my favourite.

'*Coyle*, you disgusting little bone-idle worm, you! *Move* yourself – *move* yourself or you'll be at the receiving end of my boot, young lad. Do you hear me? Come – come here, Coyle – come over here right now, right now Coyle. I've had just about enough of you and your shilly-shallying. Right, lad. This is your ear, isn't it Coyle? I say isn't it? I am correct?'

'Yes, sir.'

'Yes sir, it is sir. And here is my thumb and forefinger – see them, do you Coyle? See them in front of you?'

'Yes, sir.'

'Yes sir, you do sir. So what I do now, Coyle – stop that squirming, stand up straight, eyes front – what I do now, young Master Coyle, is I apply said thumb and forefinger to this grubby little ear of yours like so – and then I – *twist*, Coyle. *Twist*.'

'Ow! Ow!'

'Ow *what*, Coyle? Ow *what*?'

'Ow *sir*, sir. Ow! Sir.'

'Indeed, Coyle. Ow *sir*. Now get over to that rope and *climb* it boy. *Climb* it. Don't look at it – *climb* it.'

I've got my feet up on the big knot on the end of the rope and the rope it smells like Shredded Wheat, I think, which looks like pillows on your bed only made in raffia which Annette sometimes has to do flowerpots in Free Activity. If it had these big knots all the way up, then it wouldn't be so hard. And what's the point anyway, climbing up a rope? If you want to get to the top of something you can just use the stairs or shoot up in a lift like Selfridges. And Mad Man Rawlings, he's right up next to me now with his poky-out hairs and he keeps on shouting right in my ear he hurt *Up*! Up, boy! Up, you little *girl*! I wish he'd make up his mind. Anyway I'm pulling with my arms and I think I've gone up a bit and what I do now is I get the rope in my gym shoes and pull up more and I think I'm a bit higher now and then I do it again and that's when I get that squirmy feeling all down in my tuppence and it's like it was in bed last night when Annette she was all fiddling, and things. I was sad, last night. In my bed. It got me really sad. Not Annette, that was all right this time: quite liked it, and sticking my finger in and everything. I was sad because it wasn't the angels, it was only my Mummy. Why wasn't it the angels? Don't they like me any more? It's maybe because Annette, she says I'm not pious, which I don't know what it is. Or maybe they've got just heaps of teeth now and don't need any more. And then I thought maybe the angels, they went to Mummy and asked her if she wouldn't mind doling out the dosh for them because they had this really big meeting with God and mustn't be late. Except angels don't have thruppenny bits, which you would have to be quite thick not to know. Anyway – I don't know why I was sad. I was sad because it was just all different, this time.

'*Move*, Coyle – *climb* it, boy! What's wrong with you? Hey? What's wrong with you at all? Everyone else is *finished*, Coyle. You're holding up the class. *Move* yourself, you lazy little guttersnipe.'

I can't go higher and I don't want to let go or anything because then I'll slip right down and I won't feel tingly in my tuppence any more and also my hands will start to hurt – but I *have* slipped right down now, oh ow, and I'm right at the bottom and all the tingle, that's gone away and my hands, my hands have gone all burning and pigface Rawlings is shouting I'm as wet as a sponge and get over to those wall bars or else I'll be feeling the back of his hand. If I was a pirate he could walk the plank and I'd jab him with my trusty cutlass into the sea and all the sharks and stuff and then he'd be sorry and eaten up. The decent thing about the thruppenny bits though is I can go to Moores in the Lane after school and get my Spitfire, now.

After a million years, P.E. ended – Rawlings stonked off and he was going I am watching you, my lad, and don't you think for one minute that I'm not – and some people are having a shower but I never do because you get all wet and then you've got to get all dry again. Then we've got to have milk which is in these bottles that look like the ones the United Dairies bungs on our doorstep with the horse and cart except these are much littler and they're never ever cold like at home because this school, it doesn't have a Kelvinator or anything and Daddy says that with the fees they charge him they could charter the ruddy *Queen Mary* and tow in icebergs from the ruddy North Pole, but I don't think they could really. But they give you these straws which if you flatten one end they look like an oar, but then you can't suck in it. Daddy says ruddy a lot, which is a rude word, but I don't think he really means it or anything. Then there's double English and lunch which is mince today and wibbly-wobbly jelly-on-a-plate which is really really yummy and stinking Mrs Chadwick won't have to tell me to eat it all up because I jolly well will.

Stone me. That's what a man called Hancock of the television keeps on saying because I heard it at Anthony Hirsch's house when I watched it there. I don't know what it means but when I said it at Mummy she said I must never ever ever *ever* say it again and even to *promise*, so it must be quite a rude word, but Daddy doesn't say it. And Anthony told me two other things that men on the television say. One is by a tall person in a programme about the Army which Anthony says is really really funny but I haven't seen it and the tall person he says 'I only arsed'. Annette thought this was funny too but I don't quite get. She said if I said it to Mummy or Daddy they'd both have a fit, so I didn't. (They always say they're going to have them, fits, but I don't think they do; it might be like having kittens like Dismal's cat did.) And on the *Sunday Night At The London Pa-something* programme which has on people like Norman Wisdom who is even better than Mister Pastry and once they had on Cliff Richard – on that programme they've got this man called something I can't remember and he says 'I'm in charge' which I don't think is funny, and Anthony he says he doesn't think it's funny either but that's what this man keeps saying all the time. I wish we were getting a television that's got the good things on it, instead of just the boring one. When Mummy goes shopping today she says she's going to get my Jennings book from the Library (Wizzo! is what Jen would say) and then she's going to get some tea and I said can you get Horniman's because they've got Capitals of the World and Flags cards in and she said I always get PG Tips and I said I know but I don't think I'll ever get all the Birds of the World because I've only got three to get but if I start collecting all the Capitals of the World and Flags cards then I'll get one I haven't got because I haven't got any. But Mummy she just said she likes PG Tips and your father likes PG Tips and PG Tips is what I'm going to get, my lad, and sometimes with grown-ups they just don't listen to you or something because I had to say it all over again and she still didn't get so I don't think she will buy Horniman's now which is just typical – and she still won't get Rice Krispies because she says the blessed things are coming out of her ears but they're not really because I checked. I don't mind anyway now because Anthony Hirsch says in Corn Flakes they've got these proper spacemen in different colours with see-through helmets and his mother's going to get the Large Economy Size today because then you get two whole spacemen in just one packet and I suppose you can do that if you're jooish but not if you're not because then you've got to scrimp and scrape just to make ends meet which I don't know what it means but that's what we do all the time.

I can't wait till after school and I get my Airfix kit from Moores in the Lane because I can make it on Saturday and paint it and do all the transfers and stuff on Sunday and then I can go *eeeeeee-ow . . .!* with it in my hand and swoop around and dive-bomb all over and kill heaps of Germans which they well deserve for being against us in the War, and so do what Daddy says is japs. But there's still to go till the bell . . . six hours and four minutes and twenty-eight seconds . . . twenty-seven seconds . . . twenty-six seconds . . . twenty-five seconds . . . Oh gosh it's going to take just millions and millions and millions of years and I'll get old and a long white beard like Santa does while I'm waiting and then go all smelly like Grandma and die and be a skeleton. I don't know why you've got to go to school. It's stupid. Mummy says it's to learn things, but the only thing I've learned is that school, it's just completely stupid.

'You don't seem to quite understand me, Gillian. Here is merely a prudent measure in the light of circumstances. Husbanding one's resources, that's all well and good, but if we are to maintain our current levels of expenditure—'

'Oh I know Arthur – I'm not arguing at all, but—'

'Please – allow me to finish, if you would be so good. If this level of expenditure that we all enjoy is to be maintained at its current, and I might say, rather elevated level – the school fees, the housekeeping, I could go on – then additional revenue simply has to be sourced. And hence my decision. As the bread-winner.'

'I'm not – arguing, exactly, Arthur. And I know I don't work – I do know that. It's just that – well, you asking Mr Henderson over for supper – you might have discussed it with me, or at least given me a bit more notice. I mean I've only got tomorrow to look up a recipe and get in all the shopping and everything . . .

and it's really very tight, this week Arthur. I don't know if I'll stretch.'

'I sometimes am at a loss to know what it is you do with all the money I give to you, Gillian.'

'I'm sorry, Arthur. But everything's just so expensive . . .'

Arthur sighed, and made rather a show of hauling out his wallet from the inside pocket of his work suit. He placed two pound notes on the mantelpiece and carefully shifted over the bracket clock at the centre so that one of its feet would pinion their corners. He managed all this with a casual aplomb, quite as if he had in the half-light dropped down the money on to the stained and livid baize of the card table in Rosie's.

'I'm sorry, Arthur. I wouldn't ask – you know I wouldn't ask, but . . .'

'Hush – say no more. I wholly understand that I have sprung a little extra work upon you. One more little burden. But I am sure it will repay us in princely dividends. A wise investment. I foresaw that you would require a little extra, and I therefore made provision.'

Yes – yes I did foresee that. Which is why I had to borrow the two quid from good old Geoff at work. Oh Lor – not *again*, said Geoff. Sorry to do it to you, old man, Arthur had come back joshingly, but it's a bit of a must-have. Just till Friday. That's what I told him – and in plain English too. I did not call it a wise investment. I did not, God help me, tell him that we would all be repaid in princely dividends. Where do I get it from? Why doesn't Gillian ever *say* anything? Like Geoff did. Just scream at me to stop it. And never mind giving her more notice – does she think it was easy, getting Henderson to come? Well Coyle, he said – this is all very sudden. Giving himself time to think of some way, any way at all, to get out of it, I shouldn't wonder. And I said Well sir – somewhat *overdue*, is how I should put it myself. Well you see, Coyle – what with one thing and another, one is really awfully busy, just at the present. We're going to France quite shortly – and I am so wary of long-term appointments, you know: I'm much more of a spur-of-the-moment sort of a man. That's why I win in court, Coyle. Thinking on my feet – that's why I win in court! Oh well sir, I couldn't possibly agree more – which is why I thought tonight, sir: this evening. This *evening*, Coyle? (He looked startled.) Oh no, I'm afraid I couldn't possibly do this evening, no no – quite out of the question, I'm afraid. Well, I said – quick as a razor – tomorrow, then: how about tomorrow evening, sir? Tomorrow . . . is very, um – difficult. The night after – what about the night after then, sir? Please do say yes, sir – my wife, Gillian, she'll be so disappointed otherwise: she's been looking forward to meeting yourself and Mrs Henderson for just so terribly *long* . . . And I watched him flinch, go a bit greenish, but I didn't back away, didn't offer him a lifeline. And eventually he groaned with enormous reluctance: Well, um – Coyle. Well. The day after tomorrow it is, then. How very very kind of you. And of Mrs Coyle.

'Anyway, Arthur – I'll do my best not to let you down. I'll get out the good damask tablecloth and pass a bit of an iron over it. I can't remember the last time we used it, but the stain – I did get it out, eventually. It took some doing, but I did get it out.'

'I rely upon and trust you implicitly in all matters domestic.'

'Oh hang on, Arthur – I've just had a thought. There'll be a *Mrs* Henderson as well, won't there? He is married, your boss, isn't he? Mr Henderson?'

'Of course. Upright married man.'

'Oh dear. So there will – there will be a *Mrs* Henderson as well . . .'

'To move swiftly on – cast your eyes, if you will, over this card

145

I had typed up at work this afternoon. I think it covers the salient points.'

'Card, Arthur? What card? What is it? Oh wait a bit – I'll have to put on my specs if it's small like that. Now where did I leave them . . .? I had them not a minute ago . . .'

'No matter. I shall read it to you. Ready? Listening? Very well then: "A lodging is newly available in a family house in a quiet street, close to shops and public amenities. South-facing room with use of bathroom and partial hot water. Breakfast, supper and laundry included. £4.2.6d. weekly. References required. Professional gentleman preferred. No Irish, coloureds or pets." And then I have put our telephone number . . . Well, Gillian? Well? You're not talking, Gillian, which is unlike you.'

'I'm just . . . I mean – what do you *mean*, Arthur? You mean *here*? In this house? A lodger? But *where*, Arthur? And why didn't you tell me? Talk to me about it? Where will we put a lodger? The box room isn't south-facing – it's barely got a window at all . . .'

'No no. Clifford's room. It'll have to be Clifford's room – get no sort of a rent at all from the box room. The boy can move into the box room—'

'Oh Arthur . . .'

'Wait, please, until I am finished, and then of course you must feel free to express your views, such as they are. Clifford, as I say, will move into the box room and then we'll treat his old room to a little bit of a spruce-up, lick of paint – I do earnestly trust he hasn't contrary to my explicit instruction ruined all the walls. And then conceivably, Gillian, you might feel inclined to weave your magic, as it were, with the sewing machine in the curtain department – new sort of bedspread, perhaps. Whatever you see fit.'

'I've just got to sit down, Arthur. I'm stunned. But *Clifford*,

146

Arthur – what about Clifford? He's got all his bits and bobs all laid out in there – his aeroplanes, and so on. He'll be, oh – just so upset. Oh no, Arthur – we can't do that to Clifford. It's so poky, the box room – there's barely enough space for a bed in there. And then where will I put my Singer and the bureau and all those boxes and everything? Oh *must* we do this, Arthur? Isn't there some other way?'

'Alas and alack. Needs must, et cetera, et cetera. I have – you may not be surprised – devoted to this a very great deal of thought. So as soon as Clifford gets himself back from wherever the scallywag is this time – with those Jewish people again, I shouldn't wonder – he can quickly get himself round to Lawrence's in the Lane and we'll have this card in the window as soon as we possibly can.'

'You don't think that's rather rubbing it in, Arthur? Do you? Getting Clifford to take round the card?'

'I can't think what you mean. It's a perfectly straightforward errand, I should have said.'

Oh God. Oh God. Just look at her face, just look at her face. Crestfallen, is the word here. Wherever in the past my dear Gillian's crest may once have stood proud, it has utterly fallen away from her now. What have I done? What have I brought us to? And here I stand, demanding obeisance – when all I should be is just cursed and dismissed. And Clifford, poor lad – what will he think of me? Less, I dare say, than he must do already. Just about possible, presumably. Soon, all three of them – their eyes will be skulking behind half-lids so heavy and veiled, each of them, and with utter justification, nurturing to full bloom a resentment unique in all aspects, but warmly blending in secret moments without me into the sort of camaraderie, the tacit collusion that can only ever come about by way of an overspilling love, or else a mere and dogged loathing. And love here, we know, will have nothing to do with it.

'That was the door, Arthur. Annette, she's here. Don't say anything about . . . any of this.'

'I have said all I need to. I am to be found in the shed, in the unlikely event of anyone wanting me.'

'Oh Arthur! Arthur – your hand! I wondered why you were keeping it behind you, like that. I did notice it but I never said anything. Did you cut yourself? Was it at work?'

Arthur glanced down at the little finger that he had suddenly forgotten to conceal, the white strips of gauze there wound around and around, and knotted quite neatly.

'It was, yes. Minor thing. One of these paper cutters they have there, you know. Normally it's the secretaries and so on, handle that sort of thing. But I was in rather a hurry and, well – next time I know to leave all that side of things to those rather more accomplished than I.'

'Oh dear. But it's not too bad, is it? Do you want me to look at it?'

'Dear Gillian. No. Not too bad at all. You needn't look.'

And so to the shed. How often it is that I seem to end up here. There is a strange sort of comfort in this festering testimony clustered about me, a memorial to so much left undone. The paraffin heater – all it needs to be functional once more is a newly-fashioned flue, which of course it is never to receive; the smell of it is all over, though – swinishly sharp, and so familiar. There is Clifford's old tricycle – quite old when I bought it, and so much older now – and still the nut to secure that pedal, it is yet to be located and never to be fixed. Cracked Kilner jars with their rusting and unscrewable lids are ranked along the windowsill, their useless jumble of contents so stringently segregated: here we have bits, there lie bobs – and this one, this one is given over to a miscellany. In trussed-up bales along the floor there are mouldering offcuts of browning underlay, a few stray scraps of rigid lagging. The jammy paint pots with their lids all battered from repeated prising away and hammering down, each of them sporting the long and petrified spillages of age-old Brolac, Valspar and Darkaline. The kitchen clock that will lack a mainspring, now, for just ever. The burst open wicker basket, the balding broom head, the balled-up and knotted fragments of twine – and hanging above me from an oxidised meathook, perhaps the most eloquent single piece of lumber out of all of it – a severely dented and galvanised bucket with a perfectly circular hole, black-rimmed and precisely at its centre.

Well. I can now reflect with a gathering sense of – not ease, but a temporary relief, anyway, as I squat in the shed and get my mouth tight around the neck of this practically empty bottle of Haig. I seem now to have eaten the better part of these . . . what are they? Dairy Box: bit sickly. So no, it's not too bad, Gillian, in the sense that it could, of course, have been a very great deal worse. As, I am left in no doubt, it rather soon will be, quite naturally. The smell of the hospital – the numbness from whatever they put into me – these are still around. I feel, in truth, not much. I am shivering now, I notice with dispassion: if I am not mistaken, here is the aftershock. Because I did, of course – had to, did I not? – keep that appointment with Mickey (I was, as I said I would be, there on the dot) and I explained to him my situation. He, in due course and with considerable patience, explained his own situation to me – and there, more in hope than wisdom, I rather thought matters might lie. I hadn't even noticed him, the man in the shadows over there in the corner. But he came forward quite swiftly and his huge and heavy hand soon had my own (pale, unsuspecting) hand on to the surface of the table before me. He cranked up the finger so easily – as if it were Plasticine – and then it just cracked like a wishbone and I stared, quite astonished, at how very askew and rigid it appeared. Only then did the searing of pain flood into and all over me and the man's hand now was around my mouth before this shriek of the purest agony could make itself heard: instead it filled me up until it nearly burst me open. It then subsided into uncontrolled weeping. That, said Mickey so softly, was your finger, Arthur. Next time (and he made it plain, in that way that Mickey can) – next time, Arthur, it'll be yah fackin neck.

♠

I was just telling Anthony in afternoon break that I can't come round to his house tonight and he said but it's double *Popeye* and we've got this popcorn which I don't know what it is but Anthony, he says it's really good and they have it in America and I said I know but I can't come round because everything at home today, it's all just so jolly exciting, which it never is. And then Dismal, he slopes up and says Oh yeah? What's all so jolly exciting then, Cliffy? And we both went, Anthony and me, we both went Oh just get lost you *baby*, can't you? And I added on for good measure You're really *dismal*, you are Dismal – you're dismal with knobs on and your rotten brother Skimpy is the biggest bully in the whole wide universe with double treble knobs on, so nyah! And he hung about, which is just typical, and he said well what do you know about anything, *Coyle* – you don't know anything which is why you're always bottom in Meakins's class and he thinks you're really thick and I bet it *isn't* exciting, whatever it is at your mouldy house, because it never is – it's *boring* there, really boring: you haven't even got a television. And it was great when he said that because then I could say Well that's just where you're wrong Mister know-it-all clever

Dick *Dismal*, because we've got a brand-new television which is Ferguson which is a very good make *actually*, if you want to *know*, and what's more it's coming *today*. So put that in your pipe and smoke it Dismal because you're wet and a total *weed*. And Anthony went Yeah, Dismal – you're wet and a total *weed* and so that proved it and he pushed off, then.

Because it's true – it is coming today: Mummy said. She said that when she comes to get me from school it'll already be there – actually there in the sitting room – which is just so scrummy and I can't believe it, even if it does just get only the mouldy stuff. And I'm not what he said – bottom in Meakins's class, I'm not, I'm not. I'm third from bottom – well last week I was third from bottom and this week because I messed up prep because I didn't quite *get*, I'm second from bottom but I'm not bottom because Troon is bottom because Troon is always bottom in everything, which you would have to be quite thick not to know. Like Troon. But it's not my fault I'm no good with moany old Meakins. It's not my fault he's such a madman. Some people actually *like* him – they say oh he's all right, Meakins, he's quite decent. Well I don't think he is. He's third on my list of people to kill dead after horrible Mrs Chadwick and hairy loony Rawlings. I don't actually think any of the masters here are any good, and they don't like me either because you can tell in their reports which are always so unfair. They say I don't try enough and stuff but they take just ages to say it and Mummy says you've got to put in a bit more effort, Clifford – you've got to stop being a dreamer because have you any idea how much money your Daddy is spending on your fees? No I haven't but I wish he'd just give it all to me. Then I'd go to Toys Toys Toys in Kenton Road which is the best place in the world and even better than Selfridges and just piles and piles better than Moores in the Lane – but I did get my Spitfire there for only two-and-a-penny and I'm going to start it tonight after I've watched lots of *television*: crumbs. But if he'd give it all to me I'd go to Toys Toys Toys and in one window they've got all the soldiers lined up on see-through shelves and it's great because what they've got is just everything – they've got on the top World War Two soldiers from England and America and stinky Germans in grey uniforms which are actually really good and the top ones in Germany have on trousers with baggy tops like for riding horses and boots all shiny as blackcurrant fruit gums and I don't know why they got best uniforms because they're the worst and they lost the War, but anyway. And then they've got the U.S. cavalry – both sides in blue and grey – and they've got knights in armour with also horses that are all done up in coloured dresses and the knights have shields and helmets with they are called plumes sticking out of the top and in that set you can get these huge catapults that really work – not like Roger the Dodger's catty in the *Beano* for policeman's helmets which don't have plumes obviously but are on wheels and which you put great big rocks in like from our rockery and they go whoosh into the castle and hit the bad knights on the noggin and so they're dead, for a start. And there's cowboys and one I like is running so only one of his feet is on the base and he's got this sixgun in his hand and you can actually take it out of his hand and put it in his holster on his trousers, which is really small. There's one in a big hat and a fancy waistcoat and I think he's Maverick and I really really want him more than all the others but he's one-and-nine. In the cowboys bit they've got a saloon with those doors that are only in the middle and when you push them open the piano always stops and they come back and biff you like a boomerang, which is curved and what people in Australia chuck around and where the kookaburra comes from. And there's stage coaches with Wells Fargo on with barrels strapped on and luggage which you can take off and doors that open and four horses with reins so you can go Yah! Yah! and also Whoa! That costs twenty-eight-

and-six and when I told Daddy that I wanted it for my birthday he said is it made of gold, and I said no because it isn't – it's all coloured plastic and the wheels whizz round really really fast because Anthony Hirsch has got one. Anyway, I didn't get it. I got a friction Highway Patrol car which you go vrum vrum vrum with it really hard and then you let it go and it shoots off at a million miles an hour and it's good and best on carpet and then it kabloings off the end of it and goes all skiddy on the lino and crashes into the wall but not if Daddy's ever there because he says it ruins all the wainscots. And I also got some indoor shoes and marshmallows. I saw *Highway Patrol* which is a programme when I was round at Anthony Hirsch's. It's got a fat man who is a detective in America and the car is all wide and black and white and it goes eeeee-aw! eeeee-aw! when it's going and this noise frightens away the bad people and Mummy says she can't ever bear it because it reminds her of the air raids in the War which I don't get because there weren't any American detectives in the War, or not in England anyway. It's miles better than English police cars though, because English police cars are just ordinary black cars like Mr Beery's Humber Snipe or something but they've got bells on like ambulances with black windows when you're ill and going to hospital. And there's Indians obviously, in Toys Toys Toys, with also a totem pole and a fire and a cooking pot and redskins with feathers and a woman who sits on her papoose because it's what if you're a squaw the Chief tells you to do. And wigwams with sticks sticking out – they're great and a lot better than the mouldy little tents you get in Cubs. And they got Foreign Legion with hankies on their hats and Mummy says it's because they want to forget but they don't, because they've all got them. There's one with what Daddy says is a minesweeper but it looks like a Hoover to me which is the sort of thing that a squaw gets told to do. There's also not so good stuff like animals but I like the elephant which I gave a bun to one at

London Zoo and the chicken coop because the door opens downwards and you can put stuff in, like chickens which they've got. And what you do is – because they're all lined up, the same ones all behind each other, and you go outside on the pavement and you point and the man inside, he takes the one off the back of the row of them for you and when I'm really really jooish and light my cigars with a ten-shilling note I'm going to stand out there all day and point and point and point and he'll take these all off one by one and then I'll have the lot which is even more than Anthony Hirsch has got. And that's what I'd do if Daddy would stop giving the money to the school and give it all to me instead. But he won't.

And it's rotten, you know, when we get end-of-term reports because it always just sits there on the mantelpiece next to the clock and we wait for my father to get home and Mummy and me don't ever say anything but we look at it. And Daddy, he slopes in and he says Well well well what have we here, young man, which is pretty thick really because Mummy has just said Clifford's school report is on the mantelpiece, Arthur. And then he opens it and he reads a bit and he goes Mmmmmm. And Mummy looks at me and I don't look anywhere or at anything because what's the point? The trouble is, they all say the same, all the masters. They don't say I'm thick because I'm not – but I don't seem to be brainy either. What I lack is *application*, which I don't know what it is except that Annette says that it's what they put on people's heads with ringworm but I don't know what that is either and you don't ever know if anything Annette ever says is true anyway because she just fibs at everyone all the time. Mummy says, but there must be *some* subjects you like at school Clifford, aren't there my sweet? But there aren't. I don't mind art a bit, except then old Atkinson goes What's that supposed to be when it's at home, boy? And you want to say Same thing as when it's *out*, you feeble old relic, but you can't. We had one art teacher once which was a woman, which is just typical of my school, and she said to me when I was painting that the sky isn't *red*, is it? You stupid little boy. You can't have a sky that's *red*, can you? You silly little idiot. And I said I don't see why not and she picked up the paper and tore it up into pieces and everyone looked and I cried a bit but not very much and it wasn't meant to be sky anyway it was meant to be blood and it was only that I hadn't done the bleeder, yet. But I don't really like anything else. I don't like English much because I didn't do anything in the holidays as per usual, so how can I do two sides on it? Maths, that used to be OK until it got all x's and y's and triangles and stuff, which I don't get. When I was a baby I used to not get when they taught you money as well because they said there are twelve pennies in a shilling and you looked at a penny and then you looked at a shilling and you knew they were telling you just the most colossal fib ever. Jog is pathetic because I don't even know where Dogger Bank and Mendips is and I don't mind if somewhere miles and miles away there are these dopey sheep and much wool is to be had. History's just stupid because it's all dead people from even before the War so what's the point? But battles are good like 1066 and 1215 and 14-something, but I don't know what the names are called because I forgot. French is quite funny because our teacher which is another woman says Ecoutez! We've got to only speak French in all her lessons so she waltzes in with her big feet that make a slappy sound all over the floor and she picks up her chalk and she goes 'Bonjour, mes enfants' and we all take this big breath and then we've got to go 'Bonjour Madame Slingsby.' We've just started Latin which no one ever speaks any more so we've got to learn how to do it. It goes I love, you singular love, he she or it loves, we love, you plural love, they love, they love. I don't know why they have to love two times, but they do . . . or is that in French? And there's also Hick, Hike, Hock which is obviously stupid; the only decent bit is you can make LATIN into EATING on your primer with biro. P.E. is vile and so is football which we do on Thursdays and you go in a bus to a field and at the back of the bus you jam your face at the window and make your eyes go all googly until the man in the car behind starts waving his fist at you and then you stick out your tongue. That's the only good thing about football because when you get there it's all the keen types like Murchison and Dingwall and Stevenson and they're always centre forwards and things and I don't know what's worst to be because if you go on the wing then hairy old Rawlings keeps yelling at you to mark your *man*, mark your *man* you little fairy and I don't know who my man even is and I jolly well don't care. If you're a back you're meant to tackle when they all come charging at the goal but I just let them get on with it. Anthony's good at football – and P.E., he's good at that as well. And English – and he got the Maths and French prizes last year too. Dismal, he goes in goal because he can't run and he always dives the wrong way and goes splosh in the mud which is very funny because we all shout out Oh *dismal*, Dismal – you're just so wet and *dismal*! And then we all trot back to our places and we've all got to do it all over again when Rawlings blows on his stupid whistle and he shouts out Nine-One! Play up the Blues! And then you've got to bring this skewer with you from Sunday roast dinners and pick out the mud from all the studs on your boots or they won't let you on the bus and in winter your hands they all go stiff and cold and you keep on dropping the skewer and you start with using your fingers instead and you queue up and show the soles of your boots to Rawlings and he goes What's that, Coyle? It's mud, isn't it Coyle? I very much fear that it is *mud*, Coyle – get back there and clean those boots or you'll be for the high jump, my lad. On and on he goes.

So I don't like anything, really – and I suppose that's why my reports are always so mouldy. And when people say Well what do you want to do when you grow up then Clifford, I say I don't know. I used to say Nothing, I want to do nothing, but then they get all batey if you just say nothing so now I say I don't know. But I do know – I want to do nothing except get really jooish and smoke cigars and have all these slap-up meals at the Hotel de Posh. I think they want me to say that I want to be a school-master or a solicity clark or something, but I won't ever, I never ever will.

♠

'It looks huge. It looks really really huge. It's not as big as Anthony Hirsch's, but still it's jolly huge.'

Clifford was practically dancing around the thing: the very presence of a real-live proper television set in his own front room, it seemed to render him incapable of staying still for even a moment – he hopped and flipped his fingers and squatted cross-legged before it and then quickly stood up again, and every time Annette shouted over to him to oh goodness sake stop jumping *about*, can't you Clifford (you're driving me crazy!), he was genuinely surprised because until then he had been completely unaware of all this capering around – but if you actually want an answer, Annette, well then no: can't stop, just can't.

'I like the little doors,' Annette said. 'And the goldy bits on the ends of the legs.'

'It'll take a lot of polish . . .' was Gillian's judgement. 'To keep it all lovely like that. Don't either of you ever go putting your fingers all over it.'

'Is it going to stay at an angle like that?' Annette wanted to know. 'Sort of skewy?'

'Why can't we turn it *on*?' Clifford was urging. Again.

'Oh shut up, Clifford. Or is it going to go up against the wall?'

'Well the men who delivered it,' said Gillian, 'they told me that air has to circulate. It's got to have space behind it or, what did they say . . .? There's something inside, some very expensive, um – component, that if it overheats it can be very very dangerous. And anyway, if it was right up against the wall, well . . . we couldn't all see it then, could we? From the sofa we couldn't, anyway. And Daddy'll want a good view from his chair.'

'But why can't we turn it *on* . . .?'

'I've told you, Clifford. We've got to wait till your father gets home – I've told and told you, haven't I Clifford? He'll have to read all the instructions, and everything. We've got to know how to do it all properly.'

'Well at least we can plug it *in* . . .!'

'I don't like to. I don't want to damage anything. We'll wait until your father gets home.'

'What's this wiry thing?' asked Annette, fingering the metal contraption now perched quite jauntily on the corner of the set.

'You'd best not touch it. It's an aerial. Indoor aerial. But the man said that around here if you want a really good reception you have to get a proper big one – you know, outside, up on the roof like the Beerys' next door. Looks like a big aitch. They're all over, now. You see them all over. But I expect they're very expensive. It's up to your father.'

'But I still don't see why we can't just turn it *on*. It's so *unfair* . . .'

'Oh Clifford I'm not going to tell you again. Now come on everybody – we've all got things to do. Annette, have you got prep? Homework? Clifford, I expect you have, haven't you? Now come on, everyone – I've got a mountain to see to. I'm going to get on with clearing out Clifford's room, now. And I don't know

where I'm going to do all the sewing – down here, I suppose . . .
We're all at sixes and sevens, aren't we?'

'Where am I going to do my prep?' asked Clifford.

'Well I don't know – it's only temporary, as I told you, Clifford.
Once your room is all spruced up and I've got the new curtains
ready and everything, well . . . as I say, it's only temporary. Maybe
you can do your prep in Annette's room for tonight – Annette,
you won't mind, will you? He'll be very good.'

'If he's quiet. Will you be quiet, Clifford, and not hum and kick
things like you always do?'

'Yes. I'll be quiet. Course I will.'

Yes, I don't mind being quiet. I don't mind doing anything at
the moment because everything today is really really good. Not
only the television (yippee! But I still think it's mouldy we can't
even turn it *on* . . .) but on the way home from school Mummy
told me that she and Daddy had decided that my room was
looking really yucky and dingy – and it jolly is, it's all brown and
boring and I've been telling them for ages. So what they're going
to do is they're going to wash it and stuff and then Daddy's
going to get all this paint from Willis's in the Lane (I said oh
great – can I have red? And Mummy said oh don't be so silly
Clifford but I don't understand why that's being so silly because
buses are red and pillar boxes where you put letters are red and
soldiers' jackets with busbies are red and so's Mummy's
Outdoor Girl lipstick and rouge so what's wrong with red? But
she said it's going to be magno-something which I bet is
mouldy) and then Mummy's going to make these new curtains
and the thing that goes on my bed which is really good and I said
well can *they* be red then and she said they'll be in what remnants she can find in John Lewis but I bet they'll be magno-something and really boring. But it's better than brown, and I'm really
really pleased. And she even gave me a shilling, which I don't
understand but I took it and I put it away because I'm not going

to spend it on sweets or anything because when I get another ninepence, if I get another ninepence, I can add it to the shilling and then I've got one-and-ninepence (arithmetic) and then I can get Maverick in Toys Toys Toys. And also she got Corn Flakes which I don't like much but Shreddies, which are double super, they don't have anything in – because I told her all about the spacemen and I got this green one with a proper ray-gun and he's really great because you can take off his see-through helmet and after you can put it on again and Anthony Hirsch in the Large Economy Size he got a red one and a blue one because he showed me them and so he hasn't got a green one so tomorrow I can show him my green one in milk and he'll really really want it but I won't swap it for anything, not even the crocodile pencil sharpener he's got which when you roll it along his jaws go up and down and when you put your finger in it's like he's going to eat you all up and I really do like that but he said he'd never swap it for anything but I bet he'd swap it for the green space-man in Corn Flakes because then he'd only have to get the yellow one and the white one and the browny one, which is not so good but you've got to get it – but I won't ever swap the green one because I've got it and he'll really really want it badly and that just never happens, not ever. She didn't get Horniman's, of course, and in PG Tips there was the Peahen which I've got piles of and I can't even swap it because everyone's got just heaps and heaps of Peahens, even Dismal. She didn't go to the Library and get me my Jennings book, though – but it doesn't matter because I've got my Airfix kit to do and also something stupid from moany old Meakins plus some boring Latin – and all my stuff it's been put in the box room and my Hurricane and my Wellington, they've been taken down and they're on top of my bed with all piles of other stuff and my bed, it only just fits in the box room and it's really horrid and small and dark in there but I don't mind because it's only temporary and then my new room when it's done and finished will be better than Annette's room because she's not getting new paint and curtains and stuff, only I am. But she's not being beastly about it or anything or going on and on so I'm going to be really really nice and I'm going to do all my prep in her room wherever she says I can go and I'll try not to hum stuff and kick stuff which I didn't know I did.

I've never been in Annette's room when Annette's not been in it. She's allowed some pink things because she's a girl but she's not allowed things to go up on the wall like I'm not either, which we both think is just so unfair. She's got a teddy on her bed with an ear which she had when she was a ickle baby and before I was a twinkle in my Daddy's eye, is what Mummy says which I don't quite get because I've never seen him do that, twinkle – he just looks all serious like Meakins and Chadwick and Mister Churchill and all old men do. And under her bed she's got all her old *Girls* like I keep all my comics and I've still even got some *Beezers* and *Toppers* and Mummy says she's going to make me these I think she said they were orange shelves to put them all in and that will be great in my new room, when it's all done. Crumbs – she's got just piles and piles of *Girls* down here – some of them are all brown at the sides of them which are really old. And there's a clonking great book which says Dairy like in United Dairies but they've spelt it wrong or else I don't know what it is if the spelling is right. It's got her writing in. Oh I get – it's all in days of the week like a calendar and she's written in stuff about what happened, and everything. I'm glad Annette isn't in here right now because first she'd go all mental if she saw me touching anything of hers and also I've got that feeling when my ears, they go all red and really get hot and my face has gone it now and when it happens at school everyone goes Oh look at Coyle he's *blushing* . . .! Because I am because Annette she's got in really rude things about when she touched me in my bed and also she's touched – she's really touched with her fingers the bosoms of Margery! Who I don't know who is, but I do know that bosoms are on some girls and women and that men and boys don't have them but Annette doesn't either and she's not a man or a boy or anything, so that's maybe not right. I think if Annette had them on I'd like touching her more because it would be more fun than just sticking your finger in a hole which you can do anywhere like ears and noses and if you are disgusting like Turpin was in timed essay prep in the lecture room, up your own bottom and everyone went oh *urrrgh urrrgh* Turpin – you are just disgusting because he is, which you would have to be quite thick not to know. Mummy's got these pink sort of clothes under the cushion on her bed and it's got two sort of humpy holes in and also there is something else pink and stretchy and it's got all these little belt things dangling off it which go in her nylons which is Aristoc and she says is a very good make. It's all very strange, like in *Tales of the Macabre* which I don't know how you say but it's an American comic with red and drippy letters on the front that Anthony Hirsch has got and it could be that women, they have to wear all these things because they are creatures from the crypt and men wear proper clothes and are just ordinary because they come from England. I can hear Annette barging up the stairs now, oh crumbs, so I'm going to bung this Dairy back in hey presto double-quick time or else she'll go all mental and tell.

'Hello, Clifford – you OK? I'm going to do my stuff on the bed, so you can just go anywhere. Isn't it great about the television?'

Clifford looks funny – he's just sort of nodding and looking all funny now I've said that because I haven't charged in and started ordering him about like I do because I can because I'm two years older. It's just that he's going to feel so really rotten when he finds out about what's happening to his room and everything because I know what's going to happen because Mummy, she got me to take the card up to Lawrence's in the

162

Lane when I got back from school and she said to me Listen will you, Annette – I don't want you breathing one word to Clifford about any of this because it's going to be just our little secret and I said OK but he's bound to find *out*, isn't he? And she said I know but I can't bear to tell him and see his little face and your father, he'll have to do it at some point but in the meantime just don't say *anything*, all right? And at first I thought hee hee hee – Clifford's going to get stuck in the box room with all of the other junk and then I remembered something in R.I. that went you must do people as you would have them to do you, it sort of went, and I thought gosh if I was being chucked out of *my* room I'd be really really sad and probably get in a temper and shout and cry and throw things and refuse until they changed their minds and everything, so it's going to be really rotten for Clifford so I'll try to be a good Samaritan as towards God I passeth along the path (difficult to say). This is obviously a pious thing to do; in Brownies you'd get points but in the Catholic Faith what you do is you offer it up and then you just hope for the best that somebody's seen.

I moaned at first when she got me to go up to the Lane, though, because I'd only just got in and it was another pretty rotten sort of a day at school and I was tired. But she gave me a shilling to get some more cachoux there because she'd forgotten again and so I said I would then. I read the card for Lawrence's window and I said to Mummy that OK I know we don't want any coloureds obviously because Daddy says they belong in the jungle where they came from and I've only ever seen any once and they look really scary I think and like they could do spells and eat people and things and they're not all smiling like on the Robertson's labels which I used to collect and I've got two badges, the tennis player and the guitarist, but I wouldn't wear them now like I used to because I've grown out of it. Clifford, he wants them badly but I don't want to give them to him because it's me who collected all the labels. We get some other sort of jam now because Mummy, she says that Robertson's is just so expensive. Clodagh told me that coloureds are not nigger brown all over but only on the bits that show, but don't ask me how she knows because she always made up lots of things. But it's probably true – I don't think that anyone could really look like that all over because it would keep coming off in the bath; it must be horrible. But Irish is all right – there's lots of people in my convent who are Irish like Sister Geraldine and Clodagh and Deirdre with the gigantic bosoms in 4A for starters – and I know this because her second name is Milligan which everyone says is Irish and the girls in her form they all call her Goon, which isn't very nice but they just all go Oh pathetic – you don't get the joke so I have to pretend I do but I don't and even if I did I bet I wouldn't think it was even funny, or anything. Deirdre, instead of Catholic she says Cat-lick all the time. Mummy says we can't have Irish because Daddy says that all Irish are navvies who have come over here to mend the roads and drink beer in pubs and fight in the street but Sister Geraldine and Clodagh and Deirdre, they don't do even any of that. And it would be good I think if this lodger (and it'll be jolly funny, having someone new in the house; I don't think I'm going to like it) – it would be good, though, if he had a pet because Clifford and me, we've never been allowed to keep a pet, not even a not proper one like a gerbil or a goldfish which just everyone in the world has got and it's because Daddy says pets, what they do is ruin all the furniture and who's expected to take them out for walks? Muggins here, I suppose. But you don't get gerbils and goldfish ruining the furniture because they're not even on the furniture, are they? And they don't need to go walking either, especially the goldfish obviously, but he never listened as per usual and then he said the subject was closed. I wanted to know why we didn't ban Jews on the card because the Jews killed Jesus on the cross and made him wear a crown of thorns and gave him a drink of vinegar instead of something nice and I know that Clifford's friend is one of them and Clifford says he's really good and took him to the Wimpy Bar and everything, and Mummy, she's met Clifford's friend's father and she says he's very nice and everything because he gives them lifts to school and things but I wouldn't ever have a friend who is one of those Jews because of what they did to Jesus although obviously the real ones who did it to him are all dead now, but still. Mummy said you're not allowed to ban Jews because of Hitler in the War, who I didn't know *was* a Jew but he *was* against us, wasn't he? But it's not as if he's going to want to come and live in Clifford's room. Hitler's not going to go into Lawrence's, is he? That would be stupid. And anyway he's dead too because Daddy once told me that he died in his bunk like the dog he was. A bunk is a sort of a bed that dogs can sometimes use, I suppose, if it hasn't got a person in it.

So I went up to Lawrence's and it was great because I bumped into Margery there. She was bringing back these tons of R. White's Cream Soda bottles for the thruppences and she was buying a Wall's Neapolitan Family Brick (I don't know what a Neapolitan family is – probably coloured though, because the ice cream is) because her mother said she'd got these tinned loganberries to go with. And we sort of looked at each other, Margery and me, because I'd touched her little bosoms again behind the curtains on the stage after the end of Music and she touched mine too except I haven't got any but she said I had and her hands felt warm and things but I think she was only being nice to me. And Music was as pathetic as ever because as usual all that was left was the tambourine and half the bells are missing anyway; I never get to go on the trumpet and the drum got broken at the beginning of term and there aren't any sticks. And after, we were laughing, Margery and me, about how Marie-Antoinette from the class below us wouldn't go up for Holy Communion and Sister Joanna came up and whispered softly in her ear and then she pinched and twisted it and Marie-Antoinette, she just went all red and shook her head and sat there and it turned out later that she wouldn't go up because her parents told her yesterday evening they were all going to be what is called vegetarians which means you only eat vegetables like yucky old sprouts and swede and stuff and that the consecrated host as doled out by creepy old horrible Father Doobey was the body and blood of Our Lord Jesus and she wasn't allowed to eat any bodies and she couldn't go slurping down blood like we all did because if she did then her parents would kill her and Sister Joanna had told her that if she continued to sit in this holy place and refuse the sacred host that has come down as a gift straight from God, then she will be devoured by flames in the realm of the Devil and Marie-Antoinette just burst out crying and she rushed outside and screamed that she had to make herself pure and she drank all these lashings of holy water at the door of the chapel, and then she got sick in the font. She'll at least be excommunicated. They must be dotty, Marie-Antoinette's parents, though, because I mean obviously you mustn't eat any meat ever on Fridays because you go to Hell, but on other days you're meant to because it is written in the holy scriptures and I expect the Apostles were always having these Sunday roasts and maybe whatever is biblical for Wimpys right after they went to High Mass, which they had just invented. Poor old Sister Geraldine, though – she had to clean all the sick out of the font, but it's OK because afterwards she will have offered it all up.

Clifford is doing his Latin, poor thing. We do Latin but we're much more advanced – and we gets lots in the Mass, of course – like Mayor Cooper and Agnes Day and Packs Vo-bit-scum, and all of these mean things. Clifford is still on the peasy stuff – he just asked me what on earth does this mean Annette and I told him it was obvious: he she or it loves the table. He said but that's just barmy and I said I know but that's what Latin is. Clodagh once

166

said that if it's supposed to be a dead language well why don't they go and bury it then – which I think is funny and really jolly clever, actually, but we didn't ever dare tell it to anyone else because in case it was profane. I think I'm going to go down and ask Mummy if we can have some Sunfresh and biscuits till supper.

'Oh there you are, Mummy. I've been looking all over. How's it going?'

Gillian was standing at the centre of Clifford's stripped-out bedroom, her hands on her aproned hips and a bucket of grey and steaming water at her feet.

'I've done the paintwork – I'm that ashamed of the state that some of it was in, but you can't be moving around all this heavy furniture every day of the week, can you? You didn't tell him did you, Annette? You didn't say—?'

'I haven't said anything. I don't want to be around when he finds out, though. Mummy, can we have some Sunfresh and biscuits till supper? When's Daddy getting back? I can't wait till we try out the television.'

'Get them yourself, can you Annette? There's some chocolate digestives in the tin – not the Roses tin, the big tin. Tell Clifford I haven't got any fingers. And use the milk glasses on the shelf. I've just got to finish off the window, and then I'll get this carpet Hoovered. I don't know when your father's home. I've really no idea.'

No I don't; no I haven't – but when was this ever not the case? He only tells me what he thinks I need to know and for all the rest I'm left to fish for myself. I really mustn't get all worked up into a state, though – I've got to keep an even keel . . . but it's just that I've got such a mountain to see to here I simply don't know any more just what to put my hand to next. I mean to say, I thought I might be able to make a start on the curtains, but look at what time it is already. Because I was going through the old suitcase we don't use any more at the top of the wardrobe and I found all this chintz – it's sort of a rose and a quite nice blue – and I'd completely and utterly forgotten about it. Jean Beery, she'd had these loose covers made up – ooh, this is years and years back now for her three-piece in the front room (I expect she's got a new one by now – this really was ages ago, all this, and we all know what Jean's like when it comes to spending) – and she says to me, she says Here Gillian – would this be any use to you at all, this leftover, because I know you're ever so knacky with your hands whereas me, I couldn't so much as thread myself a needle. And it's true, poor Jean, she's no use at all at anything of that sort – but then married to Evelyn (but it *is* a funny name though, isn't it? For a man, I mean; no idea what he does), married to him I doubt she ever has to be: there never seems to be a shortage. Anyway there's four good yards there by the looks of it, so I'm thinking oh well that's a blessed relief, I won't have to traipse off to John Lewis now, because what with just everything else I just couldn't see how I was expected to be able to find the time. I mean if it was just a question of clearing out a room and running up a simple pair of curtains, well then I daresay I could cope. But what *about* Clifford? I mean it can't just be brushed to one side, can it? I feel the same way as Annette – *I* don't want to be around when Arthur goes and tells him, but I don't have a choice – I'll have to be, won't I? I'll have to be because he'll need me to be, though I do hope he doesn't go thinking it was me – I do hope I don't get the blame. And this whole business of a lodger – I mean yes, granted, if we can actually get the rent that Arthur's asking (he says he's been into it) then yes of course that'll make a very great difference all round. But apart from getting used to a stranger in the house (and what about at night, if you need to get up to go to the bathroom? How's that going to be? Bumping into a total stranger in the middle of the night on your way to the bathroom? Not very nice, is it? Not very nice at all, I shouldn't have said) – but apart from all that side of things (and what if the children, what if they don't take to him? Because children, you know, they can be very funny about change, new things suddenly thrust upon them, like that) – but quite apart from all of that, there's the extra work that's involved – well isn't there? Another breakfast to get (and he'll no doubt be wanting cooked) and another supper too. Will we all be eating at the same time? Arthur hasn't said. And no mention either of any more housekeeping. And laundry too – bed linen, shirts, as well as other things as well, I'm very much afraid to say. Thank goodness I've got the Hotpoint, else where on earth would I be? And Arthur says that a room like this in a street like this in this sort of area – Arthur says it'll be snapped up in no time flat, you mark his words – but we can't even have viewings, we can't let anyone come to look until Muggins here has got everything shipshape and Bristol fashion and so I doubt I'll be getting to my bed tonight, not at this rate I won't.

But what I just can't keep from fretting about for just a single moment longer is all this business of tomorrow evening (tomorrow evening! Oh heavens above) – you know, with Mr and Mrs Henderson. I mean to say I can't even remember when we last had anyone round – not properly, I mean. Anthony Hirsch, he comes over from time to time, but that's just baked beans on toast and a glass of Tizer, if they're lucky. Jean Beery, she won a bottle of Emva Cream sherry in a raffle or a tombola, some sort of charity affair it was, and she brought it round that time and said we had to celebrate (I'm going back a bit now – Clifford, I think, he must still have been in 2B) and I remember thinking oh goodness how lucky that I kept that box of langues de chats from Christmastime, else I'd have nothing in the house to offer her. They were from France: someone gave them to Mother and she didn't at all care for the sound of them so she gave them to me. But this – this is a proper three-course supper, Arthur says it has to be, with the damask cloth and the serviettes, wherever they might have got to, and the two pounds he gave me (and I thought it was quite generous at the time) – that two pounds, he says, is meant to include a bottle of wine. Wine, if you please! Well I know that they're very educated people and important and a solicitor and everything, but still – there is a limit, one would've thought. And I said to him Now look here, Arthur – I'm perfectly happy to see to all the meat and two veg side of things, and I'll do them a soup and a sweet without complaint, but if we're not having tea or water or a mineral then I'd be very much obliged if you would take care of all the necessary because I do not know the first thing about it. Jean Beery, she says that in Spain they drink it all the time, wine, and I says to her Well yes that's as may be but we're not in Spain now, are we? Arthur, he just said that the shop would advise me about what goes with what, so I've got that to worry about as well on top of just every-thing else. I wouldn't know a nice botle of wine if you hit me round the head with it. I had some of that champagne at Nora's wedding over in Hayes that time, and I said, I remember saying, well if this is champagne you can keep it, quite frankly: can't understand what all the fuss is about – it's all bitter and it's got a few bubbles in it. I expect you have to be born to it, I don't know. Maybe I'll just get a bottle of Emva Cream (it was quite nice, as far as I can recall – went straight to my head, though; one more glass and I would have been dancing the Gay Gordons all down the Kenton Road and singing It's A Long Way to Tipperary). Pale ale, I should have said, would do them – though it's why they want alcoholic beverages with their suppers at all that I don't understand, because it's all, it's all of it ever so sour and I can't think it'll go at all well with the gravy, and certainly not the custard. How Arthur gets that whisky down him I'll never know.

Oh *look* . . . work or no work I've just got to go down and make myself a nice cup of tea. You'd think, wouldn't you, in the light of all that Arthur has put upon me that he might just the once have seen fit to actually be here and, I don't know – help me a bit. I didn't say that to him, of course, but it would have been nice, I think, if he could have seen it for himself. I'm not being unreasonable, am I? And it broke my heart to have to say no to the children when they wanted the television on – I was quite eager to see it myself so that at least I could have something to say to Jean if I ran into her in the Lane – but I wouldn't dare touch it, not if he's not here, because with my luck the whole thing would catch fire or blow up or something because of the circulation of air and then who'd be to blame for that, may I ask? Yes – Muggins here. So it's as well to just let it lie, I suppose.

Mmmmmm . . . that's better – there's nothing quite like it, is there? There's just nothing in the world that beats a nice cup of tea when you're up to your eyes and you've been working like a black. And be blowed to Master Clifford and his Horniman's: Horniman's indeed! I'll stick to my PG Tips, thank you very much – tried and tested, PG Tips is: never let you down. I'm glad I got him the Corn Flakes, though – although I suppose it'll be me who's got to eat them. But you should have seen his little face when I showed him the packet. It's amazing, isn't it, how a silly little plastic toy can give them so much pleasure, these young boys. And I gave him a shilling as well because, oh – I just feel so awful about his room, and everything . . . he's got all his things there . . . and I'd already given another shilling to Annette for going up to the Lane and not telling Clifford and so's she could get her blessed cachoux, which I just keep on forgetting. And there's a point, actually, because I've only got thirty-eight shillings left now and I couldn't tell you what this blooming bottle of wine is going to cost me – we'll just have to see: I do hope it's not too much. I think I'll get a nice shoulder of pork from Barrett's in the Lane – they won't get better than that no matter how many fancy French restaurants they want to go to. But I'll think about all the rest of it tomorrow . . . can't put my mind to it now. I do hope it, you know – I do hope everything goes all right. Because of course I understand why Arthur is doing all of this, of course I do. Having the boss over to supper, well, it's hardly a new idea is it? We all know what the point of it is. And so if I do my bit and not let Arthur down, well – it can only be a good thing for all of us, can't it? In the long run. I haven't told Clifford and Annette yet, though, that Mr and Mrs Henderson are going to be here. I'll have to tomorrow of course because I'll want them to slip into something just a little bit dressy. I can maybe get Annette to wear that little frock I made for her – it's perfectly sweet and sets off her arms so well but she says it's just like *Grandma's* dresses! Honestly – the things she comes out with sometimes, that girl: where do they get it all from? Oh – and talk of the Devil, here she is now, just walked in . . . aah, she's brought back down the glasses and the plates, oh bless. That'll save me a trek upstairs later on. Right then: tea break over – shoulders to the grindstone.

I mean – it's not *my* fault, is it . . .? That we always seem to be so short of money? I mean I *try* not to be extravagant, I never ever waste. Can't abide waste in any shape or form. If I could cut down I would, but I just don't see any way at all that it's possible, to be perfectly honest with you. And I know, I know all the responsibility's on poor Arthur's shoulders because you see it *is* my fault really because I've never ever had a job, you see: never worked, so it is, it is my fault really. Oh but gosh look at this . . . sometimes, you know . . . I look at Annette . . . like now, when she's reaching over the sink to the taps, like that (mercy me – she's actually going to wash *up* the glasses and the plates: will wonders never cease?) . . . but I look at her now and I think she's maybe right about things like that little frock that I made for her. Sometimes . . . you can see the young woman there, you know. Clear as day. The young woman who will one day emerge from the little girl before me. And with that will come yet another raft of problems, of course – things to see to, things to be dealt with: new things – different things. The last time I went up to her school, you know (and I try not to, very much – I mean official days I do, quite naturally – days when you've got to – but otherwise I tend to leave well alone, as far as Annette's school's concerned. It's the nuns, if I'm honest – I find them rather frightening: isn't that silly and just the most awful thing to say? I'd never tell Annette, of course – never breathe a word). But the last time I did, went up to her school – she needed some help to carry home a project, oh yes it was a nativity scene, quite nice, but the manger kept on falling over and once on the way home we very nearly lost Baby Jesus down the drain in the road, it was a very close thing – so anyway I was up there to collect her and, I don't know, either I was early or she was a little bit late in coming out or something and against my better judgement I sort of got talking to this mother who was there (rather snooty she was, to my way of thinking) and she says, she says to me this woman, Have you talked to Annette? And I says – I remember thinking at the time well that's a terribly *strange* thing to say, isn't it? Have I talked to Annette. Of course I've, I told her – well of course I've *talked* to Annette – she's my daughter, isn't she? We talk every day. And this woman. I never caught her name – all whispering she is now, hand up around her mouth and whispering to me, she is – she says No I mean have you *talked* talked . . . about – you know. Well I just must have been very slow on the uptake that day or something because there I was at a total and utter loss as to what she could possibly mean (I told Jean Beery all about it later – oh, how she did laugh) and I just looked at her, this woman, and I said I really am most terribly sorry but I don't at all, um . . .? And she was hissing at me now, really hissing like a snake – and she says oh good heavens you *know* . . . talked to her about her, um – *development* . . . birds and bees and so forth:

173

have you? Well you could have knocked me down with a . . .! I mean to say, here we were, standing outside the gates of the Convent of the Blessed Bleeding Heart and this woman was asking me if I'd talked to my baby little child about things that should only concern you, I should have said, if you are an adult in wedlock. Except of course . . . for that terrible thing that happens to a girl that she has to bear not once, but for the whole of the rest of her life (or at least to the age where all that sort of thing, along with just about everything else, really, simply ceases to matter: just look at Mother). Oh *excuse* me, I says to this woman – not being rude I hope, but not kowtowing to this little game of hers either – I think I see my daughter now: so you will excuse me, won't you? And I just left her standing there, with her mouth catching flies: I mean to say – the *nerve* of some people.

'I'm going back up now, Annette. Finish the Hoovering and then I'm going to get at the Singer. We're having leftover hotpot tonight, so I'll warm it through when your father gets home. If it isn't one of his "out" nights: he hasn't said a word to me.'

Annette continued to rub the tea cloth to and fro across the completely dry side plate that she held in her hand. She smiled her farewell – and as soon as her mother had got to the top of the stairs and then shut the door of Clifford's room behind her, she impatiently set down the plate and the cloth just anywhere at all and darted into the front room next door where Clifford was standing awkwardly on just one leg with his fingers tightly crossed.

'Right, Clifford. She's gone back up. Let's do it. Ready? Let's do it now.'

'But what if it goes wrong, or something? What if there isn't enough air on it? Daddy'll go mad if we break it and it's only new.'

'We're not going to *break* it, are we? We're just going to turn it on. OK, now – you put the plug in, and I'll press On – but we'll have to have the volume really really low because otherwise she might hear us.'

'Are you *sure*, Annette . . .? I mean I really do want to and everything but, are you really really *sure*, Annette . . .?'

'Don't be a scaredy-cat. Look – *I've* plugged it in, all right? Now do you want to press On, or will I do it?'

Clifford confronted the gleaming television set. He glanced once with hesitation towards the door, and then he turned back with a new determination.

'*I'll* do it . . .' he said with defiance and the way he thought Maverick might have done it – and he would not give in to the thudding of his heart and these icy and glycerine fingers, all of them conspiring to reduce him to fragments as they urged him to run away screaming. He turned the knob from Off to On – he recoiled at the fizzing that resulted from this and then the next instant both he and Annette just stood there transfixed as the grey and silver rain that spattered the whole of the screen resolved itself gradually into the ghostly and barely there presence of a man at a desk, the microphone before him proudly proclaiming itself to be that of the BBC. Annette very gently eased up the volume, and straightaway a thrill ran right through Clifford as he heard the man say '. . . and that is the end of the News. And now the Weather Forecast . . .'

'Oh gosh oh gosh it actually *works* . . .'

Annette was fooling around with the aerial, now – lifting it, angling it, waving it about.

'That's a *bit* better . . . still pretty fuzzy, though.'

'What's this knob, Annette? Do you know? The one that goes one two three four five six seven eight nine nought. Why isn't the last one ten? Is that for to make it louder?'

'No – that's channels. But we've only got one. Look.'

Annette grasped the knob and clunked it heavily through every calibration – the man from the BBC was immediately lost

175

to sight and was replaced by a spitting black void. And then both Clifford and Annette, they gasped out loudly and their eyes were struck wide as a tall person suddenly swam into their vision, and when he opened his mouth . . .! Clifford, he had heard so clearly, but just couldn't believe it: I only *arsed*. This man, he said I only arsed! Clifford turned to Annette – his mouth was open and his eyes were sparkling and Annette, she put her finger under just one of those eyes and so very gently she lifted up the tears there and felt them warm and run away. *Baby* . . .! she whispered. And then she hugged him and he was winded and breathless as he hugged her back, so terribly tightly.

♠

It was, I admit, just a little bit – well, odd if you like . . . knocking on Mr Henderson's door and asking him if it would be quite all right for me to leave an hour or two early this evening. I didn't quite like to add on anything on the lines of 'Got one or two things to see to . . .' because I didn't want him thinking, I suppose, that having people around for supper was so out of the way for us that special preparation or, indeed, my presence beforehand, were of the essence. 'Leave early?' was Mr Henderson's response. 'Why – *ill*, are you Coyle?' He sounded eager, very hopeful indeed. No no sir, I assured him – just got one or two things to see to. 'Ah . . .' he said, so deflated. 'Ah yes. Quite so. Quite so.' Though perfectly plainly I *do* have to be there to supervise; I've never seen Gillian so flustered as she was this morning before I left for work. She hadn't even taken out her grips, which is a thing I've never seen. And she'd got up an hour earlier than even her usual ungodly hour – it felt to me like the middle of the night. Making lists, is what she was doing. By the time I got down to the kitchen, the table appeared to be covered with the things. I really don't understand, you know, the ways and workings of women. I mean of course I was gratified to see that the coming evening, this somewhat key evening, that it merited her attention – that she was putting her back into it, as it were – but I mean, what I mean is when all is said and done, how many lists can one simple supper require?

'Writing a book are you, Gillian?'

'Hm? What did you say, Arthur? There's some bread under the grill.'

'I say what are you doing? Writing a book?'

'Book? No. I'm doing lists for this evening.'

'Oh – lists. I never would've guessed. And here was I thinking you were writing a book.'

'Silly. You didn't *really* think I was writing a book, did you Arthur?'

'No, Gillian. No I didn't. Not really. Any tea?'

'In the pot. I'm sorry, Arthur – I'm all a bit at sixes and sevens this morning. Did I wake you, when I came up to bed? Sorry. How's your finger?'

'No, you didn't wake me. Was it late? Finger's fine, thank you. This tea looks a bit stewed to my eye.'

'I'll make some fresh. It was about two, I think, by the end. I've got one of the curtains done, anyway. When are you going to do the painting? Do you think they like peas? It's all such a worry . . . but peas should be all right, don't you think . . .?'

'I was going to say about that. You've made such a sterling job of cleaning it up, you know, that room, I think we might actually get away with the painting. It'll only hold us up. Everybody likes peas, I should have said. But not processed, obviously. How about this tea then, Gillian? Yes? Chop chop.'

I know. Still quite imperative – do this, do that, pull yourself together – but the language, the language – that's improving just a little bit, don't you think? Less arch, more – well, a bit more normal, wouldn't you say? Because it occurred to me, you see – oh yes, the reason Gillian didn't wake me up when she came in to bed last night (twenty-three minutes past two, if we are counting) is because I still had to get myself off to sleep. I'm more concerned about this evening than I dare let on – well you just take one look at her, will you? She's in enough of a tizz as it is. But it occurred to me, you see – and can't they seem endless, by the way? The nights when sleep refuses to claim you – that I so seldom encounter anyone at all when the family's around, and I'm used now I suppose to conducting conversations in these two entirely separate, um – modes, as it were. And Geoff, Geoff at work – he noticed it straight away, didn't he? It's that obvious. So what occurred to me during all those wideawake hours (which is at least a bit better, isn't it? Just a little bit better than talking about 'the nights when sleep refuses to claim you', oh God, oh God . . . it's going to take some doing, this) is that I can't, can I, throughout this little supper party of ours be talking to Gillian and the children in one way and then turning round to Mr Henderson and addressing him and his in a different manner altogether? Which is probably fairly subserviently, I really have no idea. But if, as I suspect, that is the case – well, that's another thing, then, I'll have to watch. Geoff – Geoff, he could probably tell me, but I doubt I'll be asking him: the way I'm feeling at the moment is that enough is enough, quite frankly.

'You won't be home late tonight, will you Arthur? You won't – go somewhere or anything, will you?'

'No no. Early, in fact. It is my intention to be early, as a matter of fact. Maybe have time before the off to watch the News on our television set.'

'Oh Arthur – they were thrilled, the children. They were so

disappointed, though, you didn't come home. They just can't wait to see it on.'

Yes well – I had meant to come home, be back for supper: had meant to. But then at the last minute I hopped on a bus for a very quick look-in at Rosie's – thought I'd have just the one and see if I couldn't make a bit of money for Mickey at the table to maybe defer the moment when he keeps to his word and has me not just fractured but obliterated (I try to treat it lightly but it's not, believe me, how I feel; sometimes it seems so strange, so unreal, so nothing to do with me that it's almost as if I'm watching and then dipping in and out of a film with Richard Attenborough, or someone). Anyway. I had enough for just the one Scotch, so I had three in the end, might even have been four. Then I borrowed a fiver from Hortense (she said I'll want interest, Albert – I'll want interest, but I'll do it because I love you, sweetie; goodness, the money that woman must have put away, and so much of it mine). So then I paid the drink bill and bet the rest and lost it (to the bald man, not the fat man this time) and then I left, fearful of meeting Mickey. Blowed if I didn't run into that Mrs Farlow and her blessed frumpy friend at the bus stop (do they wait for me? Look out for me?) and so I walked home in the end. What with my broken finger and my crippled feet, I am telling you . . . I'm only fit for the glue factory – which may not be that fanciful, if Mickey's got anything to do with it; and, I am very much afraid, he has, of course. Think of something else, that's what to do. I'll just finish off this bit of toast, get another cup of tea inside me, and meanwhile I'll just be thinking of something else entirely like . . . um – the television, yes – that'll do nicely. I had a quick look at it, when I got in (the Singer was rattling away thirteen to the dozen next door in the dining room). It's a handsome piece, and so it ruddy well should be for seventeen-and-six weekly (I know, I know – but seventeen-and-six, well, it hardly seems to matter in the scheme of things, these days). And if I know

my Annette at all, she will have seen it in action already –
she's never one to wait about, not Annette: something on her
mind, she gets it seen to. Gumption. And Clifford, poor
little mummy's-boy Clifford, he will have been dragged in, of
course, as an accessory to the crime. They will, I assume, have
discovered Channel Nine. Oh to have been a fly on the wall.
Maybe they've sworn a pact, or something: Now don't ever tell
Daddy it's got Channel Nine or else the old meanie, he'll send it
back: so it's just our secret, all right Clifford? Swear – go on:
swear. And if you swear and you break your word you go
straight to Hell but first they snap your fingers and then they
send you off to a factory to be boiled up for glue . . . oh God. Oh
dear God . . .

'Right then, Gillian. I shall away. I'm off, I mean: I'm off.'

'O righty-o then, Arthur. And you will, won't you? What you
said. Be back early? See I haven't forgotten anything or done
something wrong.'

'As soon as I can get away. Cheerio.'

And Arthur thought as he clanged shut the front door that
that 'cheerio' – that was rather good: 'cheerio' was much more
like it. Yesterday morning he had said to her 'Farewell to thee,
until our paths re-encounter' – not far short of 'adieu', let's face
it – but Gillian, I doubt if any more she even hears a word of it.
And Gillian, as she heard the front door clang shut, she looked
up from the Things To Borrow From Jean Beery list and she
thought Early, eh? Back early? Well there's a first time for everything, I suppose. Oh goodness – it's past my time for getting
Clifford up now, look – Annette, I think I heard her in the bathroom, not too long ago. I'll just get the kettle on again and then
I'll go up and see to him. Oh goodness, oh goodness – please
Lord help me to survive this day. I'm not much of a one for
prayers, as well you know, and I wouldn't ask but it's for
Arthur's sake, really, and I'm all at sixes and sevens and I've

just got a mountain to see to: so please God if you can make everything all right. All right? I'd be ever so grateful.

'Clifford . . .? Clifford . . .? Wakey-wakey, Clifford . . .'

'Hm? Oh what is it. Annette? Is it school time . . .?'

'It's not *Annette*, is it silly? It's Mummy. And yes it *is* school time, young man. Quickly now – get yourself dressed. There's a shirt on the handle. And don't forget your teeth and to get all of that sleep out of your little sleepy eyes. I'll put some banana on your Corn Flakes.'

'Can't I just have banana . . .?'

'Ooh, Clifford – you are a bundle, aren't you? Aren't you, hey? You're just a little bundle, you are Clifford. Now come along – quickly now.'

Oh yes of course it's Mummy. Good old Mummy. And five minutes later than usual, which she never does. Annette, she came in after we watched the television which has – it really has got all of the good programmes on it! Wait till I tell Dismal. And Annette, she said not ever to tell Daddy because if he found out he'd only send it back because he's a meanie and then all we'd have to watch is the boring old News, which is always the same and it's on every day. And I said Well all right but what about Mummy then? We've got to tell Mummy, haven't we? And Annette said Well we'll only tell Mummy if she promises to not tell Daddy and I said But we've got to tell Mummy before she promises not to tell Daddy and then if she doesn't promise not to tell Daddy well then she'll go and tell Daddy and then he'll send it back won't he? Because he's a meanie. And Annette said OK then, we won't tell Mummy either – and I don't like not telling Mummy because Mummy should know everything, I think, but I really don't want Daddy to be a meanie and send it back, the television, because we've got on it *Double Your Money* and *Take Your Pick* and *Popeye* and when the clock ticks and the man says he's in charge and the other man who is funny and says I only arsed and then best of all is *Maverick*. So I'm not going to tell Mummy: it's a secret. And then Annette, she got into my bed and touched me and everything and my tuppence it went a bit sore and Annette said it felt all different and got a bit swollen like a boil and I jolly hope it isn't a boil because I had a boil in 2B and they stick a pin in it and it goes all gooey. And I put my finger up Annette and it went in miles and I smelled it after and it's nice and a bit like what you get under icing on birthday cakes and it's green. Anthony Hirsch says that all the good programmes are in *T. V. Times* and all the rotten ones are in *Radio Times* and I said But that's just the wireless and he said It isn't just the wireless it's the rotten television programmes as well and we get *Radio Times* which is just typical.

Oh yes I will get up now because I've just remembered we're doing conkers today in break which is just great. Anthony Hirsch, he's got this zonking great conker tree at the end of his garden which is like Regent's Park but even he hasn't got a zoo and yesterday he came in with loads of them and he got on a desk and started going Quiz? Quiz? And I barged right to the front and went Eggo! Eggo! really loud and this is Latin or Roman Catholic for egg obviously, but you only ever say it if someone goes Quiz – if they don't go Quiz you just bags it. I got one-and-a-half pocketfuls and they're all lovely and shiny like the radiogram is and last night I got Mummy to put two of them in Sarson's because that makes them super strong except they go all wrinkly like if Grandma was this really old squaw, but you've got to put a hole in first which you do with a skewer from roast Sunday dinners that you dig out gunge on your football boots which doesn't work and Mummy when I got this out she said Here Clifford, give that here because you'll only go and hurt yourself and I said I won't hurt myself I can do it and she said well not on my good kitchen table you won't so just give it to me now Clifford and I'll do it over the sink because there's bound to be bits. So she made these holes and bunged them

182

in Sarson's in a jam jar because you're not allowed to bake them in the oven like you were used to be allowed to do but you're not now because everyone said it was unfair but Sarson's is all right. And then you get a gym-shoe lace and you put it in the hole and you do a knot on each end and hey presto you've got the World Heavyweight Champion Conker Of All Time In The Whole Of The Universe and I'm going to do that when I'm having my banana. First I've got to squeeze out some toothpaste down the sink and suck a bit and then I've got to mess up the towel.

Bananas are really yummy, I think, but you can never have seconds because of the poor starving children in Africa who don't even get firsts. I'm jolly glad we don't live in Africa because what's the point? Corn Flakes are boring, though – but I've got the green spaceman in the pocket of my blazer and I'm feeling it now with my thumb all over it and I'm going to show it to Anthony Hirsch in milk and he'll really really want it but I'm not ever swapping it, not for anything, and I told this to Mummy and she said I know that Clifford you've already told me which I don't remember I did. She's done a whole curtain for my room which means she's just got to do one more and then I'll have the set. I hope Anthony doesn't think it's cissy or anything, my curtains, because it's got flowers all over and his have got guitars and music notes on and one music note is really big and curly and it is called a Double Cliff which is short for Cliff Richard who Anthony Hirsch says has got a new record in the Hit Parade which is even better than 'Living Doll' which I don't think anything can be but I'm not even going to ask if I can get it because Daddy's just got a television and I got a shilling from Mummy that's put away for Maverick and I'm getting a brand newly done-up room and money doesn't grow on trees and records cost about a million pounds each – six-and-eightpence, Anthony says, and they're only small and round. I could try and hear it on my transistor but it all just goes fizzy these days like when you first pour out Tizer.

On the way to school I kept on thinking I just can't wait to tell Anthony Hirsch about the television we've got because now I can ask him round to watch my television at my house when Daddy is out and we don't have popcorn but we do get fingers. And then Mummy said some people are coming round tonight to eat our supper and so I can't have Anthony tonight and I said who are they? Is it Mr and Mrs Beery? And she said No. And I said Is it my Uncle Bob? Because somewhere which isn't near here but not in Africa I've got this Uncle Bob who I only saw when I was a baby and so Mummy says I can't remember him but I do because he had four legs and was all dark and woolly because he's a black sheep, is what Mummy said he is and I think he had LCC spectacles on like Dismal had until he broke them and now they've got Elastoplast in the middle. Uncle Bob, he maybe lives in Australia which is where the kookaburra comes from. And it's good because if anyone ever says Bob's Your Uncle I can say I *know* he is and they don't get, but I do. And then Anthony Hirsch and Anthony Hirsch's father shot up in Jaguar and Mummy said it was a blessed relief and I barged in and said to Anthony You'll never guess what and he said What and I said I can't tell you yet and he said Why can't you tell me yet and I said I just can't. But when Mummy was gone I did. I thought he'd be really really pleased when I told him about the television and Channel Nine and everything, but he just went a bit grumpy. And I said in break, Why did you go all grumpy, because I thought he didn't like me any more, and he said I didn't, it's just that you won't want to come over to my house any more and my parents say that it's all right when you come over but other boys are rough or their parents won't let them because we're jooish but I'm all right and if I don't come then no one else is allowed and I said But I *will* come round, I *will* come round – and I jolly well will as well because the popcorn they've got there is really good and they've got just buckets and also he lets me put his guitar on and he's got this really long mirror in his wardrobe and you can see what you'd look like if you were a pop star except that it looks stupid in short trousers and my hair is all so short and pathetic and when I'm older I'll have it all standing up in the front like Cliff or else I'll wear a top hat instead because I'm going to be jooish like Anthony Hirsch and I won't care if people's parents won't let them come and see me because I'll be in the Hotel de Posh so nyah to them with knobs on. He's not really a proper uncle, my Uncle Bob – not like when you get parents with brothers and sisters like me and Annette. Because my Mummy and Daddy, they haven't even got one of them because they're both just lonely children.

Well. This is just all I needed – after the day I've had, well – this is just all I blessed well needed. How could Arthur *do* this to me? How could he? And after him saying to me – didn't he say it to me? Wasn't it the very last thing he said to me before he walked out of the door? That he'd be early. That tonight he'd be early. They were his very words – that's what he said. Well just look at the time. Look at the *time*! I've got everything ready, everything's just beautiful. I've been working like a black. Clifford and Annette, I've had them sitting side by side in the front room for heaven knows how long and the fire's all lovely and everything and Mr and Mrs Henderson are due – they're actually due to arrive – in six-and-a-half minutes, nearer to six now – and where is Arthur? Where can he be? What can he be thinking? What can have happened to him? I mean to say his boss, his boss hasn't kept him at the office working late, has he? Because his boss, his boss is right now maybe parking his car in the street outside and where, where on God's earth, I should like to know, is the man who invited him to supper? Where *is* he? Because I won't be able to face it, you know – not alone I won't. And what am I expected to *say* to them? 'Oh, I'm terribly sorry Mr and Mrs Henderson, but Arthur had a previous engagement and sends his apologies.' Oh I'll just never be able to survive it – and it's much too late to put them off or anything – you know, to telephone and say something – because they're due, they're due in just over five minutes' time. They could be getting out of their car in the street outside this house right at this very moment. And where is *Arthur . . .?* Why isn't he *here . . .?*

'Daddy back yet, Mummy?'

'Clifford go straight back into that room and sit on the couch with your sister. And don't eat those nuts until people get here.'

'Well when're they getting here? And where's Daddy?'

'Now. They're getting here now. And I don't know – I don't know where your father is. Stop asking me questions. I expect he had something very important to see to. Now don't make me tell you again, Clifford. Get right back into that room and wait there nicely.'

Jean Beery – oh and what a blessing that woman has been to me today – Jean Beery, she says that the best people are always late when it comes to supper, which I don't think can be right. I can't abide being late for just anything at all and if that means that I'm not out of the top drawer then so be it. I can't for the life of me see how it can be regarded as a good thing to have bad manners. But Jean, she knows much more about all this sort of thing than I do – they're really quite gay, she and Evelyn. Quite sophisticated – not like us at all. They've already been to the Chinese restaurant in Kenton Road and she gets these little bottles of olive oil, she was telling me, from Allchin's the chemist and she sprinkles it all over her lettuce and tomatoes! What an idea – it's meant for putting in your ears, she says. She says it's very cosmopolitan, whatever that may be – to put it over salad, I mean, not in your ears. But I'm sure she's right. One thing I do know – I couldn't have coped with everything today, not without Jean I couldn't. I wish she was coming – I wish she was here now. I did think of asking her but then I would have to have asked Evelyn as well and I just can't fit eight round the table and in my little kitchen, well – I haven't the surfaces. But I don't know what I would have done without her, Jean, I really don't.

I only went round there in the first place to see if I could borrow some serviettes from her because I know I've got some, we've got a set of six of them somewhere, Irish Linen, very tasteful in a box, but for the life of me I just couldn't track them down – I couldn't find them anywhere. Can't think what on earth can have happened to them – but you can barely get into the box room now because of all my poor little Clifford's things and everything, so they might well be still at the back there, somewhere. And then I said to myself – Gillian, I said: now come along now, pull yourself together, first things first. If you spend any more time searching for those blessed serviettes then you're not going to have a single moment for all the rest of it, are you? So borrow them from Jean – she's bound to have some. Well – I wasn't wrong about that! What colour, she said to me. Is it a fairly dressy affair? Because I've got lots of white, of course. Or there's red gingham if you're going for a more Bisto look (which was silly because she knows full well I'm an Oxo woman through and through, always have been, always will be: swear by it for flavour). And so I said Oh white would be lovely, Jean – I'll pop them in the Hotpoint afterwards, of course, put a bit of Robin on them so they come up lovely again, but I don't suppose anyone will make too many marks on them or anything. Jean, she says that new Daz is what I want – it's blue, but it brings up her whites a real treat, she says (I don't

know – whatever will they think of next?). So anyway – the serviettes: if you're sure it's all right then, Jean . . .? And then she says
to me Oh for heaven's sake Gillian just take them, won't you?
Now: what about plates? And I said to her Well of course Jean I've
got *plates*, haven't I? What do you take me for? We don't all eat out
of a trough, you know. Ah, she said, but you'll need plates to put
under the plates which is what the best people do and then you'll
need sweet plates and side plates as well as dinner plates and
soup bowls and there's six of you, don't forget – and so well yes,
she had me there. So she lent me a very nice service that she says
is Royal something – By Appointment, anyway – and I says to her
Oh *very* grand, thank you Jean, we'll be ever so careful I promise
you. And then she says to me Have you got any candles and I said
Candles, no – we're putting all the lights on and she says to me
Oh no no no – you've got to have candles because candles, they
always set the mood. Cream, she said, is the most tasteful. So she
gave me a pair of these long and tapered candles – very expensive, I should have said, so I says to her Oh Jean but I'll have to, I
insist upon paying for these and she says Oh no don't be so silly
I wouldn't even hear of it because I've got a whole boxful because
Evelyn, he knows someone on the wholesale side of Price's and so
he gets them, you see: he gets them. Well I've got a very nice pair
of candlesticks on the mantelpiece that were Mother's (you take
them, she said – I'm old) so a little bit of Brasso and then I'll
pop in Jean's cream candles and that's the mood side of things
taken care of. And then she gave me these place mats with sepia
country scenes on them, quite nice, and a cut-glass vase – Mr Levy
in the Lane, he'll do me a nice mixed bouquet – and extra knives
because I've never got enough knives at the best of times and then
she mentioned glasses and that of course *reminded* me and I says
to her Oh yes, Jean – now you've *reminded* me: listen – Arthur, he
says I've got to buy a bottle of wine for this thing and you know
me, Jean – I haven't the first idea. I told her I was doing a nice

shoulder of pork and she said I should get some red wine from Italy and she wrote down the name for me and I took it into Victoria Wine and just pointed, and the man there, nice man, he said it was pronounced Key Auntie which is not, believe me, anything like what Jean had written down on the piece of paper, but there – it's foreign, isn't it? So you have to expect that sort of thing. I've no idea what it tastes like – I asked the man if it was sour and he said he was sorry but he couldn't help me there because he was a bitter man himself – but Jean, she was right about one thing: it comes in this lovely shaped bottle in its own little basket with a handle on it. It'll look very select on the table and I shall certainly keep it afterwards as an ornament. But the price! I'm still in a state of shock, if you want the truth: sixteen-and-nine! I know! So the piece of pork is smaller than I would have liked, but I'll just pick – I won't eat any. But no one would have bought in Italian wine just after the War, would they? I doubt that anyone stocked it. The man in Victoria Wine said they even have *German* now, and that did surprise me I must say: forgive and forget, I suppose – but I don't know what Mister Churchill would have to say about it all. I mean to say I can't see him smoking Italian or German cigars, if you see what I'm saying. And it was just as well that Clifford, he said he had one of those screw things on his penknife or else we never would have got the cork out because I searched the drawer but I couldn't find the one we used to have. And I could have done with just a bit of help there, I must say: nearly put my back out.

Anyway. I got the meat in Barrett's in the Lane – and Mr Barrett himself, he served me and he says to me Mrs Coyle, you've got a lovely piece of pork there – and it did look very nice, I must say: looked as if it would crackle up well, which Arthur always likes. I was going to get rhubarb for the crumble from Mr Levy, but he said he wouldn't honestly advise it so I got some Bramleys and I've done us a nice apple pie instead. Mr Levy, he says to me You can't go wrong, Mrs Coyle, with a nice apple pie all covered with Bird's, and he's right about that. And I got a nice bunch of pinks and a few marguerites and he didn't even charge me for the fern; he asked after Annette, like he always does – he's such a nice old boy, Mr Levy. The soup I'd left on the stove to simmer and I'd already put out the nuts that I put out at Christmas but nobody ate them so I put them back in their box again. Jean Beery, she says that after supper the best people like to eat a mint, that this is what is done, and I should go to Lawrence's in the Lane and ask for Bendicks but I wasn't sure she had that right because that's the name of the spin dryer that I sometimes use in the Launderette, though I didn't like to say so. Well right enough, they had a box in Lawrence's, but oh my goodness the price of it! You could have got a whole pound of Black Magic or All Gold for what they were asking and got change in return and it was only a tiny little thing. And they had only the one, and I couldn't help but notice that the cellophane, it was all dusty, so I says to the girl there, I says No thank you very much and I got a quarter of mint imperials instead, eightpence-ha'penny and very nice too – though why you should want to start eating sweets after you've just had your apple pie and custard I can only wonder: it can't be good for your teeth. Then I had to lug home the blessed tin of paraffin, of course, because that back dining room of ours – you'd freeze to death if it weren't for the little Aladdin in the corner, but the smell when you're eating, it's not very nice – and Clifford always says it makes him sick, so I'll spray around a bit of Airwick and we'll just have to hope for the best.

I was making fairly good time and the rain had kept off, which was a blessing I can tell you: it had been threatening all morning. And then didn't I just have to catch sight of . . . oh, it's been with me all day, this – I just can't shake it off . . . didn't I just at that moment have to go and catch sight of that horrible Mrs Farlow, of all people on God's earth, and just as I had done everything and was on my way home. I tried to ignore her but she says to me in that voice of hers, that voice she's got, she says Oh! Mrs Coyle! Just the person I wanted to see! I looked down and made out I was studying my shopping list and I walked on a bit faster – not easy I can tell you what with a very heavy basket and that blessed tin of paraffin banging against me. But no, she wasn't having it was she? Mrs Coyle! Mrs Coyle! Well . . . what could I do? I just had to stop and turn, didn't I? I just had to, really.

'Ooh, Mrs Coyle – I'm puffing with just trying to keep up with you. Did you not hear me? Doing your shopping, are you? That's nice. No I was hoping I might just bump into you, Mrs Coyle. Mary Jessop, she says I ought to call round, but no, I says to her. I don't like to. Much better if you just bump into someone in the Lane or somewhere and then you can just have a little chat. Much more friendly that way.'

'I'm in quite a bit of a hurry actually, Mrs Farlow. So if you wouldn't mind, I really must just—'

'Oh this won't take so much as a jiffy, Mrs Coyle. It's just that, well – there's goings-on that I think you should be a party to. Now don't you go thinking Oh, that Mrs Farlow, always poking her nose in where it doesn't belong – I don't want you to go thinking that. But it's just that there's things with Mr Coyle that I really do—'

'I'm sorry. I just really have to go now. Running late. Must go.'

'But Mrs Coyle – it's just a friendly word in your ear . . .'

'Yes I'm sure. Well goodbye then, Mrs Farlow. Must run.'

'Mrs Coyle . . .! Mrs Coyle . . .! Well that's very rude I must say – just turning your back and walking off like that when all I want to do is help. Mrs Coyle . . .! Mrs Coyle . . .!'

Oh the *nerve* of the woman . . . I'm still just boiling. On and on, she went – she just went on and on, standing as bold as brass in the middle of the street and calling my name out again and again, and with everyone just stopping and looking to see what all the kerfuffle was about. I must have run all the way, you know – I was back here in no time, and I didn't even notice the weight of my basket and the blessed tin of paraffin. My cheeks were all flushed and I was completely out of breath by the time I put my back against the front door to close it behind me – so very relieved to be home and safe. I just dumped everything down on the floor in the kitchen and straight away put the kettle on for a nice hot cup of tea (and then I checked the soup and turned it down a bit). The tea, ooh, it was such a blessed comfort – well it always is, really: it always is. And I was shivering, you know – and what with the burner on and everything, it wasn't cold in the room, it wasn't cold. And it's good in a way, I got to thinking then – it's good that I've got this mountain to see to today because then it'll take my mind off things. Right then, Gillian – finish up your tea and then let's get cracking now, shall we?

And my goodness did I! Hardly stopped all day. Got all the table done (Jean, she popped in not too long ago and she said it looked lovely); I got the meat and potatoes on, chopped up the cabbage (decided against them in the end, peas), rolled out my pastry, got the apples all cut and cored, polished the dining chairs, filled up the Aladdin heater (it's warm in there now but there's no denying the smell of it; the Airwick hasn't even made an impression). Then I cleaned the candlesticks, plumped up the cushions on the three-piece, laid the fire and got it going, had a quick Hoover round, put on the Ascot – I put sevenpence in so I could have a bit of a proper soak for once in a blue moon – and then I put out Clifford's Sunday suit with a nice clean shirt and his little tartan bow and the frock for Annette that she'll probably refuse to put on. She said she wanted to wear the little scarlet georgette scarf that I often pin with a throat brooch just at my throat there, but I'd already decided I was wearing that myself this evening because it does tone so well with the only dress I've got that I can really ever wear for a thing like this – it's satinet in a very fetching shade of maroon with contrasting cuffs (Clifford, he calls it my

Prize Day dress). And Jean, she says to me Oh Gillian – I've just so many little scarves like that and I never ever wear them: pick one out for little Annette and tell her she doesn't have to give it me back, tell her it's just a little present from her Auntie Jean. She's such a treasure, Jean is – I'm really so lucky to have her as a neighbour. So I chose a very pretty turquoise one with a bright yellow border – it'll look just beautiful with the frock that I made her, if I ever get her to put the blessed thing on. Arthur's good Burton three-piece I'd already got back from Sketchley's – it's been there for ages, I'd completely forgotten about it – and I've put out a shirt and the paisley tie for him. So all of this I got done and still it was ever so early so I didn't put my dress on until the very last minute so I didn't get anything on it, and then I ran a comb through Clifford's unruly mop (heaven only knows how he manages to get it into such a state) and then I thought I'd finally seen to everything (becoming just a little bit anxious about Arthur now, because time was marching on) and then suddenly there blew out of nothing this calamity with Annette and even now, even now as she's sitting on the couch next to Clifford, she still won't talk to me, you know – she won't say a word. She'd come into my bedroom as I was trying to manage the clasp on this blessed little bracelet that I never ever wear because it's always just so terribly fiddly.

'Can I wear it then, Mummy? I'm not wearing the dress unless I can borrow your little scarf, like I said. Can I borrow it, Mummy?'

'Hm? Oh no, Annette – I'm wearing it, I told you. But don't you worry because there's Jean's, look. On your bed. Special present.'

Well. You should just have seen her face. It was like it was Christmas morning or something. She turned and flew right out of the room and I could hear her careering down the passage and squealing like a little baby. In no time at all she was back again and she was all hot and breathless and at first I thought she might be coming down with something, but no – it was just that she was that excited.

'Where? Where on my bed? I can't see.'

'Well they're there, Annette, I can assure you of that. There's your frock, and the scarf's on top. Where are your eyes?'

'Yes I know – I know all that but where are the *jeans* . . .?'

'The—? What are you talking about, Annette? I told you you weren't getting any of those, didn't I?'

'But—! But you—!'

'I've told you a million times. Now run along and get dressed. They'll be here any minute.'

Her face was quite alarming, I have to say: she looked as if she might be about to cry.

'But you just said you got me *jeans* . . .!'

'I said—? Oh *no – no*, Annette – I said *Jean's* – the scarf that Jean next door gave you. Oh – and you thought I meant—!'

But she was gone, gone before I could even explain it to her. She's kept on her school tunic and the turquoise and yellow scarf she says she hates and won't ever wear and she hasn't spoken a single word to me since.

And now – oh my goodness! Oh heavens, oh heavens, oh dear Lord. That was the bell. That was the doorbell. They're here, oh my God they're here – and where's *Arthur*? Where *is* he? Oh where in heavens can he *be* . . .? Because I won't be able to face it, you know – not alone I won't.

♠

Were Gillian aware of the existence of Mickey, she might now be thinking – she may well have concluded that the reason for my absence (and oh dear – she must be in the most terrible state by now, poor Gillian) is that I've been . . . what are they meant to do, those gangland types? Put you in concrete and drop you into the foundations of this motorway they're supposed to be building to Birmingham, is it? She might assume that – but Gillian, of course, is far from aware of the existence of Mickey, or of anyone like him. She accepts, you see, that because our local bobby Police Constable Sugar is always around the Lane and up and down the streets, touching his helmet to the ladies and generally keeping a weather eye open, that crime simply cannot exist, not round here it can't, not with P.C. Sugar on the beat. Maybe in Soho or America, but never round here. Even that time when our red-top went missing from the step two mornings running, Gillian, she assumed that this must be down to an error on the part of this new relief milkman – she wouldn't even consider the possibility that anyone might have just come along and swiped it. And I do envy her. I do – I envy her all of that. Innocence: you can never get it back, you know. Once it's gone, it's gone.

But no – Mickey has yet to seek out and destroy me. I've got, ooh – about twenty-four, thirty more hours maybe, until the latest and last of his deadlines is breached. And breached it will be, I very much regret, because I haven't got any money, you see. No money at all. None to give him. A concept that Mickey, understandably in one way I suppose, seems singularly unable or unwilling to get a hold of. And there is little immediate prospect of this situation ever changing, it seems to me. My continued absence from the supper table will hardly be endearing me to my boss, I rather think, and the only enquiry I have so far received concerning the letting of the room was from a youngish sort of a music student who said he played a Spanish guitar, and would this be deemed acceptable at all? I said to him he had to be joking, no? So this no-show at supper can hardly be explained away by my early and violent demise, no no no. It's just that I have been sitting in this shed now for quite some time, summoning up the courage to simply face it. There is one good swig left in this flattie of Haig that I managed after one hell of a while to get chalked up in Victoria Wine, and once that is down me I shall have no alternative but to leave the peace and safety of this filthy little place and let myself in at the kitchen door and wend my way round to the bluster of the dining room, and there to face the music (though I shan't, I think, be dancing).

I had a bit of a wash, rather earlier on. Slipped in to the bathroom when Gillian was busy downstairs. Worked up a fair old lather with the Lifebuoy, a good and proper flannelling to the back of my neck – touch of Brylcreem, slick back the hair. Thinner and thinner it's getting, you know: thinner and thinner by the day. Thought I might get away without shaving. Saw the clothes that Gillian had laid out for me – I may or may not come back up and put them on later – depends, it rather depends upon just how late I am daring to stay here, and how by that time I am feeling about the stairs. I've never been much of a one for clothes, if I'm honest – but largely, I think, because I've always known that I'd never get close to the sort of clothes that I'd wanted to wear since I was just a little lad in hand-me-downs. You see these gents in town, you've seen them – lovely cloth, their suits are always made from this really quality cloth. Vicuna, barathea – beautiful cloth. You don't have to touch – you just see it and you know. And the trousers, the way they always break just so over the shoes, those shoes that look like they might have been hand-carved out of ebony, nearly patent they are, they're that well polished: people to do it, I suppose. Shirts with proper collars – and not necessarily white all the time either. One time, you know, Gillian – she made some sort of a bungle with the washing machine: something was in there that shouldn't have been, I don't pretend to be an expert, and one of my shirts, it came out all pink. I gave her merry hell for it, I can tell you that – but you know if I'm really honest I wouldn't have minded giving it a go.

I mean not *really*, of course – I wouldn't *actually* . . . Geoff at work, well – I never would've heard the end of it, and you couldn't have shown your face in the street for fear of what people would be thinking of you. And Mr Henderson, he could well have sent me home. But those gents I'm talking about – the ones you see in town – they often have shirts, I've noticed – and ties, those thick silk and woven ties – in all manner of colours. Stripes, if you can believe it – often they have all these boldly-coloured stripes into the bargain. They seem to get away with it. Mr Henderson himself is a very smart dresser, very dapper indeed. Well – you appear in court every day, you go for lunch at all these swanky restaurants, well – you've got to take a pride in your appearance, haven't you? And the clients, they expect it. They expect a man of Mr Henderson's standing to be well turned out, it goes without saying. But if you spend the better part of your working day locked up in an airless room with only filing cabinets and Geoff and tea mugs for company, if your lunch is invariably a ham and cheese on white with a spoonful of Branston taken at your desk and the next thing you know is you're queuing in the rain for the number 47 . . . well – it doesn't really matter overmuch, then. Well does it really? What in blue blazes you happen to look like. Because who in fact is looking? You see? Well there it is. There we have it. We can't all be Cary Grant, can we? No we can't. No we can't. One of us anyway was unlucky enough to have drawn the short straw fairly early on in the game and is still stuck with being, to wit, one Arthur Coyle – whose presence, I am once again reminded, is very overdue at the supper table. So I stand up . . . ooh . . . it's extraordinary, you know: a half bottle, it just slips down you so quickly, you barely even notice. But then when you stand up, well – you do then, you notice it then. I won't bother with changing – it'll only make me even later. What is the time, actually? Let's have a little look. Oh God – oh dear oh dear oh dear. Righty-o: can't put it off a single moment longer. Best foot forward then, Arthur old chum: quick march – left right, left right, pick those feet up you slovenly soldier . . .! And with these damn feet, of course, I could never even be a soldier, slovenly or otherwise. Oh well. All in the past.

My hand, it's shaking. I'm directly outside the dining room now, and the hair on my head, I feel it lightly brushing the panels of the door. I just a moment ago reached down for the handle and I noticed it, my hand – shaking, shaking quite badly. It's a reluctance, I think – a demonstration of my reluctance to grasp tight the doorknob and give the thing a good firm twist and stride on through the door and into this strange and other world beyond it – little stray and fuzzily garbled gobbets of which I seem now to be sampling: a muffled bark of stilted laughter – it's stilted, that laughter, rather forced to my ears, though I couldn't tell you which one of them in there was the laugher – and then a more general drone of ritual conversation spliced into longer silences, these pierced only by a quite gentle clatter.

'Oh – Arthur—!'

'Ah – Coyle. You've seen fit to grace us at long last.'

Arthur spread wide the palms of his hands and looked down at each of them in turn (there's some rather grubby gauze there, a wooden splint just barely protruding) – traced them to the ends of his arms which connected most surely with all of the rest of him. He would appear, then, to be here, in this room. The business with the door, clearly all of that was now well behind him. Eyes, of course – there are eyes upon me, zoning in from all quarters. Gillian, she stood up immediately I entered and her serviette, look – that's fallen on to the floor. Her face, well it's a mixture, really. There's a sort of a wide-eyed and more or less total terror there, certainly, together with the glare of accusation (which is all you would expect) just maybe tempered by a wash of engulfing relief that I've shown up at all. Enquiry, too – urgent enquiry: *Why*, she wants to know. How *could* I? And so on and so on. Well I'm not too sure, Gillian, if you want the God's truth, but doubtless we'll grapple with all the ins and the outs of it, later and for ever. And Mr Henderson – impossible, really, to read anything at all into that impassive expression of his: I've seen it before, of course. It's pretty reliable: tried and tested. He simply is waiting for a convincing explanation, and if he's remotely dissatisfied with whatever it is I imagine I'm going to come out with, he will make this well felt, without actually appearing to do anything of the sort. And as for Mrs Henderson, well, poor woman – she didn't want to be sitting here in the first place, did she? I can just see her face when it came to the moment when her husband, poor man, just had to come out with it and tell her. 'Well why couldn't you just have said *no*, James? What on earth were you thinking of? *I* don't want to go to this person's beastly little house, whoever he is.' 'Well of course I *did* say no, Fiona – of course I bloody well did. But he just went on and on, didn't he? Bloody man. Firing all these different evenings at me. Well I couldn't say we were busy *every* bloody night of the week, could I? Hm? Anyway look, my darling, I'll make it up to you, I promise – and we don't have to stay for long, or anything. We'll just pick at a bit of their ghastly little dinner, or supper as they call it – show willing – and then we're away.' Mm – something on those lines, I should have said: that's more or less how it will have gone. And she's looking down at her plate of pork, I think that must be – yes yes, it's pork, just look at the crackling, dead giveaway that, it's pork all right: good old Gillian – she knows I like that. Roast potatoes and cabbage and a big boat of gravy, look. Hm – I'm actually quite hungry now, if you want the honest truth. Think I'll just sit down, then. Head of the table – that's my place: right at the head of the table. Terrible smell coming off that heater . . . warm in here, though. I'll just flap out my serviette and smooth it down over my lap. She's a fine-looking woman though, Mrs Henderson is. Bit like Deborah Kerr, if I'm any judge. Beautiful dress, what I can see of it – sort of a green-ish kingfisher it is: little could-be – diamonds, I expect they are: little studs in each of her ears. I glance at Clifford, who's staring right at me; I glance at Annette, and she's doing the same. Probably have to say something before too long: think I'll do it now (make my presence felt).

'Sorry, everyone. Sorry, sir. Sorry Mrs Henderson. Sorry.'

'We've had the soup, Arthur,' said Gillian – rather over-energetically to Arthur's ear: the general pitch, that too seemed to be up a register on the usual (Mr Henderson – he's just wait-ing: sitting there, waiting). 'Do you want soup? I mean there is soup if you want it – I can quickly heat it up. Or do you just want . . .? Shall I just serve you with some pork, Arthur? Nice bit of pork? And vegetables? Yes? But there is soup there if you want it – you've only got to say.'

And Gillian, her eyes were rapidly blinking and she was look-ing at him earnestly, even beseechingly, because certainly within her there was the ache – she was stopped up to bursting with a pleading and desperate need for any sort of help at all just to keep her from fragmenting, because let her tell you this: right from that very first moment when she ushered the Hendersons through the hall and on into the sitting room she had felt herself poised on the verge of succumbing to if not an outright and debilitating seizure, then certainly tears and the spilling of panic. All this – this whole blessed thing was to have been testing enough, God alone knows, but with Arthur just not *here* . . . well I'll just never be able to survive it: simple as that. Simple as that.

'There we are – yes, that's it – in here, just in here, do come on through. There we are. That's it. There. Clifford, be a dear and take Mr and Mrs Henderson's coats from them, yes? Put them upstairs – just put them on Annette's bed for now, all right?'

'What a perfectly charming little room. Lovely fire . . .'

'Don't go near – you'll get chilblains.'

'Quiet, Clifford. Oh *thank* you, Mrs Henderson – how kind you are. I'm Gillian, by the way. Mrs Coyle, but Gillian's my name.'

'Fiona. Shall I, um – I'll just sit here then, shall I?'

'Oh goodness yes. Please. Please do sit. Anywhere that looks comfy. Clifford – take the coats, there's a good boy. Oh I told you not to bring your kit down, didn't I? Bits all over . . . Honestly. Children! Do *you* have, um . . . Mrs Henderson?'

'No. No none. Fiona.'

'Oh right. Jolly good. Well there we are, then. Um – do come and sit down won't you Mr Henderson? This is Annette, my daughter – well obviously. Silly. Say hallo, Annette. And Clifford. Oh Clifford do take away all your bits and pieces, there's a good boy. And the coats, Clifford. Take the coats.'

'Spitfire, isn't it?'

'Yes it is, sir. Mr Henderson, sir. Were you a fighter pilot in the War, sir? And I saw your car outside. It's super. Is it a Rolls-Royce like the Queen's got, sir?'

'Ha ha. No no – it's called an Armstrong Siddeley, Clifford.'

'Oh yes – I've got that in my I-Spy book of motor cars, so I can tick it off now, can't I sir? It jolly *looks* like a Rolls-Royce though, doesn't it sir? And were you? Were you, sir? A fighter pilot in the War? Is that why you know about Spitfires?'

'Oh Clifford – just take up the coats and stop pestering Mr Henderson.'

'No no – it's quite all right. James, by the way. Actually I was a Navy man. Commander on a destroyer. Not as exciting as it sounds.'

Clifford nodded. Not exciting a bit, I should think. Because there's one of those at school, a Commander. Commander Lacy who takes Upper Maths and Physics and we call him doiley because they're made of it. He's a lunatic. He just goes round all the time doling out commands because he's a Commander. It's a jolly funny job being a Commander if all you do is waltz about dishing out commands all the time. Why don't they just stop shouting and drive the boat?

'I think you're jolly lucky, sir – being all grown up and having a car like that. Everyone says when you're at school it's the happiest days of your life, but I don't think that a bit. I just can't wait for adultery.'

Mr Henderson grinned very rapidly and glanced over to his wife, who looked down and away.

'Annette, dear – ask Mr and Mrs Henderson if they'd maybe care to partake of a glass of sherry before their meal . . . Clifford, I'm not going to tell you again – take up the coats, there's a good boy.'

'I'll do the sherry – I can do it, Annette. Do you both want a glass? The glasses are really titchy though, I warn you. They're Mrs Beery's next door. It's called Emva Cream – it says so on the bottle. That's Mrs Beery's as well. I think Emva might be like emu which is a fast-moving and flightless bird from Australia which is also where the kookaburra comes from which isn't flightless because it flies like billy-o and there's one on the mantelpiece with a hat on. I know the word sherry because my friend Anthony Hirsch told me that in *Robin Hood*, there's this sherry for Nottingham.'

'How terribly . . . interesting . . .'

'Thank you, Mrs Henderson. Thank you, madam.'

'What a knowledgeable young man you are. And so terribly *handsome* as well . . .'

'Do you hear what Mrs Henderson is saying to you, Clifford?'

'Oh but he *is*, Gillian – so very handsome. He'll be a masher, that one, when he grows up. Mark my words – he'll be quite a masher.'

Clifford smiled lopsidedly and blushed a bit at that, but he still didn't quite get how you could be handsome and a masher because Mummy, she's got one of those in the kitchen drawer and it's just a big old metal thing and you bash up potatoes with it when it's shepherd's pie.

'I think it's better if *you* do the sherry, Annette. Clifford – you can take up the coats, can't you dear? Oh just give me the blessed coats and I'll take them up myself . . .'

'I'd *love* a glass of sherry.'

'Oh I *am* pleased. Annette – a glass of sherry for Mrs Henderson, please. And don't spill . . .!'

'Fiona. Do please call me Fiona.'

'Oh yes of course. Terribly sorry. Sherry, Annette. And for you, Mr Henderson? I'm sure you'll take a glass, won't you?'

'Oh indeed, indeed.'

'So that's two glasses then, Annette. I hope you'll forgive me for not joining you both but it goes straight to my head and I don't want to be dancing the Gay Gordons, do I? And singing "It's A Long Way To Tipperary". Not literally, of course. Pour out the sherry, Annette. And we've got Key Auntie next door for the meal which I expect you know all about. I just hope it's not sour. Well look – we'll just leave the coats over there in the corner, shall we? I think they'll be fine over there. You didn't have any trouble finding us, I hope? Straightforward was it, your journey . . .?'

'Oh quite, quite. Ah – tell me, Gillian – where is, um . . .?'

'Yes. On his way. Sorry. Here any minute, I should think. He's terribly looking forward. Well we all were. We all are. We all *do*. Sherry, Annette. Oh – you have. Oh, good girl. Is it nice? Not too sour, is it?'

'It's very interesting . . . isn't it, Fiona? Interesting.'

'Mm. Very. Oh by the way, Gillian – we brought you these. I completely forgot to give them to you.'

'Oh . . . oh you really shouldn't have gone to all that trouble and expense, Mrs Henderson. Oh look at that – look, Clifford. Look at this, Annette: Bendicks. It's funny you know because I was only just this morning thinking that's the same name as the spin, um – oh never mind. Just me being silly. Anyway. So. Here we all are, then . . .'

'Yes well – a good many of us, anyway . . .'

'*James* . . .'

'Yes well he won't be long, I promise. Annette – do the nuts. Can we interest you in a nut, Mrs Henderson? They're assorted.'

'Fiona. Thank you, Annette. So what sort of a day did you have at school, young lady? Not too bad, was it?'

'No – not too bad, I suppose. I wouldn't take that big nut if I were you because it's still got bits of peel on. We got given these money boxes of the Sacred Mission and we're supposed to put all our money in them so as to save the cripples. Whoever saves the highest score of cripples gets a proper gold badge which you're never allowed to wear on your blazers but you can wear these because they're blessed.'

'Oh I see. So it's a convent you go to then, is it Annette?'

'Tell her, Annette – tell Mrs Henderson what convent you go to.'

'It's the Convent of the Sacred Bleeding Heart but it doesn't mean you do bleed at the heart or anything. It means you weep and rend your garment because of Satan, because if you want to lead a really good life, well you've just got to get him behind you.'

'Yes I see. And you like it there, do you? You're happy there?'

'*I* go to prep school.'

'Be quiet, Clifford. Mrs Henderson's not talking to you, is she? She's talking to Annette. Answer her, Annette. Answer Mrs Henderson.'

'It's not too bad really, I suppose – except we've got this Reverend Mother who's very ferocious. She looks like a person I saw in this film round at Clodagh's called Edward G. Robinson.'

'Oh my goodness me!'

'No she does – she really really does. But she's ever so pious.

She's the most pious of all of them because she's top nun, obviously, and is always doing novenas which take nine whole days as God is my witness. We're always told to pray for her but she's the last one to need it I should think because she'll go straight up to the right hand of God and all the saints will sing in heavenly choir and then she'll be raised up on high which won't actually be all that easy because honestly, she's huge. But she's never ever broken even one of the Ten Commandments, not even telling lies – and she doesn't do murder, obviously, and if you had an ass or an ox or thy neighbour's blouse, she wouldn't ever covet it or anything. It's not blouse, it's spouse, but she wouldn't anyway. She's really really pure and it's not her fault she looks like Edward G. Robinson, it is just God's way.'

'Oh I'm *sorry*, Mrs Henderson! That Annette – once she gets going there's no stopping her. What a lot of nonsense you talk, Annette, you really do.'

'*I* played at conkers today.'

'Ah – conkers, yes yes. I well remember that from my own schooldays – long long ago in the distant past, I have to say. How did you get on, young man?'

'Not too well actually Mr Henderson, sir, because I'd got this super-duper specimen and I'd sploshed it in Sarson's and everything and Dismal, he's got this twenty-niner and he came along and hit mine and it cracked and then I hit his and my conker just smashed into all bits, which is just so unfair because now he's got a thirty-er and he just goes around swanking about it and everything which is typical Dismal, but then he is diabolical.'

'And another funny thing about my convent is that they don't have locks on the doors of the lavatories.'

'Oh Annette how *dare* you – talking like that in front of Mr and Mrs Henderson. I don't know what's come over you. I'm ever so *sorry* . . .'

'Is that true? How terribly odd.'

'Yes it is true, Fiona. It really is.'

'You call her Mrs Henderson, Annette – not Fiona. Where are your manners? Would anyone care for a drop more sherry?'

'Well it jolly well *is* true, Mrs Henderson, I can tell you that. Some people say it's because they can't afford any locks because they're very expensive but Daddy says that the fees they charge they could have the locks made out of solid gold and diamonds, so it can't be that. And some people say it's so you get humility. It's not nice, though, because whenever I'm in there I just keep on making the sign of the cross so that no one will just walk in when you're right in the middle but sometimes they do and then you just have to turn the other cheek and offer it all up. And Margery – Margery's my new best friend – Margery, she says she met someone in the holidays who goes to a different convent and there in that convent the lavatories, they don't even have *doors*.'

'Well that's just *stupid*, isn't it?'

'No it *isn't*, Clifford, actually stupid at all, Mister know-it-all Dopey. It's true because Margery *told* me.'

'Well if the lavatories haven't got any doors – how are you supposed to get *in*? That's just *stupid* . . .'

Gillian swallowed hard and repeatedly during the silence that followed, aware that her left eyelid just wouldn't stop blinking, and then she stood up and tried to laugh lightly at some imagined foolishness or other and then she smoothed down the lap of her dress and said as brightly as she could manage that she thought it might be quite a good idea if we all go next door now, yes? And Clifford, you'll show everyone where to sit and everything, won't you my sweet? And I'll pop along and see about the soup.

And when I was in the kitchen, I did – I really very nearly just broke down, you know. I couldn't remember when I'd felt this tense – and I couldn't remember either a single word of what everyone had been talking about in there. Complete blank. I just kept on looking over towards the door, listening out, praying that Arthur would just walk in and make everything all right. So I just stood there for a bit in the kitchen, holding on quite firmly to the edge of the table with my eyes tightly closed, trying to concentrate hard on all the silence and the redness swimming before me, trying to get just a little bit calm before I had to ladle out the soup and bring it on a tray into the dining room. And my face – my whole face is aching from this terrible grinning that I've been doing for it seems like just years. I must have looked like a madwoman, or something – because my eyes, my eyes too, they feel as if they are blazing. And with every single ladleful of the soup, as it poured and plopped down into the tureen, I was thinking *Where* is Arthur? *Why* isn't he here? *Where* is Arthur? *Why* isn't he here . . .? On and on. And still he didn't come. Can't put it off any longer now, can I? If I don't go back in they'll think that I've also vanished off the face of the earth and then who knows? The children might take it into their heads to go up to their rooms or something and then there'll be just Mr and Mrs Henderson sitting at the table, twiddling their thumbs and imagining they've wandered into Broadmoor, or something – I mean already they're probably doing their level best not to pass out and die due to the fumes of that heater. Oh well. At least we've got proper soup spoons, anyway. At least they'll know that I do things the way one ought. I'd put out the big dessert spoons at first and then I remembered that Mother, she'd given me a set of soup spoons, ooh – quite a time ago it must be, now. She'd said to me Here, Gillian – you take them: what does an old woman want with soup spoons? Soup spoons are for the young: you enjoy them while you've still got the chance. Young! That's a good one. I feel about a hundred – I feel old and broken and I so much don't want to go back into that dining room – I just yearn to go upstairs to my bed and turn off all the lights and sleep, just sleep, for ever and ever in perfect peace.

Well anyway: fat chance of that. No peace for the wicked, is there? So I took in the soup and of course he *hadn't*, had he? Clifford. Told anyone where they were to sit – so everyone was all just milling about in there and Mrs Henderson, she was just staring up at the ceiling (but she won't find a cobweb no matter how hard she looks) and Mr Henderson, George – oh no God it isn't, is it? It's *James*, isn't it? Yes James – of course it's James. Well he was just staring down at the floor which I was that thankful I'd Hoovered and Clifford was blathering on in that way he does when he's just that little bit over-excited about how we've got a brand-new television which is Ferguson which is a very good make – and did you see it? Did you see it when we were sitting in the sitting room? I should have showed it to you. Only we're not allowed to watch it, or anything: not till Daddy's here, anyway. Oh yes – thank you very much *indeed*, Clifford, for coming right out with it and reminding all and sundry (as if, oh heavens, any one of us is needing reminding) that Arthur, of course – he's just not *here* (and I just can't get into worrying about all of that again, I just can't – not if I'm ever going to get through this: I can't just keep nagging and nagging at it). And even as I was saying to Mrs Henderson – and I hadn't even put the soup down yet – Oh here, Mrs Henderson – won't you please be good enough to sit yourself down just here, look, and she said Oh thank you Gillian – and it's Fiona, you know, and I said Yes of course it is, I did know that Fiona, yes yes – and Mr Henderson, Jaw . . . James, you're just here, if that's quite all right with you, and we'd better all get this soup down us, hadn't we, before it goes cold – and then Clifford, he starts up thirteen to the dozen about how he's really really jolly pleased because he's having his room done up at the moment (oh dear Clifford – oh dear oh dear oh dear) and there's going to be new curtains and a bed thing and it's going to be really topping super when it's done and stacks better than Annette's little mouldy old room and *poo* . . .! It really does stink in here, doesn't it? It's that rotten old heater. It always makes me sick and once I really was sick in the middle of sweet and Mummy, she says you get used to it, the pong, but you don't ever – at least I don't, I never do anyway.

'Mmmmm, Gillian – the soup is divine.'

'Oh thank you, Mrs Henderson. There's all sorts in it. Been on for ages. Do you make soup at home, do you ever at all . . .?'

'Do you know I don't. But I possibly should – it's just the thing, isn't it? For these beastly English winters of ours. Oh how I long to get away and feel the sun on my bones. Are you going, um – anywhere nice in the summer, Gillian?'

'I want to go to *Butlin's*. You can go on everything and it's *free*.'

'Be quiet, Clifford. Use your serviette. Put it on your lap. And you, Annette. No, nothing – *planned*, as such. Last year we had a few days down at Bournemouth, which was very nice.'

'It rained. It rained all the time. Clodagh's going on retreat with Sister Jessica.'

'Oh Annette – it wasn't *that* bad . . .! We did get the odd shower. And what about you, Mrs Henderson? Going somewhere nice, are you? I thought Clodagh wasn't your friend any more, Annette? Is the soup to your liking, Mr Henderson? All right, is it? George?'

'She's not. She's not my friend. She goes with Susan and all that lot.'

'Splendid. Delicious. Splendid. It's James, actually . . .'

'And it's Fiona, Gillian: *Fiona*. Well normally of course we always go to France – we drive down to the Riviera, you know. I always say to James – don't I James? You just put me down on a boulevard somewhere warm and sunny with my little Pernod beside me and I'm as happy as Larry.'

'Yes I'm sure. And your little Purr-no is what – a poodle, maybe? One of those sweet little French poodles, is he? We love dogs but we've never had one because I don't really think it's fair . . .'

'There's a poodle in Dogs of the World in Rice Krispies, but everyone's got piles of them.'

'*Poodle* . . .? Oh no no. Pernod. It's pastis, you know.'

'Oh yes of *course*, how terribly silly of me. And I always thought that was *Italian* food – just shows you, doesn't it? Clifford – stop making those noises. I'm ever so sorry about earlier, Mr Henderson. James, I mean. You must think me terribly rude. I do know your name is James, I do know that – I can't think for the life of me really why I went and called you, um . . . do you know I can't even recall what I *did* call you now, isn't it awful? My mind. Anyway – I'll just clear away now if everyone's . . .? Oh – the rolls. I had these bread rolls for the soup and I forgot to, um . . . well it's a bit too late now, isn't it? Sorry. Never mind. Plenty more to come, though – you won't go home hungry! Shan't be a jiffy, then.'

I can't, thought Gillian – safe for now in the fug of the kitchen she trusted – I can't, I just simply can't endure a single moment longer. I mean to say what on earth is everyone *talking* about . . .? I just feel I'm going to explode, disintegrate: there's nobody here who's on my *side* . . .! Now now now, Gillian – quite enough of that sort of talk: there's work to be done so let's just knuckle down, shall we? No good being a cry-baby, is it? Well at least the pork – that's come out lovely, look. I didn't over-salt the cabbage because you never know with cabbage, people's tastes. But there's cruets on the table, with pepper as well for those that like it. Oh please God – please just help me to get through all this, will you? Just a little strength, just a little bit more, please God. And I promise I won't bother you again.

Anyway. Now I've got lids on everything to keep it nice and hot and I'm wheeling it all in on this rickety little trolley that had once belonged to Mother ('Here, Gillian – take it: my trolley days are all behind me now: you get the goodness out of it'); Arthur, I've lost track of the number of times I've asked him to do something about the wheels, though – the squeaking and squealing, it's really chronic. A little drop of Three-In-One, is what he always says – that's all it's needing, and then it'll be as right as rain. That's as maybe, but it never ever *got* it, did it? The trolley. That little drop of Three-In-One, whatever in blue blazes Three-In-One might be: you see I always leave all that side of things to Arthur, always have done.

Oh my heavens – would you believe it? Annette, she's holding forth about the blessed Holy Ghost again. How that day on Primrose Hill she became completely convinced that she herself *was* the Holy Ghost because she was there with Arthur and Clifford, you see, trying to get that kite up into the air for once – I was making the most of the opportunity to give all the bedrooms a right royal proper seeing-to with Ajax and beeswax and heaven knows what else I had up there – and she'd worked it out, little Annette, that if here were the father and the son, then it followed that she must therefore be the, oh dear me – Holy Ghost. I do wonder about that convent of hers, sometimes: the things they fill their heads with. She was disappointed when she finally had to come to terms with the fact that this wasn't the case, silly little girl, because she said she'd really been looking forward to haunting all the nuns and . . . what was it? Oh yes – carrying her head around under her arm and turning all the holy water into sherbet and no one would know it was her because everybody knows you can't see ghosts if they don't want you to and even if she was found out it would be all right because she was officially *holy*, and therefore they would all have to bow down and genuflect in her presence or else suffer the Divine wrath and perish in Hell fire which is all, she said, in God's hands. Ah, me . . .

'Here we are, everyone. Sorry to have kept you. Sorry if Annette's been going on. Have you been going on, Annette?'

'Not a bit: she's been very interesting. Very interesting.'

'Well it's very nice of you to say so. Um – I hope pork's all right for everyone . . .?'

'Oh yes indeed, very much so. I was just telling Annette, wasn't I Fiona? That we don't, um – we are not Catholic, of course, but nor, I am pleased to say, are we either – how shall I put it . . .? The 'Chosen People' as I believe the Good Book has it. Ha ha. Terrible being Jewish, I should have said: no pork, no bacon . . . Quite apart from everything *else*, of course . . .'

Well Clifford was amazed: simply astounded. He goggled now at Mr Henderson, utterly disbelieving and thoroughly confused. Because just look at his car which is Armstrong Sidney and his clothes, and everything. His suit is even nicer than Mr Barrett the Butcher's in the Lane on Sundays. He's just *got* to be jooish, Mr Henderson – he *can't* be poor, he's lying. His shirt under his jacket, the cuff bits are folded back up and he's got jewels going through them and he's got another jewel in his tie and Mrs Henderson has got them all over – she's even got them coming out of her ears. If he had a top hat, Mr Henderson, he'd be just like the toffs in the *Beano* and I bet he's in the Hotel de Posh just all the time and so how come he says he isn't jooish if he's got all these oodles and wodges of dosh? Maybe because he doesn't want people to say Can I have some, so he pretends he isn't really jooish or else someone like Annette would say to bung loads in her money box and she'll save him a cripple.

'Very nice pork, Gillian – congratulate you. Of course they're all over the place now, aren't they? Our Jewish brethren. Not around *here*, of course, I'm delighted to say, but just a bit further north and . . . well. And now in their wisdom they're shipping in blacks, coloureds, half-castes, all sorts. Soon you won't see a white face in England – and that's what we fought a War for, is it?'

'James . . .'

'Hm? Oh sorry, darling. Sorry, everyone. Rattling on a bit there. But the half-castes, I ask you – what were their parents *thinking* of, at all?'

'What's half-carts? Is there any more gravy, Mummy? It's yummy.'

'Well a half-caste, Clifford – it's, um – well, what to say? Mixed parentage, Clifford. Different, er – types of parent, you see?'

Well no I don't see because everybody's got that, haven't they? A Mummy and a Daddy. I think he's lying again, Mr Henderson.

'And *Indians* now, of course. Can't understand it. We made a perfectly good country for them, didn't we? Jewel of the British Empire. So what do they want to go leaving it for, eh? And coming over here. *We* don't want them.'

'I've got Indians. There's a fire and a cooking pot and this squaw who sits on a papoose and a wigwam.'

'Oh Clifford not *that* sort of . . .! Ooh, this boy of mine – the things he comes out with. Mind the gravy now, Clifford – careful now. Don't spill. Annette – more gravy? No? Well maybe you'd like to pass it to our guests . . .?'

Mm, yes – I don't mind passing it but Mrs Henderson, she won't want any because she's hardly been eating anything at all. Mr Henderson is – he's scoffing the lot – but Mrs Henderson, every time she goes to Mummy that something or other is really scrumptious or whatever she says, she just goes shifting it about on the plate but she's not actually eating it and I think it must have gone pretty cold by now. She's got jolly big bosoms, though – you can tell, even with the dress and everything which looks like one of Elizabeth Taylor's and so does her necklace and bracelets and earrings and everything. She's probably got on pink silk underpants but I'm not going to ask her because then everyone will just go and have a fit. Margery says you can nearly see my bosoms now, which is great. We got this fit of the giggles

213

in break today because my hand was under her vest and everything and she was touching me in my legs at the front and I
suddenly said What if the Reverend Mother and the Pope and
Cardinal Redmond and Sister Joanna all came in here right now?
And Margery screamed and her eyes went all big, but only jokey
big and then she waggled all her hands about as if she was really
really scared but she wasn't *really* but she was trying to look
as if she'd seen the Holy Ghost or something and then we
both started giggling and giggling and it got worse and worse
and we just couldn't stop and Margery, she put her hanky in
her mouth and that made me giggle even more and I held my
nose shut but my ears went all funny and then I just burst out
laughing with my mouth and Margery had slid off the bench
and was rolling on the floor and she was holding her sides and
she said all gaspy I'm aching, I'm aching, I've got a stitch and
she just couldn't stop laughing and I fell on top of her and we
were really screeching and screaming now with all this laughing
and my face was all wet with it and then that's when Helen,
she came in and she said what's all the noise about Annette?
What's so funny, Margery? And we just looked up and we
said things like Oh go *away* Helen, can't you? Go and count your
holy pictures, ickle-lickle baby, and she said she was telling on
us because talking about holy pictures like that is invoking the
name of the Lord in vain which it isn't because we didn't even
say the name of the Lord so we couldn't have *invoked* it even by
accident and then we threw all these gym shoes at her and she
ran away squealing, which is just so pathetic. And then Margery
and me – we just looked at one another and we both at the same
second, we just all burst out laughing all over again and the bell
was going and we just couldn't stop but we had to though and
we wiped our faces and went into R. I. but I didn't dare look
over to Margery for the whole of the lesson because then I would
have burst out laughing again and then there would have been

piles of prayers to write out and extra penance which would actually be better than sitting at this table and having this supper with these two funny old people who we don't even know who they are.

'No Fiona? You pass? Well then yes – I will have just a touch more gravy. Excellent potatoes, Gillian – I commend you. Thank you, Annette. Um . . . Gillian, don't think me in any way, um – but Coyle, that is to say Arthur . . . Is he, er . . .? I mean to say . . .?'

'Well you see . . . Oh—! Arthur—!'

'Ah – Coyle. You've seen fit to grace us at long last.'

Arthur paused at the door briefly and took in the scene. Then he strode over to the table as boldly as he could manage and sat down abruptly.

'Sorry, everyone. Sorry, sir. Mrs Henderson. Sorry.'

Gillian now was rather carelessly hacking at the pork and with her eyes held wide she was nodding energetically over to Annette while repeatedly jerking her head in the direction of the cabbage and potatoes – who knows, maybe one of these days the child might actually catch on to what I'm meaning, do you think, and put a bit of each on to her father's plate – but not *all* of it, Annette, because Mr Henderson, he might be wanting thirds. My stomach, that feels a little less tense now, I think it's fair to say, but I can't imagine that it's going to last. I'm worried, quite frankly. Maybe nobody noticed – I do so hope not – the way Arthur was when he just stood there at the door and then walked over to the table – but I did, I did. I've seen it before, you see, well of course I have – so many times over the years, but rather more often just lately, I have to say. I don't know where he's been – and I can't, can I? Decently ask him now, which well he knows. But wherever he's been there was drinking involved, you may depend on that: you've only got to look at him – his eyes, they're half closed and he keeps on making that noise with his lips. And everyone *is* looking. Well of course they are – well,

215

not Mrs Henderson, she's not: she's just staring down at her plate – and she's barely touched a single thing on it, you know, which I must say does seem rather rude for all her expensive dresses and jewellery – and anyway I can't abide it: any sort of waste, I just simply can't abide it. I mean it's not as if we even have a cat or anything to give it to. But oh dear – just look at Mr Henderson. He's put down his fork and knife, and now he's leaning forward. He's going to say something – I don't know what he's going to say, but whatever it is, well – it's now he's going to say it.

'So, Coyle. Or Arthur, I should say. Nice of you to come. I do hope you'll forgive us all for having started without you . . .?'

'James . . .!'

'No no Mrs Henderson – your husband, he's allowed to talk to me like that. Allowed. He's perfectly correct to, um – he's quite right to have, oh . . . word's completely escaped me, you know. Completely gone. Is there any gravy there at all? Ah Annette – thank you, thank you. *Admonish* me, I think could well be what I wanted to say. I am – I am very sorry, everyone, that I wasn't here earlier. The truth of the matter is – mm, nice bit of crackling there, Gillian, very nice indeed. Yes. No – the reason I wasn't here is that, um . . . well of course the reason I wasn't here is because I was *elsewhere*, wasn't I? Doesn't take a genius to have worked that out, I shouldn't have said. So – what've you all been nattering about? Me, I suppose.'

'On the contrary, Coyle. You did not come up.'

'Cabbage? Potatoes? Mr Henderson? Anything . . .?'

'I think I am up to capacity, thank you so very much Gillian. Our *hostess* for the evening, I must say, has been perfectly delightful. As have the children. Haven't you both? Exemplary children.'

'I'll just go and get the sweet. We were just talking, Arthur – well, Clifford brought it up – didn't you Clifford, my little one? Dessert,

I mean – I'll just get the dessert. About the, you know – new television. Clifford was just telling Mr and Mrs Henderson . . .'

'Mm. Mm. That wine any good? Pass the wine, Annette. Yes. We've got a new television. Man's coming tomorrow to fix an aerial up on the roof. Mm – not bad, bit rough. I expect you know all about wine, do you sir? I expect you do.'

'I shouldn't say I was a connoisseur . . .'

'No well – I can't afford it. Wine. Along with much else, actually. Which is what I wanted to talk to you about, sir . . .'

'I hardly think . . .'

'You didn't say, Daddy, we were getting an aerial . . .'

'Sweet! I'll just get the sweet, yes? Dessert. Apple pie all right for everyone? And I've got Eden Vale Farmer's Wife Double Devon Cream. Bit of a mouthful, but it's ever so nice. I got it specially.'

'No no but hear me out, sir – I've got a *proposition*.'

'The office, Coyle. That's the place for any talk of that sort. Um – forgive me, Gillian, but would you think us terribly rude if we took our leave of you now? It's been a perfectly splendid evening, but I really do feel . . .'

'M'yes, I think James is right. It's been *lovely*, Gillian . . .'

'Oh thank you Mrs Henderson, you're very kind. But the sweet – it won't take a jiffy. Dessert, I mean. Or there's mint imperials, if you prefer, and . . . oh *say* something, Arthur . . .!'

'I was trying to. Man won't listen. What am I supposed to do?'

'Please may I leave the table. The heater's making me sick.'

'Quiet, Clifford.'

'But it *is* – it *is* making me sick. And if I can't get down I'll be sick and then you'll be sorry. Mr and Mrs Henderson, sir and madam – would you like to come up and see my room? It's only half done but it looks really good and I can show you my planes and everything.'

'Oh shut up you little *baby*, Clifford.'

'No *you* shut up, Annette.'

'Quiet, the both of you. Clifford! Annette! Arthur – *say* something . . .!'

'No *you* shut up *actually*, Dopey Clifford, because it's not *even* your room if you want to know, because as soon as it's all done up they're going to let it to a *lodger*, so there.'

'Oh *no*, Annette . . .! I told you not to *say* any of that . . .!'

'Well I've jolly well said it. And I know it's true, Clifford, because I've seen the *card*. *You're* going in the mouldy old box room with all the other old junk, so *nyah*, cleverclogs.'

'Mrs Coyle – Gillian: we must be off. We really must be off.'

'Oh no – wait, sir! Please, sir – just wait a bit. You don't seem to understand. I've got this *proposition* – you've just got to hear me out.'

'Come, Fiona. I wonder, Clifford, if you would be so good as to fetch our coats for us? Um – Clifford . . .? Are you all right . . .?'

But Clifford wasn't moving. Clifford was rigid at the table with his shoulders hunched and steady. His eyes were glassing over with tears as he simply stared ahead of him, seeing only these glazed and liquid spangles of colour, prancing in the candlelight. Gillian had to rush over to hold him, trying so hard to shore up and stave off for as long as she could manage so much weeping of her own. And Arthur – oh no, oh my God will you just look at him! He's jerked back his chair and he's trying to get up and oh my God he's stumbling quite badly – and now he's walking round the table and he's clutching at the cloth and it's Mr Henderson who he's got in his sights – and Mr Henderson, he's sensed this, you can tell – and he's backing away now, backing away – out of the room and into the hall, his arm around Fiona – sheltering her, it looks like, from anything to come.

Arthur's resolve, if that's what he thought might have been coursing through him, it had in an instant evaporated – the sternness and determination that he imagined could possibly have been glimpsed in his eyes, they melted now into a simple and coy supplication. He placed what felt to him to be more like a paw than any hand he had ever possessed – he placed it he hoped quite gently on Mr Henderson's so perfectly tailored shoulder and he looked down at Mr Henderson's so beautiful shoes and he whispered quite slowly:

'It's just this – *proposition* I've got, you see . . .'

'Tomorrow, Coyle. We'll speak in the morning. Now, um – Gillian, if you could maybe just give us our coats . . .?'

Annette was already helping Mrs Henderson on with hers, and Mrs Henderson – her eyes were quite unnaturally bright and her mouth now was permanently cranked open into the mirthless smile that was an habitual defence in the face of any sort of unpleasantness that just had to be ignored, such as beggars, babies and certainly anything at all of the nature of this perfectly dreadful and ghastly scene that she was – and she could barely believe it – having to live through right at this moment and second by second and oh my God in heaven you just *wait*, James, you just wait till I get you in the car and I can let loose on you just everything that I *think* of all this, oh God – absolute *horror* . . .!

'No, Annette, no – that's the wrong sleeve, isn't it? It's no good tugging – it's the wrong *sleeve*, look . . .!'

'Listen, sir, just listen – this cast-iron *proposition* . . .'

Gillian was close behind him now, and she gently tugged at his elbow.

'Arthur, dear – best leave it for now, hm? Mr and Mrs Henderson, they're going home now, aren't they? You can talk to Mr Henderson in the morning, yes?'

The clatter and clang in the hall as the envelope was rammed into and through the letter flap – it made them all start and look around as if here was an emissary from hell (Mrs Henderson in particular: she was flinching quite badly) and it was Arthur who tottered the few paces to the door and wrenched it wide open and glared quite ferociously at whoever in ruddy blazes it was who thought they could get away with just ramming an envelope into and through the letter flap of his own front door at this blessed time of the evening and making it clatter, and making it ruddy well *clang* . . .!

Mrs Farlow took a quick pace backwards, really quite alarmed – but then she rallied quite strongly.

'Oh you're *in*, are you, for once? Miracles will never cease. Anyway I didn't come to see *you*. It's for you, Mrs Coyle – I see you there. The letter's for you. Coo-ee! I didn't know you had company, dear – I never meant to intrude – but I think you should know what's been going on, that's all.'

Arthur just stared at her. Then his arms were flying and now configured in the air, the fingers stiff and jagged as if he were attempting to encompass the vast and rugged dimensions of a thing from nowhere, and now his mouth was spluttering out at her not even words. Gillian barged aside Mr Henderson in her rush to reach the door; her face it was burning – she knew it just had to be scarlet and her eyes were so sore now and straining for anything even near to redemption as she hissed at Mrs Farlow that this really was not a good time, not a good time at all Mrs Farlow, and I would be very obliged Mrs Farlow if you could leave my house immediately, please (she was distantly aware of hearing Mr Henderson saying What in Christ's name *now* . . .?). And that's when Arthur began to roar.

'What in the name of the devil do you think you're *doing* here, you big fat pasty old *bag* . . .?!'

'Arthur! Oh my God, Arthur – don't—!'

'Right – that's it, Coyle. We leave now. Out of my way.'

'How *dare* you, Mr Coyle, talk to me in that tone! Honestly, Mrs Coyle – I don't know how you can *live* with such a monster, I truly don't.'

'Fiona – pick up your bag. We're leaving. Excuse me, madam.'

'Don't you talk to my husband like that. Annette! Get up to bed this instant.'

'I'll talk to him in any way I please, thank you very much. Ooh – if you just knew the half of it, Mrs Coyle, you wouldn't be protecting him I can assure you of that. You'd be packing your bags and gathering up those two little kiddies of yours and you'd be off, I can tell you.'

'Madam – if you could just please step to one side . . .'

When the phone rang so stridently, everyone froze for just that one instant and then briefly they stared in the direction. Gillian with a sudden rush of anger snatched up the receiver at the very moment that all around fell back into their stances of aggression and obstruction; not Annette, though, who was sitting at the bottom of the stairs, her chin cradled lightly in her palms, with Fiona Henderson just beside her, hugging the newel post, and close to passing out with embarrassment.

'Oh it's *you*, Mother – look, I'll have to ring you back, I'm afraid . . .'

'You just read that *letter*, Mrs Coyle – that's all. You just read that *letter* . . .!'

'I told you to *leave*, you doughy great saggy old fishwife! Go on – clear off!'

'You'll burn in hell, you will Mr Coyle. You're a sinner – a *sinner* . . .!'

'Yes I *know*, Mother, I know – but I can't talk now, I told you. It's nothing – we've just got the wireless on loud . . .'

'Madam *please* – just step away from the doorway, if you'd be so good, and then we can—'

'Don't you go pushing me, whoever you are. Don't you lay your hands on me. Who do you think you are!'

'Madam I assure you I wasn't—!'

'You another one, are you? Spend all your time whoring with

loose women and gambling and drinking till all hours? *Friend* of his, are you?'

'*Yes*, Mother, *yes* – I *did* get the sherbet lemons—'

'Step aside this *instant*, Madam, or I shall call the police. Fiona – now! We'll just have to fight our way through. Goodbye Gillian!'

'Yes, Mother – the evening went very well, thank you – oh goodbye George! See you again soon, I hope! Oh *please* get off the phone now, Mother . . .'

'Go away, you baggage! Not you, sir – not you! It's this great lardy trollop I'm talking to. Please sir wait and hear about my *proposition* . . .'

'Oh *yes*, Mr Coyle – and you'd know all about trollops, I'm not saying! I'm leaving now, Mrs Coyle. You just read that letter!'

And just as Mr Henderson rallied his resources for the supreme effort to be just, oh please God – *out* of here and into the night, his wife clinging on to his arm and babbling at him dementedly, so then did Mrs Farlow abruptly turn around and recede with so surprising an alacrity that it resulted in Mr Henderson being startlingly wrong-footed on the step and then stumbling down over its edge and coming down heavily on to the crazy paving beyond and he heard the wrenching split in the knee of his trouser before even the dullness of the pain could begin to seep into him. As Fiona was struggling to help him to his feet (and she kept on hissing I don't believe it, I don't believe it, I just simply do not *believe* all this . . .) Mr Henderson was glaring into the face of Arthur, one rigid finger stabbing at the air.

'Tomorrow morning, Coyle – understand me? Nine o'clock, first thing – on the dot. In my office, Coyle. Hear me? Hear me? Do you hear me, Coyle?!'

Arthur just twanged on and off the sort of smile that conveyed, he hoped, that nothing here could remotely be construed as in any way *funny*, and that he had in fact, yes, heard him. Oh well, he just about thought, as he hurled shut the door and slumped back against it – I was fed up anyway with wasting my life on filing, filing – just filing away all his bits of paper: making appointments with people I am never to meet, booking all these tables in restaurants I never get to go to . . . only that and filing, filing: just filing away all his bits of paper . . .

When at last Arthur raised up his eyes, there was Gillian standing limply before him. Her mouth was quivering and she was openly crying – she tried, she tried, but now she just couldn't hold it – and her head, she just gently wagged it from side to side. Maybe, Arthur thought, she is doing this because she doesn't understand; maybe, what it is is she understands completely and is just now – what? Resigned? I don't know. If she understands or if she doesn't. I don't know. What she thinks.

Gillian, when she heard Clifford's voice, was startled immediately – her face just winced and she opened her eyes, wholly unaware of ever having closed them.

'What's a trollop . . .?'

Gillian, she moaned – all she could do was just let out this long and low moaning, because everything around was suddenly and bewilderingly becoming unravelled.

'Oh *Clifford* . . .! I didn't even know you were there. Annette . . . I thought I told you to go up to bed. Come on the pair of you – upstairs. Upstairs, now. Been a very long night . . .'

'But can I go in my *room* though, Mummy . . .?'

'*No!*' barked Arthur – and they all backed away and their eyes were wide. 'No you ruddy well *can't* go to your *room*, as you call it, Clifford, because it's not any longer your room, understand? I would have thought that Annette had made that clear. It never ever *was* your room in the first place. It's *my* room – all the rooms in this house are mine. Do you all understand that? You – all of you, you're just . . . here because I *let* you be here. Kindness of my *heart*. Got it? Yes? Well just don't forget it, then. And go where you're told.'

Gillian had been just gazing at Arthur, but now she turned away abruptly. She piloted Clifford to the foot of the stairs, her hands gently pressing on his shoulders.

'You can sleep in your room, Clifford. I'll make up the bed. Come up and help me please, Annette.'

'*No* . . .!' roared out Arthur – and he was coming for them, now: he was coming for them fast. 'I said *no*! Didn't you *hear* me? Didn't you hear what I just *said*? How dare you defy me? How dare you? I said *no*! That's the trouble, you see – that's the trouble. There's no *respect* – I don't get the respect I deserve in this house, not from any one of you. There's no *respect* . . .!'

He stepped forward quite suddenly and Annette jumped up from the foot of the stairs and whimpered quite shrilly and she skittered to her mother's side and Gillian, with both of her arms, rushed her two children against the far wall and behind her, and they held on tightly to her arms.

'Oh yes that's *right* . . .!' jeered Arthur – swaying quite badly now, and swinging his arms. 'Yes yes – that's right, that's right – you all run and hide behind your mother. Very good. You all go to your mother – never mind about your father. Forget about your *father* who feeds you and clothes you and, and – does all the other, er – can't get the – all the other ruddy things I do for you, you ungrateful little . . .! Just forget all about *him*, won't you . . .? And it's you! It's *you*, Gillian – it's all your fault, this – this evening, this whole ruddy evening – It's all gone wrong and it's all your fault because if you'd just managed to cook a decent meal for once in your life and hadn't bought that terrible bottle of wine that's probably poisoned them by now – and if you'd just kept the kids out of the way so they wouldn't be under my feet and interrupting me all the time and *distracting* me . . .! How was I supposed to talk with all their . . .?! If you'd just—! If you'd just—!'

Arthur lunged forward and right up close to her and the tears were coursing freely down Gillian's face as she stuck out her chin and she *would* face up to him, her hands all the while stiffly floundering behind her to keep her two children both hidden and safe.

'Clifford! Annette! You come out here this instant! You hear your father? Hear me, do you? Step out here.'

Gillian held on to his arm.

'You leave them alone, Arthur. You just leave them alone!'

'Ah! *You* . . .! You're just—!'

And his hand and bony wrist, they thudded in that instant across her cheek and nose and the flat of his palm cracked into her forehead a slapping return and the gasp of shock was out of her mouth before even she was jarred by the burning of the blows that now clouded her eyes. Annette was screaming and close to hysterics and Clifford just tore away and rushed headlong at his father and he pummelled at the man's stomach and hacked at his shins and struggled to be free of the strength that now pinioned his arms and shrank in both fear and revulsion from the bellowing of his father and screamed into his face to just *leave* her *leave* her – you *leave* her – you just leave my Mummy *alone*, you *leave* her . . .! And Gillian, now, she wrenched her boy away from this hideous thing and she bundled him up the stairs and still he was yelping and she tugged at Annette and she huddled her close and Arthur just stood there as they clattered away from him and both of his hands were now clutching at his skull and his mouth was dragged tight and away from his teeth which were bared now and clenched into a helpless rictus of the sheerest agony and from amid a welter of torment and confusion he howled like a maddened creature stuck with barbs and alive to each one of them though yet far from succumbing to the bliss of oblivion. He sank down on to the floor and he hugged his ribs as the hacked-out sobbing had him jerking convulsively.

And later, when he was awoken as if by an artfully timed and wholly malevolent kick, he started up and was bluntly spurred into rapidly scrambling whatever he could muster – but no, there was no one there, no visible or immediate threat, and so he could melt back now into the general shambles. Still he was bent double and scattered all over the mat in the hall, one leg terribly twisted beneath him, and all of the guttural clearings and hoglike grunting that he was compelled to go through, none of it was working because his eyes, they still seemed so reluctant to open. Could he really? Could he really have fallen asleep? Keening in pain and coping badly with an implosive fury, his whole body not just juddering but turning in on itself – and then he just what . . .? Slips out and away from consciousness? Can this really have happened? Well, this at the moment is very much how it is looking – yes yes, it would certainly seem so. So what I must just gently do is first locate and then drag out this dead leg of mine – all the way back round and under to the front of me – Ah! Ah! – and then I can just – Christ my head – prop myself up against the wall, can I? Just shuffle across and nuzzle my back up against the wall – and my finger, Christ, that's just killing me – and now, and now I must try to just beg my head to please won't you only simmer down and seriously focus – for now you must give me information. Because I cannot quite remember the way it all ended – but not well, it's fair to say: it didn't end well. I'm cold. Very chilled. I think I must now try to somehow get up – there's a feeling I have that it's just not good to lie about the hall; the hall – a hall is for passing through, isn't it, on the way to somewhere else – it is not a place for sprawling.

Yes well. I'm standing, anyway. Slid my back up the wall, and now I'm on my own two feet. So I now plod through, um – which of the doors, do you think? Maybe the dining room . . . no, bad memory in the dining room – but I will just step in there and blow out that candle, yes – I will just do that. The other one, that's guttered – the wax has coursed all over the sconce: it's blackened and hard. Do you know, I didn't even notice them. I mean I was, wasn't I? Briefly, anyway – sitting at the table? I was, wasn't I? And yet I didn't even register, didn't take them in at all, those candles. Not over-surprising, when laid out into the frame of things, I suppose – but still, something of an indication of my somewhat elsewhere and distracted, um – composition at the time, if you like. I expect people noticed; I doubt I got away with it.

There's a pie over there, look. On the trolley. Looks nice, looks good. Do I feel like that? Do I? Piece of pie? And there's a jar of . . . what is it? Eden Wife Farmer Double . . . something. No. I don't think I'll do that. But just standing here wondering about it, I seem to have drunk down the last of this Italian wine, whatever it is. I must have done, you know, because I surely do find myself just gripping hard the back of a chair with one hand, the empty flask hanging down loose from the other, and a rather sour and burning insistence somewhere deep and at the gullet end of things, could be the throat – somewhere anyway low down and inside this thick and lagged balloon that my poor old neck is somehow keeping from falling away to the side and pulling me over. I'm going next door – sit down a bit. Just have a bit of a sit down on the sofa, collect my thoughts – try and work out just what I do next. Mm. Well I'm in here now – that wasn't so difficult – and it's still quite warm, which is a blessed relief. The heater in the dining room, that must have gone out. That's what must have happened there. The stench of it, though – that still hung around you: that never leaves – that never goes out. As to the hall, well – that's permanently Arctic, we all know that. But in here, the embers – the deep and orange embers all covered now in ash, they're still game and doing a bit of business.

I can put on the television. That's what I can do. Now how do you suppose one sets about that, exactly . . .? Ah yes – here we are: On. Not too difficult, was it? Bit fiddly, but nothing I couldn't deal with. Little dot – widening now . . . into what? Nothing. Just a dismal fizzing. Nothing. And I'm cranking this knob around, all the way round – right the way round to the other channel and . . . nothing. Nothing at all. Just as well then, isn't it? That I'm getting this aerial put up and seen to. Just as well. Oh but wait no – it's not that, is it? Anything to do with the aerial. It's the *time* – look at the *time*, will you? It's nearly . . . oh dear God, how did it get to be that time? I've got to sit down. Work a few things out.

Yes. Well of course I haven't *really* forgotten. I was trying to make myself feel for just a while back there that all was shrouded by a fortuitous mist, but only rarely can one spread into a luxury such as that. To have it and wallow amid it all. Of course one can, one can sometimes wallow like a bog-beast in the mire, but in terms of relief and a gentle ease, well no – they rarely if ever seem to come into play. Now let me see, just let me see . . . God my head, though: it's not letting up at all. Take something, maybe. Now let me see, just let me see . . . this – what is it? Emva Cream? Never heard of it. What is it? Oh – sherry. I don't drink sherry – I'm not a sherry person. But it doesn't seem to be at all bad, you know, once you get used to the sweetness, the very slightly sticky aspect of the first few slicks of it wrapping around your tongue and then darting off here and there, imparting all its news. Well anyway. Now – let me see, just let me see . . . Oh yes. Well of course there was the, um – all the unfortunate business with Mr and Mrs Henderson, wasn't there? What did he say . . .? Oh yes – nine o'clock, first thing, in his office: did I hear? Well I did, yes – I heard the man, of course I heard him (how could I not?). But I'm not going, am I? No, not going. What would be the point? I don't somehow think he can

228

have anything to say to me that I have not already divined. I mean to say, what? Hm? The man's going to offer me a partnership, is he? Place on the Board? I think not. I rather think not. Is he going to beg to be party to this grand and miraculous *proposition* of mine? I hardly think so. Which is, when all is said and done, really just as well, you know, because look: there isn't one, is there? Proposition. I had none – nothing to say, not even the first idea for an idea, if you want the whole truth of it – nothing, nothing at all. I just must have known, then, that it wouldn't ever get that far. Deep down, I must have sensed this. Because all I wanted him to do, all I really needed was for him to offer me much more money for doing very much the same old thing – that is to say, not much of anything at all, to speak of. And now I come to think of it, it wasn't ever likely, was it? No. No. So we might have saved all this, you know – the whole evening, it might never have occurred. The pork. The candles. The Wife Farmer's Cream. And this other Cream – what is it? Oh yes: Emva, that's it. Well that would appear to be finished now. Not too bad – not too bad a drop at all, on the whole.

Then, um – oh yes: the letter. Which wasn't in the hall. I did have a sort of a look around for it: wasn't there. So – Gillian, she will have read that, then. I imagine I can foretell the general gist, the overall tone of the thing. And then I . . . No. Can't get into that. We'll leave all that, I think. But it's very odd, you know – my behaving in that way. Like that to them. Because the really terrible part of, oh – not just this but everything, really, is that when I, you know – look at them: Gillian – Gillian in particular, sometimes – and Clifford; Annette. When I just look at them, lock into their eyes, all I feel is the burgeoning of love. I really do love them, you know, as far as I can understand it – and then I have to look away, you see; there are times I have to, oh – blow my nose or just walk out of the room or something, for fear that what I feel might just be betrayed, even by such an inkling. It's the *expression*, you see: that's what's so hard. Whenever I speak, whenever I act – God, even when I seem to be doing or saying just nothing at all . . . well then it all just goes, I don't know – awry, in some sort of a way or another: it just all comes out so strange.

But I can make it up to them. Well to Gillian, at least. I can, if not kiss, then make it all better. I can somehow get myself up those stairs – *whoa* . . .! Whoop – got to go steady . . . Yes, I'll just now get myself upstairs and then I can prove to Gillian just how much I love her – because I never ever say it and so I think on the whole she'll appreciate that. And I'll try to be, you know – a bit less . . . well, I'll try not to just be thinking of myself all the time. I *could* maybe kiss her . . . Well, we'll see. We'll see. But I don't know, now, if we will, actually – if we will see or we won't see because I've been outside our bedroom, I realise, for quite a good while now – the stairs, they just must have come and gone – and I'm twisting the handle this way and I'm turning it back again that way and it's just not, you know – it's just not working at all. And I think I've understood. She's locked it, that's what she's done. From the inside. Well obviously from the inside because on the inside is what she is, while I – me – I find myself very much on the outside of things: I just stand here, on the outside. Just looking about me. Well I'll tell you what I'll do: I think what I just have to do now is I'll quietly pad my way along and down the passage and I'll just see if I can't make sure that Annette's all right. And here – this is rather odd too, you know, because I've got the door just open and there's a small sort of a gap here but it doesn't seem to want to go any further, this door. So my hand, I've managed to worm that in and I'm flailing around a bit at the other side to try and see just what might be going on here exactly because I'm completely in the dark, quite frankly. But I've got it now – I see what the problem is. There's a chair, Annette's chair it must be, and it's sort of been tipped forward and jammed inwards against the lock, look – but I've got it now, I've freed it – I think I've just managed to knock it askew. So I'll just now slip in quietly – Shh! Shh! I don't want to make any noise – and I'll just make sure that Annette, she's all nicely tucked up. Yes. I'll just make sure she's safe, and all right.

♠

Clifford just couldn't believe it: this just never happened, not ever, not this. Things are really funny at home, lately (since finally Daddy went and had his fit). It's all sort of what Mummy says is sixes and sevens which I happen to know add up to thirteens, which is not a good number, not even one of them isn't. Mummy, she got me up really really early this morning and when I saw what the clock said I went Oh *Mummy* . . .! But she said No listen – we're leaving for school jolly early because then there'll be time to take you to Lawrence's in the Lane and get you some sweeties! And I've just had loads of everything lately so I think when Daddy gets all batey like he did, well it's quite good really because Mummy goes even nicer than her usual nice and gives you stuff. And breakfast was really quick and Mummy was whooshing about the place and kept on saying Quick quick – let's get out of the house quickly and then she went off all whooshing about again. Annette, she just sat there all moody and I said What's the matter Annette? Has the cat got your tongue? Which is silly I know because we haven't actually got a cat and even if it did have her tongue which is yucky well then she couldn't say yes and she couldn't say no like in *Take Your Pick* when you're not allowed to. I was a bit beastly to Annette because she'd been beastly to me about my room and everything and when we'd gone up to bed last night because Daddy, Mummy said, wasn't feeling very well, I'd said to Mummy but why are you going to give my room to someone else it's not fair and she said Hush, Clifford: hush. Yes I know, I said, but *why* are you? *Why* are you? And she said she'd talk to Daddy but there's no point talking to Daddy ever because he just talks back with things you don't know what they are and what they mean and then he just goes and does what he wants which grown-ups always do and why I just can't wait to be one.

But in Lawrence's it was so super because we still had about twenty minutes to go until school and Mummy said Well what do you want then, Clifford? What would you like? And I said How much have I got to spend and she said Oh you just choose something and then we'll see. So I looked at these big jars they've got there all lined up on the shelves behind the counter and they all have these little doilies hanging down in the front of them like Commander Lacy and they're mostly Batger's and Pascall and Bassets and Trebor and I always want *all* of them except aniseed balls which taste of Veno's but I know you can't really because that is childish. So I went to the penny and ha'penny trays because then you can get most and I got two blackjacks and two fruit salads and my favourite piccaninnies so you can bite their heads off and I didn't get flying saucers because I only like the outside bit and the inside stuff goes funny in your mouth and Annette always says that flying saucers are made of Holy Communion hosts which I don't know what they are but I didn't get any anyway. I always get fed up of gob-stoppers because you can't ever talk when you've got one in (which I know is why they're called it – I'm not stupid) and every time you take it out it's always white instead of colours like it's supposed to be. Dismal is good at gobstoppers, it's the only thing he can do, because what he does is he sucks and sucks and sucks and when it gets to go really really small he keeps on suck-ing until it's like a hundred and thousand or something and then he takes it out and shows you and once he did this for three hours and forty-seven minutes and also plus some seconds as well. And once he actually bought hundreds and thousands and started counting them to see how many he'd got but he gave up and he said that he didn't know how many exactly you got in a quarter but it was a jolly lot anyway, which is quite dismal really. And when I'd got all these sweets then Mummy said do you want anything else Clifford and I thought Crumbs oh golly and I got a Wagon Wheel and a Jamboree Bag which are both thruppence and then she got me a Beezer and a Topper and I really wanted a Beezer and a Topper but I said to Mummy what if you don't get me a Beezer and a Topper but you give me what they cost instead which is sixpence for both of them and then you give a thruppenny bit as well and she said oh all right then Clifford, you are a funny boy – and I knew she'd say yes because she's all sixes and sevens and now I've got this extra ninepence to put to my shilling and on Saturday I can go up to Toys Toys Toys and get Maverick.

And I was still really early by the time we got to school – even Anthony Hirsch wasn't there yet and he comes in Jaguar. There was only swots and wets and clots all standing about in the hall and waiting for Assembly and I bet they were all talking about really boring stuff like relief maps of Dogger Bank and He she or it loves the table, which is just typical of school. And Dismal came up to me and he said you'll be in bags of trouble Cliffy if anyone sees all those sweets you've got and then he said Can I have one and I said No just push off Dismal you jolly well can't and anyway I'm going down to put them in my locker for milk and maybe I'll give you one then if you're not too dismal, Dismal, and you give me your thirty-er and he said you must be joking Cliffy and anyway it's a thirty-sixer now and then Anthony Hirsch came shooting across the hall and I said Oh hey look Anthony – I've got just all these oodles and piles of sweets and stuff so you can help me stash it all in my locker and then in milk I'll whack them out and he said oh wizzo Clifford! Wizzo! And I said that's from Jennings and he said I know and then we both shot off at a hundred miles an hour down the covered way because it was nearly Assembly now and he was making these Red Indian noises he does when they put on war paint and hit their mouths and go woo woo woo like the Barn Owl which I've got in Birds of the World, only I'll never get the other three. And as we were dashing along he pulled out my tie and I knocked off his cap and I waited until he picked it up again and I went Come on come on we'll be late for Assembly and we shot off again and I said Anthony do you know what a trollop is and he said it's a sort of fish which is to be had in the North Sea which I don't know if it's true but Daddy he did call Mrs Farlow a fishwife so maybe it's Mr Farlow who's the trollop and then we zoomed off around the corner and then oh crumbs I just don't know how it all happened but then suddenly we'd smashed right into someone and I fell right over and all my blackjacks and fruit salads and piccaninnies just flew all over the place and someone was gasping and now shouting quite badly and my ear was all twisted and being pulled up and my eyes were shut all tight and I was going Ow ow ow and then Anthony was beside me and all red and looking down and bashing at me sideways for me to shut up and I looked up then and it was oh my gosh that horrible old Mrs Chadwick on the end of my ear who I hate and she was absolutely gone mad and spitting with her mouth and saying You might have *killed* me and what do you mean by it – and I wish we *had*, I jolly wish we *had* gone and killed her because she's really really nasty and she's scary but we didn't kill her, we didn't, but I jolly wish we had. And then she said Pick up all those sweets you know that sweets are forbidden and straighten your tie Coyle you shabby little guttersnipe and take off your cap Hirsch have you no manners at all? You will both of you report to the Headmaster's study directly after Assembly is that completely clear?

'Yes, Mrs Chadwick.'

'And you, Coyle? Stand up straight. Eyes front.'

'Yes, Mrs Chadwick.'

'Very well. Now cut along the pair of you. That's the bell. Go immediately.'

So we did, and all through Assembly we were looking at one another, Anthony and me, and we kept on making these faces like when you know you are in the most terrible trouble but at least there's two of you who is in it. And it was horrible after because everyone picked up their satchels from the heap outside and was going to English and they all said Hey where are you two going and Anthony said we've got to go and see Chadwick and they all went *sssssss* and started stuffing their hands underneath their arms and hopping up and down and everything and I got really frightened then because I really don't want him to hit me and I know that lots of people, they get the slipper all the time but I don't ever because I never ever have because I've always been doled out detention and impositions and lines and everything and I've just never been hit by just anybody ever and not even in a fight in the playground or anything because if anyone starts pushing you about like Derringer and Goodbody and Dobson and Smythe and all the rest of that lot then Anthony Hirsch always comes charging along and they clear off then because he's much bigger than me, Anthony is, and everybody likes him as well so I am all right. I really don't like it, hitting – I think it's not right to. I've never hit anyone except I've got this cushion which I hit like in *Maverick* if there's a fight in the saloon and someone knocks over the table and all the playing cards, they just go everywhere and someone pulls out a sixgun and someone kicks it out of his hand and then they go thwack and he goes crash through the window and into the horse trough and is run out of town and I do that with my cushion but I wouldn't ever do it to a person, not even Dismal – and it's not just because they'd hit me back, well it's a bit because they'd hit me back but it's also because I don't like hitting and Daddy, he's never hit me, not ever, and he's never hit anybody except last night when he did, he did hit my Mummy and I love my Mummy and then I hit him so I have hit someone – I've hit my Daddy – and I was crying and my Mummy was crying and then when we went up the stairs I heard that Daddy was crying too and Mummy said he was crying because he didn't feel well but I think we were all of us doing it because of the hitting because that's what happens. Annette wasn't crying, but she was at breakfast – I saw her – which proves it.

And we were standing outside Chadwick's study and the whole school had gone really quiet and you never ever hear it all quiet like that because after Assembly you're always in class. And Anthony, he knocked on the door and this red light came on above and that means you don't go in so we didn't and we stood there waiting. And I said Anthony, what do you think he'll do? And Anthony, he went like that with his shoulders and he said Two on each I should think and I felt my eyes all go a bit funny and I got a bit shaky like when you've got a tempera-ture and you have a Children's Meggezone and get Lucozade after and Mummy says you'll be as right as ninepence in just two shakes of a lamb's tail and I wish she was here now, my Mummy, because then she'd stop him, she wouldn't let him – she wouldn't let him hit me because I don't want to be hit, not ever, not by anybody, and it wasn't our fault that we barged into Mrs Chadwick and now she's taken away all of my sweets that Mummy just got for me and money doesn't grow on trees and if she's taken my sweets which is against the law anyway, then why do we have to get hit as well? It's just so unfair. And I'm scared, I'm really jolly scared now but I'm not going to say it to

Anthony who keeps just blowing through his mouth and when I look at him his eyebrows go up. And then the red light went off and the green light came on and that means you go in and I looked at Anthony and his cheeks went out like he was puffing up a Li-Lo or something and I'm glad he went in first and then I went in and we stood there and I was looking down so I don't know where Anthony was looking and it smelled of when Mummy has just polished the radiogram and the carpet was all soft and went all over the room and right up to the wall which you don't often get. Mr Chadwick was sitting at his desk and he's got this pair of spectacles that look like they've been cut in half longways and he looked at us with them and then I saw Mrs Chadwick who was sitting on a chair and she was looking too and I went all shivery and I looked at Anthony but he didn't look back. Chadwick, he took off his glasses and he sort of threw them down and then he stood up and made this breathing noise and now he was coming right at us.

'Mrs Chadwick has informed me of your quite deplorable behaviour. And Hirsch – I've seen you in here quite recently, if I'm not mistaken. Clearly you have failed to learn your lesson. Clearly I must reapply myself with vigour. Now there's absolutely no excuse whatever for this sort of hooliganism. Flouting the rule about sweets in school, running in the corridors, assaulting a member of staff . . . Anything to say for yourself? Hirsch?'

'No, sir. Sorry, sir.'

'Coyle?'

'No, sir. But sir it's just that—'

'*Quiet*, Coyle – I shan't hear another word. Put out your hand.'

And the gym shoe, it appeared from nowhere and it was in the man's grip as he reached for the tips of Clifford's shaking fingers and the shoe came down and the noise and the jolt and the sheer fear of its coming made Clifford instinctively flinch and jerk back his hand but his fingers were not to be released until such dreadful impact had been detonated and then came the cruel and sideways pain that was flooding all over his palm and already Mr Chadwick had back the ends of his fingers and the shoe cracked down again and the tears sprang right out of Clifford's eyes and he dumbly extended his other hand as bidden to do and as it was beaten, the sharpness and shock of the pain, it made him whimper as the huge and blood-red weight of the livid other beaten hand just hung down beside him and then he cried out as the shoe came down hard and again and he snatched back his hand and just stared at the colour as the pain invaded him and his eyes were bruised and his mouth was just babbling now uselessly. Before more tears were squeezed out of him as he closed tight his eyes he sighted, just glassily, the swell of Mrs Chadwick, who he had never before seen with a smile on her face.

'Outside, Coyle. What do you say? Stop blubbing. What do you say?'

'I – I . . .!'

'What do you *say* . . .?'

'I . . . Thank you . . . sir . . .'

'Right. Outside. Hirsch – give me your hand.'

And even through the closed door behind him, Clifford could hear first one, then the second swipe of the shoe on to Anthony's hand and he turned and hurtled away down the corridor and he was sobbing quite piteously as he rushed to the basin in the washroom and felt not just appalled but nearly disfigured when not one or either of his hands was coming even close to getting to grips with the tap and so he just stared at his so sore and hopeless ruddy mitts just groping at the spindles while his whole chest and stomach continued to be racked very badly with the choke of gasping and so much disbelief at the shock that now was all over him. He reached for the roller towel as he heard an approach – and here now was Anthony, his eyes quite hard as he spun at the tap and then at another on the adjacent basin and Anthony and Clifford, ignoring their reflections in the mottled mirror before them, submerged their hands and gently revolved them and Clifford said Oh *ow* at the first hit of hot water and Anthony's voice was so short and clipped as he said That bastard, he gave me three on each because he said I just had to be taught.

They blotted dry their hands and then they plunged them again under water and then once more they wrapped them softly in the towel, as if here they had flayed and cowering little animals.

'Listen,' said Anthony – and his eyes were bright with urgency. 'Let's be blood brothers. I saw it in *Hawkeye*. Let's do it now.'

'How do you mean? Oh I sting so much. Do you sting, Anthony? I do – I sting so much. I can't *hold* anything – they've all gone big, my hands . . .'

'You prick your thumb and I prick my thumb and then we press them both together and then we're brothers forever because then we're related.'

'What . . . you mean prick with a pin sort of prick? I don't want to.'

'You won't feel it. Not now because you're numb. Look – I've got this Uncle Holly badge – give me your thumb.'

'I don't want to be hurt any more, Anthony . . .'

'Just give me your thumb. It won't hurt, I promise.'

And it didn't, not really. And as they pressed their thumbs together tightly, three, four, no more than five drops of blood, they squirmed up slowly and then they oozed away and were soon rushed off into the pink and then clear of the swirling in the basin. Clifford laughed once out of maybe relief, and that deeply amazed him. He then went into one of the stalls and unhooked a roll of Bronco and tore off a few of the brittle little squares of paper and handed them over to Anthony, who wrapped them around his thumb. Clifford watched, and then he did it the way that Anthony had done it, dabbing the paper then at the ache in his eyes but the harshness made them hurt even more, so he stopped that then.

'What's "bastard" . . .?'

'It's a bad thing. It's a bad person. It's someone like Chadwick and Mrs Chadwick and we'll never be one of them because now we're blood brothers. We're a secret league, sworn to vengeance and the righting of wrongs. That's from *Robin Hood* – it's on on Sundays. Come on – we'd better get up to English now, Clifford. You know what moany old Meakins is like.'

And as they walked away, Anthony slapped at Clifford across his shoulders and he half laughed out at the pain in his hand – and Clifford, he was laughing too now, which he never thought he would: not again.

'Well, brother?' said Anthony.

'Well?' grinned Clifford. '*Brother* . . .?'

♠

It's extraordinary, you know, how having just a couple of people around for a bite to eat can result in all this pile of pots and plates and glasses. I've been at it since the moment I got in from taking Clifford up to school, and still there's just a mountain to see to. Oh well, it's good to keep occupied. Too much thinking, it can't be healthy – not to my way of thinking, anyway. Because I was doing it, wasn't I, all blessed night, thinking: didn't get a wink. Turning it all over in my mind. It all was just going around and around my head and I still don't know what to make of it all. I'm still just at sixes and sevens. But it was – it was deeply shocking, what Arthur, you know – did to me. And in front of the children, that was the worst part. I know he's got a lot to think of at the moment, but still, there was no call for any of that sort of thing – it's a very bad example. He's not done it often before, to give him his due, and never with the children there. I've heard of other women around here who are a lot worse off in that respect, so I really can't complain. But oh – little Clifford, you should have seen him: he was so upset, so upset. It took me ages to calm him down once I got him into bed – stroking his hair, saying there there there – and then he brought up all this awful business about letting out his room and then I just didn't know what to say to him, really. I mean I *will* talk to Arthur, I will try to ask him if there isn't some other way round it, this money worry, but Clifford's perfectly correct, you know, when he says that Arthur, he'll do just what he wants in the long run. Anyway, I decided the best thing to do was to get the children up and off to school quite a lot earlier than usual and before Arthur was about – avoiding any more unpleasantness all round, is how I saw it: that was the method in my madness. Annette, she was ever so quiet. Still sleepy, I expect. Because no – she couldn't still be sulking about all that nonsense over those *jeans*, could she? Surely not. And she barely touched her Corn Flakes, you know. Maybe she's like me – just not over-keen on them. And then at the door I was going Goodbye, Annette, goodbye! See you later – have a good day! And nothing, no sort of a reaction at all. Didn't turn around, didn't wave. Just trudged away as if she was carrying the entire weight of the world on her shoulders. She didn't seem sad, exactly – more as if she was really quite angry about something or other, I should've said. Well who knows? I'm just a parent, aren't I? Who can ever say what it is that goes on inside the heads of children nowadays? They get so many funny ideas, don't they? A lot of people, they blame television, but that can't be true in our case, can it? I don't even know if the blessed thing works. Oh yes and Arthur – talking of the television, Arthur, when I'd got in from spending all that – oh, just so much money in Lawrence's, I just felt I had to make it up to him, poor little Clifford, and then taking him on up to his school . . . now what was I . . .? Oh yes – Arthur, he'd gone off to work as I hoped he would've (I walked back from school ever so slowly which isn't like me, you know: not like me at all) and he'd left me this note on the kitchen table. At first, I was nervous to read it, but all it said was 'Aerial man – twelve o'clock'. Just that: nothing else. Well, I expect he had other things on his mind. Because unless Mr Henderson has simmered down a bit (and do you know I've got this awful feeling I called him George again – how dreadful) – well, it's not going to be easy, is it? It's not going to be an easy sort of a meeting at all, poor Arthur. If only he'd, oh – just *been* here – if only he'd just behaved as he always does and not acted so, oh – I don't know, I don't know: water under the bridge, I suppose. And the nip of whisky he must have had, that was not a good idea. But then poor Arthur – he does have such a lot to think of, and he never talks, you know – this is a part of it, I swear. He never sort of shares with me whatever it is he's feeling, so I'm left in the dark, really – just guessing at it, is all I can do. And then when that dreadful woman Mrs Farlow just rolls up as cool as you like! Oh what a beastly and nosy little woman she is. Her and her letter! I've not read it – I wouldn't give her the satis-faction. And I'm sure it's just lies, whatever it is she's written – as if it's any concern of hers. Once I get the fire going later in the afternoon, that'll be the first thing to go up the chimney, I can assure you of that. I don't hold with tittle-tattle and gossip; I don't hold with it at all.

Do you know, I think I'll just get the kettle on now and have a nice cup of tea. Then I'll take all these dishes and things back round to Jean's – pop the serviettes in the Hotpoint. She'll be wanting to know exactly how everything went, I suppose, and I really don't know frankly what I should say to her. Oh well – I daresay I'll think of something. But it's Annette, you know, who's preying on my mind. That face she had on her – never quite seen her like that. I do hope she's all right: I do so hope there's nothing wrong at all. Ah me: who'd be a mother? Who'd be a wife? You tell me that. Ooh look – I've just gone and opened a new packet of PG Tips here and there's a Bird of Paradise inside: I'm not sure, but I don't think he's got that one, you know – not the Bird of Paradise. Oh he *will* be pleased, poor little man. Now Annette, you see – she hasn't got any hobbies and interests, not like Clifford has with his soldiers and his kits and his teacards and his conkers. Heaven only knows what she gets up to in her room, I honestly couldn't tell you. Hours and hours she spends up there. Some mothers I've talked to, you know, they tell me they often have these little chats with their daughters about, ooh – I don't know, whatever women natter about when they're together, I suppose. But it's not like that, not with Annette and me, no. I mean maybe when she's a little bit older . . . but not now, anyway: not now, that's for sure. Oh well – doesn't matter. The main thing is I just hope she's all right: I just do so hope there's nothing wrong – that's all.

Oh – did you hear that? Now who on earth can that be? It always happens – it's always the way: we don't often have people ringing the front doorbell (Jean, she always comes round the back and does our special little knock on the kitchen door) – but whenever it happens, whenever the bell does go, you can be sure I'm all just anyhow or else up to my arms in washing up or down on my hands and knees. Well I'll just quickly slip off my pinny and give my hair just a little bit of a pat – don't want to frighten them away, do I? Don't want to look like the Wreck of the Hesperus. Whoever it is at the door. It could be the postman, I suppose, but I don't really think so because all we ever seem to get are just the household bills which I just tuck behind the clock and leave them for Arthur to find in his own good time: always feel a little guilty, you know – just handing them to him. You get samples, of course, which are always very welcome. Not too long ago seven little tiny bars of Palmolive got pushed through the door and honestly I'm telling you, they'll last us for ages. But the postman, you see, he'd only ever ring if there was a parcel or something, and we never get those. Oh goodness me I know who it is – oh of course, of course, it'd completely slipped my mind: like a sieve, these days. It's the person about the aerial, isn't it? A little bit early, but still – better that than late.

'Oh hello – good morning. Sorry to have kept you waiting. The roof is . . . oh well how silly. I expect you know perfectly well where the roof is. In your line.'

The man on the doorstep just looked at her.

'Are you not, um – here to fix the aerial?'

'Nah. Here to see Mr Coyle. Little word.'

'Well I'm afraid he's not here, not just at present. Is there, um – anything I might be able to help you with? I'm Mrs Coyle.'

'It's a little bit of business.'

'Really? Oh. Oh – I know – you're enquiring about the *room*, is that it? It's not quite finished, I'm afraid, and it may not be available after all. I'm terribly sorry if you've been inconvenienced.'

The man on the doorstep just looked at her.

'I just want to talk about the money.'

'Oh well it's four pounds two-and-six a week. But—'

'Not enough.'

'Not . . .?'

'Nah. Not by a long way. Ten pound a week. Minimum.'

'I . . . see. Well you'll have to discuss it with my husband at a later date, I'm afraid. I'm sure you'll be able to come to some sort of an arrangement . . .'

'That's what I been saying. Say to him Mickey called, yeh? Just say to him.'

'Mickey. I see. And do you have a telephone number, Mr um . . .?'

'Nah.'

'I see. An address, maybe, where you can be, um . . .?'

'Nah.'

'Righty-o. Well – I'll be sure to pass on your message, Mr um . . .'

And then he just turned around and walked away. I mean how perfectly extraordinary. Whatever is one to make of all that? I think I'd better write it down, though, such as it is, or I'll only forget. Now . . . pencil pencil pencil. Why is there never a pencil around when you . . . I always make sure I've got one in this little pot in the alcove and I'm always saying to everyone look, if you use the pencil just try to remember to put it back in the little pot in the alcove, will you? But you can talk until you're blue in the face. Oh look here's one, stub of one – not the one I was meaning, but still. Now then . . . paper paper paper. Oh I'll just use the back of this – oh bother, it's the blessed doorbell again. Oh yes it's just on twelve – well at least they're punctual, those people: I do hope they don't make a mess.

On the doorstep was Annette, and beside her was a nun.

'Mrs Coyle,' said the nun. 'You remember me?'

'Oh of *course*, um, Sister, um – Annette, what's wrong? Are you sick? Is she sick? What's wrong?'

'Mrs Coyle, I think this letter will explain the, em – basic situation. There will be further communication. But for the present, Mrs Coyle, I am empowered by the Reverend Mother to insist that you keep Annette at home. Pending investigation.'

'Pending *what* . . .? But—! Is she sick? Are you sick, Annette? What's happened? What's wrong? Will somebody please tell me—?'

'I shall take my leave now, Mrs Coyle. Please read the letter. Annette, I shall pray for you.'

And then she just turned around and walked away. Gillian's eyes were darting and frenzied as they implored Annette for information. Annette just shut tight her lips and shook her head and ran up the stairs and into her room, slamming the door behind her. And not just slamming it either, but jamming this chair I've got right up against the handle – not that it works, or anything: not that it keeps people out. I thought I'd be crying by now, but I'm not. Not crying because I was sorry or anything – just crying because when things like this happen and everyone is all quiet and ever so serious and you have to go and see Reverend Mother and everything and she just sits there like she's the Queen on the throne or something except that she looks like Edward G. Robinson and the whole room smelled of candles and peppermints and this bottle of something we've got in the bathroom which is called TCP and you can't ever put your nose in it without closing your eyes ... I didn't think nuns were allowed things from chemists – but I suppose when you're Reverend Mother you can break lots of rules like skipping Benediction and not wearing knickers which are black because no one's ever going to check. So after all this, you're meant to cry. But I'm not.

I think I'd better write it down in my diary. I don't care what happens to me. Bad things are going to happen to me because I've been bad and a sinner, but I don't care. I don't care. I mean I just *know* I'm going to burn for ever in the torments of Hell, there's no doubt about it now, so there's nothing really left to be afraid of. I don't suppose I'll ever see Margery again: she hates me, she said so – she doesn't like me any more. I don't think anyone does, not any more they don't. Mummy does, she likes me – but not as much as she likes Clifford, not nearly as much, so it doesn't really count. Daddy says he is loving me, but I think he hates me really. I think he must. Mummy isn't pious, but she'll go to Heaven anyway because mummies always do which I think is a rule. When Daddy dies, he'll go to Hell and that means we'll both be down there for all eternity and I don't want that, I don't want that. But it's where he's going to go.

I didn't know what was going to happen today. I mean you never do, not really, but most days when you're at school nothing happens anyway and so you don't sort of notice that you didn't ever know. It's only when something different happens that you know you didn't know it would. I was jolly early this morning because Mummy said we all had to be, I don't know why. I felt very sleepy and I felt something else that I don't know what it is but it's like when you feel you want to be sick but you can't and you're quite hungry but you feel like you've just eaten two helpings of stodge. I didn't sleep, or anything. I sat on the chair and I held on to my hockey stick for if he came back, but he didn't. And when I got to school it was super at first because Margery, she was already there and she said Oh hullo, Annette – you don't usually come in till much later and I said I know. And I said Let's go to the boot room Margery, shall we, and she said What – now? And I said Yes let's go there now and she said Why don't we go after Free Activity and I said I want to go now. So we did, we did go to the boot room and Margery, she's in the netball team and so she had on her Aertex shirt and she undid the buttons and I put my hand in and she was all nice and warm and then she touched me and she said Look Annette! Look! Have you seen? And I said have I seen what, and she went: *Look* – your bosoms have started! And I did look and she was right. They have definitely started and that was really sudden and everything because they hadn't started yesterday because I remember because I was pulling at them to make them. And then I put my hand in under Margery's tunic and she was wearing these huge blue knickers because of netball and she was laughing and I was laughing because it took ages for me to get in the elastic and then I did and I put my finger up and then I put another one up and Margery went Ow and I pushed in a bit harder and she said Ow ow, Annette – don't push so hard and I really did push hard then and I pushed up again and I was going faster and faster and she started shoving me away and going Ow ow *ow*, Annette – that really really hurts, you're hurting me Annette and I said I'm not, I'm not – I'm not hurting you, I'm loving you and I kept on doing it and it was really difficult because she was pulling away and trying to get her tunic down and everything and she was crying now, she was crying, and I said There's nothing to cry about is there, you big baby – it's nothing to cry about – it's nice, it's not hurting, it's nice, it's nice because I *love* you, you see – I love you I love you I love you. And she screamed – she got up and her face was all red and she shouted at me that I was *horrid* and why was I being so *horrid* and she was crying and crying and people came in and said What's wrong, what's wrong, what's all the crying about and Margery went It's *her*! It's *her*! She's been bad in the eyes of God and they all went Well why don't you go and tell on her to Sister Joanna then and Margery told them all to go away because it was none of their business and she wasn't a sneak and then she said to me I really do *hate* you Annette – I really do *hate* you Annette and I don't want to be your friend any more and I said I don't care if you hate me and I don't care if you're not my friend any more and I don't care either if you *do* go and tell rotten old Sister Joanna because all I was doing was *loving* you and the Bible says we've all got to love everybody all of the time so you can do what you want because I just don't care and she just said that as God is her witness I would perish in Hell and I said I *know* I will I *know* I will and what's more I don't even *care*! And then she ran away and she was still crying and everything, Margery – you could hear her all down the corridor – and then I got up and walked off the other way and I got to the chapel and outside the door there was Helen and Alice and Alice was doing her stupid long knitting and Helen was showing her another load of new holy pictures and then she looked up and she said Go away Annette, we don't want to talk to you Annette, just go away can't you? And I didn't say anything to Helen but I got hold of her missal and that made her go squeaky and look all scared and I took off the elastic bands around it and she was all snatching at it and going Don't! Don't! Give it back to me Annette and I just said Well if you want it so much you can go and get it and I chucked the whole thing as far as I could and all these millions and millions of holy pictures, they just went flying all over the place and Helen, she was screaming and screaming and screaming and on the floor and trying to pick them all up and then she went Alice! Alice! Please can you help me pick up all my holy pictures because they have been blessed by Father Doobey and are sacred and I said Father Doobey is a *sinner* and Alice started screaming then and I said Shut up Alice, just shut up now and she wouldn't, she wouldn't, she just went on screaming and so I got my hand on her mouth and I got her arm and I twisted it right up tight behind her back and she was yelling about how much I was hurting her and everything and I said I'm not, I'm not, I'm not hurting you, all right? So you just be quiet – but she wouldn't, she wouldn't and Helen was crying her hardest and still on the floor and picking up all of her holy pictures and I said I'm warning you Alice, just stop all your noise and she got even louder – she got louder and louder and louder and I just kept on twisting her arm and then there was this noise that came out of it and she screamed so loudly then that all these people came running in and her arm I let it go and it all sort of stuck out funnily and she screamed and screamed and then she fell right over and she looked like she was dead or something but she wasn't dead because her stomach was going all up and down and some older girls from 4A, they came along then and they got hold of me and they told someone to go and get Sister Joanna and they took me away and they said I was evil and my soul was in the hands of the Devil and I said I *know* that I *know* that and I don't even *care* . . .!

So you see it's only when something happens, I think, that you know you didn't know it was going to. And I still haven't. Cried. I still haven't.

♠

'So I do hope and trust, Coyle, that there are no hard feelings.'

That's what he said to me, Mr Henderson – that was his conclusion. And I could honestly tell him that there weren't, you know, because as I stood there before him (he had not bidden me to sit – sometimes in his office he would bid you to sit – usually, as a matter of fact; well actually *always* is the truth of it – he would always bid you to sit, but he didn't, not today, today he most certainly did not: today I remained unbidden). So as I say, I stood there before him and what there were, well – at that time were quite honestly no feelings at all – none whatever, hard or other-wise, on any single subject under the sun. I was left untouched. Apart, that is, from an insistent headache and more than a touch of dyspepsia, but when all is said and done, well – would you wonder at it? I did put away a fair old bit last night, you know – the Scotch, the wine, that unspeakable sherry. Which is why I don't remember anything about it. I don't remember anything about it.

I heard a bit of bustle going on in the morning. I was rather surprised to find myself clinging to the sofa in the sitting room.

My neck, it's still aching me now. And I thought it better, for one reason or another, to just let them all get on with it – keep my head down, as it were; stay out of sight. And then I had to decide what to do. The options were not that strong, I make no bones. When all seemed quiet, I went into the kitchen and drank down cup after cup of cold water from the tap (Adam's Ale, as I so stupidly call it, should there happen to be a member of my family within easy earshot: Adam's Ale, dear oh dear). And then I went up to the bedroom and I got out that little box of Gillian's that she keeps under her hankies in the tallboy. The priorities as I saw them were these: one, raise some cash immediately to at least partially deflect the excesses of friend Mickey for as long as I possibly could – and two, do or say anything at all that was demanded in order to ingratiate myself with Mr Henderson. Not easy; in the light of just everything that took place, let's face it, this was going to be far from easy. A third and later priority was to ascertain just what exactly it was that that awful old baggage Mrs Farlow had written in that damnable letter of hers, and quite in what manner Gillian may be seen to have reacted: that, however, could wait. That I could justify, or at least deny.

There wasn't much – not really very much at all in that little box of Gillian's – all I had ever bought her in that line were a cheap engagement ring, one or two hundred years ago, and an only slightly less cheap wedding ring, neither of which she would ever remove. There's a bangle sort of affair in here – I bought her that as well for some reason or another, lost to the mists of time. 'Rolled Gold' it says on it here: I do hope I knew that at the time. But there are one or two pieces of her mother's that look to be rather better – I mean the lord knows I'm no sort of an expert at all, but they do appear to have a bit of weight to them, if you know what I'm saying. I mean that bangle, it could float out of the window unaided. And there's a pendant, is it?

What they call these? Necklace sort of a thing with a few small, rather dull and resentful little diamonds, if diamonds they be. Not the Crown Jewels, then, but needs must when the so-and-so and so forth. And a watch. Man's watch – maybe the husband's, who knows? Anyway – bundle them all into a bag, or something, and get them down to Lawson's on the Kenton Road. I've hocked things there before, of course – always intending to redeem them, never quite managing to do so. Can't even for the life of me remember what on earth they could have been, now; nothing, clearly, that I have come to miss. But they wouldn't be open yet, Lawson's – and I was very aware that Mr Henderson, he said to me most pointedly nine o'clock sharp – said it more than once, as I recall. And I know I decided I wouldn't go, I do know I decided that – but I wasn't thinking properly, was I? Wasn't thinking it through: wasn't really thinking at all. But I am now, I am now: got to.

On the bus on the way to work – I always go on the top deck, have a pipe or two – I stared at the crossword, thought it might take my mind off things a bit, you know. I never actually *do* it, of course, this ruddy crossword. Gillian thinks I do – Gillian, I'm sure she imagines that I'm wedded to the thing, but no. I just stare at it, thinking of other matters, other matters entirely, couldn't tell you what. Well I mean to say the clues – I mean what, is it meant to be some sort of a practical joke or something, is it? All these ludicrous clues? I can never make head nor tail of them – complete and utter mystery. So I just write in any old words that come in to my mind. They've got to fit the grid, though – they do have to be the right length, the words, but farther than that I don't at all pursue it. I suck on my pipe and then I suck on my pen and then I put on a bit of a frown and then I write in the first thing I think of. Done it for years. Done it for years.

And of course it *didn't* take my mind off things – well

how could it? How could it possibly? But at least I was *early*, that was something. I was trying not to think too far ahead – trying not to over-rehearse. I thought it would not be good to pursue the idea of a raise, though. I decided that I might defer that until some later date. I thought I might compliment him on Mrs Henderson's dress and her earrings and general deportment, and then I thought I might not. Well look, nine o'clock came around, as nine o'clock will, and there I was: standing there.

'Well, Coyle. Punctual, at least.'

'Yes sir, yes sir. Nine o'clock, Spot on. Oh and may I say, sir, thank you, sir, for – and I'm awfully sorry if—'

'Coyle – I think we may dispense with all of this, don't you? Last evening has merely served to, er – bring matters to a head, shall we say.'

'To a head, sir . . .?'

'M'yes, Coyle. It's brought them to a head, as I say. I shouldn't have said that your work in the office has been quite up to mustard, would you Coyle? To be blunt, Coyle, I have found briefs where no briefs have a reason to be.'

'Not up to mustard, sir . . .?'

'And *so*, Coyle – I think it might benefit both the firm and yourself if you were to seek out, ah – were to make for yourself alternative arrangements.'

'Oh I don't think so, sir.'

'I *beg* your pardon, Coyle?'

'Can't really see how that could benefit me at all. Can't see how. I mean admittedly I can't see the *firm* suffering over much were I to, um . . .'

'Coyle. Listen to me. I am letting you go.'

'Oh but sir, I—!'

'No ifs or buts, Coyle. The time for iffing and butting is done. I should be obliged to you if you would clear your desk and be off the premises in, shall we say – one hour? Would two suit you better? Robinson will escort you.'

'Oh but sir, I—!'

'And although there is no such stipulation in your contract of employ, and therefore no obligation on my part to provide, I would without prejudice volunteer four weeks' salary in lieu. A reference – of sorts – will be provided. I think that is all. So I do hope and trust, Coyle, that there are no hard feelings.'

Well as I say: none, not really. It came as a relief, in many ways, as these things can do. I suppose I knew it had been coming, but when you are so used to living in a state of pale and meagre hope, barely sustained, it becomes altogether instinctive to give as wide a berth as possible to even the lip of the brim of despair. (*Cutting* the mustard – that's what I wasn't doing; had I merely been not *up* to something, then that would have to be scratch, of course. Mr Henderson, he's maybe loose with people he knows would never even dream of correcting him.)

I did ask him if there was any hope at all of the accounts department paying me the month's salary now, as in right this minute (I didn't go on to explain that this might avoid my having to pawn for a pittance my wife's few remaining gaudy heirlooms), and he replied that No, there wasn't: no hope at all. And then he said – and there was disdain all right, there was disdain in his voice, you could hear it quite plainly – he said to me that he could possibly organise a fiver from petty cash if this would go some way towards helping at all, and I said Oh yes please, thank you, it would, it would.

So I cleared my desk and I said goodbye to Geoff who kept on wagging his head and saying I don't believe it I don't believe it I just can't believe it Arthur, after all these years – but he didn't look even in the least bit surprised, I have to say. Here Geoff, I said – and I gave him the watch, man's watch, possibly the husband's, who knows? And he said oh I *can't*, Arthur, but he did. Because we both knew, didn't we, that it's all I had to give him. The long drink of water in accounts, he handed me the five pounds as if either the note or myself were severely contaminated, and he sneered out his Good Luck to me. And outside the building I thought well right, then – I'll just go to Lawson's (don't think, don't think – don't think of anything yet: just get yourself round to Lawson's) and see what this poor little pile of fragments will realise and put it to the fiver and get the whole lot round to Mickey, pronto. So I did, I went to Lawson's – and no, I won't tell you what he gave me, that damn Jew Lawson, because it will only make you sad; I know it did me. They weren't diamonds: marcasites, apparently, is what they are called. But far less valuable – that was the point he had been eager to convey. Anyway. And then I thought well the best place to find Mickey at this time of the day is Rosie's, really, so I went round there and Hortense, she said to me No, he's not here – he was here, he was here earlier but then he went off, I think to look for you. Oh yes and then Hortense, she said to me: and another thing, Albert – where's my fiver then, ay? So I gave her the fiver, which very much amazed the pair of us I think, and then she said I was looking peaky, bit tired, and how would I like to slip next door for a little bit and have a nice lie-down? And that sounded a reasonable and appealing proposition, what with one thing and another, and then she said well now listen to me, sweetie – why don't you buy a girl a nice big gin and orange and get yourself in a Scotch and I'll be next door making everything all cosy. So I did that. And then I came out again (she's such a fast worker, that one) and I got myself another drink and Mickey, he didn't seem to be around yet so I filled in the time with a few rounds at the table and I won them so easily – without even sweating, every card just turned up a winner, I'd never had such a streak in my life. And then I lost, of course. Lost the lot. Goes without saying. So now I naturally had to take my leave of Rosie's as fast as I decently could or else there was a very distinct danger that Mickey could just walk through the door at any moment at all (the very reason, of course – and I do not need it to be pointed out, I hardly require the irony to be underlined – why I found myself in Rosie's in the first place). It none of it, this, seems to get any easier. You know: keeping up, keeping up, keeping on up just a little while longer and trying so hard not to notice that the drag, now – the drag, it's beating the lift.

So I wandered about. Cold day, but dry anyway – just a touch of fog. Because had I gone home immediately, well . . . questions to answer, wouldn't there be? And I don't want to answer them, frankly: don't want to think about it. At some point in the park, I sat on a bench just next to the little children's playground they've got there. Used to take Clifford and Annette, you know. Well, I say *used* to – I think I did it once. I have no recollection of whether or not either of them enjoyed it, or anything: I shouldn't have thought so. Annette in particular: she's never liked anything I do. But there was a little lad here today with his mother, she must be, and he just couldn't get enough of that slide, you know. Running up the ladder as fast as his little legs would carry him and squealing in delight as he slithered on down to welcoming arms at the bottom – and the mother, she seemed to be loving it all quite as much as the little boy was. And then he'd be off again – tearing back round, up the ladder, clip-clop clip-clop, and whoosh! All the way down again. Up and down, up and down. That's all it took to make him happy. Just going up, and then coming down. Well. And while I was there, sitting on the bench, I glanced into the carrier bag from the British Home Stores that someone or other at the office had kindly furnished in order to enable me to sweep away all trace of my fractured and rickety tenure on what for a man of a different calibre, might have been not just you know a job for life, but even one with prospects. And as I peered and poked inside the bag, I couldn't for the life of me imagine why I had actually taken the trouble to remove a single item. I mean that stapler – it's never worked. I can't abide ballpoint pens. And the mug? The mug that I drank from for how long? How many hundreds and thousands of gallons of tea have I drunk in that room? And all from this mug. Which is cracked, look. How long has it been cracked? I've never noticed it had a crack. Maybe it didn't – maybe it's a very recent crack, very recent indeed. Either way, it's no use to me. And there's a diary from that firm that makes the legal pads, can't remember their name. I always meant to use that, you know – write in it. And just look: every page, pristine and white. And it's three years old. Oh dear oh dear, how the time does go. So I tipped the whole bag into the litter bin there, and then I thought right – home then, I suppose.

The television is on, predictably enough. Time for Paterfamilias to pontificate, then.

'Ah – a televisual feast I see, young Clifford. Not, I hope, to the detriment of your prep. The aerial fellow – he deigned to visit us then, did he? Did us the honour? And so I should hope. Somewhat fuzzy though, I should have said . . .'

'You don't mind it being on, do you Arthur? It's Friday – Clifford can get all his prep done tomorrow – can't you Clifford, my sweet? Um – Arthur . . .? We have to, um – can I have a word about Annette? It's quite, um . . .'

'That picture – I don't think it is perfect, you know. Not by a long chalk, I shouldn't have said. And what particular grotesque are we witnessing here, Clifford? Is it not somewhat juvenile?'

'It's *Popeye*. He's Popeye the Sailor Man – poo poo! That's what he does through his pipe. You don't, do you Daddy? Go poo poo! Through your pipe.'

It's better if I keep on talking to him – otherwise he's going to go and notice that we've got Channel Nine and then he'll send it back because he's a meanie. And it's *Take Your Pick* and *Maverick* on later. Mummy said I could watch them because it's Friday and we're having fish. We always have fish on Friday because Annette says it's pious and Mummy says it's cheap. We get cod or whiting and never anything different like trollop, or something. Annette's still all funny. She won't come down and she says *Popeye* is stupid and she says she's not going to eat her fish even if it is a sin because it doesn't matter any more. I haven't told Mummy about the slipper (I can still jolly feel it, you know) because I think it would make her sad – and I haven't told her about Anthony Hirsch and me being blood brothers for ever and ever and have vengeance and all the other stuff he said, can't remember, because she'd say I'll get germs. *Robin Hood* is on on Sunday, so I can check – but conquer doesn't mean the same as conker, but you do have to win and smash up things. And Daddy, he's looking at the television in this funny way he does – and I bet he's going to talk or something which I don't want him to do because Wimpy is on now and I wish I could eat a wimpy instead of cod or whiting or even trollop and then Bluto will be on and the spinach will whoosh up in the air and then in Popeye's mouth and this thin girl called Olive Oyl will kiss him and Mummy said are you sure that's what she's called and I said yes I am – she's called Olive Oyl and Mummy said that's funny because Jean Beery next door, she gets it from chemists and does it on her salad. Mummy, she's standing up and ironing and she said she'd never ever done the ironing in the sitting room before and there's a first time for every-thing. I like it when she does ironing because it makes this sort of sliding noise and it smells of home and warm and cosy. Popeye, he's bashed up Bluto now and won and everything but there's another one on right after but Daddy, he's still sort of looking at it funnily, and now he's started saying stuff.

'I am sure that picture could be a good deal clearer. Did he *test* it at all, our friendly local aerial fellow?'

'Oh Arthur he was fiddling with it for just ages and Annette – we just must talk to Annette, about Annette, Arthur. But don't go up now because the aerial man had to go into her room, oh – two or three times earlier because you can reach it from the window in there and every single time we had to knock and knock because she's taken to propping this, I don't know – chair or something behind her door, and she's really quite upset. Well the whole thing is just so . . .! Oh look, Arthur – we can't talk now . . . not with . . . here.'

'Why, pray, was she at home in the middle of the day? Is she ailing, the child?'

'Well that's what we've got to talk about, Arthur. No – she's not sick in the sense that she's not well, exactly, but . . .'

'I'll go up and see if I can't make this picture a little clearer, I think, and I'll have a short word with her.'

'Oh no, Arthur – I don't think that's wise until we've—'

'On the contrary. It is perfectly wise. Perfectly. Clifford – you go out into the garden – no Clifford, no argument please: no ifs, no buts – the time for iffing and butting is done. You step into the front garden, if you please, and your mother will tell you through the window what's happening to the picture and then you shout up to me if it's getting better or worse and I shall adjust accordingly. I think that with a rare show of familial cooperation we might well achieve something approaching perfection here.'

The picture looks all right to *me*. If I go out into the garden I'm going to miss the second *Popeye* and maybe the beginning of *Take Your Pick* and so I said to Daddy, I said can't we do this when *Popeye* and things are over and he just said *Now*, young man, like

I knew he would. So I've got to stand in all this sort of bog where these stalks with really pointy bits are all sticking up and in the summer they've got roses on which smell nice and Mummy sometimes takes the pencil out of the pot in the alcove and puts a rose in and says there, doesn't that smell nice? Isn't that beautiful? And I go Yes, because it is. But now it's all just wet and earth and no flowers are here and it's getting a bit dark and I should of worn my wellingtons. Mummy has opened the window in the sitting room and she says tell him to hurry up Clifford because it's freezing in here with the window open and I said Well what do you think it is out here then? And anyway I can't tell him anything because he's not even up there yet and all I can see is this big H on the roof, just like Mummy said it would be – and it's just the same as the one on Mrs Beery's house next door. It is jolly cold and I am missing *Popeye*. These sticking out bits on these branch things would be good for doing blood brothers with because with the Uncle Holly badge we had to have three goes. Oh crumbs! Gosh – that made me jump. It's Daddy, calling out my name – Clifford, Clifford, he's going – and he looks really titchy up there now, and the aerial is huge.

'What's it like now . . .? Ask your mother.'

'What's it like now, Mummy, he says.'

'Same, I think . . . Tell him it's the same.'

'It's the same! She says it's the same!'

'What about now, then . . .?'

'I don't know!'

'Well *ask* her, you stupid little boy. It's exceedingly cold up here.'

'What about now, Mummy?'

'Same. Same, as far as I can see, tell him . . .'

'It's the same! As far as she can see!'

'Well it *can't* be the same! I've turned it right round . . .! Well all right – what's that like? What's it look like now? Oh *ask* her Clifford, can't you . . .!'

'What's it like now, Mummy? He's getting batey.'

'Oh tell him it's – oh no, terrible, awful – picture's gone completely.'

'Picture's gone completely!'

'Really? Really? All right. Well what about this? *Say* it, Clifford . . .!'

'What about this, Mummy?'

'Yes . . . good . . . very good. Tell him it's perfect. Looks much the same as when we started . . . Don't say that last bit.'

'It's perfect! She says it's perfect!'

And Daddy, he makes a sort of a sign with his fingers like Mister Churchill always does, and then he sort of turns round and sticks his leg up to get in the window and then there's a bit of a bang noise on the roof bit and he sort of does a noise too and oh golly . . .! Oh my gosh – he's slipped a bit down the tile things and I'm shouting out to my Mummy now as I watch him slide down even further and his leg has hit that pipe thing and his face it's all red and his eyes are looking right down at me like he's trying to outstare you and Mummy is calling out to me and saying What's wrong? What's wrong Clifford? And I'm just waving my arms about and jumping around and stuff and I'm looking up at my Daddy and he's hanging on with only two hands and he shouts Get *help* get *help* and go and get the ladder Clifford and then one of his hands is just flying around in the air like that and then there's this awful sort of tearing noise because the pipe thing at the top is all broken and sticking out and he's hanging off it now and now he's not – he's not now hanging off it because it looks like he's sort of let go and he's dropped and he's in the air and now oh gosh he's gone crash on the ground on the crazy paving and it really made a loud bad noise and now Mummy now she's come running out and she nearly trips over him and

261

she's screaming, she's screaming at me to get an ambulance and I don't know where to get one from and I've gone all shaky and then she says oh my God, Clifford – just watch your father, watch him, and I'll go into the hall and get an ambulance but there aren't any there and she jolly well knows it but I've got to do as she says because this is really really serious because he might have broken his arm like Anthony Hirsch, like he did last term at football when we played Morecambe Court and so I've run over now and I've sort of knelt down and I've said Daddy at him and his arms and legs are all funny-looking and I've said Daddy at him and his face is on the floor and he's staring at the gate and I keep saying Daddy at him but he doesn't ever say Clifford back, and so I watch him because my Mummy, she said I had to watch him and I'm watching and watching but there's nothing to watch because he doesn't move and he doesn't speak and so I say Daddy at him again and I say it again but I just don't think he's listening. And then Mummy rushes out and she's all shaking too and she's been crying and she goes and kneels down and she says They're coming they're coming, which I don't know who it is, and then Mrs Beery, she comes in the gate and she screams and yells and comes and kneels down too and she's holding my Mummy but she's not holding me and Mummy says Oh Jean Oh Jean Oh Jean Oh Jean . . . They're coming, be here soon, they're coming, they're coming. And then all these bells start going and this super giant ambulance is whizzing up and the bells are still going and Mrs Beery is standing up and waving with both her hands and these two ambulancemen have come up with peak caps on and those beds that they carry one each end of and one of them says to me Just move aside sonny, there's a good lad, and then he says to Mummy Just give us a bit of space love, that's the way – just give us a bit of space. And then he says to Mummy Well how did it happen love and Mummy doesn't answer because of all the crying she's doing all the time now and

Mrs Beery, she's crying too and just shaking her head as if she's saying no to something and so I say he fell – he fell off the roof – and the ambulance driver says Blimey which is rude and then says to the other ambulanceman What you think Alf? And the other ambulanceman which is Alf, he stands up and he puts a hand on my Mummy's shoulder and he says I'm sorry love, I'm sorry love – there's nothing we can do. And she's hitting him with her hands and she's yelling at him there *must* be there *must* be and the ambulance driver says let's get you into the house love and Mrs Beery says Come on Gillian, come on Clifford, let's give these men a little space to work in and so I'm going to get up and then Mummy she just hugs and hugs me and my face and my shirt is all wet with all the crying she's doing and she keeps on saying that my Daddy, my Daddy, he's gone to join the angels and I didn't say he hasn't, not yet he hasn't, because he's still all lying here and anyway I didn't know that the angels collected whole people because I thought they only ever wanted just the tooth bits but I didn't say that either because I felt so funny and I felt so cold and I looked at my Mummy and I knew she was so sad and it made me sad too so I didn't look at her any more and I got up and the ambulancemen were doing all blankets and things and my Mummy was standing up too and Mrs Beery just kept on holding her arm and saying *Tea*, Gillian, *tea* yes? You come with me and we'll have a nice cup of tea and then Mummy started screaming all over again and I just ran into the hall and I bumped right into Annette and she asked me what happened and I said it's Daddy, it's Daddy, he's just off to join the angels and she just stood there and looked at me and she said Oh no Clifford, oh no, I promise you Clifford, he isn't – and I said But Mummy just said he is and Annette said No, he's going to join the others who I don't know who they are and I looked out into the garden and they were putting my Daddy into the back of the ambulance and these people in the street were all looking and everything and so where he's gone is to join the people in the hospital now and I don't really know who he's going to join after but I do know one thing and that is we're not ever going to get to watch *Take Your Pick* and even *Maverick* now because my Mummy is sad and my Daddy, he is dead. Which is just diabolical.

NOON

Oral history, autobiography, personal memoir – can any one of these be regarded as even just glancingly reliable, would you imagine? Would you, really? For myself, I do think it very much must be seen to depend, you know, the answer to that, upon whether one perceives the intention to be even in the slightest degree concealed in shadows. It is only the stripped and bare reason for the existence of the thing that can lead us to deduce whether here lies any more than merely a blatant self-righteousness, a supplication for pardon or a need for love so ardent that it can reduce the claimant to a pitiable state of mendacity before even he is aware of his own genuflection at the core of so humble a circumstance. And of course, lurking like an animal wounded but not quite spent, there can be lying beneath, can there not, the festering stench of an unchecked vengeance, and it rises up to permeate the carefully tended veneer of so miraculous a reconstruction of this many bygones, from all that time ago.

But here we deal with none of that. If I come to attribute a white and uncut evil to such, say, as the blackly glittering lady, then believe me, it is simply due and in no way a justification for my own endeavours. And believe me you really should, you know, because I neither seek nor crave an exoneration. I am not the civilised narrator – for if civilised means (and it can come down to just this) to have stolen up upon oneself in the still and dead of a shameful night and grimly slit the throat of the slumbering beast within, well then I'll happily stay wild, and beyond redemption. And the reason you must believe me is that I am base and self-serving in quite a different manner: I do all of this for me, and so I am seeking the vital truth. It is only for myself I am needing shelter as other and darker forces are tugging me elsewhere – although you too are welcome to huddle alongside of me and take what warmth it affords you; though you must accept too not just risks of deluge and a tempest, but also the threat of exposure.

And so . . . as I continue to lie here quite uselessly, I well understand now why my memory elected to take me all the way back there to my boyhood, all those tens and tens of years ago – another person, as it might be, on the planet of the past. Because after that one just diabolical day (in terms not of its event, but its consequence) all was different, all was changed. And memory, it will not be told. Like an elbow, the bend is determined by nature's direction, or else there will be fracture, and pain. And so now, although I yearn to flee into the bliss of Melissa (and is it really so strange that at this of all times I should need and love that now to flood into and over me?) it is Mary, you know – that little thing Mary who is calling me now – and doubtless there are ranks of others yet who will have somehow to be gone through before blackness or joy can eventually have me. And before that too there must be the flagrance of my Emerald, the blackly glittering lady – the only other woman who ever truly mattered: well of course before, because there is no after.

It's funny, I'd been looking forward to my sixteenth birthday for ages and ages, and now it's actually come, well . . . I don't feel any different, if I'm honest. I thought I would. But it *sounds* a whole lot better though, doesn't it? Fifteen – bit babyish; sixteen – pretty cool. I don't think I'll be doing anything special, though – you know, after work or anything – because I haven't got very much money at the moment. Got this pair of jumbo elephant cords at the weekend and that just about cleaned me out. They're really good, though – they're sort of a pinky stony colour and they're proper hipsters with patch pockets and these really wide belt loops and not too flared. The week before I'd got the belt in a market – it's amazing, huge silver buckle like a cowboy or a pirate or something and like the Manfreds wear – and then I saw how stupid it looked with my ordinary trousers (well it kept on riding all up my shirt because I just sort of had it around my waist because it wouldn't go in the loops, not on my ordinary trousers it wouldn't) and so I decided I just had to get the cords and I'm really pleased with them and everything because they didn't need altering even in the legs but they were a bit expensive, that's the trouble, and so I'm pretty much stony, more or less, so it's not going to be much of a birthday, I don't think. Unless Anthony rings me, anyway, but he hasn't so far. Oh yes – I've got this friend called Anthony Hirsch who I've only just recently hitched up with again – he used to go to my prep school and we were best mates, but I had to leave that school and go somewhere that was really shitty, hated it, but I'm out of all that now, thank God – and he's nuts on music, Anthony is, and he said to me – yesterday, I think – Isn't 'Ticket to Ride' just the greatest thing ever, I just play it again and again, over and over just all the time, and I said Well I haven't actually got it yet because I'm a bit broke this week (Anthony, he's never broke – he never was, he always had everything, lucky beggar) and he said Oh well that's OK Cliff because I can record it for you on my Grundig and I said Well yeah thanks but no good

I'm afraid because remember? I haven't got a tape recorder to play it back on, have I? (Anthony, he's just taken to calling me Cliff – he didn't use to. I always wanted people to call me that when I was a kid – because of Cliff *Richard*, if you can believe: can't stand him now.) But anyway – I listen to Alan Freeman on Sundays ('All right pop pickers? Stay bright!') and they're sometimes on *Ready Steady Go*, but not so much as they used to be, so I do *know* the song and everything, it's just that I haven't got the single yet. It's been number one for weeks and weeks. I've got this great poster of them up in my room – well I've got three, actually: the other two are the Aston Martin DB5 and Ursula Andress in a waterfall – and they're all in their stage suits, not the round-collared ones but those blue quite shiny ones with velvet lapels and they're all holding their guitars and the drum's there too with Ludwig and their name on with the T going down in the middle. They're great. The fabbest. If I had tons of money I'd go out and buy loads and loads of clothes like they've got and Chelsea boots and high collars and everything and I sometimes go down and look at them all in Lord John and Take 6 – I like Take 6 – but they're all just so expensive. Anthony's really lucky because his father actually makes a lot of this stuff for all the shops in King's Road and even in Carnaby Street, he says, and so he gets all of it for free and the way he's got his hair with the fringe and all sort of up at the top and long over his ears and everything, he looks a bit like a Holly or a Kink or something, because he's got all the gear. After prep school, Anthony went to Carmel College, but he didn't stay on to do his A levels because he said well what's the point? I'm going to join my Dad in the business anyway. (At my lousy school I only got two O levels: English and Maths, and pathetic grades.) But my hair looks quite cool at the moment, and I've got these sideburns, sort of – bit thin – but Mummy says it's too long and it doesn't suit me and it's hiding all of my face. We live in a bit of London I don't like – we had to go there when my father died. I liked the old house, but we had to give it back to whoever owned it. My father, he died when I was quite little – it sounds rather stupid but he fell off the roof. Some people at school – the crap school, the lousy one that came after – they said Jesus you're lucky, Cliff – I wish my bloody father would go and fall off the roof; I don't know if they meant it or not because they were always saying things like that, even about their mothers, sometimes. I never made a proper friend there – I don't know any of them now. They were all into girls and smoking and stuff ages before I was; some of them would bring in tins of Pale Ale and drink them behind the kitchens. I think it tastes disgusting. My mother always said they were common, and I didn't quite get what she meant at the time but I pretty much do now and I'll tell you what: she was right – they were. Anthony Hirsch, he's completely different, he's not like that at all – but I was surprised, you know, when I met up with him again because he doesn't really speak in the way he used to any more. You know – he'll say things like Hangin' Out and Cool Man and Far Out and all that, but most people do now; Mummy says I'm always saying 'fab' and it drives her mad. But the clothes he's got, Anthony – oh wow – they're just so fab. Yeh – I do say it quite a lot, I suppose. But it must be amazing to have a Dad like that – I remember him from when we were young, and he was always really great – not like my Dad, not a bit. Had this big flash car, can't remember what. Anthony and me – oh God, it's so embarrassing – we're actually 'blood brothers'. I know – it's crazy. He reminded me. I'd forgotten. Well – we were kids in those days: you do these stupid things, don't you? Mummy, dear old thing – she said to me this morning Now you promise me to get home nice and early this evening Clifford because there'll be birthday cake with all the icing and the candles. Well. I'd rather go to this Soda Fountain in Marble Arch that I went to with Anthony the other day, but still – birthday cake's nice. And I know it means a lot to her. She asked me what I wanted as a present and I thought of twenty million things but I just said, Oh anything. Because she's hardly got any money, poor old thing – she never gets anything for herself. And he had a girl with him, Anthony, when we went to this Soda Fountain – I had a hot dog and a banana milkshake – and she works as a packer or something in his Dad's factory and she had a miniskirt on and long blonde hair and all black stuff around her eyes – a proper bird, a real dolly. Looked more like Twinkle than Marianne Faithfull, though – and her accent, her voice, it was just so cockney I could barely make out what she was on about. I've met a few girls and things, but I don't really know any. Because working at Smith's and just humping things about, they all make it clear that they don't think you're much and how they're all going out with a guy in a group who's got this fab and amazing convertible E-Type: yeh yeh, girls – yeh yeh. I'm sure that Brian Jones is just desperate for some spotty little kid selling biros and *Beanos* in Smith's . . . but you know – I'd love to be rich like Anthony. When we were both at school together, Anthony and me, I knew he was Jewish and everything, but I thought this was just another word for rich – like 'lavish', or something: I didn't even know how to spell it. I'm still not quite sure what it means – I mean I know it's a religion, obviously, I do know that, but why do people make such a big deal about it? Annette – she's my older sister – she used to say it was because they were against the Catholics, but I don't suppose that's true. I don't have a religion, as far as I know. I'm nothing. Well – Church of England, obviously, but nothing really. But I don't suppose I ever will be, though – rich like Anthony, I mean – because there's nothing I actually want to do – there's nothing I'm any good at. Can't sing, can't play a guitar; I'm lousy at football. Mummy, she hates it when I go on like that – she goes Oh get *away* with you Clifford: you could do anything you turn your hand to, you're the best young man in the world. But that's just mothers, isn't it? I expect they all go on like that. She was upset when I left school early, though. Well – she was upset before that, wasn't she? Long before that when I had to leave the first school, the prep school. She cried buckets over that – but the poor old thing, that's all she ever seemed to do in those days, cry and cry. It was all beyond her, really. More than she could handle. You see, when my Dad was alive, well – he sort of took care of everything on the businessy side – except of course he didn't: that was the trouble. When he went – I only found this out quite recently, it's only recently she told me – he left us with . . . well, I was going to say nothing, but it was a whole lot worse than that. He owed money to people all over the place, apparently – including my school and Annette's convent and the, what is it? That word, when you're buying a house on the H.P.? Anyway – them too. But Annette, she'd already left her convent by then. It happened the very same day that my Dad did his high-dive act from the top of the roof. Mortgage – that's what they call it. Because I was there, you know: I saw it. We'd got this TV – I think it was new, or something, and there was this kids' programme, God knows which one – I loved the lot of them – and anyway I was desperate to watch it and he hauled me outside to, um . . . you know I don't actually know why I was outside in the garden, actually, now I come to think about it. Anyway, there he was right up on the roof, I remember that – messing about with this bloody great aerial up there, and the next minute – whoosh, splat, kerbam: finito. Anyway, according to Mummy, that was the very day Annette got expelled – so you can see that for Mummy, it wasn't a very good week, all round. Poor old thing. Annette, she didn't care, or anything – about Daddy or about the convent. And I remember thinking, hmm – that's pretty cool. God – talking of Annette, you know – I haven't seen her for years, now. She'd been to this, I don't know – some sort of a special school somewhere in London, I don't know quite, and then she went to a sort of a boarding

273

school in Ireland, for some reason – where she still is, actually. Mummy, she wanted to visit, but she couldn't afford to. I was only sad about my Dad because of Mummy, really, because she just kept on crying and crying all the time. I don't really have very clear memories of him one way or the other. I mean – he was all right, I suppose, as Dads go. Went on and on like a teacher all the time, though. I mean he wasn't in Anthony's father's league, oh God no, but then who is? But Mummy, she obviously liked him a lot – loved him, maybe. Strange.

So yeah – it's pretty crap, this job I've got at Smith's, but it's still miles better than going to that school. Even the journey back home on the bus was just, oh God – so terrible, with all the barging and the swearing – and then when all the girls from Brook Hill High got on, well that was just it, really: that was just the end. The talk would get really really loud then and all about sex of course and some girls would look so embarrassed and as if they were just going to burst out crying and I wanted to say something – wanted to tell them that we're not all like that, not all of us aren't, but . . . well, you just couldn't. You just couldn't, that's all – not unless you wanted your face bashed in. Other girls, though – and this is amazing, I still find this totally amazing – they joined in, and not just loud but they were even filthier than the boys, all the things they came out with. So yes OK, lifting up boxes from the stock room and cutting the string off all these bales of papers and magazines – it's not the best job in the world, I do know that, but all I can say is it beats being back at school, beats that hands down. One thing that is really good about it though is that they don't seem to mind if you ever read one of the magazines when you're having your tea – and behind the stock room there's this big sort of walk-in cupboard, I suppose it is, and they chuck in there any damaged books – paperbacks, Penguins, Pans and Corgis, usually – and Mr Rooney, he's my senior, he just said oh you can have them: take them. So I've actually got into reading in quite a big way, and that's something I never did at school, I can tell you that. When I was a kid I was really into this series of school stories with Jennings and Darbishire in them – there were all sorts of other boys, of course, and masters and everything . . . I used to know all of their names, but I can't remember them now. Anyway, once I'd read all those, I sort of lost interest. But the other day I was reading some stories by someone called Somerset Maugham, which I know is a pretty pathetic name (I mean how would you like to go through life with people calling out at you Oh yoo-hoo! Somerset! Yoo-hoo! Pretty bad) but he's jolly good at stories, and that's the point. And that's another example of just how crap my school was, by the way: if you'd gone around with a book in your hand they would have laughed and said you were a poof and pushed you around; if you'd said it was 'jolly good', well – they just would have beaten you half to death. Anyway. And another one I like is J. B. Priestley – he's good. And there's this old-fashioned detective called Sherlock Holmes – they're so good I've read them all twice. They're meant to be written by Dr Watson, but they're really written by somebody else – can't remember the name – who is actually dead, so there won't ever be any new ones. Best of all though are the James Bond books – they are just the fabbest. And *Goldfinger*, that's the best film I've ever seen in my whole life. If I had just loads and loads of money I'd have a DB5, no question, and I'd have suits made like double-O-seven's and a Walther PPK so everyone would just shut up when I'm speaking and then when I went to meet Anthony Hirsch I'd have somebody like Shirley Eaton to come with me. There weren't actually any James Bond books in the cupboard (I kept on checking) and so I had to do a bit of a bad thing – I had to accidentally on purpose, well – damage a few. I hope they don't find out. So anyway it's not too bad here – bit boring, but not too bad. If you're senior you get discounts on records. But I don't.

No one here actually knows it's my birthday today; I didn't like to say. I don't suppose they'd care very much anyway because I don't really know anyone properly. I only really know Anthony Hirsch, and I wouldn't even know him if I hadn't bumped into him again by the weirdest of flukes. I was in Take 6 one Saturday morning and I was looking at this amazing kipper tie that I couldn't afford with all these swirls all over it and there he was – he'd just delivered a batch of these really fab shirts – all tapered with three buttons at the collar and in a pattern that's called paisley and the Small Faces, they wear them all the time. I gave him my phone number and everything and he gave me his and it all sort of went from there, really – so that's pretty good. He hasn't changed much – not really. And it's amazing, you know, that I should just have been thinking of him at that very moment because I'm just finishing off my afternoon tea in the stock room and Mr Rooney, he's come in now and he's said to me Clifford, there's a telephone call for you – some person called Anthony? And do I have to remind you, Clifford, that you are permitted to neither make nor receive telephone calls during normal working hours? So please, Clifford, tell him goodbye, and request that he does not call you here again. And I'm on the point of saying Yes OK, sorry about that Mr Rooney – but now I just suddenly blurt out that it's my birthday – it's my *birthday* today, Mr Rooney, and he's kind of looking at me now – not knowing quite what to say, but you can see by his slitty little eyes that he's not sure he even believes me. And now he says *really*, Clifford? You promise? It really is your birthday today? And I say yes it is, honestly – and I'll bring you in my birth certificate if you don't believe me. That will not be necessary, Clifford, he goes: very well then, run along and take the call – but just this once, you hear me? And don't be all day about it.

'Hello . . .?'

'Cliff? Hey, man. Santhony.'

'Hey, man.'

'Hey. Oh yeah and look, uh – happy birthday, OK?'

'Oh right. Thanks. Thanks a lot.'

'Cool. Listen – got you a present.'

'Yeah? Really? Cool.'

'Yeah. So when're you . . . you know. Free.'

'Well five-thirty I get off. But I said I'd—'

'OK – five-thirty. See you outside. Right on.'

'Yeah great but I said I'd . . . Yeah OK. Cool.'

'Groovy. Be the coolest of the coolest – OK?'

'Um – OK. Bye, then.'

'Gotcha.'

So I was really really looking forward to home time now then, wasn't I? Because this was really great because I didn't think I'd actually see him today, Anthony – thought he might've forgotten. Because there's no reason he shouldn't have, after all. I mean I do – I forget everybody's birthday, I'm absolutely hopeless at anything like that. Like Anthony's – I know it's in the summer some time, his birthday, because he always had his parties in the garden, that enormous garden he had then – I don't know if they've moved, or anything – and there was always a clown or a magician or something and one time there was this amazing great jelly fight; God, I remember that awfully well because it was a lot of fun but I couldn't really, you know – get into it properly, because I was so *worried* all the time. I was always worried about something. What was getting to me was that some boring old grown-up or other would come along at any moment and just sort of go ape, if you know what I mean – but that was the really cool thing about Anthony's parents: they didn't ever seem to mind about anything. And Mummy – she said to me when I got back Oh *Clifford*, look at the state of your good shirt! Just slip it off now and I'll pop it into the Hotpoint. Dear old thing. Ha – but I was too busy, wasn't I, with this bag, this little bag you always got given at Anthony's parties – there was (and God, isn't it amazing actually? The things you remember and the things you forget?) . . . there was this really stinky Magic Putty in a plastic egg – mine was blue – and a Britains Red Indian which I'd already got so I swopped it for a knight in armour with someone or other – and something else as well, whistle it could have been. Amazing parties, they were. I never had one, a birthday party – well not, you know, with people coming round, or anything. And we all know why, don't we? One – two – three, now . . .! *Yes* – because money doesn't grow on *trees* . . .! Very good – well done. Anyway. But the point I'm making is that it's really cool that Anthony's remembered, because I never would have with him. Even Mummy's birthday, I'm not completely sure. September the ninth, could be eleventh – something like that. Have to look it up. I only know Annette's because it's April the second, the day after April Fool's Day, and I always said she's a day late because *she's* a fool, that's for sure – and she'd just get all sort of haughty like she did and go Oh for heaven's sake Clifford just grow *up*, can't you . . .? And God, she had a point – I really did go on and on, boring little brat. Anyway. And the other great thing is – he's got me a present! Wonder what it is.

And I was really pleased, actually, when we did meet up that he was just there on his own, for once. I'd got to thinking that whenever we went to anything he'd purposely bring along some girl or other just to show me how cool he was, or something – as if I didn't know that already – so it was good he didn't this time. (God – there was one once, and all she had to say to me was Hi, Cliffy – do you think I look like Sandie Shaw? And I said Yeah, oh yeah – spitting image, couldn't tell you apart; God – she looked more like Harold Wilson to me.) So anyway, he gave me this carrier bag, Anthony, and he said OK let's shoot off to the Soda Fountain and celebrate and I said Oh God, Anthony, I'd really like to but that's miles from here and I said to my mother

I'd be back early for . . . and God, it sounded a bit stupid to say 'cake', so I didn't. And he said Oh that's OK because I've got Sid round the corner and I went Oh yeah? Sid? Which one is Sid? Because I was thinking oh God, this'll be some other little dolly bird who thinks she's Lulu or Cathy McGowan or something – but it actually turned out to be this old guy who drove Anthony around in a sort of a, what are they called? Cars with a long bit added on at the back. Not vans – estate vans or cars or something. Anyway – one of those. And Sid, he said, he could take us to the Soda Fountain and then he could drop us both back at my place afterwards. And I nodded – well of course I nodded – but I wasn't too keen on that last bit, really. I mean I'd sort of like Anthony to come back with me and everything but, well . . . our place at the moment, it's terribly small and . . . And the street's a bit . . . I mean, poor Mummy, she does her best, of course she does, but still it's a bit . . . You see it's not a proper house we've got, or anything – it's just a bit of one. They call it a flat, and I suppose it is – but you know that 'flat' is English for apartment? And you know in American films with Cary Grant and James Coburn and all those cool old guys who live in an apartment? Well it's not like that, I can tell you: it's not like that at all. It's more like Coronation Street.

Anyway, in the car or van or whatever (and Sid – he seemed really OK: little fag in his mouth all the time and grey hair all plastered down and slicked back like they used to have it years ago) – I said to Anthony Is it OK if I, you know – look in this bag now? And he said Sure, course – told you: present. So I tipped it out and oh wow! It was one of those completely fab fab fab paisley shirts – red and green and sort of mustardy – all tapered and with three buttons on the collar which has got really long points and it's even the right size and everything! Well I tell you – that is just going to look so groovy when I put it with the elephant cords and the big belt I've got: just so fab. But I've really got to get the boots now – just got to, because my rotten old Hush Puppies are just hopeless with all this lot: have to save up. Anthony's boots were amazing – I'd never seen these ones before. They're sort of an orangey brown and really shiny and the heels are made up of sort of striped chunks of wood, it looks like, and there's zips and buckles at the side and they go up really high. I said to him once Oh wow, Anthony, you're so fantastically lucky – I didn't know your Dad did shoes as well as clothes and he said He doesn't, but my uncle does. And there's another uncle apparently who does all womenswear. I'm telling you, that family, if they owned Parlophone as well they'd have the whole of the world just about all wrapped up, as far as I can see. And then Anthony – when we were in the Soda Fountain – he said So you like the shirt? Blow you away, man? And I said yeah, it did, it does: It just completely blows me away, man. And then he said Well listen – that's just *half* my present. And I first thought Oh wow – great! *Another* present! And then I thought Oh no – I can't take anything else from him because look – when we came into the Soda Fountain and we got up on these fantastic swivel stools they've got around the counter – all silver with red seats, like they've got in America – he said OK then, Cliff: what do you want? And I said well the thing is, Anthony, I'm just a bit . . . I mean what I mean to say is I haven't at the moment actually got any, um . . . And he said Oh shut up, Cliff – my treat: it's your birthday. And I said Well . . . I'll have a glass of orange, then: thanks a lot. And he said Oh come on – get with it, man! Have something fab! So I said Well OK then – and I had this enormous great Knickerbocker Glory, and he had one too. So now – when he said all this about only *half* a present, I felt a bit . . . well – you know. Shall I tell you what it is, he went then. The other half? And I said Well yeah – sure. And then he just blew me away, man, because he said his Dad, right, had got this job going at one of his factories and so I wouldn't have to heave around piles of books and papers any more and so what did I think? And what I thought was well – that's great, I suppose. I mean OK, I'll be heaving around boxes of jackets and shirts instead, but maybe they've got a cupboard full of all damaged stuff at the back of the stock room. But no, he said – it's better than that. They want to train up someone new to cut out all these patterns and make samples and things – so how about that? And I just looked at him. I said – You're joking, right? No, he said, no – we employ a lot of school leavers, train them, and then later they can make stuff all on their own. So what he was asking me, as far as I could make it out, was would I like to – starting on Monday – be a Carnaby Street tailor? And I said . . . *yeah*.

As Gillian was getting just the tiniest bit exercised by the sixteenth and final candle that just wouldn't stand up straight at the centre of the cake – all the others seem perfectly happy in their little sugar rosettes, so why isn't this blessed one? – she was thinking too that he's a bit behind his time, Clifford, but maybe because of what day it was, all his workmates had taken him out for a cup of tea – or no, a Coca-Cola, I suppose. Well so long as he's safe, that's all. Because I mean to say well yes all right – sixteen years old, but when all's said and done he's still only a little boy, isn't he? My little boy is all he is, for all his big man talk. I hope he comes soon, though: I just can't wait to see the look on his face when he sees the surprise I've got for him. Well he deserves it, poor love – because it's not been easy for him, has it? The last few years. Well – it's not been easy for any of us, of course; not at all what we were led to expect. But then which of us ever knows, really, the way it'll all turn out?

When we first moved here, you know, I thought I'd never get used to it. It's so much more noisy, and there aren't nearly so many trees. Oh I cried and cried – what a misery I was, what an old misery. At first I thought I was just crying for Arthur, but it was me – all of us, all of us left – it was us I was crying for, really. Us, and the . . . circumstance. Because I had no idea, you see – not even the slightest idea about all the money side of things: it came as quite a shock, I can tell you. I mean, I knew things were a bit *tight*, of course I knew that – I'd lived my whole life, hadn't I, knowing all about that – but when it all came out that, oh – the school fees were owing (one term for Annette's convent – *three* for Clifford . . . they're always a bit more tolerant, I suppose, if they're not religious) and then that the mortgage was, oh – just so much in arrears I can't even begin to tell you: why did they let it go on for so long? And all that was quite apart from the usual day-to-day bills, you know – gas, electricity, all of those. I'd known there was a life insurance – Arthur, he took it out soon after we were married; silly, I'd told him at the time – it's silly, Arthur, because we're both going to live happily for ever and ever. Well. But it turned out that there wasn't, in fact, when it came right down to it – any life insurance at all. Cashed in years back, for so very very little. So all we have now – and Clifford, he's very good, he does chip in with a little bit whenever he can, but look, he's young isn't he? Life is for the young. He needs a bit of money in his pocket, so I never ever press him – wouldn't ever dream of doing that. Life is for the young . . . that's what Mother – that's what she was always saying to me, poor old thing. She's just about hanging on – it's hard to know now just how much she's taking in, these days. Still a martyr to her blessed sherbet lemons, though. The doctor there, he says they can't be good, but I say to him Well where can be the harm? If it gives her a little bit of pleasure. I try to walk there if the weather's fine, but my old pins now are not what they were – but there, just grin and bear it, that's all we can do. Isn't it? When all's said and done. But little Clifford – Never mind Mummy, he says: one day I'll have loads and loads of money and I'll buy us a mansion – would you like that? I say to him You just work hard and earn the money, young man, and then we'll talk about it. Little sweetheart. So no – until that day when Clifford becomes a millionaire, all I really have to live on now is the little pension they give me from Arthur's work, and I think I only get that because that man, Arthur's boss, what was he called again? Henderson, that's it – George Henderson, yes – I think he only gave it to me, you know, because he felt a bit, I don't know – embarrassed? Guilty? I don't know – about, you know, giving Arthur the sack the very day he . . . I mean who knows? Who can tell what Arthur was thinking that day? What was going on in his mind? And the number of times I've thought, Oh – if only I'd stopped him from going up on that blessed roof! If only I'd just stopped him! I mean the picture was fine – there was nothing whatever wrong with the blessed picture, was there? What did he have to go up on the roof for? Especially with his feet. Anyway – that went back. The television, I mean. That didn't last two minutes: couldn't keep up with the payments. Kept the Hotpoint, though – just about managed to hold on to the Hotpoint. It's still going strong. And the Singer – I had to keep the Singer. We've got another little television set now – bit small, but perfectly all right. Jean Beery – she gave it to me, said she had no use for it any more and I'd be doing her a favour if I could just take it off her hands. She's been such a good friend to me, Jean has; just as well – because I still don't know a single soul round this area, you know. Even after all these years. The one or two I have spoken to, well – they either seem to be rather common or else they're very high and mighty, and I can't see they've got any call to be. It was one of the very hardest things, you know – leaving. Not just my little house, but having Jean there, next door. And she wrote to the Council, you know, Jean did. She said that I was a ratepayer and had lived in the area for all these years and that they had a duty to rehouse me in something similar nearby. The Council, they didn't see it that way, I'm afraid to say. Apparently a summons was pending due to non-payment of rates, and they were obliged only to offer me whatever was currently available. Well it's a large borough this, very large, and where we are now, well – it just couldn't be farther away from where I used to be, not if it tried. Jean, she's got a Triumph Herald all of her own, now – passed her test the very first time, I don't know how she did it. Me, I'd all be at sixes and sevens. How she manages the gears I do not understand because she's not a big woman or anything and you seem to need so much strength for it. I used to test her on the Highway Code. It's a lovely little car, the Triumph, pale blue and white – and she drives over and fetches me, time to time. She says the people in my old house are not a patch – not a patch Gillian, she says to me. It's difficult when I go over to Jean's, though, because I find it impossible to look, to look at the house I used to live in, where I brought up the children and everything. I did once, look at it, the first time, and it seemed so strange because the pebbledash, it wasn't buttermilk any more but this really bright white like a Kelvinator or something, and the curtains at the windows, well – they weren't mine, they weren't mine, you see. Jean – she's got an extension now, and they've had the front porch all covered in. I always wanted that, the porch covered in. Because in winter, the draughts in the hall were that bad I'm telling you, and . . . Well; doesn't matter now. I help out old Mr Levy in the Lane on Saturdays – he's getting on now, poor old Mr Levy, his arthritis is chronic, but he's still a cheery soul. The bus fare to and fro, though, it does eat into the little bit he gives me, but we're never short of fruit and veg, that's the big thing in its favour. Some of the things they just get rid of, you know, it makes you weep when you keep on reading about how much starvation there is in the world; if you cut away the bad parts, throw away the outer leaves, there's a lot of goodness there to be had, you know: a lot of goodness. Over Christmas I made us a little shelf unit out of an old orange box I brought back with me, something I'd always been meaning to do. And he still, old Mr Levy, he still always asks after Annette, dear old soul: never forgets.

And Annette – yes, well. She's been nothing but an ordeal, that one, for as long as I can remember – but you go on loving them, don't you? Despite everything. If you're a mother you do – you just go on loving them, no matter what. But the nuns at that convent of hers, you know – they were badgering me right from the start, night and day, and they wouldn't stop, they just wouldn't ever leave me alone. The very morning after they'd brought her home – that very morning they were on the telephone. *Look*, I says to them – and I was crying, crying – look, I says, I don't know if you know or care but my husband has just *died*! There was a pause, just a bit of a pause, and then this woman – nun, presumably – this person on the other end, she says to me she says I offer you our sincere condolences at this most difficult of times – keep the Faith, the Lord will provide, and I shall pray for you. Oh I see, I thought: so that's all right, then. And then I'll be blowed if she didn't just carry on in exactly the same way that she was going before – about how Annette would have to be taken away from the convent and all the rest of it – on and on and on. And then she says to me that they would be obliged if I could pay the outstanding term's fees at my earliest convenience. I just told her she should keep the Faith and that I was sure that the Lord would provide and that I'd pray for *her*. Jean, she just roared when I told her that. I don't know where I found the nerve – it's not like me, you know, to

just come out with something like that. Anyway, the Council –
they put her, Annette, in this, oh – I don't know what it was,
really . . . they kept on calling it 'special', this school – well, I
went there once (just once though – I couldn't face it again) and
it looked extremely ordinary to me, I can certainly tell you that.
She shouldn't have been there. I mean whatever it was she had
or hadn't done – and I'm not condoning her, I'm not at all saying
that what she did was right because I actually think it was
dreadful, just dreadful – but she really shouldn't have been at
school with all these, well . . . quite mad, they seemed, some of
them, poor little children, you know. Big staring eyes – rocking
from side to side. Shouting. They even had some coloureds
there. Which yes I know is perfectly all right nowadays – now
that we're all 'swinging' and all the rest of it – but I tell you this:
it was certainly a lot different in those days. And then . . . when
she did the other bad thing . . . the worse, much worse thing . . .
still can't talk . . . well then they said that she had to go to this
sort of a boarding convent on the coast of Ireland somewhere –
a place of correction for girls – and so poor little Annette, there
she was back with the nuns again. She screamed when I told
her – screamed and screamed and she wouldn't stop. Quite
hysterical. Well young lady, I says to her – you should have
thought of that, shouldn't you? You should have thought of that
before you did what you did to that poor little boy. She was
lucky, you know, it wasn't reform school or even Borstal – and it
would've been if she'd been any older. And I was told, they told
me this, that it was touch and go that the police weren't
involved. Oh my goodness – can you imagine? Can you *imagine*?
I was just crying – crying, crying. The little boy's parents, they
were up in arms – demanding a full-scale prosecution – and I
mean to say can you blame them? If it'd been *my* little boy . . .
Anyway. But it was her age, you see – that was what saved her.
By law, no one so young can be that bad.

What took up much more of my time, though, I have to admit, was trying in the face of just so much disaster to get the best I could for my Clifford. Because Clifford, if you think about it – if you just stop and think about it for a moment, well – my Clifford, he was the innocent party here, wasn't he? He was the *victim* in all of this. *He* hadn't done anything wrong, assaulted anybody. It wasn't *his* fault his blessed father went and fell off the roof. But my options, well . . . well I didn't have any, plain and simple. Rather like with the flat – they call it a flat but all it is is just a couple of tiny rooms and a boxed-off bathroom and kitchenette, when all's said and done, but they call it a flat. There was barely even room for the radiogram – it just about fitted in over there, look, very tight squeeze, and I've got the little kookaburra lamp on the top of it. I still keep it nicely polished; I never play records on it, though. I didn't care at all for any of Arthur's records – hated them, really – and I never could think of buying any new. And the lamp, the little kookaburra lamp: I hate that too.

But what I'm saying is that it was the same situation when it came to choosing a new school for Clifford: I couldn't, is what it came down to. Like it or lump it. He would go where he was put. And so it was – no matter what I did or said, so it was, so it was, so it had to be. Oh and goodness, he did so hate it. Well for a start he had to leave all his friends behind, didn't he? Anthony, and all the rest of them. And the journey, the journey in the morning, Well – often we had to leave when it was still pitch-black outside. And the boys there – not at all what he was used to, were they? I think he got quite a shock. 'They talk funny' – that's what he said to me: 'They talk funny.' And soon he was making all sorts of excuses – you know, so that he didn't have to go in. Headaches, tummy aches, leg pains, fevers – leprosy once, he said . . . and some mornings I'm telling you, the weather was that bad I was tempted to let him get away with it, but then I thought no. It's bad – it's a bad lesson for life isn't it, that? Dodging your responsibilities; being a coward. We'd had quite enough of that in this family for one lifetime, I thought – quite enough of all that. So on with the duffel coat and the wellingtons and out we went. I wept, though, when he came home with his dear little eye all closed up and blue, it was – all red and blue, and it looked so painful, the poor little man. What happened, I said. Who did it to you? Nothing, is all he answered me: no one, no one did it. And I'm pleased, you know – I'm so relieved that it's me he takes after. I'm not saying Arthur was a bad man – because I don't think he was, not bad; it's just that he wasn't very good, that's all. But I was disappointed when Clifford left school so early – yes I was, but I understood. I mean I always assumed he'd go on to one of the public schools, get his A levels – even university, maybe: that would've been a first in this family. But well – the way it all turned out I couldn't really blame him, could I? For leaving when he did. And what with all the injuries he kept on coming home with, well – I'm just thankful he got out of the place alive, really. But he'll need it, you know, Clifford – in life, he'll need to be a bit like me, the things that get thrown at you. Resilience, that's what you want – that's what's needed. Never duck – never attack, just be resilient, and then you'll survive.

Is that . . .? Was that . . .? I thought I heard . . . oh yes it is, oh good, oh good – I was just you know beginning to get a little bit worried. It's Clifford, he's home, my birthday boy, he's back . . . and oh . . . he's got someone with him by the sounds of it. Oh dear – I do wish he'd *told* me he was going to . . . I mean it's not that I . . . but it's only a very *small* cake and – well *I* don't have to have any, of course . . . but there's no time to worry about any of that – door's opening, you see, so let's just see what's what then, shall we? And deal with it, accordingly.

'Hi, Mummy – look who I've brought. Member?'

'Hello, Mrs Coyle. Member me?'

'Oh my! Why yes of *course* I . . . but what a *man* you've grown into, Anthony – why I'd barely recognise . . . and so *tall*, so very tall and handsome. Clifford said he'd run into you again – I was so pleased to hear that. Oh well now come in – come in and sit down, the pair of you – I'm afraid there's not a lot of room, not with all you grown-up young men; there isn't. There – that's it, squeeze in. That's it. All right? Not too squashed? Oh good. Well look now tell me, Anthony – tell me all that's been going on with you. Goodness, it's been so long. So long. You were both just babies. And you've left school too now, have you? Clifford was telling me.'

'Fab-looking cake, Mummy. Guess what – Anthony's Dad has offered me a job.'

'A . . . *job*? Really? But you've *got* a . . . what sort of a . . .? Don't *pick*, Clifford – we'll do the cake later. We can't do the cake yet. What sort of a job? Anthony?'

'Oh – you know. Clearing the drains. Rat-catching. Usual thing. No – not *really*, Mrs Coyle. Don't worry. No, it's pretty good – pattern cutting, basically, is what it is. Training.'

'Tailoring, Mummy. I'm going to be a tailor for Carnaby Street.'

'Oh well that *does* sound nice. I always hoped you'd learn to do something – oh no I mean, I didn't mean that to sound—!'

'Sall right, Mummy! I know what you mean. Hey – why don't I do the candles on the cake and then we can whack it out. We've actually just had these most enormous Knickerbocker Glories and I was bursting on the way over here – weren't you, Anthony? I thought I was going to burst. But I'm actually quite starving now.'

'He always was a pig – wasn't he, Mrs Coyle? Except when it came to old Mrs Chadwick's cheese pie. Member that, Cliff?'

'Do not, please, mention that woman's name. She was a lunatic, you know. She should've been locked up. Even now, you know – just the mention of her makes me go all . . . oh yuck, I don't want to talk about her. Come on, Mummy – let's do the cake.'

'Well, um – we *can't*. Not just yet. No look – on the table, Clifford. Birthday present. The envelope, look.'

'Oh yes – *birthday* present. Look at this shirt! Where is it . . .? Hang on – yeh, here. Look – look at this amazing shirt! Isn't it just the grooviest thing you've ever seen? Anthony, he just gave it to me.'

'Oh Anthony – how terribly kind of you. You really shouldn't have.'

'Oh it's only an old sample I found on the floor. Don't worry, Mrs Coyle – I wouldn't actually spend any *money* on him.'

'Oh you two boys! You're just the same – just the same as you always were. Still just two naughty little boys, aren't you?'

'Not me, Mrs Coyle. I'm pure as the driven. *He* is – Cliff is – he's as bad as they come. But not me. What have you got there, Cliff? What's in the envelope? Million-pound cheque?'

'Don't *think* that's what it is . . . it's, um . . . I don't quite *know* what it is, to be honest. Oh hang on – it's tickets, sort of. What's it say here . . .? Oh wow – it's ferry tickets, a couple of ferry tickets to, um – *Jersey* . . .'

'Hey man – you've got a ticket to ride!'

'Ha. I've heard of Jersey, I think – it's where the cows come from, isn't it? Gold top. And a couple of nights in a guesthouse, sort of thing. Oh wow. How great – oh thanks, Mummy – thanks a lot. But hey – this must have been awfully *expensive* . . .'

Gillian was grinning with delight, one hand flapping away all idea of any of that. But no, as it happens, it wasn't expensive, wasn't expensive at all – completely free, as a matter of fact, and all thanks to, well – guess who? Yes, my dear friend Jean Beery. She gave it to me just the other day, and I can't tell you what a godsend it was because I was at my wits' end to know what on earth to get Clifford for his birthday. I mean money was tight, it goes without saying – but I'd been putting a little bit by, a little every week, and I know he'd been going on about some tie he'd seen somewhere – said it looked like a 'kipper', if you can believe it, and I said to him are you sure, Clifford? Are you sure you've got the right word there? A *kipper*, did you say? And Clifford, he's terribly amused by his mother's 'squareness', is what they say. Well *I* didn't know that a tie could look like a kipper, did I? How was I to know? Just so long as it doesn't *smell* like one, I said . . . (Arthur, he quite liked a kipper of a Sunday breakfast, when he didn't have to rush off to work.) But anyway – I couldn't go and look for this tie, could I? I wouldn't even know where to go. So I thought I'd maybe just get him, oh – a record token as usual, or something – and then Jean Beery, she says to me now sit down and listen to me, Gillian – Evelyn, he booked us up this little trip to Jersey, so sweet of him, but I'm no good at all on boats and it's completely non-returnable apparently and so you'd be doing me the most tremendous favour if you could take it off my hands – make use of it, maybe. Do you good, the pair of you – always cooped up in that flat. Give you and Clifford a nice breath of sea air. What do you say, Gillian? Oh *please* do take it – else I'll just have to drop the whole caboodle in the bin, and you know how you just can't abide any form of *waste* . . . Ooh, she's a crafty one, Jean is – and so kind, so terribly kind to me. And it's true what she says, of course – me and Clifford, we haven't been away anywhere for, oh – I just can't remember how long. And Jersey too! I've never been abroad. So the little bit of cash I've put by, that'll be spending money for him. Oh I'm so looking forward to it, you know. Can you imagine? Going on a boat and staying in a *guesthouse*, if you please. Just me and my handsome young man. And you can see he's pleased – you've just got to look at him to see how pleased he is.

When the doorbell went, Clifford glanced across and was really quite surprised because the doorbell here, well – it just never went. But looking at Mummy, now, I can tell she was expecting whoever is there. Normally she'd be flapping around all over the place and patting her hair and jabbering on about well who can *that* be? Who in the world can *that* be . . .? But all she's said to me now is Well open the *door*, Clifford, there's a good boy . . . So OK, I'll do that then – I just raise up my eyebrows for the benefit of Anthony – and now I'll just squeeze myself out of the room and then into the – well, we call it the hall, but that's a bit of a joke really because it's just about the size of a wardrobe. So right – haul open the door, and . . . oh. Oh my God. I don't . . . I don't *believe* it because . . . and she does look so different . . . it's *Annette*, look: it's Annette. There's someone else as well here, but the main thing is it's Annette! And now she puts her arms around me and pulls me in close and her cheek it's cold and soft and she smells of flowers and the weather outside. I feel so . . . I mean to say I can't really say what I feel, how I'm feeling . . . but I watch her face, looking for something, and I can hear Mummy's laughter coming out of the room – she knew she was coming, this was clearly arranged – and there's a girl behind Annette, and she's holding right back, she seems so shy – and Mummy's got to be telling Anthony now about how astonished I'd be – and I am, I am, I just can't remember how long it can be since I last saw Annette because now, my God, she's eighteen years old. I'm just sixteen and she's eighteen years old – and she's here, she's here, and now I'm saying something to her I think, but not too much – *wow* is all that seems to be coming out of me now, with nothing at all but nonsense in between – the girl, she can't get in, that's what it is, because there just isn't any room; she's got thick and brown hair, straight with a fringe – so I think I'll back my way into the room while everyone's gabbling and then they can follow (*Annette*'s here – can you believe it?)

and now I'm there, I'm in there now, and Mummy's up and clapping her hands and she's crying again, look, but in a good way this time, and I'm sort of miming over to Anthony some sort of a message or other, but I'm not sure what I'm meaning because I just feel so strange – the girl, she's just about in now too and she's looking down and her eyelashes are long, I can see that at least – and it's just such a tight scrum in the room now because everyone's standing up and jostling and Mummy's said oh look Annette – it's Anthony, you remember Anthony, from Clifford's old school, and I don't know what she says then because Mummy's now said to her so let's all meet your friend, Annette – come on in dear, that's right, don't be frightened, sorry there aren't enough chairs – and Anthony, he's just staring at Annette which I suppose he would do, looking at Annette – she's just so different, I can't get over it, I can't take my eyes off her myself – and the girl, she says she's Mary: she says her name is Mary, and Mummy now she's lit up all the candles on the cake and the light's out now and I get myself over there and there's all this sparkle in all these eyes around me and they're glittering now and I bend down low and right over the cake and I blow and blow again and then whoosh they're all out now and the smell of their smoke, it comes up and hits me, and Mary is here and she says Happy Birthday, happy birthday to you, and I only notice then that everyone else, they've just finished singing it. Her voice, it's so soft and there's something about it – she looks up at me now for the very first time and her eyes are pale but I don't know what colour and there's, what are they? Freckles around them and I think she's just lovely.

'Here, Mary, here,' Gillian was now urging her – patting the seat of the studio couch and beaming so broadly, as if encouraging a bashful puppy to leap up on it and settle down. Oops – I'll just quickly tuck away my roll-on and nightie back under the cushion – I hope no one has seen. Well you see I sleep on the couch – there's only two rooms and I've nowhere else to put them. 'Oh Annette it's *so* good to see you, just can't tell you. We've been nattering all day, Clifford, but I told her to go out for a little walk and come back later and surprise you. She only left Ireland yesterday, didn't you Annette? It's so *nice* that it's Clifford's birthday – such a happy coincidence. And Mary, she's just been released too, haven't you dear? Oh no – of course I didn't mean released, I meant that she's just left the, um – was it a convent, Annette, where you were? I was never quite sure.'

Annette had removed a deep pink birthday candle from its pale blue sugar rosette, and this she crunched down on hard.

'Do you want some cake, Mary? We didn't eat much today, did we? No, Mummy, no – it wasn't a convent, no. Was it Mary? It was a workhouse. A prison, basically, is what it was.'

Gillian paled. 'Oh for goodness sake, Annette. We've got guests – Anthony is here, look. Mary – do please help yourself to cake. Cut it for her, Clifford.'

'Oh don't mind about me, Mrs Coyle,' grinned Anthony. 'I'm just part of the furniture. So it was pretty grim, was it Annette? Where you were?'

Annette, she smiled, and sucked on the wiry spindle.

'I'll tell you about it some time. Mary, though – she'd done nothing wrong, had you Mary? Not like me. I was the sinner – but the only reason Mary was there was that she's an orphan. She was sixteen this week, and that's when they get rid of them. The sinners they keep in longer.'

'Oh *Mary* . . .' deplored Gillian. 'I am *so* sorry – no mummy and no daddy. Oh I *am* sorry. So what will you be doing now, dear?'

'That's what we've been discussing,' said Annette. 'We've no plans, have we Mary? Job, I suppose. Some sort. Somewhere to live . . .'

'Oh I do wish we still had the old house . . .' Gillian was practically moaning. 'But you can see, Annette – the way we are now, well . . .'

Annette, she laughed once and quite ringingly. 'Mm – yes I don't think we could quite fit in here – do you Mary? Oh I don't know, though – you could take the top shelf in this little orange crate here, and I could sleep underneath. Suit you?'

'Well where *will* you go . . .?' worried Gillian. 'You saw it was an orange crate then, did you . . .?'

'Oh – we'll find something. The State, they give you a few quid to get started. We'll be OK.'

The room was quite suddenly electrified by the still of the hush that surrounded Mary's voice:

'I'd like – to maybe see a little bit of London. I've not been here before. Not even to England.'

'Mary's Irish,' explained Annette. 'God – I never want to *see* Ireland again, I can tell you that . . . Nothing to do with you, Mary, but you know how it was . . .'

Oh I *see*, thought Clifford – yes of course, that's what it is. That's what it is, what I heard in her voice. When she spoke, it was almost like a shushing noise – as if she was whispering something and it was only for you and she was calming you down and making you feel that everything was going to be just so good.

'Oh well I'm sure that *Clifford* . . .' rushed in Gillian. 'Clifford – he'd love to show you around a bit. Wouldn't you, Clifford? Forever taking trips on the tops of buses, my Clifford. He's quite the expert on London now. What do you have to say for yourself, Clifford? Hm?'

'Oh . . . please . . .' said Mary, so quietly. 'I'm not wanting to be any sort of a bother at all . . .'

'No no,' said Clifford quite hastily – and he could feel the vile and familiar creeping flush of blood-heat engorging his neck and could only hope that no one was looking. 'I'd love to – like to very much. It would be my, um. Pleasure. Yup.'

'Good!' said Gillian. 'Now listen, everybody – I'm just slipping out to the little shop on the corner very quickly – he's always open late. You don't have to rush off, do you? Any of you? No? Oh good. It's so nice having all these young people around. Because it's such a special day I'm going to get us some sausages and bacon for our tea, and I'll get us a Family Brick as well. And something to drink – what do you all drink these days? Hm? Coca-Cola, is it? Oh Anthony I forgot – um, sausages and bacon, are they, um . . .?'

'They're fine,' smiled Anthony. 'And Coke's fine too. Thanks, Mrs Coyle.'

'Meths,' said Annette. 'That's what I drink. No Mummy – just kidding. Coke would be great. All right with you, Mary?'

Mary nodded. 'I've only ever had it the once. I liked the bubbles . . .'

Clifford just stared at her – and then he stopped that because it's rude. And then he thought oh look, what the hell – it's my birthday, isn't it? And so he stared at her again. He sort of wanted her to catch him at it – he was ready for the sizzle that would come as soon as their eyes should chance to meet and then he could glance away quickly, but all the time she sat in the chair and the heaviness of her fringe toppled over her eyes as she continued to look down at the twisting of her fingers.

'Nice clothes, Anthony,' said Annette. 'Why are you laughing . . .?'

'Sorry – I didn't mean to. I'm not laughing, really. It's just when you said "nice clothes", like that – that's all.'

'Look at this shirt that Anthony gave me,' said Clifford quite eagerly, waving it about. 'And I've got these elephant cords. I don't always dress like this – it's just that I've been at work. That's the only reason I'm dressed in all this.'

'What's so funny about saying "nice clothes"?' Annette demanded to know – and her eyes (and Clifford remembered how they could do this), they were glinting like swords in the sun, and ready to clash.

'It's not funny – it's not. It's nice. Good, I mean. It's just that everybody these days, they go "Oh – cool gear, man" and, you know – "dig the threads". Junk like that. I do it myself, but it's the business. It was just – different, that's all. I didn't mean anything. It's cool.'

Annette nodded. 'Yeah. Right. I sort of heard that London was swinging. We didn't get to know about any of that – did we Mary? No television. No magazines . . . the only music we got was in Latin. It's a kind of brainwashing, but it doesn't work. It didn't work on me, anyway. No matter what they did. The only thing swinging where we were was the whip. Mary doesn't know anything about that. But I do.'

Clifford was watching Annette and wary, a bit like he used to be. 'You're joking . . .' he said.

Annette shrugged her shoulders and then she looked down. She started to blot up cake crumbs with the just-licked pad of a finger. 'If you like. But talking of clothes – or "gear" or whatever you want to say – don't tell me either of you that you haven't noticed what Mary and me are wearing. I daresay it isn't the height of fashion. I mean I don't actually know what the height of fashion is, but I'm guessing that this isn't it. A grey hessian sack – not "cool gear" is it Anthony? I mean you'd *know* . . .'

'Well actually,' said Anthony quite rapidly, 'sack dresses were quite the rage this spring, but A-line and minis are more the thing now. Sorry – but I'm in the business. Oh hey – Cliff! Everybody! I've just had the greatest thought. Sid!'

Annette looked up from the cake plate and narrowed her eyes. 'It's not that great a thought, Anthony. Clifford – what's he talking about?'

'No listen,' went on Anthony, really quite excitedly. 'Sid is my – well, he sort of drives me about until I'm old enough to get my licence – about nine months or so, bit more, and then I'll be able to get my own wheels. But you see there's always samples and proper stock in the back of the car because we drop off things for my uncle as well. He's in womenswear – we do styling for the younger man. Look – he's only down the street, Sid – isn't he Cliff? Why don't I buzz round there now and see what he's got? Yeh? What size are you Annette? Ten?'

Annette was smiling – tugging at the corners of her lips was the beginning of a look and a feeling that Clifford could maybe recognise from so very long ago.

'I haven't any idea what size I am. I expect that sounds stupid. Just guess. What about you, Mary? Do you know what size you are?'

Mary tugged disconsolately at the hem of her tunic.

'I *hate* these clothes . . .' she whispered. 'I hate them so much . . .'

'Right then!' said Anthony decisively, clapping together his hands. 'That's settled then. Cliff – I'm off. You coming with? Help me carry? I mean I'm not *promising*, Annette – but there must be *something* there . . .'

And Clifford thought he would – go with, help him carry. In one way he wanted to stay, though – but the, um – what would you call it? Atmosphere? No – not atmosphere. The whole just sort of *feeling* in the room is a bit kind of strange. I mean, God – all I thought would happen today is that I'd get a bit of birthday cake and a thirty-bob record token as usual – which means I'd have to put half-a-crown to it before I could get an LP – and now all this. There's piles of things I want to say to Annette, ask her about, but I can't actually think what they all are. And Mary – I don't think she'd ever talk, say anything, not to me, not if there are people about. So yeh I will – I'll push off with Anthony and see what he can scrounge off of Sid, from Sid, and then we'll shoot back here with all this gear, with a bit of luck, and then Mummy will be back from shopping and cooking us the sausages and bacon and then there'll be ice cream and while the girls are all trying on stuff, I – oh I know, I can be next door with Anthony in my room and I can show him all the things I've kept since we were at school – it'll be really funny, he'll really laugh. I've still got all the free gifts from the cereals that I used to drive poor old Mummy crazy to keep buying for me, week after week – the spacemen, the Dogs of the World, even the rotten little submarines, the whole lot. And I've got all my Matchboxes and the cavalry and the knights in armour and the cowboys – oh yeh, the *cowboys*: there was this one with a big black hat and a waistcoat and I'd decided he was Maverick. *Maverick* was a TV programme I used to like – forget who was in it, but I saw him in an old film a month or two ago with Doris somebody-or-other and I recognised him immediately and I thought Oh my God look – that's Maverick! I really used to like him. I haven't dug out all this old stuff for just years and years – I hope Anthony doesn't think it's stupid, me still having it all. I don't think he will. I wonder if he's hung on to his old toys and stuff. He'd need a warehouse to keep them all in. Oh hang on – he's calling me now, so OK then: I'm off. I hope Annette was, you know – joking, when she said that. You know – about a whip. Because I felt just so funny inside; still do, a bit.

Oh my goodness – what a to-do! The shop on the corner – it's always open late, that shop, sometimes till eight o'clock I've seen that shop open – but not tonight, oh no, oh dear me no. So I had to trudge all the way to the Parade because there's this sort of a, oh – they call it a mini-mart which is a silly little name, really, but it's much smaller than the Co-op but it's not an ordinary shop either – and oh my heavens the prices! A dozen sausages – ninepence more than I'm used to spending, and the bacon, well, I just wouldn't pay it, I'm afraid: I just wouldn't give them the satisfaction. So I got some nice ripe Jersey tomatoes instead, just under two pounds, and a loaf of Sunblest – that should do us. I didn't use to buy bread wrapped and sliced like that, not when it first came out I didn't, but I have to admit it's ever so handy and it does keep for longer, there's no denying it. Jersey tomatoes! I'll be picking my own before I know it: ooh – what a day this is! I couldn't tell you if the Wall's Family Brick was more expensive than it normally is – I mean to say I'm sure it *was* because everything in that shop was just, oh – wickedly priced (I won't be back there again in a hurry, I can tell you that), but it's that long since I bought any ice cream I just wouldn't be in a position to tell you, quite frankly. I got strawberry and vanilla, half and half, seeing as it's a special occasion – and a big bottle of something that says it's a cola. And it came on to spits and spots of rain on the way back but I always keep my little rain hat in the compartment of my handbag, so at least my hair hasn't all frizzed up on me – I just hate it when it does that: makes me look like a gollywog.

And then I walk in the door and – oh! I've never seen anything like it. There's Annette and little Mary – sweet girl, could be quite pretty if she'd only give us a smile, thin little thing though – there they were the both of them, jumping about and squealing like they were still in kindergarten – and there's the sofa, all covered in dresses and blouses and heaven only knows what else, like it was the first day of the January sales, it looked. And there was Annette in a little corduroy skirt – well, she might call it a skirt, but I've seen belts that were more substantial – and she's got me by the hands, look, and she's dancing me around the room and I've just got to laugh now despite myself and all I'm doing is trying to get some *sense* out of the girl and I'm saying to her oh for goodness *sake*, Annette, what on earth do you think you're doing? What are you up to, at all? Mary – you're a sensible girl – you tell me if you please just what exactly is going on here? Where have all these things come from? Where's Clifford? Has Anthony gone? And then I look back to Annette . . . and oh, I just see now in her face, just the way her face is turned away and against the light, like that, I just see the little girl I once had – when she was just so young and fresh and pure and happy, she seemed then: she seemed to be happy. Ah me, the passing of time – the things it can do to us all . . .

'Hello? Hello? Is everybody decent? Hello? Can you hear me?'

Anthony had been knocking on the door for quite some time now but with all the girly squeaking, no one was hearing it, clearly.

'Is that you, Anthony?' called out Gillian. 'Oh hush, you two girls – it's Anthony. Annette – do up those buttons. Mary – here Mary, come over here for a minute, will you, and I'll zip you up. There. Done. All tidy. All right you two boys! You can come in now! Come on – come in. That's it. Now will somebody please tell me what on earth has been going on here? I leave you for just two minutes and when I come back . . .!'

'Oh look look *look* Mummy – look at this skirt! Isn't it just wonderful? Oh I love it, Anthony – I just love it. Oh thank you thank you thank you. And Mary – oh you look so sweet in that dress. The colour – the colour! I've never ever seen you just wearing a *colour*!'

Mary looked down at her dress, her forefingers and thumbs nipping hard at the hem. When at last she raised her eyes, they were filled with the brimming of tears, on the verge of falling.

She appeared to be rapt, and yet eager to make some sort of expression – her mouth was moving, but there were no words. Annette, to her own amazement, was quite suddenly overcome and she rushed across to embrace her and the two of them simply stood there with their arms so tightly clinging, mutually racked now with the sobbing and laughter and locked into something of their own. Anthony glanced over at Clifford who quite automatically raised up his eyebrows. Mummy, look – she's very moved by this, and yes I can see why, I think – it's strange, though, what's going on here. It's because – I think this is why – it's from somewhere else. We don't ever know about other people and other places, Mummy and me. But my mind isn't on it. This can't affect me. My mind is still all caught up. I mean it was OK at first when Anthony and me, we went into my room, because we both started talking about, well – Annette and Mary, obviously, is what we were talking about, and Anthony, he said Jesus Cliff, that sister of yours – she's an absolute knockout . . . and it sounds a bit odd but I knew what he meant but all I said was Well look Anthony, she's a little bit old isn't she? She's eighteen – we're not. We're sixteen, aren't we? Like Mary is. And he said Yeh yeh yeh I know, but still, she's really really fab – I mean, she needs the clothes and the make-up and the hair and all that but Jesus, what a knockout! And I said, I really like Mary. And he said Oh yeh, she's a sweet kid I suppose, but she's not in Annette's league is she? I mean I'm telling you – what a knockout! I mean, um – sorry, Cliff, if I'm . . . I mean I know she's your sister and everything, but Jesus – what a knockout! And I said . . . I really like Mary. And Anthony, he went Yeh yeh, you've already said. So anyway, Cliff – what about all these old toys you were talking about, then? And that's what I mean when I say that my mind, it's still all caught up in a sort of a shock as if somebody's died and I feel all jittery because I know this sounds stupid and everyone else is so happy and I know it's my birthday and it's all just old junk anyway and I shouldn't even care because I'm now sixteen but I went to the shelf on the top of the wardrobe and the box that I keep all my stuff in was gone. And all I could say to Anthony – and he was going Well come on then, Cliff, let's see all the gear, God this'll be a laugh, won't it? This'll be good – and all I could say to him was Well look this is all very funny because this is where it always used to be and I suppose it could have been put somewhere else but in this titchy little so-called flat there's not a lot of somewhere else to put it and so all I can do now is wait for when Mummy gets back from the shop and she'll tell me – and that's when I heard her come in and I said to Anthony OK then, Anthony – she's here, she's back, I can ask her now, and he said No hang on old china you can't go in now because of the girls and everything and so what I'll do, Cliff, is I'll knock – I'll knock on the door and see that every-body's decent and then we can go in and your mother can sort us all out and I'm quite looking forward to some bangers now, actually – and blimey they're making such a row in there, Cliff – I mean I'm knocking and knocking but I don't think they can hear me. Yes and then they did hear, they did hear Anthony knocking and so we came in then, the two of us, and here's Annette and Mary going all a bit dippy over a couple of skirts and dresses which aren't anyway nearly as good as my red and green paisley shirt but that's not got anything to do with it because the point is Mummy, she's not *listening* to me, is she? I've asked her once and I don't think she heard and I've asked her again and all she does is put on that sort of half-smiley face and that means she's just not *listening* and so now Annette has finally shut up all of her yakking and so now at last I can ask her again.

'I *said* – didn't you hear me, Mummy? I said where's that box that was on top of my wardrobe? My box. Where is it? What have you done with it?'

'But you couldn't go *out*, Annette, not in a skirt like that – showing all your legs. I mean I know you see it on the television, yes – but they're *paid* to, those women.'

'Mummy – you're not *listening* . . .!'

'It's not *that* short. I'll have to get stockings, though. Got any stockings, Anthony?'

'Tights. It's tights you'll need. Not a line we carry, I'm afraid.'

'Mummy – *listen*—!'

'What is it, Clifford? Can't you see we're talking?'

'My *box*. The box on top of my wardrobe – it's not there any more. Where's it gone? Where have you put it?'

'Where's it *gone* – where have you *put* it . . .? Dopey *baby* . . .!'

'Oh shut up Annette, can't you?'

'Don't talk to your sister like that, Clifford – she's only just got here. I've got to get these sausages on or else we won't be eating till midnight. What box? What box are you talking about, Clifford?'

'The *box* – the *box* – there's only *one* box. The box with all my old things in. You know – the *box*. And I'm allowed to talk to her any way I want because it's my *birthday* . . .'

'Childish, Clifford. Oh – you mean . . . Annette, make yourself useful – start unwrapping the sausages and chop up the tomatoes, there's a good girl. Oh and the ice cream! That's got to go straight into the fridge. You don't mean, Clifford – you don't mean all your little plastic toys and things, do you? It's not that box you're talking about?'

'*Yes* – yes that's exactly what I'm talking about. Where is it?'

'Where do you keep your knives? Come on Mary, come and help me – but you'd better wear an apron – you don't want to mess up that dress. Got an apron, Mummy?'

'Under the sink. In the drawer. Oh but Clifford I got rid of all those things just, well – years ago now. It was just taking up space. I mean it was all your baby things – I didn't think you'd

want them again. They went out years ago, Clifford. Clifford . . .?
Oh – don't look at me like that! How was I to know you'd want
them? They were only *plastic* – I thought there'd be some poor
little kiddies who'd be grateful for them. Oh for heaven's sake
Clifford stop *looking* like that. Oh you tell him, Anthony – you
won't see Anthony wanting to keep all his old toys and things,
will you? Anthony's far too sensible for that. Far too grown up.'

'He's got *all* his stuff. *All* of it. He just told me.'

'Really? Well I expect he's got a good deal more space at home
than we have. We can't keep everything, can we Clifford? I mean
to say it's the first time you've even noticed and they've been
gone for *years* . . . How are you getting on in there, Annette? Oh
no, dear – not that knife! You don't use *that* knife for tomatoes,
do you? What are you thinking of?'

As Gillian now squeezed herself into the kitchenette and
started shooing away Mary, Anthony placed one hand quite
softly on Clifford's shoulder and he said to him Oh Jesus I'm
sorry, mate – I know how you must feel. Still – blood brothers for
ever, ay? Ay, mate . . .? Clifford just shook his head and stared out
in front of him. You don't – you don't know how I feel. You *can't*
know how I feel because it's all right for you, you've got all your
old stuff – it's *always* all right for you because you've just got
everything, everything in the whole wide world, and you always
have had, you always have, and you always will because we're
not blood brothers, we can't be, because you got the Dad who was
fab and got to be so rich and gave you stuff and I got the Dad with
a broomstick up his backside who never had a penny and talked
like a lunatic and then he went and fell off the sodding roof and
broke his neck. And that's the bloody difference between us.

It's extraordinary, you know, how having just a couple of people over for a bite to eat can result in all this pile of pots and plates and glasses. It was worth it, though – oh it was lovely. I can't remember when I was around just so much bustle and noise and laughter. Well – I never was, that's the simple truth of the matter; not in this flat, and not in the old house either. And as for the washing up and Hoovering, well – I really don't mind it a bit, I'm grateful for it really because it gives me something to put my mind to. This little flat we're in, you see, it really is so terribly small – it's hard to convey if you haven't actually been here – and what with it being just Clifford and me, well, there's never exactly a mountain to see to. Anyway.

It seemed so quiet when they'd all gone away. Annette and Mary, they're staying in some sort of a hostel for the time being – I think she said, Annette, that they're allowed just a few days more there and then they have to find something for themselves. Together with a means of paying for it, of course. Oh dear – I do wish I were in some sort of a position to, well – help out a bit, but it's all I can manage to keep body and soul together as it is. But that's life, I suppose – I mean to say I do have to keep reminding myself that Annette, she's eighteen years old now, not a baby any more – quite the young woman. I must say she does appear to be very well developed – not unlike Elizabeth Taylor, who she always doted on as a child. So all those years in Ireland don't seem to have done her any harm, anyway. Her time in the convent. She never even mentioned all of my letters – and I sent them religiously. Of course it goes without saying that she didn't ever so much as once think she might have written back to me – but there, that's the young for you, isn't it? It's what you come to expect. Maybe she'll meet a nice young man with prospects in the fullness of time and then start court-ing and well – who knows? Perhaps settle down, become a little homemaker, a mother herself with two or three kiddies. Well it's possible, I suppose; I mean to say, anything's possible. Anthony – such a nice boy, Anthony, so very well-mannered he is, and terribly generous, terribly generous – he said he'd drop them both off, which was sweet of him. Clifford went along as well – for the ride, he said. It must have been quite a squash with all of them in the one car, but then the young, they don't mind a little bit of discomfort, do they? A bit of mucking in; it's all part and parcel.

When he came back in, Clifford, I'd got everything back in order and nicely sorted out and everything, and I'd just that minute made myself a good strong cup of tea and I was doing a bit of jigsaw on the table. Clifford, you know, he used to just love doing jigsaws when he was a little boy; many's the evening we'd pass, just Clifford and me, slotting in the pieces as merry as you like. He's gone off them, these days – well I suppose it's understandable. He's young, isn't he? Life is for the young – not messing around with a blessed jigsaw with his poor old Mum! He got it for me, the jigsaw – he found it in the damaged cupboard at the back of the stock room at work, he said. I can't see it's damaged, to be honest. It's ever so nice, though – a lovely little old thatched cottage all surrounded in flowers and a rickety garden fence. How lovely, I said to him, to be able to live in a pretty little house like that. Oh don't worry Mummy, he says to me – you wait, you just wait till I've got loads and loads of money: I'll buy you a house that's much better than that one – a castle with a moat, if you like. Well that's very *kind* of you, Clifford – and I was laughing, I couldn't help it, the ideas that get into that head of his – very kind *indeed*, Master Clifford, but a little thatched cottage will do me very nicely, thank you: you can keep your castle – I'm not grand. (I hope they didn't mean by damaged that there's a piece missing, or anything . . .)

He seemed – oh, maybe it was just me, maybe it was just the contrast with how everything had been before – but I don't know, he was very quiet, it seemed to me, rather subdued, when he came back home. Everyone get off all right? I says to him. He didn't even nod: not even a sign. I've made some tea, Clifford, just made it freshly – shall I pour you out a cup? Would you like that? No answer, no response at all. I think, Mummy, is all he has to say to me – I think I might actually just go straight to bed, if that's all right with you. Well of course, I says to him – you please yourself; you're not ill though, are you Clifford? You don't feel you're coming down with something? Because I'll make you some hot milk and honey and I can always give you a note for work tomorrow. He says he's fine – and they don't take notes, it's not like school. So that was me put very firmly back in my place. He sat there for a while though, saying nothing. Well something's got to him, I was thinking. Well – be fair, it's been quite a birthday for him, hasn't it? What with everything. Annette just turning up like that out of the blue after all these years; this new job he's been offered . . . sounds a little odd, is what I think – I mean, do they really employ young lads to be tailors these days? My Clifford, he's never so much as threaded a needle, so he'll certainly have his work cut out for him. But I suppose when you're young, you can put your hand to any-thing; that's what I'm always telling him, anyway. And then he says something, suddenly. It made me jump, I can tell you that. He'd been sitting there so quietly for just so long I'd even for-gotten he was still in the room with me. 'I wish you hadn't . . .' – that's what he says. And I know that's what he said, word for word, because I asked him to repeat it. What was that, Clifford? What did you say? You wish I what, dear . . .? And then he just says it again – and his voice, so very flat it was, so very very dull it sounded. 'I wish,' he says to me, 'you hadn't.' So now I'm going through everything in my head that could be this thing he wishes I hadn't done. Asked Annette round to surprise him? Going to buy the sausages? Not buying the bacon? Getting a cola that he said wasn't the proper one, wasn't the real one? No – no

I know it was none of these really. I knew what he meant, and don't think I didn't feel badly about it; it was evident to me now, though, that I was meant to feel badly about it, and very possibly not for the last time, either. Aren't they funny, young people though? The things that seem to affect them, and the things that pass them by. And then he says: 'I've made an arrangement with her, Mary – to take her on some bus trips.' And I says to him Oh good, Clifford, that's nice, she will be pleased, seemed ever such a nice girl even if she was a little on the thin side. I'm left to see to my jigsaw for quite a while then. And then he says Yes, and I've asked her if she'd like to come and see Jersey with me too because she's never ever been anywhere at all in her whole life except around and about the place she was born and I think she'd very much like to. And I says to him Oh *what* a nice idea – yes yes I'm sure you're right about that, Clifford – anyone who had never ever been anywhere at all in her whole life except around and about the place she was born would just adore to go and see Jersey with you, yes I do, I do, I do quite see that.

I could've got angry with Clifford, you know; just like I could've got angry with Arthur, for all he did to me. But I mustn't. Look: it's for the young, isn't it? Life. It is – it is: life is for the young. And men, it seems. So let them get on with it.

♠

Mary – nice enough child, I suppose, but the time has come when she's going to have to learn about what little truth there is in life, and then the lies. And I'm not going to be her teacher. I don't ever want to teach, and I've nothing left to learn: I'm on my own now, and I'm not having Mary slowing me down. All morning now she's been looking through this filthy little window in this filthy little room we're in and saying and saying Oh Mother in Heaven, Annette, I've never seen a street as big as that one, I never have, I never have. Can we not explore a bit, Annette? Should we not be looking for jobs, at all? What will we eat today? How will we find the Catholic church? Where is it we'll be living, Annette? We we we. Not good – not for me. I said I'd get her safely over to England and I've done that now. I'm not going to be her guardian: the Lord is her shepherd – if she doesn't know that by now, then when in Christ's name will she? The doctrines, they are all that have ever been told to her. I said she should do what they wanted her to do and stay and become one of them; she said she lacked the vocation. So having deemed herself inadequate and unprepared for the extraordinarily difficult and arduous self-immolation that is the taking of orders, the wearing of black – hurting children, living off the backs of broken drudges, idolising the stupid and spoiled whiskey-sodden priests, embracing chastisement as the one true ecstasy and doing nothing whatever useful or even decent for any living thing . . . instead of committing her body and soul to so glorious a calling, she has opted instead for throwing in her lot with the easy option: real life. Never imagining that the Calvary cross might not ever be the only one to be borne – never foreseeing that the crisis that overwhelms you could be other than one of Faith.

I am relieved. Relieved and quite astonished to so suddenly be rid of Ireland. The hum and grime of London, the clamour and the edge – I never knew I missed it all because I think I was wholly unaware of ever having noticed it . . . or needing it. The clean and dampening air of Ireland, the green and eternal silence – they as much as anything fractured my spirit. I was no more than a child when they took me. I had known, of course, when I hurt so badly that stupid little boy – and in a minute I'll remember his name, it will come to me – I had known, oh yes I had, that bad things and then worse would be bound to hound and savage me, but had I only known too that it would be the nuns in Ireland, that the terms of my expiation could be so severe, then I would never have spilled over into sinning so gorgeously. Had they simply informed me that the perpetration on my part of any further misdemeanour would inevitably and at once make me subject once again to the swishing of those choirs of fustian habits and the cold and endless echoing corridors and the rattling and clack of all those waist-bound rosaries and the dull and lowering clanking of the bell, the bell, the bloody bloody bell – the hawk-faced witches and their ritual cruelty that at first I had considered to be both instinctive and random, long before I knew it to be not just premeditated but so thoroughly ogled and met with gloating. The palls of incense, setting fire to the eyes, clutching at the throat and easily smothering the odour of – no, not sanctity, no, nothing like it – but an ominously shifting and deep putrefaction, a terrible decay kept somehow just at bay and blinded beneath a simple gauze of gossamer purity. Had they only warned me that this, for all those years and years and years, was to be the unremitting dimension of the walls of my punishment, then by my behaviour I should have made all the saints known to you seem tainted beside me. And the stupid little boy, I would not have hit hard in the face and pulled and pulled on his foolish little penis until it was red and nearly hard and raw and even pappy (and he cried out so loud); I would not then have hit him hard in the face once more, and this time causing those spectacles to splinter; I would never have twisted his arm so tightly behind his back and slapped and slapped at his foolish little penis and nor then would I have hit him even harder in the face, and this time splitting open his lip, and I would never have twisted his arm so much more tightly back and again behind his back until I felt it taut and heard it crack, and then just let him fall down amid a puddle of his own making, and he was sick then and all the time shrieking. They only had to warn me of the coming of the nuns, and then that stupid little boy – who was, apart from stupid, quite pitiably blameless – he would never have been hurt nor bothered. But they let me believe that any reprisal that would surely come my way would be grimly bearable, merely one more fresh challenge to my expanding resources, to be met head-on and countered by defiance. But no, they did not tell me, they did not warn me that I would be instantly subject to a death without end, a withering of my heart and the excision of my soul, and all beneath the marble eyes of judgement and at the pink-rinsed hands of the Sisters of Mercy. Simon. Was his name: the stupid little boy. Later in life, he'll strive to overcome; people like Simon and me, we have to.

On the boat over to Ireland, I was so very ill amid the awful welter of it that there could be only room for amazement that this could be happening. It was as if my whole body was determined to turn itself inside out, dead set on my hacking out blood and organs and leaving me ripped apart, flayed and jagged bones exposed to the scourge of the brine and gale that lashed us. The slavey who was with me – a novice, she told me she was, and she made the sign of the cross as she said it – she made me stay on deck, and she dragged away from me the coat that my mother had insisted I take; she said there were poor and good people who deserved such a benefit so much more than I. I lay in the slime, yearning for death – though as I dashed away the insistency of vomit and spume that was slathered all over my lips and chin, I was trying so hard not to make it a prayer. Later, when the storm subsided and I felt just liquid, I regarded the mauve of my poor bare legs, and then the dappling of white that came to overlay it. No one had said to me 'Ireland'. I thought we must surely be headed to the end of the world; all I remember is the grey and climbing sea, so angry around me, and it just went on for ever. We did land – the boat, it did stop moving, but my limbs were no help to me and I practically fell on to the shore. The thin and hard Irish girl, the slavey, the novice – and how many years older than I can she have been, that little chit? Not really many – but the gulf between us, she made so clear, was wholly immeasurable; she openly smirked as I stood on the quayside and angled my head and grasped in both hands the two great and sopping hanks of my hair and wrung out of them a splattering cold and salty cascade. I was wet beyond wet, and shivering badly. It was raining; I do not think I passed a single day in Ireland when the rain did not fall, or else just glazed the air. Only the sluggish discontentment of the sea could distinguish it from the iron and menacing sky that seemed so very much lower than any sky I had ever seen before. There was a rusty bus, pockmarked by the bullets of decades of rain, but it was not for the likes of me. We climbed into a wagon and a man made big by a carapace of oilskin goaded now the bored and broken donkey into trudging on back the way it had come, through the ruttings and the mud. Slung across hoops and over the wagon was a torn and canvas covering, whipped up suddenly by the rush of wind. Each time a corner was hurtled away with the muted drumroll of a startled pigeon, there swept in a spattering of rain so hard and cold it hurt you, and I could see outside just deep green grass, humps and tussocks flat and beaten down by just centuries of this. As the wagon trundled on, lurching badly in the deeper gutters, I tried to get some feeling back into my legs. The soon-to-be nun, she broke off from her intense and mumbled rosary and clutching hard the bead to which she was currently devoting her being, instructed me sharply to not rub and not touch and to sit up straight and to never forget that the eyes of God, they were always upon me.

Grey. It's hard to not keep coming back to that one word, grey. Grey was all around, lapping, and soon it came to pervade me.

When the wagon ceased its pitching and we reached the place – and what place is this? – all I saw were walls that were grey against a sky that was grey and the cold grey rain, it continued to fall. The hall was lit by just two thick candles in big iron sconces and from far away I heard a determined footfall – a heavy step, and then came a lighter one, as if the walker could be lame or had a rolling gait, though it seemed quite natural to me. Then there came the swishing, the forbidding swish of the damnable habit – the thing I was sure that the nuns loved most about the visible aspect, anyway, of their raven calling. Behind closed doors, of course, there was so much more to delight them; this I had yet to know. The slavey who had brought me, she lowered her eyes at the approach of the nun; when finally the swishing had ceased and I sensed her before us, the slavey, she punched my side and I looked at her, startled. She was urging me with her eyes to mimic a little bobbing motion she was making continually, somewhere between a curtsey and a genuflection. I had not seen this before; the movement, though, it so soon came to be a part of my instinctive condition.

'It is here, Reverend Mother,' she whispered.

'I see it is,' came the cold and – what was it . . .? Strange, somehow strange to me, the tone of the nun's response. I still was looking at the floor, and I tried not to shake. The slabs of stone around my feet were spotted dark as water plopped down from me like the ticking of a clock.

'You run along now, girl. There's bread and tea in the refectory for you. Pray for me, child.'

'I will, Reverend Mother. And thank you, Reverend Mother. Are you quite sure it is all right to leave you alone with it . . .?'

'Quite all right. Quite all right. Run along, now.'

Strange. So strange. What was so strange, and why was I so much more disturbed now than ever I had been?

'We are old friends, are we not Annette?'

My throat was clutched by a strangler in the dark. My breaths came in gasps, and I thought I must not cry.

'But I am no longer the Sister Joanna, as you now may see Annette. You will, when you encounter me again, address me as Reverend Mother. Look at me, child.'

I was shuddering so badly that I thought I might fall. If I did not look up, then it might not be real.

'Look up at me, child. I forgive your impudence this once. You have had a long journey. Look up at me, child.'

'Please . . . let me go. Let me go home . . .!'

'Home. Ah yes – home. Alas alas, Annette, home is forfeit. You are a sinner. You are a black-hearted sinner, and you are here to be cleansed. And you will be, Annette – oh as God is my witness, believe me you will be. You will stay here for as long as the process requires. Sometimes, when a child allows the Lord back into her soul, oh – it is but a few years. For others, well . . . some of our children, they never leave us. We cannot expose them to the Devil in the outside world, and so we keep them safe and sheltered. The cemetery, Annette, is full of them. Now. Someone will come directly, take your clothes, burn them, and allocate to you a cell. For tonight, all you must do is sleep and pray, sleep and pray. And then tomorrow at dawn, you will be taught our little ways. And tomorrow too, if we deem you deserving, you will be given bread and some water. Welcome, Annette. Welcome. I might have known when I came here that our paths might cross again. But fear not, child – wherever within you the evil is lurking, we shall seek it out and put an end to it. You will be purged. Ah – here is your guide. God bless you, Eileen.'

'God bless you, Reverend Mother.'

'Eileen – this is Annette. You know what to do. No talking further than is strictly necessary. Goodnight, Annette. Goodnight. And may God have mercy on you.'

And Eileen, my first sight of Eileen – the poor little girl, she reminded me of nothing so much as the defeated and broken-backed donkey that had dragged me here on a wagon. She did not smile. I followed her down corridors, silent and grey, up two flights of stairs, all silent and grey, and then into a box of stone where I was to live alone, for all those years. It was numbingly silent in there; and grey. A nightdress, grey, lay across a straw-stuffed palette, hardly bigger than I was. Eileen, she indicated this and turned away. I took off my sodden clothes and dropped them on to the floor. She scooped them up and she said God bless you and suddenly I was gripped by a terrible alarm and I cried out oh *please* don't go and I made to clutch at her arm and she flinched and whinnied and ran, and clanged shut the door behind her. Poor Eileen. Nearly two years later, she lost her mind. She tried to bury herself alive in the vegetable garden, and then she started drinking from the drains. One of the nuns said she needed further guidance. Poor Eileen. None of us ever laid eyes on her again. It would be nice, you know, to be so feeble-minded as to believe in Heaven, if only to think of sweet Eileen just being there. But all I believe in and can think of is Hell, and the villains I am determined to send there.

The induction into The Mission, it was neither slow nor caring. The other poor girls, it was hardly their fault – when later I was forced to become a guide myself, I'm sure I was similarly resentful, and just as cool. We had all had the life beaten out of us, in many cases not just literally, but often. And when the bell, the bloody bloody bell that came to dog my every waking hour, when it clanged out discordantly that very first morning, I was just so surprised to find myself asleep. The mattress, it was so small and hard, and the one thin blanket had nothing to do with comfort; there was no pillow. I had cried in the night. And then I must have stopped. And that very first morning, like the thousands that followed, it was as grey and as wet and even more cold, it seemed to be to me, than the night before it. There had been a dish of cold water, I presumed for washing, but I had drunk all that, drunk it in the night. I put on the black and heavy woollen singlet and bloomers, the grey and hessian shift that I now saw hanging there. It was much too large and it stuck out stiffly, but soon it came to bulge and crease up in the manner of sacking, hanging from you shapelessly, in common with all the others (the scratching alone could make you crazy). As I left my cell I was just in time to catch a fleeting glimpse of the rapidly receding forms of one or two other girls at the end of the corridor, and I rushed to catch them, to see where they were going. We went into the chapel – oh but of course the chapel, where else might we have been destined but the lowering and ice-bound dim-lit chapel? The other girls, they each had a sort of a cloth tied over and around their heads – the same grey hessian of the dresses. Had I failed to see mine? Was it still there on the peg in my cell? Was I already to be punished for failing to demonstrate due humility in the house of God? No. No no. The humility that was about to be thrust upon me, it would have crushed a titan. A nun came towards me and took my by the hair and hauled me to the altar. She pressed down upon my shoulders and I was forced to my knees and my eyes now could see only the belt of her rosary and the panel of fustian that might have been expected, were we dealing with humanity, to have concealed a groin and even inner organs. She lifted up the skeins of my hair and the shears, they did their work fast and deliberately badly – the clunk and slicing of the blades, I can hear it now, and I willed myself not to cry, to make no noise, as the heavy chunks and hanks of me fell down before my eyes and to the floor. When she was done, she instructed me, the nun, to make the sign of the cross and to pray to God to make me humble. Then she handed me a square of grey hessian, and then I started to cry and she told me to cease that immediately and I think I must have been wailing by then and she slapped my face and then she slapped it again and she would have continued had not the pain and amazement immediately quietened me. A girl came forward and escorted me to the back of the chapel. Throughout morning prayers, I felt my head beneath the scarf: tufts, clumps, patches of scalp – it was like the flogged to death fields of Ireland around me. Only the nuns had hassocks. My knees, they were aching already. Even now, I cannot kneel. All of us – our knees were deformed, as the years slipped by. A collective gasp of pain was all there was ever to be heard whenever once again the bell was tolling and we all knelt down for yet more prayers, yet more devotions, oblations, vespers and benedictions. The cartilage now, it is gone for ever. There are other wounds too, much deeper.

At first, I suppose, I behaved as a new girl might be expected to. Not out of fear, and not because I felt I should be seen to be capable of any such deference – and nor because I was so desperate to, I don't know . . . how can you honestly phrase it in a place such as that? Fit in? No one fitted in. No one could. It was a citadel of misfits misruled by a lunatic hierarchy that reached all the way up from the compliancy of drones at its base to the giddiness of psychopaths and criminals at its sainted apex. So no – at first, I simply concentrated upon learning where everything was, fundamentally – learning the routes so that I would not continue to be punished for always being the last to arrive. Learning how to crouch down in a certain way when sowing or picking potatoes so as not to stay bent over and crippled for days to come. Learning never to be at the wall end of a refectory table, where no food ever reached you. And learning to do this strange little bob and curtsey whenever a nun should cross one's path, and never to look them in the eye – not, in my case, out of a show of humility, but in order to ensure that no fresh instruction might then occur to them that they would be eager to assign to you. Because already the age-long day was filled to capacity with prayers and labour, prayers and toil, prayers and sweating and obeisance. I wrote a letter to my mother; they tore it up before my eyes. They said it wasn't pious. I wrote a letter that I thought might be seen to be pious – I do not know if they ever sent it or, if they did, what in heaven's name my mother might have made of it. On two occasions, I was presented with a ripped-open envelope – pale blue, Basildon Bond – and my name and the address of this place was written in my mother's hand with my father's old Parker in blue-black washable Quink; at the top right-hand corner was a thruppenny stamp in mauve with the head of the Queen of England, smudged over heavily with a postmark reading London N.W. The letters themselves, they said, had been quite unsuitable. So I kept the envelopes, and read and read my name, and where the flap was torn away, I fancied I could sense and inhale my mother's saliva.

Later, I began to look out for myself. I learned this from no one, for everyone around me, they did as they were told. Barring, of course, Belinda. But I discovered that if you are careful, the pouch in your work apron, it can easily conceal a very large potato – and when you are behind the woodshed and burning garden rubbish, an old handleless bucket from the back of the scullery can serve very well as a saucepan. Because we were all of us hungry, just all of the time. Bread, potatoes, cabbage – and then potato soup, cabbage soup and bread to dip into it – here were the staples. We grew tomatoes and strawberries, but only for the nuns. Apples, in season. Sometimes the soup would contain little bits of fat and gristle and even shreds of meat – said to be the scrapings from the gargantuan joints that were roasted together with chickens and geese whenever Father O'Doyle would pay us a visit, to hear our confessions. So a purloined potato was, yes – just one more potato, but the method of its obtaining, it made it taste so sweet.

I began to read in the library. The books were drab – religious tracts, sermons – but the language was often inspiring. I tore out the blank flyleaves and began to try to write myself: I enjoyed the formation of words, and the sounds they made. We were not allowed to ever remove a book from the library, but I soon found a way. And I collected the stumps of candles from under the holy statues and I stole a box of matches from the vestry. Mea culpa. I would read and write in my cell till all hours, each dawn carefully concealing the results, so motley, beneath a flagstone in the floor just by the corner. It took me five days, every spare second I had, to chip away the surrounding mortar with a snapped-off screwdriver I found in the garage, and all my strength then to heave it aside: it soon became easier. And then from the vestry, I stole some wine. I had never drunk wine, and I thought it tasted, oh – just so bad, so awful. But the thrill of just having it, and the giddy feeling later – these were the few rare moments when I approached delight. Tiny, precious moments. But for eighteen hours a day, every day, every day, I was scalding myself in the laundry, blinded by steam and exhausted by the wet weight of washing, cracking my knees at the endless prayers, and crouching into a huddle to sow and pick potatoes; and the rain, it continued to fall.

I don't know how long it was that passed – days, seasons, there was no way to tell: it was always dull, always wet, so often dark. I very rarely even glimpsed Sister Joanna – or Reverend Mother, as I had to think of her now. Not for a long time. That was to change. And Belinda – she, in a way, was the beginning of that. In that she was, had to be I think, the catalyst. Catalyst is a good word: I kept up with my reading, you know – I actually read the whole of the Oxford Dictionary, and I wrote down words I liked the look and sound of: learned them. Invigorating, I found – that one could forever be vainly and badly striving to describe, I don't know – an action or a feeling, say, while all the time there existed this one so perfect word that expressed it completely. Always assuming, of course, that it was known to the other party. But then that is always the case: whatever you want to do, there must be someone receptive that you can do it to – or else what you have is worthless, no? An impotent thing. No? Anyway: Belinda. Some girls, I had noticed early on – their hair was not regularly and horribly shorn. Belinda was one of these – a beautiful girl, I thought. Wide blue eyes still alive with a vitality that the forces here had somehow failed to kill. She would laugh at times when the rest of us would never even have dreamed of doing. Instead of dropping a newly gouged-out potato into a sack at her side, she would lob it from a distance, each time singing out Allez-*oop*! Allez-*oop*! Sometimes she would miss her target, and then she would laugh again, and casually retrieve the potato. Once, she put a large potato down deep inside her knickers and made a sort of thrusting and grinding motion forwards with her hips, which I thought was terribly funny and mortally brave and both of us were laughing quite uncontrolledly. Of course, a nun would just have to notice this, wouldn't she? She came over to Belinda – oh don't ask me which one of them it was: they all just blurred into a drifting and wicked, swishing and vindictive mass of nun. You would have thought, wouldn't you, that there might have been a good one, a kind one, even a not-too-bad one but no, in this place there wasn't; such bad faith born of anti-charity, and leaking all hope. They must each of them have been hand-picked by Rome for scoring so highly in some sort of a twisted examination to seek out the closest to the antithesis of Christianity, as any merely moral layman might understand the word (rather in the way, I imagine, the Gestapo was recruited). So one of these witches, she went up to Belinda and I was too far away to hear – but Belinda, she lowered her head and nodded then and mumbled something and followed the nun quite meekly inside. Later I asked her: what happened? What happened to you? And she said they whipped me: they whipped me. The thrill of the impossibility of their having actually done such a thing, it rushed into and coursed right through and over me. She would say no more, though: not a word about it.

We became quite close, Belinda and me – though not as you might understand it. The day was structured so as to entirely sublimate all trace of the individual, allowing no time or scope for freedom of expression, and virtually no opportunity for togetherness, save of course at the eternity of prayers. But Belinda and I, we burned the garden rubbish behind the woodshed and we boiled our illicit potatoes and then in the woodshed itself we would touch each other gently, and then not gently at all; it was Belinda who taught me to bring her to what she said was called an orgasm, and then – oh, the rapture, I will never forget, the first time – she gave it to me. The nuns, she said, did it with candles. And priests. Candles and priests; the Reverend Mother, she used a crucifix. And then she showed me, Belinda, how I could do it to myself, and from that moment on, I barely ceased. It was the only thing at night that could lure me away from my writing and my reading. I looked it up, orgasm, in the Oxford Dictionary, and it wasn't there. I think they must print a special edition for Rome. The full Oxford, I can only assume, is on the Index – which one day, I fully intend to seek out in its entirety, and read my way through; I am sure I am headed for disappointment. Currently I was engrossed by *Foxe's Book of Martyrs*, which still I think is the most exciting book I have read in my life: it is most satisfyingly explicit.

Belinda, she would protect me too, because she was strong and much bigger than me. Because that place, it was full of mad and dangerous girls, many of them much worse even than myself. One girl, in the dark of just before Vespers, she hit me in the face with the Holy Bible, and then she drew back the hard and heavy book and banged it back into my face again. I was stunned and my nose was bleeding and I had to cover my face in Vespers with the corners of my headcloth. Why did you do that, I asked her afterwards – shivering, still shivering: why did you hit me in the face? And she turned and sneered at me – Shona was her name, two broken teeth and fists like a pair of pile-drivers – she just spat at me that the reason she had hit me in the face was that my face was just *there*, did I see? And strangely, I sort of did, yes I did: this is what happened in a place like this. I told Belinda though, and I don't know what she said to her but Shona, she never did trouble me again.

It was around this time that my hair was due for its ritual hacking; whenever you could get a hold of it, twist a curl around your finger, imagine how a full head of it could frame your face and make you pretty again as it used to (before they took you away from you), then that is when the clanking shears would reappear. But instead, I was ignored. No one said to me that I could or should allow my hair to grow back: I was simply ignored. So with my thickening hair and my friendship, and I think it was a friendship, with Belinda, I began to quite gingerly at first, and then more assuredly, assert myself in any small way that was allowed to me. I cut two inches off the bottom of my shift, and for this I was strapped to the down pipe on the water butt for two hours in the rain; this was one of the milder punishments. Another was to be made to kneel on the marble of the baptistry floor, and then a nun would pile about thirty hymnals on to the backs of your calves. One stayed so, reciting the Hail Mary to the outstretched arms of her plaster effigy with its exposed and radiant heart, until someone remembered you were doing this and despatched some other downtrodden girl, herself near mad with sleeplessness and prayers, to somehow coax you back to your feet and from the brink of delirium – help you, then, limping and useless, back into your cell. Sometimes, a tumbler of holy water would be balanced upon each of your upturned palms and you would be left outside, standing in a gale, to contemplate the thoroughness of the damnation to come should you let so much as a single drop spill over. Other punishments came closer to a naked sadism: sticking plaster would be applied to our unshaven legs, and torn away in slow and agonising strips. And then there was the penultimate penalty, the whip. I had assumed that this would form the pinnacle of their criminal and lustful cruelty, but they had just one more instrument in reserve. As I was one of the few to discover.

Belinda and I were scrubbing the pulpit – a huge, carved-oak and quite laughable structure, it seemed to me, from which Father O'Doyle would drunkenly bellow out his quite preposterous platitudes and dire imprecations; for him, the Lord thy God was no more than a machine of retribution, bent upon wreaking a terrible vengeance. And I came upon a stack of holy pictures. Maybe they trigger a reaction within me, holy pictures, I truly cannot say; but there is something about the badness of the art, the smugness, the complacency of the limpid portrayals of St Joseph, St Benedict and St Francis and of course the Virgin Mary that just immediately infuriates me beyond all measure. So I tore all their heads off. Belinda – she gasped at the audacity, and then she laughed out ringingly, and so did I: the undoing of us, as it transpired. And that is why that evening I was due to re-encounter the Reverend Mother.

'I wondered,' she said – and her voice, it was so nearly languorous – 'how long it would be. How long you would take. It was always, of course, no more than a matter of simple time. Which is, along with all else on earth, in God's hands.'

The nun rose up from her chair behind the broad and clear desktop. She picked up a ruler and confronted Annette.

'Make the sign of the cross, child. Kneel down before me, and make the sign of the cross. Speak. Speak out the words to me, child.'

She waved the ruler as if conducting an orchestra.

'In the name of the Father . . .'

'The Lord – he cannot hear you, child.'

'In the name of the *Father* . . .'

'The Father, yes – the heavenly Father –'

'And the Son . . .'

'The Son, the blessed Son, who died on the cross for our sins –'

'And of the Holy Ghost . . .'

'The most holy Spirit – most holy –'

'Amen.'

The Reverend Mother now carelessly cast aside the ruler, as if holding it had suddenly exhausted her.

'Amen . . .! Amen . . .! Amen . . .! Rise, child.'

Annette stood before her, and lowered her eyes. She could not even bear to look at this woman; it was merely convenient that to do so was forbidden. The room she found herself standing in now, it was quite sparsely furnished, though each of the pieces was of a very dark wood and gleaming unnaturally. A dull red Persian carpet was spread across a table and to the left of the mullioned window was a heavily framed and mounted chromolithograph of the averted head of Jesus, his pale eyes pleading, the gauntness of his cheek and the elongated throat each thinly lined by the perfectly delineated rivulets of blood that snaked their way down so gracefully from his embedded crown of thorns. Annette had a good deal of time to observe all of this, even with her head hung low, for the Reverend Mother was silent, and seemingly uninterested in speaking any further. Behind her wimpled head there hung the crucifix, Annette could only assume, that she rammed up and between her vile and chalky stockinged thighs in order to achieve an ecstasy that would leave St Teresa merely coping only with no more than the stirrings of arousal. She spoke, then.

'Why, child, did God make you?'

'God made me to know Him, love Him and –'

'And the saints. Does God wish you also to love all the saints?'

'Yes – yes.'

'*Yes . . .?*'

'Yes, Reverend Mother.'

'Yes, Reverend Mother . . . That's right isn't it, child? And what of the Virgin Mary?'

'What . . . what of the Virgin Mary? Reverend Mother?'

'Must we love her? Does God wish for us to love her also, child?'

'Oh – yes. Yes, Reverend Mother.'

'Yes. Yes, Reverend Mother . . . You see you know all this, do you not my child? You are not a stupid girl.'

'No. No, Reverend Mother.'

'No. No, Reverend Mother . . . And yet you do defile them, do you not? The images of the saints. The mother of Christ. You do defile them. Do you not? Child?'

'I'm – sorry. Sorry, truly sorry, Reverend Mother.'

The nun looked over to the window and narrowed her eyes. Her voice took on a wistful and pale, rather faraway tone.

'I'm . . . sorry. Yes, child. You are sorry, truly sorry. Reverend Mother . . .'

'Yes. Yes.'

'*Yes . . .?*'

'Yes – Reverend Mother.'

'Mm. Mm. Yes. Reverend Mother . . . Good. Good. I am pleased to hear it, child. It means our work here, it is not in vain. Sorrow and penitence – these are to be encouraged. Penance is to be endured. I shall whip you, child. I shall whip you this instant, child. Extremely severely.'

Annette now raised her eyes, and they fused with a shock into the mutely furious gleaming from the nun's. The woman had now in her hand a four-foot-long and flexible thong, tightly wrapped around in a tiny and painstaking latticework of leather, a doubled-over flap at its tip.

'You will walk to the table, child, and prostrate yourself across the rug there. Place your feet on the tray. You will lift your tunic, and lower your undergarment.'

Annette's mouth, it opened to speak and she closed it. There was loathing but also a quick and beating dread now within her, both of them clamouring for if not an uprising, then at least expression. She opened her mouth and she closed it. She turned and moved away towards the table. The grey hessian dress dragged away coarsely on her thigh as she hoiked it up. The warmth of her bloomers was a passing comfort as they were slid away and down. She lay across the table and her heart was now hurriedly throbbing like a cornered creature sent wild and mad by the first smell of fear. She heard a slicing through the air and felt but a short kiss of impact and only when again she heard the slicing did a rush of burning sear her to her centre, exploding into so shocking an agony as the slicing came again that she screamed and no scream came as her fingers were claws now and ripping at the carpet as the whole of her lower body was left just raw and boiling in a cauldron of white-hot torment. The whip, it spread and coiled and flayed her as it was dragged away to fly again and come back down to set alight and electrify her nerve-ends and take them up to melting point. She prayed for oblivion, as the Devil tore her limb from limb. And, when she was bidden, twice, to rise, she could not move, she could not breathe.

'Rise, child – *rise*. Obey me at once. *Rise*, I say!'

Annette lifted up her sweat- and tear-soaked face from the scorch of the rug. She could not straighten her body which was bulbous and roaring and now just lost to her. Trickles of warmth ran away down her legs and into the tray where she stood. She raised herself a little more and saw the perfectly delineated rivulets of blood snaking their way down so gracefully from her embedded crown of thorns.

'Speak to me, child.'

'I – I – *can't* – I—!'

'*Speak* to me, child.'

'I – thank you . . . *Thank* you, Reverend Mother . . .'

'The Lord has bestowed upon you this degree of mortal pain in order to concentrate your mind. You will be humbly grateful. Now go in peace, child. Begone.'

Annette, cracking and broken-backed, staggered with her legs as stumpy struts, her arms hanging forward like an imploring ape. Every movement set up jolts of deep and fiery pain, all overladen by so vast and seething a body-ridden hurt. Somehow, she reached the door of the room, her eyes made blind by a wash of tears.

'Child – you are a sinner. You are a wicked and evil sinner, and I will pray for you.'

Then they made me pick potatoes. Then they had me kneeling for prayers, and then longer for a penance. And when finally and halfway into the night I could crawl away and back to my cell and tend to my wounds with no more than a dish of cold water and a rag, a nun came in to tell me that at bedtime we lie down on our bed, do we not Annette? So lie down – lie down, Annette. And she pressed me flat on my back and continued to do so until I could no longer hold back the racking of my shrieks. Only then would she leave, and tell me she would pray for me.

The next day, before dawn, I took down the ladder from the garage and somehow I managed to drag it all the way to the chapel and I leaned it against the wall between the seventh and eighth Stations of the Cross and climbed up to the big oak crucifix that hung there and unhooked it from its rusty bearing and it was so much heavier than I imagined it would be but I did eventually get it down and then I laid it on the ground. I covered it with my blanket and I hauled back the ladder and hung it in the garage and then came back to the chapel and lifted up my shrouded cross and happily bore the full weight of it across my shoulder and got it around to the back of the woodshed and left it there hidden and the bell for morning prayers was clanging so dolefully and the thin and ceaseless rain had now soaked me so completely. During prayers, I traced the ridges of my blood-hardened weals through the thickness of the hessian. Here was a pain that I would not offer up. This was a pain just for me alone. I wanted to carry the tang of it within me for ever, so that when the time was ripe for inflictions of my own, its sharp reminder would point up my utter determination.

Later that day, when Belinda and I were burning all the garden rubbish behind the woodshed, I laid the crucifix with ceremony across the smouldering pyre. Belinda – as I had hoped she would be – was gleeful. Then Mary just happened along – I barely knew Mary – and she wept and appeared quite hysterical. It's only a piece of wood, I said: we burn wood all the time – it's just like burning a chair, no more and no less. And Mary, she screamed that it wasn't, it wasn't at all! And Belinda and I, we knew her to be right. We poked ferociously with sticks as the flames enveloped it (Mary – she'd run away now in a paroxysm of torment) and we sizzled with pleasure as the body of Jesus became at first just distorted before it split away and practically dissolved. Here was an intense delight, on a glorious scale.

Poor Mary, though: she was one of the innocents. Unlike most of us, she had done no wrong. When she was born, her father was long gone and her mother could bear neither the burden nor the shame and so God in his mercy despatched the baby to hell, and here she has lived ever after. I thought she would be released well before me – non-sinning orphans were usually freed at sixteen – but it did not turn out that way, and all wholly as a result of this impromptu immolation of Christ. When you left this place, it depended so often upon your usefulness to the nuns. The eager and the sycophants, the skilled and the pious, these they would retain for as long as they could manage before some or other law could no longer be sidestepped – one of the few they appeared to be bound by. The wicked, the beautiful and the damned, such as myself and Belinda, they would often be held back as well, for so many baser reasons. Some girls of no more than thirteen or fourteen would be sold into virtual slavery, or worse, to some or other worthy in a neighbouring village (a Catholic family, of course, but further than that no enquiry was made). A suitable donation to the continuance of God's work would be duly deposited, and then the child would be given a brand-new grey hessian dress and was abandoned to her fate. I would have been kept, I swear, until I was twenty-one years of age – three years hence – but for the scandal that was now to unfold.

As a result of my bonfire party – and I had told them quite brazenly, my accusers and then my captors, that here was no more than a deeply pious ritual of sacrifice and sweet purification – I was put into a cell underground in which you cannot stand up fully erect and there is no natural light; straw on the floor and a hole in the corner. I was to be left, said the appalled and I think she was frightened, the nun who threw me in there, until the Reverend Mother had decided what was next to be done with me. She might have considered that a further whipping so hard upon the last could easily have resulted in a rather gaudy murder, news of which they would wish to reach the attention of neither God nor the Garda: my miserable skin was hardly worth the assumption of mortal sin, nor yet civil prosecution. So instead, they turned me over to the highest court of all.

There was no light at all in this skulking dungeon of mine – no light, not a chink, for reading or writing . . . not that they had left me books or paper. I had been instructed to pray (and when was

I not?) but instead I just pleasured myself to an obsessive degree
– I do not know the true word for it – and blessing Belinda as
I did it. The focus of my fantasy was merely the image of all I
was doing – the thrill of the thought of my doing it, this alone
was easily ample; the tentative fingers of sensation would then
rapidly scurry over me and the first lapping wave before the
deeper rippling would make me breathless and take me to the
lip . . . the softest touch of all, then, and I could give myself up
and fall away on a float of so much pleasure into the warmth and
satisfaction of a languorous elsewhere, and peace. Then I would
nibble just a tiny bit more of the one hard lump of bread that was
all they had left me, doze for a while, and then once more I
would coax myself along and rise up to the plateau, and dreamily
tumble over into a bath of true bliss – a fleeting rapture that was
saving me from madness, and hence the need for more and
more. I could sit now with much less discomfort – I sat, I
crouched, I stretched out my arms as far as the walls would
allow me and blocking dread, I kept my mind from wandering.

I was so shocked when they opened the door – I shied from
the light as if it might burn me. I do not know how much time
had now passed – it might have been no more than a day and a
night; it may well have been much much longer. A nun – the
same one who had imprisoned me? A different one altogether? –
she did not enter but silently bade me follow her. All was silent
as I padded behind in my grubby bare feet, so numb with cold
that only now I noticed how very chilled I was throughout.
Walking was difficult, but we did not go far. There was a room I
had never known existed (I suppose there were dozens of them)
and at its centre stood a deep and scuttle-shaped burnished
copper tub. Before I could speak, the nun was gone, locking
the door behind her. Steam arose from the water in the tub – I
dipped in a finger and recoiled in delight at the softness and
the heat. On a chair alongside, there was a glass-stoppered

bottle – the sweetness of the just greenish crystals inside, the scent, it had me reeling (there were no good smells in this place ever, save maybe the maturing tomatoes in the glasshouse). And here was a sachet of something I remembered and it was called shampoo: that, that was the trigger for my tears – so simple a reminder of an ordinary life of so long ago and beyond my reach and maybe lost to me now, for ever and ever. Hanging by the window was a plain white cotton maybe nightdress, it was. I looked down at the stained and stinking grey sack that still clung to me and yes, I cried again and my fists were wringing out my eyes. Draped there alongside were two lengths of silky ribbon, one white, the other so delicate a pink, like a tender rosebud.

And there I was – taking a bath! Of all things, this was most beyond belief. The lapping heat, made milky by the crystals, it was all the way up to my neck and I stared quite giddily at my two pink and glistening knees breaking like globes through the surface of the water. I could at that moment have happily died there, hugged by warmth and in a space of my own. For all their carping and insistence in this terrible place about the paramountcy of the spotlessness of the soul, no devotion was ever bestowed upon its tainted carrier, the body. On Fridays, you would stand behind a blanket strung up between beams, strip off your lousy clothes and wait for a nun on a ladder to tip over you a bucket of cold water; for fifteen seconds then you would rub the bar of household soap across any part of you that was reachable and then, teeth clattering now with the cold and exposure, you waited still for the final deluge. A greyish rag would be handed to you then by another of the grim-faced nuns; if it was the time of month for the scourge, we called it, you received a second rag. I did not hate my periods, which I now know to be the word. The first, I thought I was dying from within, but Belinda, she explained it to me. From then on, I suppose I rather looked forward to them. They were evidence of not only my new maturity, but also the passing of time – that would maybe one day lead me somewhere . . .? Proof too that on this level, at least, I was functioning, anyway, as do other and ordinary women; also, I liked the colour – I loved to watch the spreading seep of all that vividness, before it dulled and hardened.

But this! A bath – and in clean hot water with scented crystals. The only good and kind thing that had happened to me in, oh – just years and years and years. And no, I did not wonder why: I could not. As the water began to cool, I just gave myself up wholly to a passing enjoyment. I massaged my head with the creamy shampoo – my hair, it must have been six inches long now, more at the back, and I even had nearly a fringe. I held my breath beneath the water for as long as I could, wishing I could swim away down and then strike out into the length of an underground torrent urged on excitedly by the insistent tumble of a current that would hurtle me farther, and then I would rise up vertically, my arms to my sides, my feet as treadles, as the water grew clearer and now just dappled by the white of daylight and then my head would burst up with joy through the glassy surface of a pale green sheltered and sunlit lagoon, and as I rid the streaming water from my mouth and nose and eyes, smiling natives, covered in flowers, would row and wade out to me, proffering a sarong and blood-red fruit, and then I would be saved . . .

There were towels – clean white towels, and with a nap to them. I wrapped myself in the softness of the larger one and rubbed at my head with the other, before I draped it over me, like a cowl. Now that I felt so clean, my blemishes offended me. My hands were big and raw, the fingernails splintered and so very dull and lifeless. My feet were swollen and livid about the ankles from when in the potato fields the coarse stalks had stabbed me, and from around the woodshed, where the tangle of brambles had pierced, the rash of nettles burning. My forearms were reddened by the rain and cold, elbows hardened and grazed – my knees so blue and bony from all those penances and prayers. And then behind the hanging white nightdress (it might easily have been) – just behind, when I took it down, I saw this thing and gaped. A mirror. A small and mottled mirror, hanging on twine from a bent-over nail. Only sometimes in a darkened window could I glimpse the grey and hollowed-out shadow of a ghost that I may or may not have become. I stopped even trying to imagine how I truly appeared when one day, there was the blackened blur of me in a twilit mullion, and next to me was Belinda and we both looked the same. All that was there was the mean and just about symmetry of the human face – all else had flooded away from me. So I could not ignore the mirror – what woman could? – and yet my approach was so slow – so slow and fearful. I edged into the rim of it, so that just my hair, and now an earlobe were visible to me; I was startled by the first glimpse of my eye – there was a sadness there, an element of the forlorn, though nothing even close to despair. Behind that eye there still lay the resolve of someone I knew, biding her time. The face – it was not a bad face; my nose, still straight – lips, full, yet so very bloodless. Cheekbones high, hair as black as anthracite – and both dark eyes, now, giving me strength (making me a promise). I pinched hard at each of my cheeks, and a little colour came that almost instantly faded, and then it was gone. I slipped on the nightdress – it was, it had to be a nightdress, I had decided now – and it felt so gentle and cool. I forced my stiffened fingers in and through the tussocks of my hair – there was no comb, no brush: I looked – and then I passed the slippery silk of the ribbons over the palms of my hands, to and fro, to and fro. The pink one I looped and then lifted around my hair so that it rose at the crown, and then I somehow tied a bow at the back. The white one I slipped around my waist and knotted loosely – let it fall down, like a sash. There was no more to be done, now: I had used up all of my props. I sat on the chair and pressed my nose right into the neck of the bottle of just greenish crystals, dizzily breathing into me their scent and freshness, my eyes so tightly closed. But whenever you are waiting for the moment to last, you know that its end has come. The door of the room was noiselessly unlocked, as I was sure must happen, and I was silently summoned, as I knew I had to be.

I followed the nun up a narrower staircase – we were in the very oldest part of the building now, the part I had no place to be. It was the waft of hot and hearty cooking that took me over so completely – the forgotten smells of roasting meats in the place of just the steam and clog of boiling that was always a watery broth, or else just laundry. The glitter of the room she eventually left me in was at first just so disconcerting – all these candles in gleaming plate, a fire in the grate with flames that were dancing, not just damp and feebly alive beneath a spadeful of dusty slag and ashes. Father O'Doyle, he put down his knife and scraped back his chair away from the table.

'Approach, child. Approach. Bow, now. Good girl. Well now, child? Have you nothing to say for yourself? You do not? Then let me do all the speaking for you. You will not have met before Father Sheridan . . .? And Father Morton.'

Annette looked up, and fleetingly to the left and right of her. The room was as full of priests as a small room could be. One of them seemed to be almost nun-like in his blank and hawkish, mean disapproval, the other was a huge man, broad-backed and well-rounded, his face as red and cooked as the litter of meats and poultry on the table before her. She could not take her eyes away from all that food – so spiked was her appetite that it was for now even quelling a deep and creeping unease. Father O'Doyle poured out more wine – indicating with a flourish of a soft pink and plumpish hand that the other two priests should feel quite free to follow his example.

'Well now . . . Annette, isn't it? Ah yes – 'tis indeed, 'tis indeed. Have you partaken of supper, Annette? Can I not just coax you into maybe forcing down you, well now – a leg of chicken, perhaps? Or a cut off the joint? There are peaches here, my child: peaches. Hm? Still nothing to say for yourself? Well now this is what I'll do for you, Annette. I'll lay out a little assortment of things for you to eat, all right now? And you just pick away at them, as it takes your fancy. Do you hear me now, Annette? Are you listening to your priest?'

Annette bobbed her head very briefly, and without at all planning to do any such thing, she reached out immediately with both of her hands and lifted up the meat and the chicken and tore at them both and was choking now in her eagerness to get them both down her and grab and then to chew, chew, chew up more. As the huge priest Father Sheridan was chuckling in a deep and contented sort of a way, the other, Father Morton, was tut-tut-tutting through his teeth.

'She is a sinner,' he said. 'It is evident. She is behaving like a sinner and should be treated as such. Why do we indulge her?'

'Oh now come, Father Morton. 'Tis but she's hungry, that's all. And when was it a sin to be hungry? Did not Our Lord feed the five thousand starving?'

'I do not refer, O'Doyle, to her craving for food. It is her other appetites I am meaning, as has been made perfectly clear to us by the Reverend Mother. Do you not think, Sheridan, you have had enough of that wine for one evening . . .?'

'Well now since it is you who is doing the asking, my dear Father Morton – then no, no sir I do not, I most sincerely do believe that for this evening, no – not enough, not yet. No no.'

'We are in the presence of a *sinner*. It is not seemly to indulge in levity. She is a *sinner*, O'Doyle. Is that not why we are here?'

336

'Well sure it *is*, Father Morton. Is that not right, Father O'Doyle? But beneath the starch of our surplices, which one of us is not a sinner? Is that not right?'

'Sir! How can you speak this way? *Sir* . . .?!'

'Are you forgetting the Original Sin, Father Morton?'

'Sheridan! How do you dare speak to me in this manner! O'Doyle – will you tell him? And in the presence of so base a *thing* . . .!'

'Be calm, my dear Father Morton. Father Sheridan – you shouldn't be talking that way, you know. But let us be asking of our guest here, will we? What, child, of the taint of Original Sin?'

Annette's whole mouth was slathered with the juice of peaches. Still she was standing, and the food and heat were now making her dizzy.

'It is my understanding from my reading of theology . . .' she began quite carefully, 'that we need not all be sinners, for Original Sin has not left a permanent blight on mankind . . .'

'Has it not now? And why should that be so?'

'Because . . . because it has been redeemed, redeemed by Jesus Christ's sacrifice in dying for Man's sins . . . and redeemed also, Father, by the sacrament of baptism. Is it not so that all those who are baptised in Christ have the stain of Original Sin washed away from them? That they are cleansed? That they are no longer in thrall to evil?'

'That is so, child – quite so. And what may we deduce from this?'

'That . . . wickedness is not a natural and inevitable condition . . .'

'You use words well, child. You use the words well. And you are correct – is she not correct in this, Father Morton? Wickedness, thanks be to our Saviour Jesus Christ, is not a natural and inevitable condition.'

'*Indeed* this is so, O'Doyle. It is an *aberration* – a sign of the serpent within. And this – *girl* . . . is riddled with sin and wickedness and evil. She is an *aberration* – an insult to God and the baptism.'

Father O'Doyle nodded slowly, and then he sipped more wine.

'My child . . . I fear that what Father Morton has to say to us is no more than God's truth. Are you penitent, my child? Speak. Speak up, Annette. Are you in a state of penitence?'

'I am sorry . . . to be here . . .'

The outraged explosion of breath from Father Morton was overladen by a hissing from Father O'Doyle and an eruption of laughter from Father Sheridan at the end of the table; and then he poured more wine.

'You are a clever girl, Annette . . .' said Father O'Doyle, very measuredly. 'But foolish too. There are lessons, child – lessons that must now be taught you.'

'Oh enough of all this – let us *purge* the child, O'Doyle. Is that not the reason we are here?'

'Indeed. Very well, then. Father Sheridan – if you would be so kind . . .?'

Father Sheridan set down his glass, grunted peremptorily, and with enormous difficulty struggled to his feet. When he tugged once and harshly at Annette's two arms, she felt as if she had been launched into the air by a force beneath her. She gasped as her back was forced down upon the divan, the bulk and weight of Father Sheridan pinioning back her shoulders with a terrible ease. Annette looked up once into his mauve and deeply veined great globe of a face, and the beads of his sweat fell down singly, and struck her cheek. When he laughed, the breath of wine and whiskey was near overpowering. She closed her eyes so tightly, and then she felt the hands on her breasts that were kneading her, and roaming.

'You see, Father Morton – lookit, Father Sheridan – she feels like a good and clean Catholic girl. She smells . . . oh yes, she smells so clean and good. Can we be mistaken, do you suppose . . .?'

'There's no *mistake*, O'Doyle. It is within! Within! The cancer is within and it must be excised – for the good of whatever remains of her Catholic *soul* . . .!'

'I fear you are right, Father Morton. This thigh, now – does this feel to you like the thigh of a sinner? Father Sheridan – could I trouble you to place just one of your hands over the mouth of the child? She is beginning now to utter the words of the Devil, and there is no place for talk of that kind in a place of consecration. I am obliged to you, Father Sheridan. And lookit – if we follow this seemingly pure and altogether blameless thigh of the child – up, and now yes just a small way further, look, we can maybe see now clearly the gateway into Hell. But sure I feel is it not the duty of a priest to put to the sword the kingdom of Satan . . .? With an army – a Holy Crusade? A flood of purity, to expunge the sin, and to save the sinner . . .?!'

'It must be done! Yes, O'Doyle – it must be done!'

Annette was stifling and panicked by the weight of the big and fleshy hand across her face, and the screams that rose up in her now were damped and throttled as a terrible and thunderous pain, it just tore her asunder and the champ and bruising at her hips was so sharp and rapacious, it was as if ravenous little animals were gnawing at and into her, so intensely eager to be part of and close to this massive invasion. Her legs were warm now with the trickling: she remembered being maimed by a whipping, and so here must be the fullness and ritual of a stark disembowelment. The vast weight of the hand was removed from her mouth and she sucked at air and rolled away her eyes and then shut down for ever the sight then of the wild eyes and glory of the whiskey-sodden priests and a new hand now clamped down on her hard and an explosion of sheer raw and blood-hot hurt now, it simply engulfed her and she fought for just breath at the jolt of each giant kick of the mule that was jarring her and battering into her guts. As more hands came and the whiffs of other sweat were borne in and away from her wet cold face by a new short breeze and the shifting of weights, she willed herself with all she had left to her to just pass away and yet still be a silent and abstract witness to each blunt moment of this mortification so that the depth of their graves that these three ambassadors to Jesus were clawing so assiduously from out of the very blood and roots of her should extend in profundity to the core of the earth.

After they were done with her, she fell on to the floor. Her jaw was distorted, her arms near deadened, and the rest of her in trauma, ugly and scattered after so total a collision. The nuns who came in silently and carried her away were encumbered by her dead-weight, and further by the need to bow down in unison to each of the priests on their way through the door. All Annette heard before at last she lost consciousness was the further indulgence of Father O'Doyle – so sorry, he said he was, to be adding to the burden of the good Sisters, but when they had dealt with all that, did they think they could find it in their hearts to bring us just a drop maybe more of this very excellent wine? And then from Father Sheridan, a muted rumble of deep amusement, and then the banging on the table of his glass, and then his fist.

Annette was taken back to her underground dungeon. The white nightdress – ripped now, and streaked so badly – that was briskly stripped off and bundled away; the ribbon in her hair – so delicate a pink, like a tender rosebud – was tugged at and torn from her and hurled with distaste on to the heap of tatters. The old grey hessian dress was then thrown into her face. She was not sure for just how long they kept her there – it might have been no more than a day and a night; it may well have been much much longer. Her own small cell, when at last she got back there, it seemed to Annette to be almost a kindly place, now – it nearly seemed good to just be there. As the days continued, as they always had done – prayers, toil, toil and prayers – Annette was quite mute. She did what was expected of her, still keeping a secret and frantic hold upon her sanity by the old means of reading and rereading anything at all, writing down her thoughts if ever she had paper, and spilling over into a welter of orgasm with or without Belinda at the merest opportunity. Are you all right? Belinda, she asked her again and again. Annette – speak to me: are you all right? You seem the same, but different. And Annette, she answered her quietly: I am the same. And different. It was Belinda who noticed that for so many months now, Annette, she had not bled. Annette acknowledged airily the flimsy truth of this – had little awareness, now, of the passing of time. And then just a few days later she was summoned to see the Reverend Mother.

'We meet again, child. I had known we would. I learn that once more you have been touched by the finger of sin. Your body, child – your body is sinning as it stands before me. When you leave this room, a Sister will escort you to an address in a neighbouring village. There you will be dealt with. You will not speak. To anyone. Is that perfectly clear to you, child? And then you will return. Oh but of *course* you will return. Eternal punishment is all that is left you. You are aware, I trust, that you will never ever leave this place?'

It did feel like that – I had, I suppose, very nearly given up all hope of ever being human again, if ever I had been. But as to being 'dealt with' – I knew what this meant. Belinda, she had told me all about everything to do with the whole awful horror of women and men and for so long I had condemned her for a liar. But then I just knew it to be right. I knew too the state I was in – and being 'dealt with', I knew what that meant too. And that part I would go along with: this might serve me well, I was thinking.

The journey in the rain was to be in a car, this time – an old and rounded rusting thing; maybe over the years – how many years? How many? – the crocked and dip-backed ass had been finally granted the mercy of peace, the wagon just crumbled into dust. But oh – what exhilaration as we drove through the gates! I can never forget that, the lift to my heart. The giddiness and speed of the passing trees! I laughed at the tottering cloud of sheep who croaked in protest and fled from the car – and the nun who was gripping the wheel so tightly, she told me to be silent, and to pray. The village was no more than a cluster of ancient buildings huddled in shame under the thunder and weight of a sky that was constantly weeping. We drove a little way beyond and turned down into a heavily rutted dirt track made mallow in the rain, and then the silence as the engine sighed away was full and over-powering. I had to duck my head as I entered the cottage – it was spare and grimy, but I wanted to touch a curtain, a cloth, the shade of a lamp – I barely remembered them, all these so ordinary things. The man just nodded, and scratched at the bristles on his face. In the room next door there was yet another sacrificial divan on which I was instructed to lie. A tall and yellow metal cylinder stood close by, and a thick rubber mask was now held to my face and as it was wheezing I gulped in and was immediately sick and the man, he tutted and passed me a cloth and I wiped my chin and then he clamped back the mask to my face. When he took it away I was no more than groggy; I would have protested at this state of still consciousness as I saw him now pick up a long grey rod, or could be needle – but I just had to remain aware: I would have to take the pain, because I so needed to be aware, now. And there was pain – searing: too sharp and bad to remember. It seemed to be all that my innards were for, then – to be gouged at, and cause me such pain. And here was just another whiskey-sodden and dirty man, just one more – they put things in, and they take things from you.

I was shaking so badly, but I made no sound, when I heard something not too heavy but dripping wet get clanged into a bucket. The pain, that too was still so severe, but I was becoming a master at biting down hard, choking it back. When the man left the room, I stayed stock-still. When I heard the dull rumble of conversation through the door, I carefully made to get up. I had to ram my hands into my mouth then just to stop the shrieking that rushed to my throat. I did not expect it to be so very terrible, the gash of huge and hidden pain. I looked down into the bucket, and all I felt was nothing.

I wrapped the cloth between my legs and climbed up on to the ledge – eased open gently the tiny window. It was just so small I had to squirm my way through it and I could feel again that trickling along and down my legs, the ultimate disgrace after a fresh round of punishment. My feet sank deep into the mud outside and the ooze of the sopping grassy hillocks felt clean to me now and I was excited and my eyes grew bright as I set my mind to fleeing. I carefully circled the cottage, bending so low and trying not to whimper with the deep cramping hurt that every single step was causing me. I crouched down tight to the side of the car and swept away the ceaseless drizzle from the lids of my eyes, wringing out the splat of my hair (for it still had not been cut: the priests, they maybe thought they might have to again redeem me). And then I was on the road, and limping and hobbling in so awkward a way that I could not even be sure that I made progress at all. At last I got to the village proper, and people in the street there, they all were eyeing me. I clutched at an old woman and said Garda! Where? Please tell me – I need help. She brushed me aside as if I were a spider that had dropped down beside her. A man, then – chewing on a pipe, leaning against a wall, seemingly unaware of the worsening rain. Will you help me? Garda? Please help me – I need help. He narrowed his eyes and pulled the peak of his cap down over his forehead. Help, is it? Is what he said. And I maybe started to panic and I pulled at his coat and I nearly screamed at him for Help! Yes help – why do you not listen to me? I need *help*! And I heard the car just a moment too late – there was nowhere to turn and the man, he had me anyway. He said to the nun – This one, is she giving you trouble, Sister? Will you want her in the car? And the nun, she smiled so sweetly and she said Bless you, my son – and he threw me into the back of the car and I screamed out in pain and he slammed shut the door and now we were moving and the trees were flying away from me and the nun was spitting with hatred and rage and I am sure a deep-seated fear of the Reverend Mother who now, she promised, would have me flayed alive.

She didn't, though. I think she might have – but before I was summoned to see her, I had in desperation devised a plan – my only chance, I really did believe, of being allowed now to live. And when I went in, all her cruel and easy urbanity had left her, and all I saw was a barely reined-in and so cold fury. And doubt. Yes! That was the beauty – that one small chink of it that I had to work at now as surely as I did the flagstone in the floor of my cell – it had to be prised at and finally riven asunder: my only way out of here.

'I never – in all my lifetime of serving the Lord, I never thought I could ever encounter so black and wicked a sinner as yourself . . .! You will—'

'You have to release me.'

She was so shocked. She was quite literally stricken dumb. And then she was white with rage.

'You will wish to God in heaven that you never—!'

'Listen to me. You have to release me. If you do not, they will come for me. And then I will tell them *everything*.'

Her eyes, they were nearly closed, and flickering.

'What are you saying, you Godless and impertinent child?!'

'I spoke. I spoke to a man who is bringing the Garda. He will tell a Dublin newspaper. If I am here when they come, I will tell them *everything*.'

'Nonsense. You lie. You spoke with no one.'

'I spoke. They are coming now. They are coming now.'

She seethed. She seethed at me. And her eyes were blinking hard.

'I should have had you buried alive while I still had the chance . . .'

'You maybe should. But it's too late now. They are coming.'

'I shall refuse permission for anyone to talk to you.'

'They know I am here. They will not leave it. They will not stop. And I will tell them all that goes on. *Everything*. And why I was in the village.'

'I will simply say you were in the village to – buy provisions . . .'

'And I will say that I was in the village to be rid of some damned whiskey-sodden priest's little bastard child . . .!'

She clutched at the corner of the desk, and I swear she was swaying. Then she seemed to regain at least some of her composure. She closed her eyes, and coughed once gently.

'What is it . . . that you suggest?'

'I suggest that I am seen to leave here of my own free will. I will then agree to anyone who asks me that of course I was lying. Leave you in peace to continue your abuse of the innocents . . .'

'You are a *sinner* . . .!'

'Am I leaving? Time passes . . .'

And while it did so, yet one more trickle of my blood was wending its way down the length of my thigh – further, now: it touched my ankle, and soon it would be staining the floor. I was hoping to anything but God that I would not faint now.

'You – ! Are leaving. I had decided anyway that you had to go. You are a highly disruptive and evil influence. A detriment to all the good we do here. I will see to it. You will stay in this room until all is arranged.'

'I'll go where I want. I'm free now. I'm *free* now, Sister Joanna.'

Her face was tight with anger.

'Reverend *Mother* . . .!'

'No. You're Sister Joanna. You always will be. To me you always will.'

'You – are – a – *sinner* . . .!'

'No. You're all wrong when you say that. It's worse than that. What you must now understand, Sister Joanna, is that me, I'm not the sinner – I am the *sin*.'

I was trembling with an appalling terror and elation as I walked out of the room, as steadily as the fear of discovery and the still raw pain inside me would allow. A nun was assigned to me – and one more I saw was despatched to the gates with I am sure strict instructions to keep well at bay anyone at all who should call. I collected my papers from beneath the flagstone – the nun, she just gaped at me – I changed into a clean grey hessian dress that was handed to me by yet one more scared and so very incredulous nun, and then I sought out Belinda who was burning rubbish as usual at the side of the woodshed. We slipped around to the other side and shouted out our joy as she at least was almost at once and gorgeously orgasmic as a result of my coaxing, while my own legs stayed tightly entwined, to stop up the blood and the pain. She cried when I told her I was leaving, and I told her too that it may seem strange, but I loved her; and then I kissed her on the lips (which I had never done before). I just happened upon Shona, whitewashing a new wooden fence around the cowshed. I said to her hello, I'm leaving now – and then I reminded her of the time she had hit me with the Bible. She sniffed and glanced away: I don't remember, she said. Oh well there it is, is all I replied – it's funny, really, because I do, you see, I remember it. Yes well, is all she had to say to me. Well goodbye anyway, Shona, I said to her; yes, she said, goodbye Annette. And I turned to go and then I turned back to her again and I picked up a length of paling that was leaning against the wall and swept it hard into both of her shins and it splintered as she screamed and fell down so awkwardly and clutched at her legs and I picked up her head by the tight little tufts of her hair and I dunked it stiffly into the billycan of whitewash and lifted it up and rammed it back in and then I just kicked her aside as she clawed at the paint in her eyes and her mouth and her nose and she was choking on her screams and one of her legs was angled out so strangely now and I kicked her again and she doubled right over and her face through the clogging of paint was scared and pleading and so I kicked it hard until she fell back against the wall and just lay there. A slick of red had bubbled up over the white: she looked like a melted clown.

They gave me a bundle of ripped-open envelopes – pale blue, Basildon Bond – dozens and dozens of them – and my name and the address of this place was written in my mother's hand with my father's old Parker in blue-black washable Quink; at the top right-hand corners were these thruppenny stamps in mauve with the head of the Queen of England, smudged over heavily with a postmark reading London N.W. The letters, they said, had been quite unsuitable. They gave me too my birth certificate, and I read it then and there – I had never laid eyes on it before. I asked what year it was now, and they told me. I had no idea I was eighteen years old, but now I knew. Then they gave me some money, and then Mary appeared – see she gets to England, they said to me. I said I would: I did not see why I shouldn't. Here was a cover for them, I could only presume: two little Christians, leaving their place of education as a result of the kindness and wisdom of the nuns and priests of the Catholic faith.

We were on the boat and halfway across the sea before Mary said a single word to me.

'Where will we go, Annette . . .?'

'We'll go and see my little brother. In London N.W.'

Just these simple words were so thrilling to me – and yet I was numbed now by a total disbelief. I could not believe I had left there – could not believe I was in the middle of the ocean: could not believe I had got back my *life* (my soul – that could go to the Devil: he'd worked so hard – just let him have it).

And then later:

'They said, the nuns – that you are a sinner . . . There's white on your shoe, Annette . . .'

'It's not true, Mary. Don't believe them, Me, I'm not the sinner, The truth is, I am the *sin*. White . . . oh. That'll come off.'

So the very next morning, I chucked in my job at Smith's, which was quite grown-up, yeah OK it was, but also pretty scary. Mr Rooney, he said he was very disappointed in me – and might he enquire as to why I had arrived at so foolhardy a decision, and how instead I intended to spend my working day? I told him I was going to be a Carnaby Street tailor and the look on his face, then – he just seemed so utterly disgusted that I thought he might be going to be sick. Flash in the pan, he said – you don't want to let your head be turned by any of that nonsense, lad; at W. H. Smith's, you've got a job for life – work hard, do as you're told, smart young man such as yourself – no reason why in ten years' time you couldn't become, ooh, I don't know – branch assistant under-manager, maybe: look at me, Clifford – just you look at me. I've been with Smith's ever since the day after I left school at the age of fifteen, and I've not put a foot wrong. *History*, lad – that's what you want being aware of: Smith's – it's got *history* behind it, see? Two weeks paid holiday a year, staff discount – rising incrementally – voluntary pension scheme . . . do I really want to throw all that away for the sake of a bit of gimcrack fly-by-night tomfoolery in so-called ruddy trendy Swinging London? And I told him yes, I do – I do I do I *do*. He shook his head in sorrow – it was as if he had failed to dissuade me from leaping off the summit of the Empire State Building. Collect your cards, he said – you'll be docked for the whole of today – but it's not goodbye, Clifford. You'll be back, lad, after this here-today-and-gone-tomorrow little set-up of yours has shut up shop like all the others: I've seen it a thousand times. You'll be back – and don't think you won't, my lad.

So that was that – this is what is known as burning your boats – or bridges, is it? Burning something, anyway. I jolly well hoped that Anthony's Dad hadn't gone and changed his mind or anything, because I just couldn't now, could I, go back to Mr Rooney? Not after all he'd just said to me (and I noticed he said 'ruddy', which is just so square; my father, he used to say that, but that was in the Fifties).

But it was all OK: Anthony got Sid to drive me over to the factory which is in somewhere called Hayes – I can get there on the Tube, I think, or on some little railway or other – and a really nice sort of a bloke called Dave, miles younger than Mr Rooney, he showed me around. Basically what my job comes down to is guiding this huge sort of cutting machine and then tidying up the raw edges with this funny sort of pair of scissors with zigzag blades – they're called pinking shears, apparently, but they've got nothing to do with pink, or anything – it's just what they're called. Then I've got to sweep up all the trimmings and bag them and haul them round to this sort of bay place at the back. So there's still a bit of heaving involved – well, I knew there

349

had to be, really – but Dave, he said that if I was quick to learn I could soon go on to proper hand-cutting for what he called 'our more select line of garments for the discerning young gentleman about town' – which he then translated as a pricier bit of schmutter for all the chinless wonders who've got a few bob. I laughed, but I didn't actually know what 'schmutter' meant. I asked Anthony later and he said schmutter, Cliff, it's the name of the game – and I said oh, OK (I didn't want to push it; I mean I didn't know what a chinless wonder was either, to be perfectly honest, but you don't want to look stupid, do you? You know – *asking* all the time).

The other good bit about all this job thing was that I didn't actually have to start till the following Monday, but they gave me a whole week's pay in advance (two pounds more than mingy old Smith's) and so I suddenly had all this time on my hands and money in my pocket and the weather was all sunny and everything and so what I did was I went round to Annette's to see if Mary still wanted to go on that bus trip. And talking of Annette, you know – I felt really funny when I first saw her that evening, after all this time. I sort of realised how much I'd missed her. Which quite surprised me. Because I mean it's not as if we were twins, or anything, but when I was a little kid . . . I don't know, everything had something to do with her, if you know what I mean. Well I mean it *would* do, wouldn't it? Same house, same parents, both of us at school . . . she was older, and a girl of course – but still, I think at the time we must have been a lot closer, you know, than I actually realised. I don't know if she felt that – feels that: couldn't tell you. But it seems like we've got a lot to say to each other – although I still can't, you know . . . work out exactly what . . . but there must be, mustn't there? After all this time? Stuff to say. I don't think I want to ask her too much about Ireland, though – I get the feeling it wasn't good. Bad for her, it could have been. I mean, I'll listen – if she wants to speak, I'll listen, course I will; but otherwise, I don't think I'll bring it up, or anything. Won't actually mention it.

Grotty little room they've got. Makes where I live look like Buckingham Palace. Annette, she said she's got an interview for a job lined up (I don't know what sort of a job: she didn't say, I didn't ask – not Smith's, I hope) and so soon, she says, she'll get something better, somewhere nicer. I said to her, So is it OK, then – with you? If I, you know – take out Mary? On a bus or something?

'Jesus, Cliff – what are you asking *me* for? Do what you want.'

'Well – it's just that, you know – she's with you and everything, and—'

'She's not. She's not with me. We came over in the same boat – that's it. No one's with me. Do what you want with her. In fact, Cliff, you'd be doing me a very big favour if you *would* take her out. She's getting clingy. I can't bear clingy. Just can't bear it.'

'Oh. OK, then. Why are you calling me Cliff all of a sudden, Annette?'

'Am I? Was I? Didn't notice. You were always on at me to call you that, when you were at school.'

'Yeh well – that's when I was at school. I mean I don't *mind*, or anything – it's just that you never used to. You used to call me *Dopey* . . .'

And then Annette, she stepped forward quickly and kissed Clifford full on the lips, and then she held him there.

'It may seem strange to you, Cliff – but I love you. Oh God look at you now . . .! You've gone all red!'

'Yeh well – I do that. Don't I? You know I do that.'

'I love you, Cliff . . '

'Yeh. Well. I do. I do – love you too, Annette. And I'm pleased you're – you know. Back, and everything . . .'

'Good to be back. I can promise you that. Maybe, Cliff – if I can find somewhere, you know – decent, somewhere decent . . . you could maybe share it with me? So we're not alone.'

'Gosh. Well. That would be . . . But what about Mummy?'

'She should be used to it by now. Being alone.'

'Yes but I mean – I mean, then she'd *really* be alone, wouldn't she? With me gone. I mean – yeh, she's recovered from the death of . . . oh God – what should we call him? What do we say? It sounds stupid now, doesn't it? Saying Daddy. Sounds so stupid. Our *father* . . .? That sounds stupid too – our *father* . . !'

'. . . who aren't in Heaven. Call him nothing. He's gone. Doesn't matter. Anyway – think about it. OK, Cliff? And I'll let you know when I find somewhere. Oh yeh – I wanted to ask you: how do I join a library, Cliff? I'm desperate for books.'

'Really? Oh God – that's great. I'm really into reading and everything too. How funny. I can lend you books. But we never did it at home, did we?'

'Wasn't anything to read. Phone directories. *Woman's Own*. That was about it. Oh look – it's little Mary. Come in, Mary – don't be shy. Cliff wants to ask you something – don't you, Cliff?'

Yes well – not quite how I would have gone about it, but still. She looked all right, Mary – nice hair (I think she must have washed it, or something – it was only short, but really shiny) and she was small, smaller than me, which I liked: made me feel quite good. She was wearing the clothes that Anthony had given her – pink and blue floral little dress thing – and so was Annette. Well so was I too, come to that – the paisley shirt, so fab, with my elephant cords and the really wide belt. Shame about the Hush Puppies, though, but what could I do? If I spent all my week's wages on a pair of boots I'd have nothing at all left over for the other stuff I want to do. She kept on looking down though, Mary – it was just so hard always to even catch her eye. Anyway, she was still keen, apparently, to see a bit of London, but she'd assumed – and you just should've seen Annette's face! – that we were all of us going: the three of us on a bus. Oh no, Annette said very firmly – you can put that idea right out of your head: I don't want to go on some damn bus – I've seen London, Mary: seen it. Anyway – I've got an awful lot to do here. What was going on was – and this is quite funny, I suppose, in a creepy sort of a way – it wasn't that Mary particularly wanted Annette's company so much as she had believed that if she was with a boy, i.e. me, then she would have to have a chaperone! I know – hard to believe. So Annette, she said to her Look, Mary – forget, you've just got to forget all the lies and nonsense that the nuns filled your head with. Forget about *sin* – living, it isn't a sin, it's what you should *do*. This is the nineteen-sixties, Mary, and we are in London now. You just do whatever you want. Got it? Understand? Yes? Good. Now for God's sake get out of here, you two – I've got a mountain to see to. God. Did I really just say that? Eighteen years old, and already I'm turning into my mother . . . oh God oh God oh God.

It felt funny. It felt really strange, just walking down the street with a, you know – girl beside me. Because I know that Anthony was just always with girls, and things – God knows where they all came from; he's maybe got an uncle who makes them, or something (wow – wouldn't *that* be good . . .?). But me, well – the only girls I've ever met have either been with Anthony and all they ever talk about is how great Anthony is and how he gave them these miniskirts and won't they look great when they're on *Top of the Pops* (really thick, most of them are – but they've all got these really fab legs and all the other bits which are a hell of a turn-on, actually, even if they are all really thick). So either those or else the girls in Smith's who were what my mother calls common, which wouldn't have been so bad if they hadn't been just so rude all the time. All you had to do was just put your head around the door and they'd all be whistling and cackling and pretending to undo the buttons on their overalls and telling me to pull down my trousers and show them what I'd got and betting each other that I was still a virgin. Well of *course* I'm still a virgin – I'm sixteen years old. I mean, I suppose *they're* only about that too, most of them, but they all seem to be what Anthony calls slags. Not sure exactly what that is, but I get the idea. So Mary, you see – well, she couldn't have been more different. I doubt if she's even heard of *Top of the Pops* or Lulu or Cilla or any of that lot, and I don't think she could be rude to anyone even if she was paid to. It's all you could do to get her to even speak to you, actually, so at first it was pretty heavy going. She loved the Routemaster, though – she'd seen one, she said, on a postcard one time. I loved it too – I only ever went on Routemasters, and I always sat on the top deck, right at the very front – used to go with Daddy sometimes, but it's better without him because of that stinky pipe he was always smoking. And anyway, that's where we were now, Mary and me: the number 13, on its way to the West End.

'So you see over there, Mary? On the right? Quick – look quickly, or we'll pass it. See? That's Lord's. That's where they play all the cricket matches. See it? Did you see it? It's gone now.'

'The Lord's . . .? Is it like a church?'

'No – no it's – oh never mind. It's gone now anyway. At the end of this long road is Baker Street. Have you heard of Baker Street?'

'No. I've not. I know what a baker is, though.'

'No – it's got nothing to do with bakers. It's just called that. Have you heard of Sherlock Holmes?'

'Where is that?'

'No it's – it's not a . . . It's a person. The Great Detective. He lived in Baker Street, you see.'

'And he's passed on now, is he? God rest his soul.'

'No he's – well *yes*, I mean – well no, he's not passed on, he's not dead because he wasn't ever real. He's in books. He's character in stories, you see.'

'I've not read any stories. I've only ever read the Bible.'

'Oh right. OK. Well he's not in that. Look! There – just there, that's the site of 221b – that's where he lived.'

'But – he *didn't* live, is that right?'

'Um. Yeah. Never mind. It's gone now. At the end of this road there's this huge great shop. One of the biggest in all of London – Selfridges. Ever hear of that?'

'They sell fridges?'

'No! Well yes they *do*, I suppose – but they sell piles of other things too. They've got everything in there. There's nothing they haven't got. It's like Harrods – that's the other big one. They're both famous for selling just everything.'

'Oh that's a miracle. So they sell motor cars and—'

'Well no – no they don't actually sell motor cars, but they sell—'

'Dogs and horses? I love them, dogs and horses.'

'Um. I don't actually think they do, er – sell those, actually. Not sure. But everything else they've got. Look – there it is. See it? Isn't it huge? See all the flags and everything?'

' 'Tis like a cathedral. That's where the Church must buy the altars and the pews and the crucifixes and all.'

'Well . . . I shouldn't think they actually do sell all that. I doubt it.'

'But sure you said—'

'Yes I *know* – I *know* what I said, but they sell everything *else*, OK?'

'Have I upset you, Clifford?'

'No. No of course not.'

'You sound as if I have.'

'Well you haven't. Just leave it, all right?'

'You want me to leave you . . .?'

'No – I didn't say that. I said leave *it*, the subject, not me.'

'Because I wouldn't know where I was to go . . .'

'You don't *have* to – you're not going anywhere. Oh God. Look – we're coming up to Regent Street now, OK? And then at the end of that there's Piccadilly Circus.'

'Oh I've heard of the circus!'

'Oh my God. No – it's not a circus like a *circus* circus – there aren't any animals and things.'

'No dogs and horses?'

'No. Well there *might* be, I suppose, but it's not a show, it's just a place. Piccadilly.'

'Is that like – when you . . . pick a daisy?'

'*No*. It's not *pick* – it's Piccadilly, all one word. It means, um. Well I don't actually know what it means, but that's what it's called. And there's this statue there called Eros. That's the god of love.'

'God *is* love.'

'Yeh – yeh I know. But this is a different god – he's got a bow and arrow.'

'There is but the one true God.'

'Yeh I *know* that, but this is a god of *erotic* love. You know? Yes? No. No you don't. Well erotic love is when – well, it's what men and women do. Together. You know? Do you? Mary? What's wrong? Why are you looking down at the floor again? Mary? What's wrong? Why don't you say something? Look! Look! There it is! See it? Eros. The statue. See it? No you didn't see it, did you? Because you keep on looking *down*. Anyway – it's gone now. Look – we're turning into Haymarket. And no it's *not* a market, and there isn't any *hay*, all right? Oh God I'm *sorry*, Mary – no look – don't cry. Please don't cry. Look – we'll get off now, shall we? Yes? We'll get off now and then we'll walk to Trafalgar Square and we can see Nelson's Column yes? And the lions. No no – don't be frightened – they're not *real* lions, Mary . . .'

So yes – pretty heavy going, that first outing, really. The weather was lovely, though – so we went into the park and I sat down under the shade of a plane tree and Mary, she just stood there. I said, Well why don't you sit down? Mary? And she said You want me to sit down? And I said Well . . . not if you don't want to, but it's a jolly sight more comfortable than standing up, I would have thought. And she said So what you want is for me to sit down there beside you, is it? And I said Well yeah – but only if you want to, you know. And she said Well how would it be if I just sat over there, and I could call over to you? And I said Look – you can sit over there, you can stay standing up – you can go and find a different park altogether if it'll make you feel any better about it . . . and then I said Oh look, Mary – I'm – I'm – sorry – I didn't mean to – no don't cry, don't start crying again – I'll stand up, all right? Better? I'll stand up – look, I'm standing up now. See? I'm up. Is this OK for you? And then she said No, no no, it's all right Clifford – I will, I will: I'll come down there beside you. Bloody hell: I mean all I'd done was sit down and then stand up again and I was completely worn out.

So anyway, she did – she squatted down and wrapped her arms tight around her knees and buried her face into the crook of her elbows and then she said it was kind of my friend Anthony to have given her the dress – it was all so muffled, I could barely make her out – and that he would be repaid a thousandfold in the kingdom of heaven, but still she had to admit that she could wish it was a good deal longer. So she changed her position – sat with her legs swung under her now, one arm keeping her steady, but that lasted no time and then she lay down flat on her front and that was clearly no good because she then sat up and hunched her back away from me and was trying to swallow the whole of her head, it looked like to me – it was as if she was severely cross with all the young and pretty parts of her body for – exerting themselves, putting themselves forward, even being there at all, though I have to say that for

357

me the gathering effect of her continual motion was really very exciting – the complete reverse of all she intended, I'm absolutely sure of that – but just the curves and the elegance of her limbs and then the sheer wonder at the dark and hidden places where all were connected . . . I shuffled a bit closer and sort of circled round her a bit, but still she'd look just everywhere so long as it wasn't at me, but generally speaking just down at her feet as usual – they seemed to fascinate her a good deal more than all of her other bits and pieces put together. From my point of view, her feet were fine – I mean, feet are feet, if you know what I'm saying, and as feet went, well, hers were, as I say, fine, just fine – but as for all the rest of her, well wow. Wow, is all I can really say, you know, because I'd never been just sitting alone with a girl like this. I mean admittedly she was behaving as if I was about as attractive as a spadeful of contaminated waste, but at least she wasn't screaming and actually running away. But I realised that if I went any further towards her, there was a real possibility that she would unhesitatingly get up and do not just all of that but maybe even throw a hysterical fit or even an attack upon my person – because let me tell you: 'shy', it doesn't really come even close, you know, that word, to describing little Mary's condition. It was as if she was willing her whole self to be invisible, unwarm, unlovely, to dissolve into the air around us (she maybe wanted to join the angels). I said It's nice this, isn't it? Just sitting on the grass. And a couple of birds, they twittered above us in the tree and I said It's nice this, isn't it? Just sitting on the grass. A little boy, he tottered up, squealing and laughing, to retrieve his ball – and I said It's nice this, isn't it? Just sitting on the grass – and she nodded quite hurriedly and I thought she might even have spoken so I then rushed in with What? Did you say, Mary? Did you say something, Mary? And then she just went mmp and I said to her *Mmp*? What's mmp, Mary? Sorry, I didn't quite catch . . .? And then she said Damp, it's just a bit damp, is all.

The sunlight filtered through the branches of the tree and it dappled and lit her two rosy cheeks and the fall of her hair – it made just one of her arms so pink and warm-looking, and all the little hairs there were golden and downy. Oh dear. I was having the most terrible trouble with my own body, of course, like I did about a hundred times a day – at least now there was a reason why I had to squirm about and as subtly as I could manage to sort of tug and shift around a bit in my elephant cords; the tightness of them, and that socking great buckle on my belt, I'm telling you – they were just about killing me. Sometimes I could be, I don't know – looking at a pile of loaves in a bakery window and I'd become so bloody aroused that it was actually frightening. Other times, the TV would be droning out football scores for all the fools who do the pools – Queen of the South, Wolverhampton Wanderers, Lake and Orient, is it? – and there I'd be as if Ursula Andress had just stepped down from her poster and was pulling at her nipples, or something. I once got this magazine called *Parade* (not from Smith's, though – no, not from Smith's) and it was full of these nice and clean young girls, they seemed to me, and they're not wearing any clothes on the whole, and are all just grinning and with beach balls and poodles and parasols and things and their bosoms are really quite perky, really good, no complaints whatever, but where all their legs join up and boys have got all this stuff, there's just a blurry sort of nothingness, like a mortared-up air vent or something and it puzzled me for ages because I knew there just had to be a hole in there of some shape and description, just like there was in Annette, or else it just all of it, well – it just wasn't going to work, was it? Anthony told me that it has to look like that for legal reasons. I had this vision then of all the young and good-looking women in the whole of the country having nothing in their knickers except this dirty great trowelful of solid pink cement (for legal reasons). Anyway, the pictures in *Parade*, they certainly work for me – sometimes I don't have time to even get my trousers off, which I know, yeah, is actually pretty yucky, I admit that, but at least it shows how, well – eager I am, doesn't it? Mind you, I can be trawling the small ads in *Exchange & Mart* and the same thing can happen, so all I can assume is that I'm primed and ready – raring to go. God – if I so much as even looked at a climbing rope in a gym these days, well, I'd just about explode on the spot. And now the very first girl I get to be sitting alone with has to be Mary. Oh dear.

'So, Mary. Looking forward to going to Jersey? With me. Are you?'

'I'm not sure . . . what Jersey is, Clifford.'

'It's an island. I mean I don't know the first thing about it myself, if I'm completely honest with you. Never been there, or anything. Never been anywhere, really. But it's an island. You get there on a boat, on the ferry.'

'Is it like Ireland?'

'Much smaller. Better weather. People say it's a bit like France. I don't know. We'll find out though, won't we?'

'And Annette – will she not be coming?'

'She – no. No. There's just two tickets. It's just you and me.'

'Maybe . . . it's Annette you should be taking.'

'Why? Why should I want to take Annette?'

'Sure she's your sister.'

'I know. I know that. I know she's my sister. So why should I want to take Annette? I asked you. It's you I want to come. Why? Don't you want to go any more? Is that it? You don't want to come?'

Clifford now stared at her hungrily, but very aware that he had just somehow and clumsily opened wide the gate to a big disappointment. Maybe what she'll say now is Oh dear,

I'm awfully sorry but I just don't feel I should. Or ought to – however she puts it. Maybe she'll say that. Maybe she'll bang on about Annette again, I don't know. Or maybe – maybe she'll just say Oh no I'd *love* to come to Jersey with you, Clifford: I can't wait – when is it we're going? Maybe she'll say that. Look, face it – I just didn't know, did I, what in blue blazes the girl was going to come out with, but what she did eventually say – well, I gaped at her in silence, and then I just burst out laughing.

'Oh Clifford . . . I would, I would like to see this place, this island. But if we go together, just the both of us, then of course we must be married in the sight of God.'

It's then I gaped. And it's now I'm laughing.

'You – ! You're *joking*, yes? This is – sense of humour, is it? Mary? You look very serious. You're not joking, are you? No – no sense of humour going on here. Right. OK. Well – let's talk about that, Mary. Shall we? I mean – you do know, don't you, we're only sixteen, the two of us? Sixteen years old. That's very young, isn't it? We've got the whole of our lives before us, you know. All the things we can do. And also – look: we don't really know too much about one another, do we Mary? I mean – we've only just met. All we've done together is share a bus ride. It's maybe not the best basis, you know, the most solid foundation. For marriage. Not yet, anyway. Not at this stage. Don't you think? Don't you?'

'You're maybe right. It's a shame. I would have liked to have seen the island.'

'What? Wait – are you saying . . . you're not saying, are you, that we can't go to Jersey for a couple of days because we're not *married* . . .? You're not, are you? Mary? Saying that? Oh God you *are*, aren't you? Oh my God. Oh my God . . .'

'Please – do not take the name of the Lord in vain.'

'Hm? Oh – OK, then. Right. Sorry. But *listen* to me, Mary – people, they go away all the time, people do. They don't have to get married first. I mean – remember what Annette said to you, yes? It's the nineteen-sixties – we're in London. You do what you *want*. Life isn't a sin, is it? And, um – well I can't remember all the rest of what she said but you get the *idea*, don't you Mary? Hm? Don't you?'

'But this *is* what I want. I would like that very much. I think you are a good man. Clifford. We could the both of us raise a fine big Catholic family.'

'A fine big – ! Oh my God – sorry, sorry: *not* God, not – but, oh God, I don't know what you're meant to say if you can't say God. But I mean – how did we get on to a *family*, now? All we've done is sit on the top of the number 13 *bus*. Unlucky for some, right? No? Never mind. But look – we're barely more than children ourselves, for God's – for something's sake, Mary. I mean you've got to see that's *sensible* . . .'

'I regret your decision. I am sure you are wise.'

'Hm? No – no I don't want to be *wise*. I just want to go to Jersey, is all I want. With you. Why can't we?'

'We can.'

'We—? Oh. Oh good. Well that's all right, then. That's all sorted out, then.'

'But we must be married first. God is watching us at all times.'

Mm, yes – well I just bet he was peering down and having one hell of a laugh at this little lot. I just goggled at her – just goggled; it was all I could do. Her eyes were cast down – well of *course* her eyes were cast down – and her little nose, it's all covered, you know, with these sweet little freckles; her arms, they seem so long and graceful. Her bosoms are just filling out that little floral dress of hers so perfectly. So what a bloody pity, on the whole, that the girl's a complete and utter nutcase. She's got to be told – I've got to tell her. I mean she's just got to be put *right*.

'Well look, Mary – OK. Fine. All right. Whatever you say.'

'You mean you will?'

'Yup. Absolutely. We'll get married on the boat. They can do that.'

'There's a priest on the boat?'

'Sort of priest, yes. Naval . . . sort of priest. They can do that.'

'But sure a boat . . . it's not the house of God.'

'Well it is in some ways, Mary. I mean, the house of the Lord has many mansions, I think it is. And boats – they're sort of floating houses in one way, and God, he made the sea, didn't he? In his own image. Created it. Along with the earth. And if you want, we can do it in a proper church later. Some time later. All right? All right?'

'Well . . . you're sure it's . . .?'

'Oh yes. No doubt. No doubt at all. No doubt on that score.'

'Well . . . all right then, Clifford. But you must ask me.'

'Ask you? I did ask you.'

'Ask me properly.'

'Um. OK. Will you come to Jersey with me?'

'No. Not that. Our betrothal in the sight of God.'

'Oh right. That. Well, Mary – will you, um. Marry me?'

'Oh I *will*, Clifford. I *will*.'

'Good. Well that's all that arranged. Can I kiss you, Mary? I'd really like to.'

'Oh yes, Clifford. Yes! But only when we're married.'

'I see. Right. Well look – let's go tomorrow, Mary. Tomorrow – we'll do it tomorrow. OK?'

Yes: tomorrow it has to be. Because just looking at her legs and her face and her bosoms and everything, all I can tell you is this: if I don't get married really really soon, I'll just about explode on the spot.

It was only lately, I think, that I'd realised that I didn't actually know how to do anything – you know, the sorts of things that proper grown-ups have been getting on with for years without ever thinking about and just more or less take completely for granted. Like getting to the coast, for instance. I mean I knew where we had to be and when we had to be there and everything, and that obviously this would involve a train, I did understand that, but where did we get the train? You see? And how do you go about buying the tickets? And also, rather crucially, how much do they cost? Ordinary things like that. Packing: I'd never packed for a trip before, so what are you supposed to bring along? Not too difficult, this, as it turned out, because I didn't actually have very much, and I was wearing most of it. I did ask Anthony if there was a discount scheme for people who were nearly on the staff and he said Why? What do you want? And I said Well I could do with another shirt, and I just thought that if it wasn't too expensive . . . And he said I'll send Sid round in the car and you can pick one out, don't have to pay, free sample. And I said But oh God look, Anthony, you've already given me one shirt and I didn't say all that so you'd, you know – actually *give* me another, I mean I'm perfectly willing to – and he just cut me short and said No no no no no – that was a birthday present: this is a free sample. OK? And I said Well if you're absolutely *sure* . . . it's jolly decent of you: thanks a lot, Anthony: thanks a lot. So that and a toothbrush and I was pretty much sorted out. And Sid, he's really great, Sid is – he drove us to the right railway station, Mary and me, and saw us on to the train and everything . . . which was, OK, just a little bit embarrassing because I was after all sort of trying to be cool here, but it was a hell of a relief really because otherwise God alone knows where we might have ended up.

And all the way there on the train, Mary – who'd brought even less than I had, it looked like: just a little shoulder bag that was mainly filled with apples, it turned out. She crunched them just about ceaselessly. She was wearing the same floral dress she'd got from Anthony: all she had, I suppose. So Mary, all the way there on the train, the only thing she was talking about, when she spoke at all, was the naval priest who did the weddings: had he been ordained by a cardinal, did I know? Oh yes, I assured her – God, she did look lovely – Oh yes, a cardinal, a cardinal – one of the very top cardinals, I should think: maybe even the Pope himself. That shut her up for quite a long time; I mean I've no idea what she made of it, what I'd been saying, but it certainly did shut her up, anyway. So: this was going to be tricky, wasn't it? I'd been hoping in a pretty lily-livered and pathetic sort of a way that she might possibly have forgotten all about this marriage nonsense, but clearly she'd been thinking of nothing else at all. I'd tried to whisper to Annette to talk a bit of sense into the girl, but Annette just said that she'd no desire to talk to her at all and that it was my concern and nothing to do with her. I didn't mention any of all this to Mummy, obviously: well, obviously. She was pretty quiet when I left her – packed me up a lunch and gave me a Thermos with I'm not sure what it's got inside it, could be soup, and gave me an extra two pounds which I know she can't afford and then she said she hoped I had a really lovely time and not to bother with sending her a card or anything because I'd be back before it would arrive – and it honestly hadn't so much as crossed my mind to do any such thing – and then she said I should be careful. You will, won't you Clifford? Be careful. And I said Yeah, sure, course I will (don't know what she meant, but I think that's what she wanted to hear), and then she said Well just make sure you are. And I said I would. Be.

There was this person I found on the ferry. He had a navy blue blazer with brass buttons and a whitish beard and he looked the part, I thought – could have spent his whole life flogging Bird's Eye fish fingers. I was as red as blood, I could feel it, when I told him what I wanted. He stared at me and kept on saying *Married*? You want to be *married*? And I kept on saying Well yes – well *no*, not really I don't, but yes in a way. And he said I was very young, and I said I know. And then he said How much? And I blinked a bit and was going, How much . . .? How do you mean, how much? How much do I want to get married, do you mean? And he was roaring his head off at that (I think he was a bit drunk, to be perfectly honest with you) and he went No – no no: I mean how much money are you going to give me to pretend to marry you so that you can have your evil way with this guileless little innocent? Which did pretty much sum up the whole situation, to be fair to the man – I mean he did seem to grasp the gist of it – so I said, Well, I haven't actually got very much, to tell you the truth. And he said Now why doesn't that surprise me? Well how much have you got, laddie? And I said, Um . . . two pounds? And then he said – Two pounds? And I said I know it's not an awful lot, but . . . um – how about two pounds ten? And then he was off with his laughing again, and eventually he managed to splutter out No no – two pounds it is: you keep back the ten bob for your honeymoon.

So believe it or not, the terrible thing actually did happen. He put his peak cap on, pretty smart, and he gabbled on about Do you, Mary, take this man, Clifford – waffle waffle waffle, probably got it off of some film or other, I should think. From some film or other, I shouldn't wonder. I've no idea if the words were right or anything and I don't think Mary did either – hope not, anyway – and then he said to me: Do you have the ring? And well no of course I didn't have the ring. Did I? Didn't have anything. Between the two of us, Mary and me, all we seemed to possess were a couple of paisley shirts and a bagful of apples. So anyway, give him his due, the sailor man, whoever he was – he took out his packet of Player's and he pulled out the little bit of silver paper inside and he sort of twisted it around into a kind of spiral and he ended up with a pretty good wedding ring, actually. Mary, when I slid it on her finger, she gazed at it as if it had been solid gold and studded with rubies, and then she gazed at me as if I was a Beatle, or something. I now pronounce you . . . man and wife (bloody bloody hell) . . . and now you may kiss the bride. Which I did, like a shot, and God she did taste so good: so soft, so warm – all those things that girls are meant to be, she really really was. You get to thinking it's all just a rumour, you know – the softness and warmth of girls, but no, it's true: they really have got it. So then I sat Mary down in the cafeteria with a nice cup of tea – she was looking out to sea and in that whispery voice of hers she kept on saying Mrs Coyle . . . Mrs Coyle . . . Mrs Coyle . . . which is my Mummy's name, so it was all a bit strange – and then I went back to give the sailor man his couple of quid (amazing he hadn't asked for it before, really) and he was still just laughing like a drain and slapping at his legs – and I was absolutely sure that he was pretty pickled by this time – and I said to him Well thanks for that – and are you actually the captain of this boat then, are you? So then you had to hang around a bit more while he kills himself laughing again and then he says to me Nah, laddie: nah nah – not me. Turned out he was in charge of on-board catering: basically spent his whole life flogging Bird's Eye fish fingers. Still. He did the job. And then I thought well, I'd better get back to the wife.

The boarding house place was OK, I suppose – nothing really to compare it with. Two iron beds, we had: I thought maybe later I could push them together. The woman, owner of the place, she said the door was locked at ten-thirty prompt every evening and we were to let her know if we wanted an egg or just cereal in the morning. When Mary was upstairs, I'd told the woman that she was my sister. I've no idea whether or not she believed me – but you had to face it, it was a whole lot more credible than saying we'd just got married on the boat over, you know, and there's the silver paper ring to prove it – hand-formed by a sozzled ship's caterer who conducted the service; and the certificate . . .? It's in the post.

I was prodding one of the beds (Mary wasn't) and the sun came just suddenly and straight through the window and all that bright white light, it made her look, little Mary, oh just so very lovely, and so I went up behind her and I stroked her hair and she turned around and she said to me: Prayers. What? I said. *Prayers*, she said – why were there no prayers when we were wed? Well you see they save them for the big church service later – there's a rule about weddings at sea: prayers, they're thought to be bad luck. Like cats. I think it's cats. Anyway, one day when we're back in London we'll go to a cathedral and have all the organ and the choirs and as many prayers as you could wish for, Mary – more prayers than you can shake a stick at.

'Then let us kneel and say a prayer now, will we Clifford? To bless our sacred union.'

'Um – OK. Is it a long prayer, Mary? Only if it's a long prayer you want to say, we could maybe do it later. No? I don't actually know any prayers except going to bed prayers and grace and things. So you'd better say it for me. Mary . . .? Hello . . .? You're looking at me oddly again, Mary. You do keep doing that.'

'How can you not know any prayers? You're a Catholic.'

'Hm? No – no I'm not, actually. No I'm not. Mary . . .? What's wrong? What's wrong now? I never *said* I was a Catholic. Did I?'

'But sure you *must* be. Annette – your sister: *she's* a Catholic.'

'Well yes I suppose she is, sort of. I mean I don't actually know if she was baptised, or anything. She might have been. Don't know.'

'She wasn't *baptised* . . .?!'

'Well she *could* have been. As I said, I really don't know. I wasn't, anyway. At least I'm pretty sure I wasn't . . . I'm not anything, really. I mean yes – Annette, I suppose she's about as

Catholic as you're ever going to get, and Anthony – well he's Jewish, of course. But me, well – I'm just not anything.'

'You're a . . . *Protestant*?'

'No. I'm not. I don't think I am, anyway . . . I'm just a bloke. I'm not anything. Look, Mary – you must be tired. We've done a lot of travelling, haven't we? Today. Why don't you come and lie down – have a little bit of a rest? Hm? Look – look: *I'm* lying down. Why don't you come here and lie down beside me? Hey? Mary? Yes? Lie down? Hm? What do you say? Oh for God's sake come *on*, Mary. Sorry! I didn't mean God – for *my* sake, Mary: for my sake. Yes . . .?'

'If she was not baptised . . . if Annette was not baptised . . .'

'But she *might* have been. Look, let's just say she *was*. Shall we? OK? Leave it at that.'

'If she was not baptised . . .'

'Oh God. Not God. Sorry.'

'It would explain . . . if she was not baptised, it would explain how the serpent could have corrupted her – could have willed her to burn the holy crucifix.'

'Burn? Did she? Did she really? What – set fire to, you mean? How odd. Well I expect she had her reasons . . .'

'It was a wicked act.'

'Well they've probably got plenty more. Place like that – they'd make sure they never ran out, wouldn't they? Look, Mary – let's not talk about Annette and religion and all the rest of it any more, hm? Let's just – look, you come over here, yes? And just lie down beside me. OK? That's right – come on, come on, Mary . . . that's it, that's it – good girl, good girl, Mary. There. There you are. That wasn't so hard now, was it? No – wasn't hard a bit. So are you all comfy now, Mary? All right, are you?'

So she was lying beside me on this really narrow bed and her eyes were tightly closed and it didn't seem that she was ever going to speak to me or anything . . . and then I just suddenly went quite nuts. Everything I felt I should be doing or saying to her with a maybe coating of tenderness, it just got blasted away – I couldn't coax, I couldn't cajole, and to hell, quite frankly, with any more sweet talk. My need to do this, fast and now, just burned me up completely. I shoved my hand right on up her dress and she sort of yelped but her eyes stayed closed and I nearly screamed out at all that I was feeling there, this blood-hot mound and the papery creaminess of her thighs around it – I was raging, just raging – and I pulled and then I pulled and then I yanked at her pants and I tore the little things right off her then and she was breathing so hard and I must have been panting like a bloody locomotive or something and I was fighting with the zip and the catch and this great big buckle and then I was squirming down my trousers just away and around my knees and I fell on her then, just collapsed on to the top of her and I was battering hard and I couldn't get in and I hauled aside the two of her legs and I jerked up a finger and the heat that flooded over me there, it shocked me so much and I thought of Annette and I was so very wildly excited and I felt so scared and I rammed my way in and she squealed out once and I ploughed my way in deeper and she screamed so loudly and I put both my hands right on top of her mouth and I thundered in and out of her and I thought of Annette and then I just jackknifed up and juddered so hard as I exploded inside her and the sweetness and rippling of the gush of all that made me roar out now as I went stock-still and then I eased right away and I fell back flat and the oozing trickle away down my leg was all I was aware of now as my heaving chest, it began to subside and I just touched again that bounce of her hair on that little tight mound and I thought of Annette and it was all so strange.

And so having done with unsmilingly raping her, I cranked round my head now and looked at her profile. Her eyes, still closed, the lashes lit up by the sun; the cheeks just touched with a flush of warmth. And then she said Oh Clifford – and I was startled when she did it. Oh Clifford – now we have consummated our blessed union. I breathed out quite heavily and then I said to her Yes, yes we have – we did do that, Mary, we did. And the amazing thing was, I wanted it to happen again – right here and now, I wanted to do the whole thing all over again. But already she was standing now and batting at her dress as if it could be covered in crumbs. There's blood on the sheets, not too much, and all over my hand as well: I just now noticed it.

'Shall we pray together now?'

'You do. You pray, Mary. But come back here first. Come back.'

'Well shall we go and explore this island, Clifford?'

'Mm. Maybe later. Come over here, Mary. Come on.'

'Are you not hungry? I'm quite hungry now, Clifford.'

'We can eat something later. Come on, Mary. Come *on* . . .'

It went like that for the whole of the day, and well on into the next. Mary, she wanted to do all of these perfectly natural things (apart from the praying, of course – that didn't seem natural at all); she wanted to go walking, and eat some fried fish and maybe find somewhere we could have a cup of tea – and all I could think of was to drill her on the bed, grimly and again with an utter determination, and then I wanted to stroke and inhale her, and then I wanted to do it to her one more time. So she didn't ever get to leave the room, poor Mary. I'm sore, she said – Clifford, she said: I'm sore. And I said so am I: come over here, will you Mary . . .? And she said would they maybe bring us up a sandwich, do you suppose? And I said I was sure they would and I'd go down and ask them in just a minute's time – but listen, Mary, listen to me – just come over here now, will you? Just come over here.

Towards the end of the following day, something rather

terrible, I think it really must have been – something terrible just suddenly happened. I was, finally, sated – I couldn't think of slamming into her, not even one more time. And as I looked at Mary sleeping, I just knew I couldn't stand the very sight of her. She looked so pale and stupid, just lying there now – and I knew too that as soon as she was awake she'd want us both to pray, or else to eat a sandwich, and I was dreading the hushing whisper of her maddening little voice – it just so drove me crazy. Because apart from that bloody hole in her, I didn't even want a single part. So I put my spare paisley shirt into my bag and I got my toothbrush and the Thermos (it had been soup: chicken noodle with peas) and I bent down to kiss her but I found I didn't want, no, to kiss her and then on an impulse I took my pocket knife and I oh so carefully sawed away just this one little curly tuft of her hair. I put it in this tin that I carry around – one of my Daddy's old tobacco tins it is, and I keep in there what? A stamp, just a few coins and the little black Scottie from the Dogs of the World, the only thing that had somehow survived. I placed two pound notes and three half-crowns on the bedside table. I had got to the door and my hand was on the knob now and I twisted it slowly and the hinges yawned so jarringly and then she sighed out to me Clifford . . .? Clifford . . .? Is that you . . .? I said it was, and that there was nothing to worry about and she should just go back to sleep. Are you going, Clifford? Where are you going . . .? Just downstairs, I said – to get you a sandwich. Oh thank you, Clifford – thank you so much: you are my husband, and I do so love you. And God, he loves you too.

The sea was quite choppy on the crossing to the mainland. And I felt so free.

Mummy said to me There, Clifford – there on the table, look: see it? That's Annette's new address, and there's a phone number there too. She said to give it to you. She's worked like lightning, that girl; I don't know the street – it's not round here, anyway. West One – that's, well – West End, isn't it? I'd never want to live there, not with all the big shops and the to-ing and fro-ing and all the rest of it – no, I wouldn't care for it. And I said to Mummy, yeah – I've heard of this street. I could have passed it on the bus: pretty posh, I think. How did she afford it? Broke, wasn't she? Have you been round there? What's it like?

'Ooh you're asking the wrong person, Clifford. Annette, she never ever did confide in me. I can't imagine how she afforded it. I would've given her a little bit, just a bit, if she'd asked. But she didn't. You go, and tell me all about it and if she needs anything from the shops – tea or milk, maybe. Anything like that. She didn't ask me to go round. I would have, but she didn't ask. Anyway – so long as you're safe and sound, Clifford, and back in one piece. You haven't said much about it. Was it nice? Is it nice there? What was the weather like? We had spits and spots in the morning. Did brighten up in the afternoons . . .'

'It was fine, it was great. Don't think it rained. Look, Mummy – I think I'll go over and see her now, if that's OK.'

'Of course, dear. Please yourself. How's Mary?'

'Right – I'll go now then.'

'Leave your dirty things out and I'll pop them in the Hotpoint. And Mary – she enjoyed herself, did she?'

'It was fine. It was great. See you.'

Well – I didn't want to get into it, did I? I couldn't say I've no idea if she enjoyed it or not, being starved and rutted – and anyway I abandoned her. Could barely believe it myself – so I didn't want to think: didn't want to get into it.

I was right, though: it was posh. I looked it up in the *A–Z* and it's just off Baker Street – a leisurely stroll and in no time you could be consulting the Great Detective himself – you know, the one that Mary had never even heard of. I mean – that's one of the things that would've driven me totally crazy – well wouldn't it? I mean – you say: Sherlock Holmes, and she says: where's that? Unbelievable. Mind you, I wouldn't object to – you know: doing her again. But it's no good, is it? If you're just all over a girl and then after it's done and everything, you just . . . well, not *hate* her – I didn't hate her, didn't want to harm her, or anything. I just wanted her not to be there. Until the next time. It would've been good if she'd been like, I don't know – one of these portable tellies you can get now. You bring it out of a cupboard, watch the programme, turn it off and stick it back in the cupboard again. Well I mean obviously you can't expect *people* to, you know – be like that. Be good, though.

It's a flat-fronted terrace house and there's a sort of a half-circle window, fanlight I think it is, over the front door, and a hanging light. There are bells, and one of them says 'A. Coyle' – typed out. They're funny, these old houses, you know, because from the outside they look like, well – nothing at all, really – just a wall with windows and a door – but once you get inside, they're absolutely huge. Well this one was, anyway. Great big hall, black and white floor, marble I should think it is, and a winding staircase that just goes up and up and up. Annette had answered the door and said Hi and I said Hi and then she said I'm right up on the top floor I'm afraid and I said Well you just lead the way, and she did. You know – when I last saw Annette, she seemed to me to be, well – far more grown-up, fairly obviously, but still only a larger and curvier version of just my sister from all those years ago. But she looked different now, very – and I was trying to count the ways. Hair – very sleek, it is – and more new clothes, it seems to me. She looks a bit like Elizabeth Taylor, which is fairly amazing in itself. But it was the scent she was trailing behind her – that was really getting to me now – just so fresh and heady: not like anything I've ever smelled before. Mummy, she has her lavender water, but it's nothing like this.

Quite a climb, actually – fourth floor – but the flat she'd got up there was, oh – really terrific. I just loved it straight away. It's so much bigger than where Mummy and I are – the living room alone, I think – you could fit our entire little flat into the living room alone. Carpets going right up to the walls – sort of creamy colour. And the views are amazing – all these rooftops and chimneys and loads of trees beyond – Regent's Park, pretty sure: think it must be. And there's three bedrooms and a bathroom and a kitchen with all these fitted cupboards and everything, looks brand-new, and another little sort of a storeroom, box room thing.

'God it's fantastic, Annette. Amazing. Really cool. It's the sort of place Steed would live in. Really really cool . . .'

'Who's Steed? Do you want a drink, or something? There's some beer in the fridge. Or orange. Or I could make us some tea, if you like.'

'God – I haven't had a beer in ages. I'm still not actually quite sure if I like it or not, beer. Yeh – a beer, that would be good. Steed, he's this really smart bloke in a TV series. *Avengers*. Wears these amazing suits and goes around in a vintage Bentley.'

'Role model, is he Cliff? There's some glasses somewhere . . .'

'Well – not much chance of that, I don't think. Although I am going to be a tailor – did I say? Oh yeh, I did. So maybe I could make my own. Can't make the Bentley, though.'

'I'll buy you one, one day, Cliff. You just pick out the colour.'

'Ha! Thanks a lot, Annette. Thanks a lot. Hey but listen – talking of, you know . . . how are you actually paying for this place? I mean – it's expensive, isn't it? You said you were broke.'

'I can't quite believe how expensive it is. I thought for the money they were asking I'd own the whole house. But it's just for the rent of this one floor. And next month I've got to pay it all over again. I stole it. The money. Here – you pour it. I'm no good at things like that.'

'You . . . *stole* it? You stole the money? How? Who from? What do you mean you *stole* it, Annette?'

'I went to the shops and I stole all these clothes. It's very easy. No one seems to look. And then I brought them back again later and I said I'd changed my mind and I'd lost the receipt and they gave me the money. I've got a trustworthy face: I'm a nice little convent girl. Three times I did that. Different shops, of course. And then I did it one more time, but those I kept. They're really nice. Then I got my hair done, and everything. Manicure, make-up – anything they had to offer me. It's not completely worked yet, though. I still don't feel quite clean. OK, is it? The beer?'

'Mm? Oh, yes yes. It is actually. Quite nice. Well *blimey*, Annette . . . what else did these nuns have to teach you?'

'Quite a lot. One way or another. So anyway – what do you think, Cliff?'

'What about? Your new life as a criminal? Be seeing you on Wanted posters . . .'

'The flat. What do you think of the flat?'

'Oh the flat – well I told you. It's brilliant. Terrific.'

'So . . . do you want to, then? Share it with me?'

'Well gosh, Annette . . . I mean *yeah*, love to, but . . . and it's actually really near the Tube to work and everything too. I mean I think it's fab, but . . .'

'Mummy. Right?'

'Well yeah . . . can't just – *leave* her, can I?'

'Why not? People do. Leave. I'm assuming you just left Mary?'

'Hm? Well . . . yeh I did, as a matter of fact. How did you know that?'

'I would've. She's very boring. I daresay she'll go back to the hostel. I didn't leave an address.'

'Oh. So – that's the end of Mary, then.'

'Mm. I assume you fucked her, though.'

Clifford set down his glass, and looked away. Then he brought up his eyes and gazed over frankly at Annette. Her eyes were alight with maybe amusement, and they were maybe alight with something else too.

'I, um – did, yes. Many times, matter of fact . . .'

'Mm. I would. If I were a man I would. I do understand it. I hate men – for doing it. But I do understand. Do you want another one? Beer?'

'Mm? Oh – no. Haven't finished this one yet. Well, Annette – this is a rather strange conversation we seem to be having . . .'

'Everything's strange, I think. All of it is. So you enjoyed it, did you? Fucking her. Fucking little Mary?'

Annette's eyes, they were blazing now – she seemed to be suddenly so excited.

'I – did. Yes.'

'In her cunt. Liked it, did you? Fucking her in her cunt?'

Clifford licked his lips: sipped some beer.

'I did – yes. I did very much. Here – this might make you laugh. Or something. I don't know why I did this, but I did. Look – in this tin. See? That's a chunk of her hair. Don't know why I did that . . .'

'I remember those tins.'

'Huh? Oh yeah – it's one of Daddy's. Our father's . . .'

Annette just stared at the tin.

'Three Nuns,' she said. 'Would be. Of course. He was a bastard, you know. Our father. Who aren't in heaven . . .'

'Was he? Don't really remember. Why was he?'

'He sexually assaulted his daughter. Molested her. Did you know that?'

'I . . . no. I didn't know that. He did that? To you?'

'Mm. Well that's why I killed him, of course. I don't suppose I would've otherwise. That's why I pushed him off the roof.'

377

Clifford was standing now, and holding her shoulders.

'You did? You did that . . .?'

'Yup. The only thing that worried me was that he might not be dead when he hit the ground. But he was. So that was OK. So anyway listen, Cliff – what do you think? Do you want to? Come and live here? Be here with me? I think it would be really good. Do you want to?'

Clifford looked into her eyes.

'I . . . do, yes. I will, Annette. I will.'

'Why don't you kiss me, Cliff?'

'You smell . . . God you smell quite fantastic.'

'I know. Did you like it? When I talked like that?'

Clifford touched her cheek.

'Yes. I did.'

'I know. Well do it then. Kiss me.'

'I love you, Annette . . .'

'I know. And I love you. Kiss me.'

Her lips were soft, and sweeter than Mary's.

NIGHT

How much more time, I really have to wonder, can be granted to me now? As I do all I can do, and continue to lie here quite uselessly. There is the rest of my life to relive on this day; my life, of course – it is all I had; this day, is all that's left me. But few of us are so stupid as to imagine, I may only assume, that there really can exist some preordained structure to our mean existences – the very word, structure: it conveys to me an unquestionable solidity, the implication of symmetry and a rigid stability owing all to the diligence of its origin, an architect of stature. But this speaks only of a blameless building, erect but insensate, powerless in the face of its casual occupation, accepting of its periodic refurbishment and resigned to a coming demolition. There never was a life lived like this. And so rather, we might envision a lush and panoramic landscape – easy prey to the capricious and absolute powers of the elements and yet at the same time so sure and familiar and apparently negotiable, the peaks and chasms our ups and downs, the warmth of the sun before the lowering skies our highs, and then our lows: the very nature of the beast.

But no. If it is a structure, then it lacks foundation: it groans in the wind, only able to conceal so rank an inner and rising decay for just as long as slapdash masking continues to be guiltily applied. Then it will be listing and openly ramshackle; and soon after, it is condemned. And the only landscape that we can ever inhabit is that of the desert: a pitiless heat and the

381

mocking contours, the constant and imperceptible movement of the rolling and eternal dunes. We build on sand, and later lie among the ruins parched and blinded by the light as we clutch and are raving at yet another mirage when all that is real is the shadow of the buzzards, menacingly patient and wheeling up above us. And should we ever feel the whisper of their lazy undulations, glimpse the gleam in a rapacious eye, then we idly set to wondering about the identity of whichever unfortunate it can possibly be who is now so close to very extinction, soon to be a whitened carcass, later to be whitened dust. The desert – it is the waste of life; the desert is the waste of it.

Memory, though, it swoops down like a missile so unerringly and always to the centre of the heat of the moment. So I am entering, now, into the bliss of Melissa – so long after, so very many years after I ceased even to wonder myself over how I could not ever mind that Annette, she had killed my father. Why I had been so careless about the duping and abandoning of Mary. And how I did so smilingly leave my mother alone, and to her poor resources (and Christ in heaven, just look, will you, at what happened then). But by the time of Melissa, I no longer was amazed by any single thing that I did; though still I was to be ever more astounded – brought as I am to the very point of death – by the actions of Emerald, my blackly glittering lady.

And *still*, you know, it won't let me . . . the tug of my memory, again it is taking me elsewhere. To one more stop along the way. Sonya. A strange love, and another of my wives.

'Was there something wrong with the meat, Clifford? Something not quite right? Not to your liking, was it? Clifford? The meat? Tell me.'

'Mm? Meat? No no. Fine. It was fine. Just a bit too much. That's all.'

'Because if there was something wrong with it, you know, I'd really prefer it if you told me. I won't be offended. I'd really like to know because then I'll be in a position, won't I? Not to make the same mistake again.'

'There's no mistake. None. It was good. It was fine.'

'Truly? Truly good? Or fine? When you said fine, Clifford – and I know I go on about this, I know I do, and I hope you will forgive me – it's just that I need to get it all clear, you see. Cut and dried. Out in the open. I can't bear, what is it . . .? Ambiguity. Is that the right word, Clifford? You're so wonderful – so very wonderful with words. Is that what I mean? Ambiguity. Is that the right word?'

'It's *a* word, certainly, Sonya. I can't be expected, however, can I? To know beforehand whatever it is you are trying to say.'

'Well that I want everything to be – not confused in any sort of a way. Black and white.'

'Mm. Yes. Then you do indeed wish to avoid any trace of ambiguity. Will all this take long, do you imagine . . .?'

'Am I tiring you? Are you tired? I must be, I suppose. Tiresome, sometimes. To you.'

'Say what you mean to say, Sonya. And then we can leave it alone.'

'Well all I'm meaning, Clifford, is that when you said just then that the meat was . . . well you said two things, you see. You said it was good – well that's good, good is good – but then just afterwards you said it was fine, you see. Didn't you? You said it was fine. And I just need to know, Clifford – and then I'll leave it alone, leave you alone, I promise you I will – it's just that I need to know if you meant it was "fine" as in – supreme, excellent, at the top of the tree, sort of thing, or just "fine" meaning, you know – OK, so-so, perfectly sort of . . . adequate. That's all. Because – well *you* know this, Clifford, with all your words. You know that the language, well – it can be funny, can't it? Sometimes. With words we use nearly every single day of our lives, and maybe we – or the other person, that's more to the point, isn't it? Maybe we don't ever really quite know what exactly we're saying to one another.'

'Mm. There are many such words. "Nice" is one. "Nice" is certainly one of those.'

'Nice? Nice is . . . pleasant. Isn't it?'

'Often. Usually. But it means "exact". Exact is what it actually means. Not that anyone would know, I suppose, these days. Or care. "Quite" is another. Quite, it used to mean absolute, you know. Utter. So "quite nice", strictly speaking – it means completely and totally precise. Whereas now, of course – well . . . it has simply come to rather sloppily denote a sort of a . . .'

'Pleasantness. Yes. Sorry to have interrupted you, Clifford.'

'Quite all right. And I'll leave it to you to decide the nuance of my meaning there, Sonya. "Love". That's another one.'

'Love?'

'Oh yes. Many shades – many colours. Quite apart from the working-class habit of using the word as a casual endearment. They used to say "ducks" or "dearie". Then they started to say "love". A gift, really, to these haughty bloody feminists. These Women's Lib types. To draw themselves up . . . or in . . . up and in, I should imagine, and retort so bloody cleverly: "I am not your *love* . . ." Tedious. Very tedious.'

'I've no time for women like that. Have we, Clifford? But anyway, look – about the meat, yes? Which way did you mean it? Just so I know for the next time.'

'Very well, Sonya. There is nothing amiss with the seeking out of accuracy. I meant that it was a very superior piece of beef, most

384

satisfactorily cooked, presented and garnished, with vegetables that were both suitable and suitably al dente. Not the "finest" meal since the creation of the world, but very much higher than an even generous average. All right? Clear now, is it?'

'Yes. It is. Thank you, Clifford. Would you like me to . . . what would you like me to do for you now? Would you like to go to bed? Would you like me to put my mouth around you?'

'I think I am content to read now, Sonya. Why don't you do the same? Plenty of books you have yet to get to, Sonya.'

'Some of the books you give me, Clifford . . . I find them quite hard, you know. I'm never quite sure that I understand what the author is saying – *underneath*. All these novels, they've got layers, haven't they? The characters, they can be saying one thing, but then there is a . . . what did you say it was? When something is unspoken, but still undeniably *there* . . .? Subtext? Was it? Anyway, I think it's just that I like things to be plain. You know? If these characters, these characters in a novel, if they just came out with exactly what they *meant*, well . . . we wouldn't have to, would we? Dig around. For all the things that are underneath. All their secrets.'

'Maybe, Sonya, I shall have just a drop more wine. This Pauillac, I have to say – it really is most singularly good. Shame you don't like claret.'

'Or any red wine, really . . . I find it a bit . . . It's nearly finished, this one. I'll open another one for you, Clifford. *Heavy*, really . . .'

'Thank you, my dear. And do you know . . . your mouth, your sweet little lips . . . suddenly they do assume a charm of their own . . .'

'I will, Clifford, I will. I love to. I'll just open the wine first, shall I? Oh – Clifford . . .?'

'My dear . . .?'

'It wasn't beef, you know. Actually. It was lamb, the meat.'

'Ah yes – but *nice*, Sonya. Quite nice, was what I was meaning. Wasn't it? Now then . . . you do all those things. Yes? And then I think an early night would not be too bad an idea.'

'Oh I do so *love* you, Clifford. I really really do.'

'I know you do, my sweet. And the love I have for you – it really is, quite extraordinary.'

♠

Sometimes, with Sonya, it's rather as if the two of us have only just recently been introduced. As if she is aching to please (which, of course, she is – often quite literally) and keenly divining in me any recent little whim or peccadillo. Now there's a word: peccadillo. Annette, she had not heard of this one – this one was new to her – and it incensed her beyond measure, I am so delighted to say. We test each other out, you know, with any new word, and virtually daily – she catches me, of course, but less and less frequently. Her reading is still quite voracious, I have to say (how she packs it in with all that she is doing, well – I do take my hat off to her), though it remains I who seek out the more esoteric writers, the more out-of-the-way fiction, far less mainstream; and of course nightly I still keep on trawling my Chambers, ever on the lookout for tidbits and gems. But anyway: Sonya, yes. I am aware that many would envy me. I am in the grip of the eternal honeymoon. Excellent in many ways, of course, though the fundamental unreality of so rose-tinted a condition, it would seem to have precluded the building of any more solid foundation. She seems to greet each morning as a brand-new and gleaming opportunity to please me, and she is ever ready to dissolve into an almost delirious delight at the merest whiff of any little treat, no matter how spurious, that she imagines might be coming her way. She is, as the phrase goes, easily pleased – though her constant and sometimes pathological enthusiasm for pleasing me in turn, well . . . it can become a trifle wearing: wearing will do. There are many husbands – and of course I do know this – who conversely feel quite totally ignored – snubbed and redundant. It is the balance that seems to be the so elusive thing: the plateau of contentment, mutually achieved. But although I have many escapes in place – wholly courtesy of Annette, of course (but of course) – I do have to confess that having made my escape, it is then my great pleasure to return. Sonya is really a most excellent person to return to; and her gratitude when I do so, it is suitably overwhelming and in addition, I must say, so perfectly satisfactory. Money, quite naturally, is the great enabler; without it, one of us by now would most surely be dead. And the money, well . . . I suppose it is Annette whom once again I have to thank for all of that. Suppose . . .? No shilly-shally: there can be no 'suppose' about it: the indulgence is wholly Annette's, however far she goes to dressing it differently: Annette is the hostess of all our parties. Oh it's not to say that I don't earn money – I do, I do. I have a small but very select portfolio of customers, and sometimes there is so much work to be done that I am impelled to turn down more, even if they come with the very best introduction.

It is such a long time since I was merely a bright-eyed pattern-cutter in that dingy old factory in Hayes – all been flattened now, I understand: another of these out-of-town shopping centres, according to my information (and who is it, please tell me, who actually would of their own free will elect to visit such a place?). But I remain indebted to young Hirsch and his father, because without them I might never have discovered my talent. It is the only one. I have never been able to do anything at all, so you may imagine that the discovery of a seemingly genuine ability was a matter for some rejoicing. I found I could cut cloth with shears, and even freehand with a knife – usually this takes years, they told me (and I have to assume that here was more than mere blandishment), and so I was quite rapidly promoted to the made-to-measure side of things. Just pockets and waistbands at first, of course (I was, I shiver to remember, only a little more than what can I have been, by now? Seventeen? I doubt I was yet eighteen), and then later, under supervision, my very first jacket – or coat, we call them. I made it for Anthony – and this cluster of wizened old Jewish tailors, they were watching my every single move, suggesting the occasional minor adjustment, and always so patient and very kind to me: I'll never forget them. The coat, the whole venture took a ridiculous amount of time, of course – they really were so very indulgent towards me – though the result, I have to say, was not wholly discreditable. Anthony, dear old chap – he pronounced himself quite thoroughly delighted with this really very standard little garment I'd made for him (although what he probably said to me was 'Groovy!' . . . if still we said all that sort of thing by then: it's so long ago now, I honestly can't remember) – and to give him his due, he not only wore it and wore it, this damned little coat of mine – blue-grey herringbone, twelve-ounce Holland & Sherry, as I recall – but he never ceased to broadcast to just anyone he encountered the identity of its creator. It did most thoroughly inspire me: my confidence was high, as a young man's confidence simply has to be. I remained there for quite some years, learning the trade, quickening the process, and filling in what leisure hours were left to me (and gradually and quite voluntarily, they became fewer and fewer) with pubs and girls, the usual thing. The girls, they were Anthony's cast-offs, to start with: stupid, beautiful, often stoned and thoroughly lacking in any concept of morals: a perfect combination at the time. And then the pubs became wine bars, and the girls became my own and not – as Anthony enjoyed to say – secondhand, but in really good nick (I took the quip upon the chin – and then I took the bird: we called them birds). The girls I met in the wine bars were, yes – far less stupid (not altogether too difficult) and generally far less beautiful as well; it took me a while to decide which combination I preferred (because the marrying of the two better halves, that for now appeared not to exist). For a long time I lied to myself that of course intelligent and homely was the wise man's choice. The fool in me, however, was ever drawn back to the pink-lipped, long-haired, false eyelash-batting thick and pretty pushovers; it is only quite recently – and again I am indebted to Annette – that I feel quite comfortable with embracing the truth, and then this quite wonderfully easy option, grabbed with both hands. Whereupon I return to Sonya . . . Because she'd known, Annette, hadn't she? Known me through and through, like she always did. Knew that Sonya would be good for me. That's what she said when she brought us together: you come to me whenever you choose, Cliff – but you need a base. You need something to go back to. And that something is Sonya: she's no good to me, not in what I do – but for you, Cliff, for now: I think she's just perfect. Annette, on the rare occasions that she comes over here, she can be very cruel, you know, to Sonya. Jeers at her, laughs at her humility – tells her she would have made a quite perfect nun. It used to make me uncomfortable. Sonya, though, she accepted it all. She sometimes even appeared to thrive on it, so far as I could see. You should try it, Annette said: abuse her. I've no need to, I told her. No, she said, but maybe Sonya – maybe she does; do you beat her? No, I said: no. You maybe should, said Annette: do you want me to? No. I said: no. My marriage to Sonya, it had been a very low-key affair indeed; Annette, she arranged it all: saw to everything.

So anyway – there I was, cutting away and stitching. The money was getting better; pitiful, of course, by today's standards – but way back then, a pound was a pound, if you know what I'm saying to you. So I could help out my mother rather more than formerly – and it was my very great pleasure to do so, you know, because she never quite got over, poor old thing, my leaving her the way I did. Quite literally, I was here with her one day, and gone to Annette the next. How callous, how unthinkingly selfish the young can be (and not just the young, of course: not just them). I visited her often – at first I did, and I gave her as much as I could. And then, as the twin demands of girls and wine bars made themselves ever more felt, I visited infrequently: gave her less. Then it got to the stage where I would drop her just a card, and on Annette's answering machine there would then be a plaintive message, largely about how she loathed to speak on this blessed machine, and eventually to merely convey to the two of us, Annette and myself, that she hoped we continued to stay well and that she for her part was blooming, and so not to go worrying ourselves on that score. It was only after Annette had bought me a flat of my own (her business then, it had started to expand) that I felt I had to say it: Look, I said – we really have to do something, you know. We can't let Mummy live there any longer, in that pair of horrid little rooms. OK, said Annette – I'll get her somewhere else: not too near, though. What do you think she'd like? And I laughed – a bittersweet memory of all the rose-strewn cottages and castles that I had promised her down the years. Oh, I said – just a decent little flat and somewhere acceptable, I should have thought: garden flat, maybe, so she can get out a bit, grow a few flowers. Fine, said Annette – I'll see what I can manage. And then I said, Um – look, Annette, would you mind terribly if, um . . . well, would it be OK if it seemed as if it were *me*, I who was buying the flat? For her? It's just that I so often said I would, and . . . Oh *God*, Cliff, went Annette: you can tell her whatever in Christ's name you please – choose it, if you want. God knows I don't have the time: just square the money side of things with Tumulty, OK?

(That's Edgar Tumulty, I might say – Annette's sort of right-hand man, I suppose, and general fixer.) He's good, she said, at squeezing a bit more from that creepy little bank manager that I seem to be stuck with. OK, I said: and thank you, Annette. You don't have to thank me, Cliff – not for anything, not ever. She kissed me, then – quite tenderly at first, and then with her more customary ardour. We drank some champagne, and then we went back to her bed.

Years ago, of course, all of that – though the pattern remains substantially unaltered, spiked though it is with the odd diversion. Annette, she is not a jealous person, which I must admit does continue to astound me. She'll lend me a girl for the afternoon, quite often gift-wrapped; Oh, I say – what a touching thought, how terribly sweet, you know you really shouldn't have, Annette. And as to my being with Sonya, of course – well, Annette's idea, wasn't it? The whole thing. Nothing at all to do with me. She really has done so very much for me, all down the years, this sister of mine – but do you know what it was that gave me the greatest thrill? The thing that I appreciated most? Well, that flat; not my flat – not the one I live in with Sonya, no (perfectly nice though it is), but the one that, courtesy of Annette, I – or the bank – was finally able to buy for my mother. And the moment I loved most of all was when she finally saw that this time and at last I was no longer the prattling child, promising her the world, but her grown-up man, making good.

We looked at quite a few, Mummy and I, before we found 'the one'. The estate agent – and where on earth do they find these people actually? With their damned awful suits and such implacable pride in their fathomless ignorance? – he would keep on insisting, this shabby little huckster, that the pokiest sort of a hole was actually deceptively light and spacious, but then of course he was quite perceptibly vile and stupid and evidently imagined that we were too – huddled together in a small dark warren, demonstrably unable to appreciate its bright and latent roominess. The flat we eventually went for – I found it quite by fluke, as is so very often the way. I was driving around Hampstead one sunny afternoon in my . . . did I say this? Have I mentioned that I've got one? In my Bentley. I do so love just saying it; it's from the Sixties – an S2 – dark blue with a pale grey interior. Very beautiful in every way and remarkably reasonable, you know, these fine old cars are; for the same money you could very easily come away with a garish and plasticky little play-thing – and people do, of course: people do. Annette, she'd urged me to get any model I wanted, but you know I do some-times feel that she is rather too profligate for her ultimate good. I mean to say *yes* she's doing well in her chosen profession, but there is a limit, you know: money doesn't grow on trees (I dared to say it – she practically brained me). Anyway, I'd become rather lost – I can't have been concentrating – and I'd found myself down at the bottom of this rather narrow road not too far from the edge of the Heath; I was idly supposing that I might have to back my way out of there (that's the drawback about the Bentley – it's all things but nifty; the turning circle, it's that of a bus) and out of the corner of my eye I glimpsed this little For Sale board, modest thing, nailed on to a tree, some tiny agency I'd never even heard of. There seemed to be a separate entrance to this garden flat – the unmade path wound around to the side beneath a rustic arch well laden with wisteria. Early nineteenth-century, the house was, I should have said – full-length windows with the slenderest of glazing bars: rather worth viewing, I con-sidered. Mummy, her initial enthusiasm over making the move had evaporated by this time – she became actually physically diminished, you know, every time we looked over yet one more dank and charmless little hovel (I watched her spirits sink) and it was all I could do, you know, to make her come with me. I think we both of us knew, the moment we stepped through the door. A beautifully light front room, half-panelled and with a working fireplace; Rayburn in the kitchen – two good-sized bedrooms. The garden was a place of enchantment: the glitter in her eyes was a thing to behold. I haggled over the price, of course – Hampstead, it's never been known for bargains – but they were barely budging. Annette, she said to me: that flat – done the deal? Well not exactly – they're being awfully stubborn about the price. But she likes it, yeah? Oh yes: it's terrific. Well pay them the bloody money and be done with it, Cliff – what the hell's wrong with you? (Mm – she can be very forthright, Annette: says what she means. Maybe why Sonya absorbs the abuse: at least she knows where she stands.) So I did – I paid them the bloody money, and then I was done with it.

We had the place decorated, well naturally we did – all her own choice of papers and colours: she was surprisingly efficient, Mummy, you know, and endlessly enthusiastic about the whole business. She specified the sort of light fittings she wanted, and while demurring at her taste, I set to tracking them down: they looked magnificent, once they were installed – quite perfect. I found her a little Regency bureau (I had to dip into my savings, but God knows she's worth it) and she was thrilled with that – all the little cubbyholes. The kitchen was in a very good state, so we left that pretty much intact – changed the tiling, though: Mummy wanted red. Red? Are you sure, Mummy? What, red as in *red* red, do you mean? You've never had anything red before – do you remember when I wanted my room to be red, at the old house? You said to me not to be stupid. Poor Clifford, she said: poor Clifford. Yes – *red* red: like blood. It was generally around this time she began to be surprising. You hear about older people, don't you, acquiring a 'new lease of life' when something fundamental occurs. Well here, somewhat belatedly, it rather seemed to be. What are you taking from the old flat, Mummy? Nothing, she said: nothing at all. What – literally nothing, do you mean? Yes, she insisted: nothing at all, literally.

Well, I said, there's not an awful lot to take, of course – but the radiogram, presumably . . .? Particularly not the radiogram, she said – I never ever want to see it again. Rather predictably, she changed her mind about that at the very last moment. Where do you want it, the old radiogram, Missus? That's what one of the removal men asked her, as he held it aloft in his two mighty arms. In the garden, she said – up against the far wall. The *garden*, Missus? You sure? Positive, she said so quietly: positive. So he heaved it out there, did as he was told; for myself, I said nothing. Later in the week I went round there, and kicked at its ashes; she had so much enjoyed that, she told me: setting it ablaze. It was a way of ridding herself, she said – ridding herself of the guilt and burden of all those wasted years when all she ever did was polish and polish the thing, so that her Arthur could take a pride when he put on his records. Which she had smashed to pieces; those that wouldn't break she had thoroughly contorted and scored with a knife. Amid the crunch of debris, I spotted the occasional shard from the kookaburra lamp, the one with the hat on. As I said, this was the time she began to be surprising. We toasted the new flat with champagne, Mummy and I (Annette, she said she was too busy), and Mummy said two things about that: the bubbles, they tickled her nose, and the taste, she very much liked. But that very same week, when everything was sweet and so much more settled than ever it had been, that very same week we got the call about Grandma.

We drove over in the Bentley, Mummy and I (Annette, she said she was too busy), and I was gratified to learn that we were not too late. All the way over, Mummy did not talk about Grandma at all – all she spoke of was the car. It's such a shame, she said, that Daddy never had one: the days out we could have had, the picnics we all might have gone on. Do you know, Clifford – and I hate to ask, because you've already been so very good to your old mother: I had no idea that your tailoring was going so terribly well (I let it lie). But do you know, Clifford, I would very much like a little car of my own. A car? Really? But Mummy you can't drive. Well of course I know *that*, don't I Clifford? I should have to learn – I do understand that: Jean Beery, she learned to drive, so I don't see why I shouldn't be able to as well. Well no of course not, Mummy – but Mrs Beery, well . . . that was an awfully long time ago. Well, Clifford – better late than never, no? And I laughed – it was delightful, really, all of this. All right then, Mummy – I'll see about lessons: I'll see about it in the morning.

Grandma, she was unrecognisable. Not unrecognisable as Grandma, I don't mean, but unrecognisably human. She seemed stranded in a desert, the texture (not that I touched) of her hand and withered body – quite close to tree bark, or maybe air-dried jerky, her eyes two milky egg whites. Her last whispered words to my mother were that she wanted her to have the electroplated biscuit barrel, because of what use now could it possibly be to her? Biscuit barrels are for the young – and just look at me, Gillian: I'm old. I'm old. And then she sighed out her last. It was difficult to judge, Mummy's mood. All she said on the way back home was that Grandma, she wasn't old. Well, I said – she was *really*, wasn't she? Old? Grandma? And then she replied quite testily that I didn't at all understand her: when she said that Grandma was not old, what she meant to convey was the truth that she had been beyond even ancient: she had been virtually dead for just years and years and years. I, Clifford, am not going to be like that, not ever – do I hear her? And I said Yes, Mummy, I do: I hear you well. I dropped her back, got her settled and then before I drove away (I had a funeral to arrange, and also a course of driving lessons) I said to her Well, Mummy – what a sad day. Are you sure you're going to be all right?

'Well of course I'm going to be all right, Clifford. What an extraordinary thing to say. Why shouldn't I be all right? I've always been all right.'

Well – not quite true, but Clifford, I doubt if he listens to half of what I say – probably thinks I'm just a dotty old woman. But I haven't, not always, I haven't always been all right. But I am now. And it's going to get better. I don't know yet what direction I shall take, but something, I feel sure, will soon be presenting itself. And then I shall be unstoppable. Because I *have* to be, you see. I owe it. To myself. I am in debt. To myself. And it may sound stupid (which is why I would not voice it) but I feel it is time now to pay me back. Because it may well be true, you know, that life is for the young – that's what Mother always said, and me, I said it too. But where was life, then, when I was young myself? I never had it; I never saw it. If I could have come close to defining life – a thing I would never have presumed to do – then I should have said that it was either merely a rumour, or else a light that would come on somewhere else entirely. A woman's liberation is long overdue. And so what little life there might now be left to me, well . . . I'm just going to get on with it.

'I've got the figures here, Miss Annette. Just leave them for you, will I? Have a glance?'

'Oh thank you, Tumulty. How are they looking?'

'Well . . . they're a bit . . . well to be honest they're just a bit . . .'

'Bad. They're just a bit bad, right? Again. How bad? Very bad?'

'No no – not *very* bad. Not *good*, it's fair to say . . .'

'Mm. Well just leave them, will you, Tumulty? I'll get to them. Oh Christ. It's all going wrong.'

'It's the girls, Miss Annette. If we could just get more girls . . .'

'Yeh well. We've tried, haven't we? Done all the usual. They're just not around like they used to be. It's not like it was in the old days, is it Tumulty? When we had our pick. Couldn't put a foot wrong . . .'

'Happy times, Miss Annette. Maybe things'll look up soon, ay?'

'Let's hope.'

Yes. Let's do that. We can hope – we surely can't bloody pray, but yeah – we can go on hoping. Until hope runs out, and then what? Got to *do* something – and for the first time ever, I just don't know what. Because it's *not* like in the old days, no it bloody isn't. Christ – back then, when I was new to it . . . couldn't put a foot wrong. I didn't even, I don't think, ever make a conscious decision that this is eventually what I was determined to do – it was almost a sort of destiny, in a way, if that doesn't sound mawkish, or simply ridiculous. It was just that I knew, when finally I got back to London, away from all that Irish air, so that I could breathe again – and I was only a girl, only a child, barely eighteen years of age – that there was no sort of penury nor enclosure that ever again I could dream of enduring: the tyranny of a drab and stupid job, for how miserable a wage? The dinginess of a small back room, somewhere bleak – the very thought, it made me shudder. And nor could I have borne it even for the interim. I remember – God, and I remember Cliff's face too, when I told him so simply (he was only a kid, remember: only a kid in those days) how I had just coolly lifted all those clothes and got back from the idiots the money I needed and rented this really rather excellent flat near Regent's Park (I really enjoyed living there, for however long it was) and then I just had to treat my body – my body needed balm, after all those years of harshness and abuse. I had no idea, of course, how the following month's rent was to be dealt with – and in order to eat, well I couldn't be relying upon stealing coats and jackets, could I? Apart from its inherent unsuitability

397

as a long-term career prospect, I was all too aware that luck, it shouldn't ever be pushed. It just needed one single store detective who wasn't completely idle and stupid, and that was me finished before I'd even begun. These days, of course, with all the security cameras wherever you look – well, I wouldn't have stood a dog's chance. Luck, you see? That shouldn't be pushed.

So I sat down and frankly assessed my situation. I had no education, no technical skills bar the setting of bonfires and the steeping of laundry, and of course no, oh God – contacts. I did, though, have my beauty (on a good day I am still not too unlike Elizabeth Taylor – when she was young, I mean) and my guile and my wit – those things that The Mission had failed to destroy in me – and I also was possessed of a determination to not just survive (I had been doing that, hadn't I? All my life on earth) but to conquer, to overcome, to be fully in control. Of something. (God, I daresay, knew what; well – being all-seeing he would, wouldn't he? I wonder if he liked what he saw? I do so hope that he was at least severely wounded.) All I had to sell was myself – this much had to be faced – but it was going to be on my terms. I was frightened – of course I was frightened – but right from the beginning, anyone concerned would just have to understand that this: it was going to be on my terms. Because were it not so, well then . . . well then they had won, hadn't they? The nuns and priests. They then would have made me into a humiliated slavey, forever at the beck and call of those I most despised. So what I did was, I bought a copy of – I think it was called *What's On*, or something like that. It listed all the cinemas and clubs and everything else that went on in London. There was a section with advertisements for models and French teachers and all the rest of it (innocent times – all so very different now) and I simply rang a few numbers, completely at random. Well – total nightmare. Cockney women on the end of the phone who actually did call me 'dearie' and seemed to imagine that I wished to avail myself of their unspeakable services. I wandered around Soho and Paddington – you saw cards pinned up in hallways, the door just ajar; within, you would glimpse a yellowish dado made grimy and shiny by the swish and abrasion of all those comings and goings. I did not enter one of them. I had no one to talk to, and seemingly nowhere to go. That was a low point – a point of desperation. I stole more clothes, converted them back into money. I also stole a cocktail dress, shot blue silk, hideous and tarty little thing – I would never allow one of my girls to even contemplate such a rag – but it suited my purpose at the time. I swept my hair over to one side of my head, and let it loll there. I wore stilettos – and just to cram my poor peasant's feet into them, the suffering was considerable (not helped by the fact that I had stolen a size too small: the pain, I offered it up). A cigarette holder, quite long, and a coloured cigarette – unlit. At first the thought of smoking appalled me, and then it didn't. Got through packs and packs as the years went by; I've kicked it now, I hope – still quite often get the craving, though. Anyway – if I'd got the look right, then I was a sophisticated young woman about town, her own boss, who was to be seen in only the very best places; if I had misunderstood the symbols and imagery – and it is a delicate thing, a convincing imposture – then a bouncer would have me back out into the street in no time flat. It would have to be tested. I arrived one evening in a taxi at the London Hilton, and made my way up to the bar at its summit – I had read all about it in *What's On*, if that was the name of the magazine I had bought: my one-and-sixpenny passport to simply getting close to even the sight of a pithead – proof, at least, of the existence of all the deep black and glinting seams and strata that I knew had to be seething beneath.

It was quite dark and intimate; over towards the sweep of window (and the lit-up panorama of London, so terribly beautiful) a man in a gold and spangly suit was touching the keys of a white grand piano, and so there was borne on the air – sometimes lost in the mingle with the drone of conversation – an occasional ripple, the sporadic tinkle of nothing approaching a definable tune. I settled myself into a red plush banquette in a moody corner, and was immediately very startled indeed by the speed of a waiter in a little maroon bolero, fast bearing down on me – I gripped the upholstery, prepared to resist all attempts to evict me. But no – he was deferential; his manner, it flooded me with a wholly disproportionate delight – he was smiling, calling me madam, and asking me how he could help me, what I would like. It's a memory that still makes me shiver, and I shall always hug it: no one before had ever called me such a thing, asked me such a thing. I ordered a glass of champagne – of which I had heard, of course, but never had I tasted it. It arrived very quickly in a flute like a vase, with a little paper doiley set beneath it. The waiter laid down on to the thick glass table a selection of small deep dishes containing very salty nuts, some little tubular biscuits and an oily cluster of wickedly gleaming berries that I had never before seen (olives, of course: but I didn't know). I had not requested all this food, but I set about eating it anyway – quite properly finishing off one bowl before I dutifully progressed to the next. The olives I thought bitter, the champagne I considered to be sour. By the end of the evening, I was wedded to both.

'You look lonely,' said the man. 'May I join you . . .?'

Annette looked up, as if in total surprise; in fact she had been concerned that an approach had taken this long: was her costume or demeanour in any way defective? But here finally, anyway, was a man. He was old – maybe nearly forty. A seemingly genuine smile, a suit that shimmered in the lamplight. He was not, Annette knew, the man she was seeking, but he was most definitely a beginning – a signpost. Maybe – who knew? – even an envoy.

'Please do. It appears as if my friend . . . isn't coming.'

'Then,' said the man, sitting to the side of her, 'it's your friend's great loss – and, I am delighted to say, very much my gain. Richard, by the way. And you are . . .?'

'Annette. Do you, um . . .?'

'Come here often? It's me, isn't it? Who's meant to say that. No – not often. Well – no more than anywhere else, anyway. I certainly haven't seen you here before, though. I should most definitely have remembered. Ivan! Yes – Ivan! Good. Bottle, please – Clicquot, I think. My account. So, Annette – what brings you to the Top of the World? Can I light that for you . . .?'

'Hm? Oh – no no. I don't want to light it. I'm trying to give them up. Lift.'

'Um – I'm sorry . . .?'

'What brought me here. Lift. Sorry. Not very funny.'

'Ah yes – lift. Very good. Lift. Yes. Ah – champagne. Excellent. Pour away, Ivan – that's it: pour away, old lad. Well, Annette – your very good health. Cheers. Mmm – hit the spot. Look, um, Annette – by the damnedest coincidence, I've been stood up myself, you know. What terrible people we both of us seem to know. So I was rather wondering whether we couldn't form a sort of a, well – a jilted parties club, if you like, and maybe, um – grab ourselves a little spot of dinner, or something? What do you say?'

'I'm rather full of nuts and biscuits . . .'

'Doesn't have to be anything elaborate. Jolly decent place just around the corner, as a matter of fact. Be there in no time. They know me there – I don't think you'll be disappointed.'

'I'm sure I won't. Well, um. Thank you, Richard. Yes. That would be lovely.'

I remember it all so clearly. We left most of the bottle of Veuve Clicquot, so eager was Richard to be out and away with me (and God alone could tell you – are you still watching me, God? – just what the poor sap imagined would be his prize at the end of the evening; whatever it was, he didn't get it – not even some small consolation). I thought this a terrible waste – the Clicquot I was meaning – and I said to him Oh, can't we take it with us? And he seemed to think that was so fantastically funny ('You do love your jokes, don't you Annette? Lift! Very funny'); but I wasn't joking – I wasn't. I wouldn't give it so much as a second thought these days, of course – but back then, the waste just appalled me. So anyway, we drove round the corner to this restaurant – he had an E-Type Jaguar, Richard, convertible, which I now see he just had to have, didn't he really? – and it was a rather nice place, I considered. But then I would: it was the very first restaurant I had entered in my life. Italian. I insisted that Richard order for me, which of course he was delighted to do. It was, I do remember, quite the most wonderful food I had ever tasted: well of course it was. The waiters, they were even more oily than the olives in the bar.

I think he was quite surprised, Richard, when I urged him afterwards to take me on somewhere. On somewhere . . .? What, um – do you mean exactly, Annette? I mean to say my flat's just up the road, you know, if you feel like a change of scenery . . .? No no, I said – a nightclub, somewhere delicious: somewhere *dangerous*. To give him his due, he coped quite bravely: *dangerous*, he kept on muttering to himself: *dangerous*, ay? . . . Oh, right-o, then – I think I know the place.

Well he didn't know the place – hadn't understood me at all. It was just like somebody's front room, the dive we pitched up at, with an apology for a bar wedged into the corner, surrounded by men drinking hard because the pubs were now shut. There were a couple of tarts, quite shy at the edges – it's only much later that I understand why they had both been so coy and unforthcoming: new faces, could be anybody – Vice, Mob: could be anybody (though could Richard or I possibly have been mistaken for either thing . . .?). But there was one man there who was more what I was meaning. I had to work very quickly: when Richard went off to the, oh God, 'little boys' room', as he called it, I approached this startled man (Greek, as it turned out) and said to him I wanted to go somewhere rather better than here, if he knew what I meant, but it had to be now, this instant, immediately. One minute later, the two of us were in a taxi, heading west (contemptible, isn't it? The way men do whatever you tell them). But poor Richard, though: he was really quite a nice man. But that wasn't what I was needing. (I am still fearful, you know, for my younger self: the risks I took, while not even knowing I was taking them. Just manically pursuing some nebulous ambition that was not even yet of my own invention. I was alone and driven: I had to be.)

All the way to the Embassy Club, the Greek was all hands, hot eyes and saliva – he had obviously misunderstood, as men do seem to. He had a name, the Greek, lost to me now, though I do recall that I couldn't pronounce it anyway because it had, I think, rather too many esses. The Embassy, though – and I do remember that name, anyway, because it did turn out to be somewhat key – this club, it was just the sort of place I had envisioned. There was about it an established warmth, the quietest hum of measured confidence. The walls were covered in baize, a sort of violet shade, and there appeared to be just hundreds of tiny and gleaming brass wall lights, each one bestowing little more than a candleglow to the gilt-framed pictures and the plumply-buttoned leather. Close to the bar (the Greek, now, he was becoming annoying – insisting we just quickly had the one, and then there was this small hotel close by: I'd like it, he said) – but close to the bar, there was the most beautiful woman I had ever laid eyes upon. She was at once so demure and aware – perfectly capturing my own, I saw now, previous and embarrassingly clumsy intention: worldly sophistication – the effortless air of quality and belonging, and yet so wide-eyed and alert to any new and shifting nuance. The Greek, I think, was rather surprised when I sat down beside her; no more so, though, than the woman herself.

'Do I know you?' she said.

I shook my head. 'I think you are so beautiful.'

'You're . . . kind. You are too. In a way. Is there something you, um . . .? Is this gentleman with you?'

I glanced up at the Greek, who was hovering greedily. He did not know whether or not to be offended and angry, not quite yet.

'No,' I said. 'I want to talk to *you*.'

Now he knew: he started making all sorts of horrid foreign noises (Greek, presumably) and waving about his hands. Why didn't he see he was a stepping stone? He had got me here – now he could go. Why was that so hard to understand? Men, so simple in themselves, can never seem to see what is really so terribly clear. Anyway, he did go eventually – one of the staff murmured to him that it might be a sound idea. Called me every name under the sun, of course (he was back to English now, of a type). Most of them I had never before heard, but you knew from the blaze of fury in his eyes and his staccato delivery, that he wasn't being at all nice to me. No matter – he was gone now. And so I could talk to Amanda: her name, this beauty, was Amanda (or rather it wasn't, I was later to discover, but here anyway for now was the name she went by). In my eagerness and gaucherie, I'm afraid I must have come over as most frighteningly direct.

'Do you work here? Are you contracted to work here? Or do you just happen to be here now? Do they know you're here? The owners? Or whoever. Do they like it? Do they mind?'

'Look. I don't think I need to answer any of your questions, thank you very much. I'm actually waiting for someone as a matter of fact, so if you wouldn't mind just, um . . . whatever your name is . . .'

'It's Annette. And I'm it. I am she. The person you are waiting for. Look – I've got money. Forty pounds. If I give it to you, will you talk to me? Answer my questions?'

'Forty pounds . . .? Let me see it.'

'Here. It's here. Take it. Now will you? Talk to me?'

She raised an eyebrow (delicious) and then she shrugged, quite elaborately.

'Well . . . all right. If that's what you want.'

'It is, yes. I would get us both a glass of something, but I've just given you all the money I have.'

She laughed at that, Amanda. Bought us each a flute of champagne, which I loved by now. She had the most beautiful speaking voice (I think, consciously or not, from that evening on I modelled my own upon its example). Her hands and nails were like you might see in a glossy magazine feature that concentrated upon nothing but hands and nails. Her suit and bag, she told me, were Chanel – I had not then heard of Chanel; I get a lot of my things from them now – because grooming and deportment, she told me – discretion and class, of course – were of the utmost importance if one wanted to generate serious money. And do you? (I pressed her.) Do you? Generate serious money? Oh yes, she said: very serious indeed. And so this forty pounds I've just given you – is that serious? Or is that not serious? How serious, tell me, is forty pounds (because remember, we're going right back to the Sixties, now)? Forty pounds, she told me, well – it's not silly, but it is far from serious: did I follow? Well, I was beginning to. But I now had to know what exactly she did in return for all this serious money – when she did it, how she did it: with whom, and where. I was very lucky that it was Amanda who I encountered that night: she was immediately so very forthcoming. I think she must have made so very much serious money in the past, that she didn't seem at all to mind spending, oh – it must have been well over an hour, an hour and a half with me by the end, you know; and that forty pounds I gave her, she must have spent all of that and more on champagne for the two of us. She told me that the Embassy was one of just four or five extremely select places where she would come in the evenings and sit, radiating beauty, and simply wait: it never usually, she said, took long – tonight, for some reason, it's very quiet. She paid the management to ignore the blatancy. Home – and work – was a ground-floor flat just behind Eaton Square (nearly paid for) and her clients tended generally to be rather the older man – fifty, sixty, even more – and their tastes were broadly similar. Traditional and rather scrumptious (her word) underwear and lingerie seemed to be the key to it: that and red lipstick, and long and lacquered nails. They wished to be admired and adored, and they expected both her flattery and gratitude which, in return for sometimes many hundreds of pounds, she was pleased to supply. She had to control their keenness for spanking her, however, because an unblemished skin was a mandatory requirement. Oral sex, of course, was a given. I had not heard of this: I presumed her to have said aural sex, and it all rather confused me, until she explained (I would never do that, for all the money in the world). Some men, she told me – not her own clients, but those of associates and colleagues – needed to be severely beaten and humiliated without mercy. Did they? I said. Did they? Mm, she nodded – it's quite big business, I'm told: but I wouldn't care for it. Wouldn't you? Wouldn't you? Wouldn't you? I kept on asking her: Christ in heaven – I would.

There was, of course, her minder to be taken into the equation. Her minder? Who was her minder? What is a minder? For the very first time she became evasive – didn't wish to linger, it very much seemed, around this aspect of the conversation. After a fair deal of wheedling on my part, however, I eventually got out of her that there was this man (and wouldn't there just be?) – she refused to expand upon any single aspect – and this man, he took from her half of her income. Why? Why would you do that? Give it to him? It's not his money – it's yours. What does he do for you in return? In return, said Amanda so quietly, he allows me to keep my face, so that I may continue to work on our mutual behalf. I took hold of both of her hands and I said to her, Amanda – please listen to me: Will you come and work for me? I won't take half your income. And I won't ever threaten you either. She stared, and then she laughed at me, quite ringingly. Work for *you*?! What on earth are you talking about, Annette! You're a young girl – you're pretty much penniless: what are you talking about, work for *you* . . .? Oh not *now* – I didn't mean now – of course not *now*. But one day. When it's all different. Will you then? She laughed again and wagged her head from side to side as if in so fond despair at the breadth of my illusion. No but *will* you? Please say yes, Amanda – please say you will. And then she must have decided that it was time now to humour me: oh all right then, Annette – I will, I promise: you call me, and then I'll come to you. Oh and by the way, Annette – I'm not really called Amanda. My real name, it's Gillian. And then *I* laughed – I had to laugh too, then (and she kept on asking me why).

We left soon afterwards – her flat, quite spacious, and so very tastefully decorated: really rather charming. Before we fell asleep, we joyfully engaged in what I now know to be tribady. I tried the word on Clifford not so very long ago: he didn't know it, as I was sure he wouldn't. I very much enjoyed telling him that it is an exclusively lesbian activity, where the two women simulate heterosexual intercourse in the missionary position; during this instance with Amanda – I could not, would not call her by her real name – I assumed the male and dominant position, which evidently gave pleasure to us both. It is not unlike the behaviour of Cliff and myself, now that I come to think of it. Because never would I consider penetration: never will that

407

happen to me again – because all men do is, they put things in and they take things from you. Cliff is the only man in the world whom I would ever become close to: what we do is we caress, and feel each other tenderly; we giggle and whisper in a frenzy of nerves, lest someone should happen to walk in on us (and yes I purposely do leave the door unlocked). People might think it strange, but I don't because I love him. And Amanda, oh, years and years later – but I did, you know, call her, and then she just came to me. She helps with the management, these days, of course, but for a long time she was my very best girl. Twenty per cent is all I asked for (the money she has made is so far north of serious as to transcend even solemn for terminally earnest). And I never ever threatened the beauty of her face.

But way back then, there had to initially be a man involved. At first I refused to accept this, but the delay, it cost me so much precious time – because now I had made my decision (pledged myself to a singular future) I had to have it, stake it, nail it down right now. At first, though in far too dilatory a manner, I had attempted to merely ape the antics of Amanda – simply positioning myself at or close to the centre of a ready-made web, trusting to the allure of its filaments and the glamour of its bait. It could not work, though. I did not dare try to steal from the Bond Street boutiques, and these were the clothes that I knew I had to have: I had no money. I could not possibly keep up with the constant tipping of commissionaires, barmen, the management: I had no money. Amanda – it was she who maybe took pity and gave me a name and a number: Angelo. Go and see Angelo, she said: but do be careful, Annette – promise me you'll be careful (you maybe don't understand this world you're getting into). And of course I was, careful – it had become my nature; I was aware of my vulnerability, the supreme fragility of all my aspirations, and yet – it was so curious – I felt myself at the same time to be also the rapacious prowler, seeking the scent, so eager to pounce without pity upon my unsuspecting prey (strip it to the bone).

'So . . . Annette, is it? Drink? You want a drink?'

'A glass of champagne would be very nice, Angelo. Thank you.'

'Expensive tastes. I like that. Maybe means you're willing to work hard. How you get my name?'

'Does it matter?'

'Not too much, I guess. Here, Annette: champagne. Annette – that's your real name?'

'It is, yes. Is Angelo yours?'

'You being funny?'

'Not especially.'

'You being, what . . .? Clever, are you Annette?'

'Just talking. Why shouldn't it be my real name?'

'This business . . . a lot of girls, they don't maybe want too many associations with their other life. The legit life. Get me?'

'I don't have another life. Don't have any life at all. That's why I'm here. I'll tell you what I'll do and what I won't.'

'You reckon? You'll tell *me*? Wrong, girly. Annette, or whatever your goddam name is. You work for me – *if* you work for me, because so far, I tell you, I'm not too loving your attitude. But if you work for me, you do what the fuck *I* say. Get me?'

'No. It can't be like that. You give me a target. You tell me how much money I've got to make, and I'll make it. But it has to be on my terms.'

'Ha. You kill me. You really do kill me, Annette. Your *terms*? You got *terms* now? You know who you talking to? What makes you think you're so special? You ain't the only pretty face. What makes you different from all the other girls I got?'

'I am. I am special. You'll find out. But it's got to be on my terms. Is there any more champagne, possibly?'

'You really do, you know, Annette: you kill me. You really do kill me. Bottle's in the bucket – you want it, you get it. So OK:

humour me. These terms – these big terms of yours, Annette. Hit me.'

'Well yes, That would be what I do. I will beat men. I will string them up, tie them down, rack them, spit on them, make them bleed, make them beg, whip them to a pulp, gag them, starve and bloody well half-kill them, if that's what I feel like. I'll chain them up in the cold, I'll burn their skin with cigarette ends – I'll scream at them until they are weeping, and then I'll kick them in the face. That is what I shall do. You're not speaking, Angelo . . . you're just looking at me. Well speak. Because I have told you: that is what I shall do. And – this is important – that is *all* I shall do.'

'There *is* a market . . .'

'So I have been told. I want to make money, Angelo. A lot of money, as fast as I can. I will work harder than any girl you have ever known. And I will give you twenty per cent.'

'You . . . will . . . give . . . *me* . . . twenty per cent. You know, Annette, I was just beginning to like you, and here you come again with the attitude. Listen. Without my say-so, you don't work at all. Get me? Not just here, but anywhere. You don't be nice to me, Annette, then you're over before you even begun.'

'Take your hand off me.'

'Or what?'

'Or I'll smash this bottle across your bloody face.'

'Jesus. You maybe don't like living, girly. I could have you hurt so bad . . .'

'Stop. This is stupid. Are you or aren't you going to let me prove to you what I can do? You tell me the figure you want from me every week: I'll get it. You take twenty per cent.'

'You're full of bullshit, but I'll tell you what I'll do. I set you up in an apartment in this very building. Get me? You pay rent. I give you a number. You give me that amount of money, every week, every fucking week, mind. If that's only twenty per cent of your take, well good. But if it's one hundred per cent well then that's just tough, baby: because that's the number I want. You take it. You leave it. Either way, time's up.'

'I'll take it.'

'Aha. Good girl. So we're in business. Oh yeh and – Annette? You cross me, you get cut. Then you're catfood. Get me?'

'Do you always talk like this? Take your hand off me.'

'Or – the bottle, right?'

'Right.'

'When can you start?'

'I already have.'

And I was – this should not be surprising – quite true to my word. I worked so hard that my upper arms began to develop these really quite highly-defined and bulging hard muscles. There was no shortage of slavering ninnies who came to me. One in particular I recall often seeing interviewed on television later the same evening. He looked both rosy and solemn, as a Minister should, and talked about the State of the Nation. Beneath his Savile Row suit lay a body so thoroughly excoriated as to resemble the aftermath of a primitive and pitiless inquisition. Before he left me, he would always rinse out the urine from his mouth with a twenty-one-year-old malt whisky. I learned from one girl in a flat below mine that she was far too scared and squeamish for my line of work – a view, apparently, held by a lot of them. Maybe why Angelo was so keen to get me (and despite all his blather, I knew, I knew from the first moment, that he was so

411

keen to get me). Looking back on it all now, you know, I really do feel rather proud of all that I achieved in those first early years. I made no money at all at the very beginning, of course: Angelo saw to that (a pride thing, I can only suppose, though he soon grew out of it). But men with a taste for torture, all they know is to come back for more. News of me spread (and who is it, I wonder, who does the talking?) and soon I had a stable of regulars and any number of pathetic little worms who had been skimping on their wives' housekeeping and eagerly hoarding their pennies for a one-off journey into hell (which was never, of course, nearly enough for them). I raised my prices on a virtually weekly basis, and this seemed to strangely thrill them. It did not take too long before Angelo was taking his agreed amount, and still I was left with the eighty per cent.

And so I spent my days: plucking individual hairs with tweezers from the chest of a man whose nipples were clamped into the serrated jaws of jump leads connected to a battery that would be fizzily activated if ever he whimpered (and he whimpered a lot). Immersing the head of another into a bath full of ice and water – keeping him under until he turned so blue, and feebly beat at the floor with the palms of his hands. Locking another into an understairs cupboard, bound in parcel tape, his mouth stopped up with a rubber ball, only one nostril active. Whipping and beating just dozens of them until they saw the perfectly delineated rivulets of blood snaking their way down so gracefully from their embedded crown of thorns. There was a priest. Who had had just such a thing made up for him; he urged me to press it ever tighter into his forehead. He wore a wig, to hide the scars. His eternal yearning was to be nailed to the cross; he said the only reason he did not pay me to do this was that there could be no disguising the wounds and no longer would he be able to hold aloft the chalice at the blessed Mass, nor dispense the body of Christ in the form of a host at the Holy

Communion. I would have done it – I would have nailed his hands and feet; I would have driven a nail right through his bloody skull, if he'd paid me to (and maybe if he hadn't). With some of the men there was a prearranged signal – some gesture or sign when a barrier was close to being breached and they urgently needed me to desist now from whatever form of pain or deprivation I was currently meting out to them, on an escalating scale. I often ignored this; their gratification later was practically boundless. Once there was a man – a Harley Street physician of about sixty-five, he could easily have been. He was sitting on the commode with the usual lead weights suspended from his genitals, and I was wrapping his head in the swaddling of a mummy. He tapped out his emergency tattoo on the arm of the commode but I just slapped at his penis with a riding crop, and kept on winding around his head the great wads of gauze. It was only later that I knew he was dead. A colleague who was also a client managed to hush the whole thing up – got him out of the building, signed his death certificate, paid me more to guarantee my silence. According to the obituary in *The Times*, he died unexpectedly of a coronary, while holidaying in the Norfolk Broads.

Clifford, I remember – he seemed so very oddly incurious about how I was spending my days, my evenings; sometimes I worked on into the night, but whatever time it was when I eventually got home to our little flat off Baker Street – no matter that I was exhausted and just fell into my bed – Cliff, he kept the conversation light, confined it to generalities. He was already making suits by this time, you know, and he's done so terribly well since: I feel very proud. The moment arrived, however, when I had to tell him – had to let him in on it all. I had known for a long time that however hard I was working, no matter how much money I could make in a week (and it was really quite a lot now, even as much as Amanda, and far more than I needed if

413

all I required was a well-feathered nest: but no – I wanted more; I had to be, didn't I? In control) . . . so I knew that until I was an employer, until I could establish a toehold in proprietorship, until that day I should always and ultimately be beholden to such people as Angelo. And that was not to be the way. The moment, then, as I say, for the next stage had now come. And so I put it to Clifford – didn't go into a great deal of detail, or anything – not at that point I didn't; just laid out for him the bare bones of the thing. He was wonderfully calm – quite unworried; I had sort of known he would be.

'So what you're saying then is, Annette, that there will be some, um – girls here then? In the flat.'

'Well yes – not all the time. Not living here. But yes – in the rooms we don't use. It's got to be quite cleverly staggered, actually, because if the neighbours get a whiff of it then the landlord's just bound to find out and then there'll be all sorts of trouble. But the plan is, Cliff, that soon I'll be able to buy a proper house some-where – don't quite know where yet. But a house of our own. Could be round here – but somewhere good, somewhere really smart, it's got to be. Mayfair. Chelsea. Somewhere.'

'I see. And this house, then, wherever it is. We'll live in it, will we? Is that the idea?'

'Yes – I think so. I really want to do this, you know, if I can. Do you think I can? Do this, Cliff?'

'I think you can do anything – anything in the world, if you really want to. And I'll help, if you like. If you want me to I will.'

'Cliff. I do so love you.'

'And I do you, Annette. I love you too. Um. Just one thing . . .'

'What is it, Cliff? What's worrying you?'

'Well – not *worrying* me, exactly . . . it's just, um – well, these men, Annette. These men you see . . . what do you . . .? I mean – ?'

'What I do is I beat them senseless. And more. They love it. They need it. I'm helping them. They pay me. Not one of

414

them – not ever – lays even a finger on me. Was that it, Cliff? Was that what was on your mind?'

'Um. You know, I think it was, yes. Yes – I think that's what must have been troubling me, you know.'

'Dear Cliff. There's only one man who I'd ever be close to.'

'Really? Who's that?'

'Who's *that*?! Do you really not know, Cliff? It's you. It's you. It could only ever be you. Did you really not know that?'

'It's nice . . . to hear it. Well I'll back you, Annette. I'll do anything you want me to.'

'And you don't hate your sister for turning out so strangely . . .?'

'Hate you? Ha! I don't *think* so. No, I don't *think* so, Annette. And you're not strange, I don't think you're strange at all – I don't think either of us is. It's everyone else, I think. It's everyone else – they're the strange ones.'

♠

And that, you know, is frankly pretty much how it went: according to plan. I had to saddle myself with a quite shocking mortgage to secure the very first house – Sloane Street, and I still have such a fondness for it – but as soon as I managed to reduce the monthly outgoing to slightly less frightening figures (it took such a long time, though – even though I drew out nothing at all from the business for myself in those days – the business was just everything to me: I suppose it still is) – well then I took out a second mortgage on Ebury Street. The girls – the lifeblood – they were largely introductions, recommendations, friends of friends who had heard about the rewards that such a pursuit could offer you. Amanda, she brought along with her one or two in the early days. She also introduced me to Edgar Tumulty, who I trusted from the first; I was right to – he's been with me ever since: not a friend, exactly, but a very staunch colleague and ally. And Tumulty in turn (I call him Tumulty: could never quite accept the Edgar side of things), he introduced a few more men – for security purposes. I don't really care to call them 'the muscle' but that, in essence I suppose, is more or less what they are.

I have always been very strict when it comes to selection: many is the girl I have had to turn down. Sonya, in point of fact, was one of the girls who never frankly stood a chance. I knew at once that she would be doing it all just solely for the life of ease; the best girls, they have to want the sex, or – difficult to explain – it's never quite right: you know them immediately. And although she was terribly humble, which men, of course, always adore (well, she wasn't really very much short of grovelling, if I'm honest), the humility within her was so very deep-seated that it could, professionally speaking, become very wearing for a client, you know: you need a bit of guts in this job. But I instantly knew that she'd be a perfect little thing for Clifford, and so I gave her to him. Paired them off. Happy ending, really.

No but my girls, they have to look as if they have just stepped out of the pages of . . . no, not a girlie magazine, no no – but *Vogue, Tatler*, that sort of thing. My girls must never look as if they are what they are. I think my clients very much appreciate that – and I can see that it would add to the excitement factor. So until quite recently, all was working well. Oh I'm not saying there hadn't been problems in the past: I don't at all see the past with myself cast as some sort of a benign and indulgent mother hen, clucking away over her chirruping brood of happy hookers, no no. Of course there were problems; sometimes a girl would refuse to cooperate with the proper and regular medical check-ups that

I absolutely insist upon. There is usually a reason, I'm afraid, and so the girl in question will then have to leave me. There is always the matter of ensuring an enormous and unquestioned supply of the Pill, as well as the full range of alternative contraceptive devices; and yet there has been the occasional abortion to arrange – it is, after all, these days the merest formality (if only they knew how it used to be). Some girls, of course, they choose to keep the baby – in which case yet again, alas, we have to then part company. So generally speaking, the way it works is that Amanda and I, we take care of the girls and all the appointments and so on and Tumulty sees to security and the money side of things. I trust him completely. He filters all the cash in some terribly clever way that I must admit I don't altogether understand, and then when I come to invest it or – more likely – pledge a fortune to the latest prohibitive pay-out (and I will get on to the pay-outs very soon: they have come to haunt not just my every waking moment, but they even invade my dreams) – its provenance then, the cash, appears to be impeccable. And dear Cliff, he imagines he's helping me too, but he isn't, not really; I give him the odd little thing to keep him busy, you know – make him feel useful. I don't want to worry him with the nuts and bolts. And the girls, of course – I give him the free run of all the girls; it's so nice to see him enjoying himself. Because I do understand – men, they have to do this, it is how they are programmed. And of course he can't do any of that with me, he knows that, and Sonya, well – I can't think that she's terribly moving, you know (she really is such a bore, quite frankly), and so it all works out quite nicely. It's rather like Iris Murdoch said – we both of us, Cliff and I, we both love Iris Murdoch. From one of the later novels, I think: 'Every man needs two women, a quiet homemaker and a thrilling nymph.' Well that's how it is for Clifford, now – except that he has all the thrilling nymphs he can handle. As well as me, of course.

There are fashions, you know, in sexual fads and fetishes, in common with everything else, I suppose. At the moment there seems to be a rising enthusiasm for being wrapped up snugly in a terry-towelling nappy, then being gently suckled. There is a rather sweet and lovely part-time wet nurse, Anastasia – ah! The names they select, the girls – who is, I am told by an appreciative clientele, so happily accommodating in that particular predilection. And even now, you know, I am not myself averse to stepping in and thrashing and kicking and pounding to a mulch anyone at all who should babblingly implore me to do so. Lavinia, she sometimes dresses up as a nun. Do you know, I can never bear to see her – would not maybe dare: I would hate to do her harm. Once I happened into her room and I just saw it all hanging there – the habit, the wimple, the bloody clanking rosary – and I felt quite faint. With fury. Faint with fury. Hatred, of course . . .

But. It is hurt I feel, really. So many of my girls just lately have been, leaving me – loyalty, in this business, is never dominant. The thing is, they have all earned so very much money – for who else would allow them to retain a full eighty per cent of everything they make? – that they have decided to do now whatever it is that girls in their late twenties, early thirties, want to get up to these days. One opened a boutique that specialised in what she termed as 'vintage clothing'; there were no hard feelings – I sold her a mountain at a knock-down price of our barely-worn cast-offs. The girls, you see, only get dressed in order to get more or less immediately undressed, so there's very little wear and tear. Most of the girls seem eager to secure for themselves, as they put it, a foot on the first rung of the property ladder, for which I can hardly blame them. Others, of course, have met a nice young man (and I do wonder where and quite how they manage this) and wish to draw to a close their colourful pasts, I can only suppose – maybe deny to themselves the reality of what they have been (a thing I could never contemplate doing myself). And of course my girls, as I said – they look and sound so terribly classy that quite a few of my older and richer clients have promised to make a lady of them (silly, really – because they are, they are that already: I insist upon it – I have made them so) and of course they have accepted, these impressionable girls. And very eagerly too, should the man have a title, as so many of them do. Terrible. I lose a girl and a client in the one swingeing blow (although I have to say that given a little time, the client, he generally returns; marrying your favourite whore, it can never be a good idea in the long run, can it really? You know what they say about familiarity. And with their backgrounds, do these newly installed wives ever wonder where their husbands might have got to? When they just slip away for an hour or two in the afternoon?).

The outcome of not just these defections but also some powerful exterior forces is that I am now – have been, actually, for longer than I care to consider – losing money on a perfectly frightening scale. There is a limit to how much I can sustain – a limit that is now being very rapidly approached. You see, I don't suppose for a moment that a normal and everyday sort of a person could ever be moved to sit down and contemplate the economics involved in the running of these two quite simple little houses. Quite apart from the givens: mortgage repayments – not just on the houses but Clifford's little flat (our mother's flat too, of course), rates and so on . . . a cumulative fortune in themselves, these, I have to say, but not by any means close to the heart of the matter. You see it has to be understood that no expense I am put to can ever be either fair or legitimate. Everyone – and I mean everyone – has at any price to be kept silent. We cannot employ cleaners, for example, in the way that the normal and everyday sort of person might easily do. They each take, oh – just so much money, this squad of cleaners, in return for keeping everything they see very strictly to themselves. It is a similar story with, well – you name it, really: plumbers, decorators, delivery people – even the window-cleaner (who I have constantly argued, and not wholly in jest, ought in a just world to be rewarding *me*: but there). One of Tumulty's people, you know, is constantly engaged with the replacement of light bulbs; we buy them – pink, sixty-watt – by the gross (Osram told him that they make them now exclusively for us). Clothes, lingerie – they're just sky-high. Scent – bubble bath, massage oils, all the paraphernalia: prohibitive. As is the eternal laundry. Tumulty and his cohorts, of course, they have to be very generously rewarded. There's Clifford's allowance – he does so much appreciate the very best of everything; but I love him, you see, so it's really no hardship. Cars, of course (we have two – a black Mercedes and a BMW, both secondhand, but quite impressive), for the rather lucrative hotel work, you see . . . fallen right away now, I very much regret to say: all the rich tourists, they're just not coming to London in the numbers that they used to. But by far the biggest outlay of all . . . well, the pay-outs, of course. We had some trouble from nearby rivals in the early days, but they quite soon seemed to lose interest: not big enough fry, I can only think. But nowadays it tends to be just the police who are intent upon causing me grief. There is a detective-sergeant – everyone knows him, knows he is as crooked as a spiral – and yet he seems to get away with it all. All he has to do, he says to me – I know that he's speaking the truth and I know that he'd do it as well, quite without hesitation – is to pick up the phone: have a swift word with Vice, Annette – down on you like the proverbial, aren't they Annette? (He talks like this, repellent little man.) So be clever Annette, ay? Mm – well. It's these payments now that have become utterly crippling. And he thinks he owns the girls, this bastard detective. Susannah, she told me one time that Hanson – his name is Hanson – he had the handcuffs on her (his own, not the recreational leather and fur ones) and he repeatedly slapped her hard around the face and then her breasts: she was in tears – not as a result of pain, I think, but at the sight of the yellow and indigo bruises. I paid her money until they had faded, until she could work again. I remonstrated with Hanson: he laughed at me.

Oh look. I can't – I just can't think about it for even another minute. I'm going to have a glass of champagne, and then I'll do the crossword. Cliff and myself, we both started doing the *Times* crossword, oh – quite a few years ago now, I suppose. We were so completely out of our depth at the very beginning, of course – I'm not sure which of us was the more frustrated by our patent inability to simply *understand*. But Cliff, he bought a book – it explained quite a few of the devices. Slowly, we began to pick it up. God – the day, I'll never forget it, the day we jointly completed our first *Times* crossword! We were in raptures. Didn't get even close with the following day's, though, which sobered us up a fair deal. But now, we're really good. I don't know which of us is better. Me, I think – but I wouldn't ever say that to Cliff. We each do it individually these days, of course – we phone one another and say how long it took us (we're both very honest) and we practically always do finish the thing. And I wonder if Clifford is aware . . .? That now we are 'cruciverbalists'? I wonder if he has ever come across that word. I only recently did myself, in Chambers: it comes just after 'crucify'. I'll try it out on him when he next comes round. I don't know if he is coming over this evening or not. He's gone to see our mother. He does that rather a lot. Don't know why. But he might – he might call round and see me, at some point later on. And then I'll try it out on him. Cruciverbalism: rather lovely, isn't it? I bet he doesn't know it. Now then – let's have a look at today's (mm – this champagne: quite divine). One across, let's see . . . it's wonderful, the crossword, you know: takes my mind off, oh – just all of it, really. For a time.

And when Cliff and I cuddle, of course – that always helps me such a lot. But you see he's just so close to the centre of everything, here's the trouble of it, this is why my headlong escape can sometimes be blocked. I often think, you know, that if it weren't for Cliff, I might now just lay it all down: stop it abruptly, and amble away. It used to be for me, it was certainly for me at the beginning . . . but now I feel bound to supplying shelter, to be something to depend upon. And once you're the supplier, you know, you really shouldn't hold back: you just must replenish the reservoir of goodness, you have to keep on filling up the void. Amanda – she used to be a comfort for a long while, of course, but we both of us sensed – I knew this to be true – that first our hearts and then our eyes and finally and inevitably the warmth of our bodies were seldom and then hardly at all flooding into unity, not like once they seemed to. And for a good while after, impact had been supplanted by collision. We smiled our agreement to do this no more, and Amanda, she gave me the most beautiful doll (it looked like her, of course it did) and this doll of mine, I called her Belinda. When I was a little girl, my Mummy was constantly urging me to play with the mawkish dolls I so thoroughly neglected. She made all these sets of clothes for them (with the remnants of remnants) but I never got around to even undoing the little pink poppers to so much as see if they fitted (they would have fitted, of course – they would have fitted quite perfectly). Belinda is so fleshlike to the feel, her golden hair not those angry and punched-in divots of crackling synthetic, but so shockingly silky, so touchable, and seemingly growing away from a blood-fed scalp, and tumbling into life. I don't think I ever gave names to my dollies in childhood; I called this one Belinda, though, because it's simple, and because it's so clean. I take her to bed, and I talk to her, you know. About how tired we both are now, and how we're going to drift away into a dreamless sleep. If it works, it so pleases me;

sometimes, though, these tiny tears, they seep out of Belinda's quite spectacular eyes, gathering briefly on the upswept lashes before they course on down and run away, when I need to hug her just close to me, the two of us clinging, and weeping so softly. But in grief we are apart . . . and then I have to disappear into a longer fiction.

She loves the Ritz, now – she says it's her favourite. Long ago, though, when I first brought Mummy here for lunch, she was very uneasy (Oh but it's so *posh*, Clifford – it's just so terribly *posh* – which had reminded me suddenly, oh . . . of all sorts of silly things from so very long ago: made me smile). But these days, well – you would swear, you know, that she had been born to it all. Well we've all of us changed, of course, but the transformation in her, there was nothing tentative or gradual about it – it was as rapid as it was (well to me, anyway) so very extraordinary. Even now I catch myself forgetting that here before me is in fact the very same mother who raised me, the very same woman from that other world. It is only when she momentarily relapses into being just that woman from a different era that I suddenly am jolted – I come to, and remember. She looks so different, you see. Well the face – that hasn't changed, no not really: it's gently lined, of course – her eyes are much darker (she says it's the contacts) – but her hair now, it's like the plumage of a raven, so appallingly sleek. Her clothes too – terribly smart: she has a visiting tailor and a sempstress, which I'm more than happy to pay for. Or at least Annette is, anyway: it hardly matters – we're both of us her

423

children, aren't we? After all. The utterly disconcerting thing about her, though – I don't, in truth, know quite how to handle it, and nor can I dwell upon its possible significance – is that one minute we can be having a perfectly natural conversation (or as natural, anyway, as it ever can or will be between us) and then suddenly she will come out with some or other quite extraordinary remark that is so detached, so utterly surprising, and sometimes in a tone that is not just wholly unconnected from the previous easy and general delivery, but undercut too with a hint of maybe even menace; I flounder around, trying to fathom its justification, trace back to source any slight or casual comment that might conceivably have prompted it. I fail, invariably – and by then she is chatting away merrily again, quite as if it never happened at all. You begin to question your reason, you know; you begin to wonder if it's you. I spoke to Annette about it one time, but you see, well . . . Annette and our mother, they so very rarely encounter now that I doubt if Annette has ever at first hand witnessed such a thing and so it is left up to me to rather galumphingly attempt to recount and describe it, and I never seem to do it very well. She's old, is all Annette says. As if that explained everything. Well she *is* old – well, pretty old, anyway – but that's not it at all. The reverse: when she behaves in this way, she seems so very youthful, so vital; it is I who feel slow, and apart. I assumed I'd get used to it or – better – cease to even notice. Maybe I would come to simply put it down to a vagary of nature, the merest human foible – but every single time it happens (because sometimes it won't, you know, not for days – and it can lull you, that; and then suddenly she has that glare in her eyes, and the words that come out of her, they can be sometimes beyond all belief) . . . and every single time it happens, it seems not just as if I am stupid and excluded (although I do feel both of these) but as if these seemingly chance and throwaway comments are not at all just a disparate string of periodic ramblings, a latent undercurrent of anger, momentarily surfacing – but are in some way unknown to me, part of a darker and elaborate pattern; it is almost as if she is determined upon structure, struggling to connect them all, link them up into a chain. Or – maybe this is better – that despite the customarily still and placid surface, deep beneath there is something brewing. Annette, she said I'm crazy; I sometimes used to hope that she was right. The first time I was aware of all of this, I think – it's the first time, anyway, I can remember – was quite soon after she had passed her driving test. I had signed her up for thirty lessons, assuming that either she would drop out after the first two or three, or that I should be booking up a further block of thirty every three or four months, and possibly into eternity. She took just twelve lessons: passed the test. I – Annette – bought her a Golf; she said to me Why can't I have a Triumph Herald? Jean Beery, she had the sweetest little Triumph Herald. Well they don't make them any more, Mummy – that was quite a long time ago, remember. And then, by one of those freak coincidences or ironies that seem to happen all the time in life (though a wise author would hesitate before making them into fiction) – just two days later Mummy learned that Mrs Beery, she had died: in a car crash. How awful. My mother, she did not cry – but her face, it was livid; it appeared as if she were boiling with fury. When eventually she spoke, she just kept repeatedly spitting out that it was not *fair*, it was so *unfair* that this should happen to Jean, of all people. Why do they never take the bad ones? Hey? Jean, she was always so good to me – good to all of us, Clifford, even more than you know. Do you remember that time when you went to Jersey? With that tiresome little girl? Oh, I said: vaguely. Well that was a present from your Auntie Jean. She was always so kind. And now she's dead. And why did I not make the effort to see her, when she was still alive? And now she's dead. And I never ever had another friend, you know – never had a youth, never had a life. There was just your father. And Jean. And now she's dead. But there's nothing to stop me now, though, is there? Nothing, no – there's nothing to stop me now (and so it was then, I suppose, that she started). I never really imagined I'd ever get to the bottom of her moods – become a part of whatever she seemed often to be brooding over, so grimly. But I was wrong. At this latest lunch of ours at the Ritz, she evidently decided to make it all clear to me: and oh my God, I do so wish she hadn't.

'Do you eat it, Clifford, simply because you imagine it's the, oh – I don't know . . . smart thing to do? Or do you really enjoy it?'

'What? Caviar, you mean? Adore it. Loved it from the first moment I tasted it. Why won't you even try it? I'm sure you'd like it. It's exquisite.'

'No thank you, Cliford. I know it sounds silly, but I always feel it looks just a little bit, well – dirty. I always remember when your father, he'd be oiling whatever part of your tricycle one used to oil in those days, and his fingers, they always ended up looking like that: black and oily.'

'He oiled my tricycle? Daddy did?'

'Well I can't imagine what else he can have been oiling. Certainly not my trolley – he never did that. Maybe it was the lawnmower. He was oiling something, anyway . . .'

'He never even put the pedal back on that tricycle. I only rode it a couple of times. It just rusted up in the shed. And then I grew out of it.'

'Yes well. Isn't that often the way. These scallops, though – quite marvellous. So terribly juicy. And clean.'

'Do you miss him ever? Daddy?'

'Miss him? Your father? Oh good heavens no. Why ever should I miss him? I do miss Jean, though. Think about her rather often. It's awful, you know, when someone close to you just goes and dies, like that.'

'Well you'd better start getting used to it. Would you like a drop more Chablis? Wonderful with scallops, I should have said.'

'What do you mean? What do you mean by that? Get *used* to it – what on earth can you mean?'

'Well I just meant that . . . all I meant was, Mummy, that you do seem to be becoming ever more, well – youthful, really. Defying age altogether. So you'll be seeing us all out, I shouldn't wonder.'

'Oh that's just a terrible thing to say. How could you say such a thing? What – *you*, you mean? Oh I simply couldn't survive it. You – you will live for ever. You are my little boy. The only man I could ever be close to. I will have some more Chablis actually, Clifford – it's quite delightful. Thank you. Of course . . . if something isn't done very soon, well – I doubt we'll be having too many more of our splendid lunches, will we Clifford? Not unless Mummy does something, anyway. Which I do, of course, intend to. It's just that it would have been rather nice if someone had asked me, that's all. Well Annette, of course, I'm talking about. But then, she imagines me to be stupid. Or too old. Or both. Either way, I doubt she'll ever speak. I really do think, you know, they might have cleared away our plates, by now. We've obviously both of us finished. It's not really what you expect, is it? Place like this.'

'I think the waiter's coming now . . . yes, here he is, he's here now. Um . . . what, um . . . Mummy . . . are you talking about, exactly? What do you mean – *do* something? Why shouldn't we go on having lunch together? Do you not want to any more? Is that it? Is there something wrong?'

'Well of course there's something *wrong*. Where are your eyes, Clifford? Honestly – if you didn't have your Mummy to look out for you, what on earth would become of you? Hm? Oh not wrong with *you* – there's nothing wrong with *you*, of course

427

there isn't, Clifford. It's Annette's little business, isn't it? From what I can gather, it's coming apart at the seams. Ah – spring lamb! How lovely. It looks as if it's done quite perfectly, doesn't it? Don't you love it when they take off the silver domes, like they do? All at the same time. Even though you know perfectly well what's underneath, it's still always so terribly exciting, I think. And do take some greens this time, Clifford. If you don't eat your greens, then you'll never grow up to be big and strong.'

'But I am grown up, aren't I Mummy? Grown-up man, now.'

'Hm? Oh yes well of *course* you are – of course you are, Clifford. But you'll always be a little boy to your Mummy, you know. And your sister – she I know feels exactly the same. There's something about you, Clifford, that just never ever changes.'

'But what you said earlier, Mummy – about Annette's, um – "business", did you say? Wait a minute – what do you mean I haven't changed? Of course I've changed. Just look at me, for God's sake . . .!'

'Oh yes *externally*, oh yes I agree. Big tall man – those beautiful suits of yours: so terribly clever you are, Clifford, to be able to make with your own two hands such a thing of beauty. Your big posh car. Those enormous cigars . . . not good for you, you know, Clifford. I do wish you wouldn't.'

'It's one of the things . . . that men do. But look – never mind all that. What was it you were saying? About our lunches. About this – "business", whatever it is. What "business"?'

'Clifford. I can't believe you are that naïve. I happen to know to the contrary. And please don't think me blind. You can't seriously imagine that I have no idea of what's been going on for all these years? Surely you can't believe that? Have you had gravy? Yes? But you still haven't taken any greens, look.'

'I'm all right with potato just for the moment, thank you very much.'

428

'Now you're blushing. Just like you always have done. Don't look away from me, Clifford. It's no good staring down at your plate now, is it? Did you really, then? Believe I knew nothing? How very disappointing. The broccoli's excellent – oh *do* have some, Clifford – just to please Mummy. Here – I'll put some on your plate. There. You see – I was very much like you for a long time. Oh yes I was. Well, most of my life, really. Just burying my head in the sand – not at all wanting to know what was really going on because then I'd be expected to do something – and in all honesty, you know Clifford, I always rather felt that I had quite enough to attend to as it was. I mean when you two were very young, well – there was always a mountain to see to. And so whatever it was your father was getting up to, well – I made it not my business. And when he neglected the basics, failed to see to the very necessities – well then that too was just his concern: nothing to do with me. But I see now, Clifford, that this was wrong. Because we all of us, didn't we? Suffered in the end. And that's what you're doing now, Clifford: burying your head in the sand. And to a lesser degree, of course, Annette, she's doing it too. Oh she was fine, quite wonderful, wasn't she? When everything was plain sailing. When everything was going to plan. But now, well . . . she's just not *dealing* with it. She's ignoring it. But it won't go away, you know. It never ever does, this sort of thing. So I just can't sit by, can I? Until it just gets worse and then it's too late altogether. Not any more I can't. Because it wouldn't do, you see. It simply wouldn't do. Clifford – if you don't finish up all that broccoli, and right this minute, young man – well then I'm going to get quite upset with you. And we don't want that now, do we? I'll feed you myself and then everyone will look over and think Oh my goodness, what a little baby – still needs his Mummy to feed him his greens. I suppose we shouldn't order more Chablis, should we? Although I can't actually imagine why not. I'm not sure I'm going to have room for pudding, you know. Such a feast. Oh do eat *up*, Clifford. What's wrong with you?'

'I'm, um . . . not hungry. Look, Mummy . . . I don't really know if I thought you knew or not, quite frankly. It's just something, I suppose, I chose not to think about. But . . . all this about something being *wrong* – you know, with the "business", as you call it. Well – I just don't know what you're talking about, I'm afraid. I mean I'm being completely honest with you, you know.'

'Oh I *believe* you, Clifford. But isn't that exactly what I was saying? Your head is in the sand. You have to have eyes and ears, don't you? Or else how are you ever going to know what on earth is going on? And Annette – of course she's not going to *tell* you, is she? It's not in her nature. Firstly, of course, she's still your big sister – she feels responsible for you, which is just as it should be. And in the second place, she wouldn't want to, well – put it all into words, would she? Because then it would become too real. Then she would have to face it. The only people in the world who understand the gravity of the situation – because it is, Clifford: it's really very serious, you know – are Annette and Edgar. And myself, of course. Edgar, Annette and myself.'

'What – Tumulty, you mean?'

'How many Edgars do we know, Clifford? Of course Tumulty. He is my source. He tells me everything. At first he wouldn't – very discreet, very tight-lipped. Then I imagine he thought that it could do no harm to humour a dotty old lady. Then I think he came to see that we were all on the same side. That I actually *cared*, you see. We've talked a great deal since. So you see I've done all my homework – or no, it was prep you called it at your school, wasn't it? Yes: prep. You do know he's in love with Annette, don't you Clifford? No – you probably don't. Well strange though it may seem, he is, very much, has been for years. I shouldn't wonder he realises there's nothing there for him, of course. And do you know, Clifford – despite your and Annette's little, um – arrangement, shall we call it, he doesn't resent you even the tiniest little bit. Such a gentleman. So anyway – I've decided now. I've worked it all out. Well Edgar and I: we've come up with a plan. Plan of action. Shall I tell you now? Or shall we wait until we're all of us together? Annette, Edgar – all of us.'

'A . . . *plan* . . .?'

'Mm. Maybe a crème brulée. Maybe I could just go a crème brulée . . .'

'But what sort of a plan? What is *wrong*, exactly? You haven't yet told me what on earth is meant to be *wrong* . . .'

'Well basically, my sweet – if nothing is done, if the situation is permitted to deteriorate, then I estimate that within no more than a few months, well – none of us really will have anything left. You see. I expect you've no idea what I'm talking about, have you? No, I thought not. And then of course there is the matter of the police. There is a very good case, you know, for us all to be convicted of living off immoral earnings. Sounds so sordid, I know. But there it is. Or maybe a crêpe suzette. Terribly fattening. Hard to resist. What are *you* having, Clifford? You know – it would be too awful now, it really really would. Giving up all these lovely things – we're all so used to them. So it mustn't happen. We have to stop the rot. Why don't you just have some jelly? I know you like jelly. Wibbly-wobbly, on a plate . . .'

'I'll just have a coffee, Mummy. You have whatever you want. But . . . I think . . . no, don't tell me now. Whatever it is. The plan. We'll all meet round at Annette's. Yes? Think that's best. Can't take in any more. Not just at the moment, I can't.'

'Mm. Yes. I can see that you're all at sixes and sevens. Well all right then, Clifford. Let's just enjoy the rest of our meal then, shall we? I bet you would have given your eye teeth, wouldn't you Clifford? For a lunch like this, when you were a little schoolboy. Who was that beastly woman? At your school?

431

The one who forced you to eat all that terrible pie, or whatever it was?'

'Oh God don't. Chadwick. Hate her. Hate her for that. Always will. So anyway, Mummy – are you having a pudding or not? Because if you aren't, we could maybe take coffee in the lounge. Quite like a cigar . . .'

'Ooh, Clifford – you and all your big man's toys. Well we'll just have to make sure, won't we? That we can all hold on to our toys. Because I love you, Clifford – you do know that? You're the only man I could ever be close to. Oh yes! Oh yes goodness – I nearly forgot. Look – look: I have something for you. Been in my bag for days. There. You haven't got it, have you? You haven't already got that one, I hope?'

'What . . . is it?'

'Well open the little packet and *see*, silly. It's either Snap, Crackle or Pop. And they're each of them playing an instrument. Rice Krispies – I like them now. Oh let *me* do it then . . . there, let's see. Oh it's a yellow Pop. And he's blowing a trumpet. How sweet. Have you got Pop, Clifford? Blowing a trumpet?'

'Um. No, Mummy. Haven't got him.'

'Not even in a different colour?'

'No. Haven't got him at all.'

'Oh good. I am so pleased. Well get the bill then, Clifford, and then we'll go and have our coffee. Maybe some petits fours. Would you like that, Clifford? Would you?'

'I would, Mummy. Yes I would. Very much indeed.'

'I've got another packet at home. New one. Wonder who's in it . . .?'

'I wonder.'

'You'll have the whole set in no time. Two shakes of a lamb's tail. You've dropped your serviette on to the floor, Clifford, look.'

'Napkin, Mummy. It's called a napkin.'

'That may be so, but it's still on the floor, isn't it? Pick it up, there's a good boy. Now do you want to go off to the lavatory or anything? Because now's the time if you do.'

'I'm fine thank you, Mummy. I'm fine.'

'Dear Clifford. Love you. Just love you . . .'

'I know you do, Mummy. And I love you too.'

It's the cutting, you know – that's the part I most enjoy. When I've laid out my paper patterns, seen to all the chalking, and then I can shear away into this beautiful cloth with these subtle and sweeping actions that come from the elbow, and then they are lightened on the final flourish by just the merest little twist of the wrist. One always has in mind, I think, that here is to be a soft but sturdy three-dimensional thing, close to the body's contours and yet affording all the swing and easy latitude that such a garment demands. Part of the reason, this, why the coat is always put together around a bloated little hessian sort of a cushion affair; sew it flat, and flat it will always be, you see.

This particular coat I was cutting out now was very much on the grander scale. It's for Judge Fenton, one of Annette's more profitable clients. He's a very big man, I have to say; he quips that he has a body of a god, and that it is merely unfortunate that of all the gods in the Pantheon, it was his body that was plucked out to correspond broadly with that of the mighty Buddha. He does everything in twos, Judge Fenton. Maybe big people, they do this quite naturally. Two suits at a time – and two girls as well (and hence the considerable expense). The girls, they draw lots, they've told me, for which of them is to ease off as much of his weight as ever can be possible by means of an endless repertoire of erotic and diversionary stunts and titillations (the girls, believe me – they are really so terribly versed), the other girl – and usually it's Marilyn – coping with the crush of the rest of him. But the point I am making is that it is always a great pleasure to be cutting out a coat for Judge Fenton because the canvas is large, the scope quite exhilarating. All the very detailed stitching, I must admit, I farm out to a workshop in Soho, these days – very fine craftsmen, all of them there: Savile Row uses them all the time. There's one woman, Edie, must be ninety, partially blind, and she does all the silk-threaded buttonholes. I've never seen one that is less than immaculate, and she can turn around a coat – that's up to sixteen buttonholes, you know, if we're talking double-breasted – in rarely more than a couple of mornings.

'Is there anything I can do for you, Clifford? Tea, maybe? Anything you need? Anything you'd like?'

'No thank you, Sonya. I'm quite all right at the moment. I'm just going to cut out the sleeves and then I'm going over to Annette's. Little bit of a meeting.'

'Meeting? What – a family meeting? Am I to come? I can very quickly change, if you'd like me to come.'

'Oh . . . no, not really. I don't think so, Sonya. It's not that sort of meeting. It's just . . . well, you know: a meeting.'

'I'd be no bother. I wouldn't speak, Clifford, if you didn't want me to.'

'No, I'm sure. But really, Sonya – I'd be much happier if you just stayed here. I shouldn't be very long.'

'Well all right then, Clifford. Just as you say. I'll have everything ready and beautiful for you, for when you return. Yes? Is there anything special I can get you for dinner? We've got fillet steak, rack of lamb, pork chops – some beautiful veal . . .'

'Mm – any of those would be quite delightful. Thank you, Sonya.'

'Or fish? Maybe you'd like some fish. We've got sole, trout, proper wild salmon, monkfish – I could get you a lobster. You love lobster.'

'Mm – any of those would be quite delightful. Thank you, Sonya.'

And I would offer even more, just to keep him here longer, but all of my options are used. Even as I am listing this tedious menu (and it's always the same – simply the best of everything, never ever anything but the cream for my Clifford) I can see his eyes shifting, the tensions in his body that are urging him elsewhere, and of course without me. I ask him questions so that he is forced to answer; were I simply to pass comment, he would be nodding with energy or lazily smile, having listened to nothing. To keep silent is to lose him all the sooner. I must be as dull as Annette keeps on telling me I am – and her mother too, now: she tells me as well. Or could it be the bludgeon of so repeated a drubbing? Could this have subdued me into barely being? I know that for Clifford I can never be sparkling, but if only and if ever I could learn to even gleam . . . It's just that my love for him, it makes me so weak – weak in my blithe acceptance of all that comes to me, feeble to the brink of swooning whenever I measure the breadth and depth of it, this sweepingly hopeless great love that I have for him. And whatever I utter my eyes are pleading: oh God don't leave me, Clifford – not now, and not ever. As you walk through the door, I slightly die and I ache for your return. Were you never to walk back, well then it would be killing. I must never let it happen – I must blithely be accepting of all that comes to me. I forgave him the girls – Annette I tried so hard to understand, and then I gave up even trying to at all: now I just get down the bile, and ignore its burning. And even at this very moment as I just am standing here, mumming maybe like an imbecile, the tears disguised as the shining in my eyes, I feel him so edgy towards me. His mind is on the door, and he is surely determined.

'And what about dessert, Clifford? What can I get you after . . .?'

I had to say that, and now I curse myself as usual. Even as I take a loud breath and launch now so pitifully into the litany of available pies and pavlovas, mousses and meringues, crêpes and (I curse myself again) those crème caramels, I can see him now edgier, and closer to the door. Goodbye then, Clifford: goodbye again, my love.

'Mm – any of those would be quite delightful. Thank you, Sonya.'

I think I have to leave, now. These inventories – they can go on into the night (she's quite a sweet thing, Sonya, I suppose – but I'm telling you, it can become extremely wearing, you know: thanking her all the time). Also – I've just looked at my watch. I really must be going. I offered to pick up Mummy in the Bentley, but No, she said: she'd drive over herself because from now on, she said, I'm going to be completely independent. Oh and Clifford? I don't, you know, if I'm perfectly honest, terribly like this little Golf of mine any more. I did – I used to: at the beginning I thought it was perfect. But you won't think me ungrateful, will you Clifford, if I replace it with something a little bit roomier, something with a bit more power, and maybe a greater degree of comfort? No no, I assured her – whatever you like, of course: anything particular in mind? Or would you like me to have a look around and then report back to you? Well as a matter of fact, Clifford, all I would like you to do is dispose of the Golf – get what you can for it. I ordered a new car a little while ago: it's coming tomorrow morning. Oh really? Really? Well that was, um – fast work. What is it? What did you go for? Oh it's a Jaguar, Clifford: the new Jaguar. All we've got to do now is ensure that I can pay for it. Which is the purpose, isn't it? Of this little meeting of ours.

Yes well. Heaven only knows, quite frankly, what exactly was the purpose of this, as she says, little meeting of ours, and as to its outcome, well – I simply couldn't project. Annette, she was quite incredulous when I came to sort of fill her in. I felt rather stupid, if I'm honest, because here I was confiding in Annette that our mother was now wholly apprised of the extent of the problem, and that she and Tumulty had come up with a plan – while all the time I was ignorant, of course, of the nature and scale of the problem myself; it was only due to Mummy, indeed, that I was aware of the existence of a problem in the first place. Annette was wild, at first – screamed at Tumulty (I'm glad it wasn't me) and he, of course, just crossed his hands in front of his crotch, the way he always did, and looked down at the floor. Here was no display of contrition – he just was calmly waiting for the rant to be done with, whereupon she would become calmer (and she did) and see without prompting that the situation could be denied no longer (and she did) and that now, with all of us behind her, Annette should be feeling at least a modicum of relief that the burden now was no longer hers alone. And she did. Or she appeared to, anyway. When Mummy began to speak, though, there was on Annette's face only the rigid mask of just about tolerance, her mouth not still and so ready to pucker up into scorn.

'I must say you've done this room out very beautifully, Annette. So long since I was here. That rug – is that new? I haven't seen it before, have I? Really? Well I just can't have noticed it, then. Oh Edgar – don't be standing over there like that – come, come and sit down beside me. We're a team now, aren't we? All of us. What was that you said, dear? Nothing? Well it was a very funny noise, Annette. Maybe you've just a touch of the collywobbles. I swear by Eno's. Anyway look – I know you

437

don't want to hear me rambling away like a dotty old lady, so let's get down to the point, shall we?'

'That would be refreshing.'

'Ooh, Annette – I don't think we're at home to Little Miss Sarcastic, are we dear? She was always like this you know, Edgar. Well – working for her as long as you have, I expect you know all too well. Anyway, dear – and Edgar, you will speak up, won't you? If I leave something out or I get something not quite right? Because I do think it's important that we all of us *understand*. Now the first thing to be addressed, of course, is the matter of the girls themselves. Without the girls, I think we all agree, there's really nothing to discuss. We have to stop the very best of them leaving.'

'Oh I see. That's what we have to do, is it? Honestly – do you think I haven't *thought* of that? Do you think I haven't *tried*?'

'Well of course you have, Annette. I do not think you stupid. I so admire you for having built up such a wonderful organisation in the first place. And all on your own, too – I'm sure I could never have done it. But you see, Annette – and do you know, I never thought, not when you were growing up, that I'd ever be saying this to you – but you see, dear, what it is – you're being too *nice*. You're being far too *kind*. And I know you've thought it too. You've asked them to stay, the girls, of course you have, and they have politely declined your invitation, and there the matter now rests. But it can't. It mustn't. They have to be . . . persuaded. Am I not right, Edgar? Edgar knows – Edgar knows I am right.'

'Persuaded. Right. I see. And how do you suggest we—?'

'Well of course I don't really mean, do I – *persuaded*. I mean they must be made to see the error of their ways. They must be *made* to stay. The girls must be, well – threatened with repercussions. I know, I know – I know it sounds horrid. But Edgar has assured me that his men, they can be very, um – convincing. They are

438

sorely underused, you know Annette. These men, well – they are among the very best in London at all this sort of thing, and yet here you have them just running round as chauffeurs, doormen, changing the light bulbs . . . it's time they were allowed to . . . oh dear me: flex their muscles. Also, Annette – this twenty per cent business: quite ridiculous – and a contributory cause, of course, to so many of the walkouts. You must raise this immediately to fifty per cent.'

'I can't. I gave them my word.'

'Yes – but they have broken theirs. It's all about survival, Annette. I should have thought that you of all people, with all you've been through, would have understood that. And anyway – fifty per cent, it's still a great deal more than they'd be getting anywhere else. Edgar told me. Even so, Edgar's men will still not have nearly enough to do. I suggest that they lean on people, I believe is what you say. The better-known clients must know that their continued anonymity is only consistent with their latest payment. To ensure it. No no – no arguments quite yet, please Annette. We'll all have our say. I know you're going to talk about trust and loyalty and all the rest of it, but we're rather beyond all that now, aren't we dear? Just let me put it to you – think about it, as I have. I have been thinking about it for such a long time, you know. You shouldn't have left me festering in those awful two rooms for so terribly long. I had too much time, and in a bad place too. And that's another thing, Annette, that you might have considered, in the light of your past. Anyway – a lot of money, I feel confident, will be generated soon. Very soon indeed. This should not be invested, as you have been doing, Annette. It should be lent. At a certain level of interest, needless to say. To people who can go nowhere else. Edgar assures me that Lenny – is it Lenny, Edgar? Yes. Yes it is. It's Lenny. He's very good at this, Edgar tells me. Now then—'

'Oh there's more. There's more of this, is there?'

'Oh you can be so *moody*, Annette. Just *listen* to your mother, can't you? I've an old head on my shoulders. You might, you know, actually learn something, if only you'll just listen to me.'

'I think you're mad. But I'm listening . . .'

'You can think whatever you please, although I think you're very rude to say that to your mother, but there. Now – the policeman. When he next demands even more money than the last time, you, Annette – you ask him up here, offer him a drink – do your best to put on a *smile*, Annette, and say you would like to discuss it. Hanson, isn't it? Yes. Well anyway – you're chatting away, Annette, arguing your case, and Edgar next door is videotaping the whole event. And then we show our gallant detective a film he will never forget. Quite simple, but effective. I doubt he'll bother us again. The remaining problem is how to get more girls of the necessary quality.'

'We've tried. They're not around. And particularly now, if we're going to be taking fifty per cent . . .'

'We are not taking fifty per cent – we are leaving them with half. And they are – they are. Of course they're around. Beautiful, hungry women – they're always around. It's just a question of knowing where to look for them, that's all.'

'Uh-huh. I see. And you do. I don't – but you do. Is that it?'

'Well *apparently*, Annette – I'm very much afraid that that *is* it, isn't it Edgar? Dear Edgar – too loyal, you see, to speak out. There are Russian girls, Annette. Floods of them. Most of them illegal, many of them quite beautiful: looking for rich men. Czechs, Estonians, Latvians. Certain Africans. All seeking visas, marriage, passports . . . They must be persuaded. Edgar's men will take care of the willing ones, but others may need to be captured. There are things, you know, that you can put in people's drinks. Ketamine, I believe, is the chemical term. Rohypnol the brand name. Very effective. I'm told. It sounds a bit extreme, I'm quite aware of that

440

– but all it is is a slightly quicker way of just getting them here, you see. They'll love it, I'm sure, once they get used to the idea. And should they not, well . . . then one of Edgar's men can talk them out of leaving. Clifford – I rather thought you'd like to help out in this little area, you know. You're such a charmer – but this would just give you that little extra edge. You get them back here – and if I know you, my lad, you'll only be picking the very best of them – and then, well – Edgar, he'll take care of things from that stage on. Won't you, Edgar? Of course you will. So now tell me, Annette: what do you think?'

'Oh now look, Mummy – you can't really expect me to—!'

'Quiet, Clifford. I'm talking to Annette. Well, Annette?'

'Mm. Well let me see now. Unless I've forgotten some little detail along the way, what you are suggesting – no no, not suggesting: *insisting* upon, isn't that right? Is that we supplement the simple business of prostitution with, um, let me see . . . protection, extortion, intimidation, blackmail . . . and oh yes, kidnapping as well. That about it? Sum it up?'

'Ooh Annette – you'd get twenty out of twenty in a vocab test, wouldn't you dear? Yes – I mean I think I put it all a little more graciously, if you'll forgive me, but yes – I think you've grasped the essence. Oh and also, dear – I nearly quite forgot. Like with you the other day, Clifford – do you remember? At lunch? When I nearly forgot to give you the yellow Pop? With the trumpet? Yes? Well it's just the same now with this photo, look – I've got this photo, and you know it nearly completely slipped my mind to give it to Annette. Here, dear: photo for you. Oh and Clifford – something little for you too, but you'll have to pick it up when you next come round because Mummy has very stupidly forgotten to put it in her bag – but I've got Crackle for you now! Red: hitting a drum.'

'What . . . is this? What is this a picture of? I can't make it out . . .'

441

'Honestly, Edgar – you had one of your people go to all that trouble to take the photo, and now the girl can't even make out what it is. Well what does it *look* like, Annette?'

'It looks . . . I don't know what it looks like . . . grass, bundle of rags . . . is that a hand there? It's terribly dark . . .'

'Oh it's no good. Do you give up, then? I'd better tell you. I mean I know it's not a very good likeness, but I did think you'd recognise her. It's Sister Joanna! Don't tell me you don't remember her because I just know you do. Honestly, Edgar – never stopped talking about her, how she hated her so much. Well there – you don't have to hate her any more. Because she's gone. Say *thank* you, Mummy . . .'

'This is . . .? But . . . I don't understand. How can . . .?'

'Well it wasn't easy – was it, Edgar? Apparently she only ever left that awful place in Ireland on Friday mornings. Was Fridays, wasn't it? Yes. Fridays. So Edgar's connection there, he had to wait and wait in the pouring rain, poor dear. And then he shot her through the head. You can't see the head – I don't think there was a great deal of it left. She was terribly old, of course – would've died soon anyway. But you see, Annette – I thought you'd appreciate the gesture. And also, I suppose it was a way of proving to you that certain things, well . . . they can be quickly and efficiently carried out. You see? Oh and Clifford – I didn't want you to feel left out. Because I've learned, Edgar, you know – as a mother, if you give one of them a little gift, well then you just have to do the same for the other or else they go into the most awful huff, you know, and so—'

'I . . . can't *believe* it . . .! . . .'

'Oh be quiet, Annette. I'm still talking. But I'm afraid, Clifford, that I've got a disappointment for you. Your Mrs Chadwick – yes? Remember? Well of course you do. She died, Clifford – oh, about five years ago, I think. I'm so sorry – I so wanted to have her killed for you, but there – what could I do? At least she's dead, hey? Let's hope it was lingering or something, shall we? And the same thing happened with that horrid Mrs Farlow – I expect you were both too young at the time to remember Mrs Farlow. Well *you* might, I suppose, Annette. Remember her. Perfectly horrid woman, she was. Anyway – Edgar, he tracked her down to her last address, and wouldn't you know, she as well – she'd already died. Strange, isn't it, how these women have haunted us . . . So anyway, that was another big disappointment. Still – never mind. At least I was able to help Annette. Oh and Clifford – just to make up, I've got something else for you. Oh no no – I don't mean *Crackle*, no no: of course not. That's not a proper present, is it? No look – afterwards . . . because Annette, she might think to offer us some tea, you never know . . . and then afterwards, Clifford, you come back home with me and just see what it is that I've got for you! So do you think that would be a good idea then, Annette? Some tea? Oh for goodness sake stop *glaring* at me like that, can't you? What's wrong? It was only an old *nun* that you hated, wasn't it? Who was cruel to you? Thought you'd be happy. Children today – no matter what you do to try to please them, they're always just so terribly ungrateful. I didn't see you caring very much about all that sort of thing when you were little. I didn't glare at *you*, did I? When you killed your father, that time. So just stop now behaving like a spoilt little girl and let's for goodness sake all of us sit down and have a nice hot cup of tea. Oh yes – I looked in the last packet I opened, but I think they've done away with them now, you know, Clifford. Tea cards . . .'

The three of us – Annette, Tumulty and myself – we all appeared to be stricken silent during the stark and suspended moments after Mummy's quite breezy departure. The silence, it seemed all the more shocking and thoroughly unreal because throughout her measured and very assured outpourings (and she had been, hadn't she? So terribly assured) the room had been alive with all manner of interjection, exclamations of disbelief, thwarted attempts to talk her down, intaken hisses of outrage – sometimes even a gobbet of delirious laughter (some from me, most of them from Annette) and then quite fearful pauses as we were once again left dangling over an unexplained abyss, stepping back with energy as seemingly solid ground was cracked asunder into sudden fissure and a beckoning chasm (alarmed by the distant rumble of a coming avalanche). It was Annette, as it had to be, who first broke the silence.

'Well. She's mad, right? I mean we all do agree, don't we, that she's gone completely mental? And why is she suddenly so bloody . . . *articulate*? She was never that, was she Cliff? So articulate. Speaking that way. Where did all that suddenly come from?'

'We're all of us different now . . .'

'Yes I know – but we've worked at it, haven't we Cliff? She's just – suddenly become this . . . *thing*. Jesus. Well look come on, Tumulty – you, it was you who brought her into the magic circle. What have you got to say? You haven't said a single word. Well? Tell me. She's nuts. Right?'

Tumulty, he simply expanded his mouth into the tight and joyless smile, his eyes opaque (devoid of all amusement), and stretched out the fingers on each of his large and bony hands; his eyebrows were raised up practically to the hairline. That, I thought, was all we were going to get out of Tumulty: we could make what we would of it.

'It wasn't . . .' I ventured – and quite carefully, because

444

Annette, she was teetering, you know, between something and something else entirely (I didn't know what, and I didn't at all care to) . . . 'It wasn't . . . altogether nonsense, though. Was it? I mean to say – you, Annette, it's you who knows all the ins and outs of the business. Well you too, Tumulty, of course. Me – I'm just, well – on the sidelines, aren't I really? But if the problems really are all that severe, well . . . it seemed to me that there was quite a lot of good sense then, actually. Brave . . . Daring, I mean. Quite bloody frightening, really. But maybe practicable. I mean I'm guessing, but I don't think Tumulty would have been sitting here – confided in her in the first place – if he didn't go along with it all, broadly speaking. Well – the plan, it's a joint effort, from what we've heard. Isn't that so, Tumulty?'

Tumulty, he slowly closed his eyes – and equally slowly, opened them wide again. There was ample time for both Annette and myself to have observed the exhibition, and then to draw our own conclusions.

'There are certainly . . . things to think about . . .' conceded Annette – and the tone, it was not nearly so grudging as I had expected it to be. 'Look, Tumulty – you know I trust you. And of course you know we're in one hell of a hole, here. If all this could really *work* . . . I mean – you wouldn't, would you? Take us into this, if you didn't really believe that it all could actually work? No. You wouldn't. Well. We have to think. We have to think. Um – Tumulty . . .? This picture. It's really her, is it? It's really . . . Sister Joanna? No mistake? It's not some other witch . . . it is actually *the* witch. Right? Sure?'

Tumulty closed his eyes once more, and this time he nodded, slowly and sombrely: his most absolute assurance.

'Christ . . .! . . .' breathed out Annette.

'Are you, um – sorry, Annette?'

I didn't quite know what else I should say; it wasn't even what I meant – but there, I said it anyway.

'Sorry? Yes, I'm sorry. I'm bloody sorry I wasn't *there*. I would have loved to have *seen* it. See her recognise me – see the fear, the uncontrolled, the uncut fear as that gun was raised up to her head. Why are they always so terrified of death, these vile old crones? All their lives they've been praying to God – well now it's time to meet in person the star of the show, so why aren't you *laughing*? Hey? Why aren't you *laughing*, you vile and disgusting – *creature*?!'

'Annette? You all right? You're shaking. Do you want a drink of something?'

'Hm? No. No. I'm fine. I'm perfectly fine. OK, Cliff – you go now. I've got to talk to Tumulty. Get into the detail, now. Work out all the detail. You go and see her. See she hasn't just bought a machine gun, or something. Maybe that's what it is she said she'd got for you, Cliff: maybe she's just gone out and bought you a machine gun.'

Well no – it wasn't that that she'd got for me. It turned out to be very small and, I suppose, eternally precious. When I drove round there, I was surprised to see an unfamiliar car in the place where the Golf had always been parked – a gleaming, dark blue Jaguar – and even more surprised to make out through the green tinted glass – Mummy, still in the driving seat, and gripping the wheel. Oh Christ, I thought – she's had a seizure, or something: the excitement, the strain, it's all been too much for her. But no no – nothing of the sort. She was beaming delightedly. She liked to sit there, she said, because of the heady smell of all the leather, and also because the seat, the seat itself, it just held the small of her back, cradled it in quite the most perfect position – far more comfortable than her armchair in the living room; because she gets, you know, just the tiniest little touch of lumbago, these days, nothing at all for me to be even the least bit concerned about, though – hardly anything at all, really: not even worth mentioning. And then she stepped out of the car and began to urge me into the flat (prodding at me from behind: 'Come on – come on, Clifford: get a move on, can't you? You always were such a terrible *dawdler* . . .').

Did I want tea? No – no tea, thank you Mummy. Champagne? There's a bottle in the fridge, if I didn't mind seeing to it. No no – I'm absolutely fine, thank you Mummy – but can I get *you* something, maybe? Oh heavens *no*, Clifford – I'm far too excited to think about anything of that sort. So tell me, Clifford: what did she say? When I'd gone. I expect she said that I was a completely ga-ga old woman and that I should be left to my knitting and quietly forgotten. Or somesuch. Did she? Ah – I can see by your eyes that she did: you can't keep anything from your Mummy, can you now Clifford? Read you like an open book – always could, always could. But then – a bit later – she thought but oh hold on a minute! What about Edgar? *He's* not a dotty old woman, is he? And then she will have begun to think about everything that I actually *said*, won't she? And by now she will know that it all makes sense. Desperate remedies, you see Clifford? Desperate remedies. Had to be done. And when everything's up and running, Annette of course will be the first to claim all of the credit – you know: for making it work – and do you know what, Clifford? Shall I tell you? I shan't mind a bit. Just so long as we're all of us *saved* – that's all I care about. Because I really do think that we deserve it, you know. Don't you, Clifford? Salvation. I do believe it's our due.

I hadn't noticed (I don't think I had been meant to) that while she had been so gaily prattling away to me there, she had placed on the table between us a small drawstring bag, just pink, and I think it might have been kidskin – it was anyway quite heavenly to the touch.

'Oh don't *touch*, Clifford – always grabbing, aren't you? Just wait your turn like a good little boy. Now then – close your eyes.

447

No no – don't argue. Just close your eyes, and hold out your hand. And when I put something into your palm, then you close your hand right up, right up tight into a fist – and no *peeking*, Clifford: promise me now.'

I did exactly as she asked me to (well of course I did exactly as she asked me to) and I soon was aware of something small and cold and hard and quite light in my hand.

'Can I open my eyes now?'

'Not yet. Wait until you're told. Wait . . . wait . . . just let me . . . right. All right. Now, Clifford – now you can open your eyes.'

And so I sat there opposite her, one of my hands still balled up – and over there was Mummy, and she too seemed to be gripping something tightly. And although the room was not dark, she had lit a candle, and it glowed between us.

'I . . . open my hand now . . .?'

'Yes, Clifford. Now you do. You open your hand.'

So I did that then – and I gazed down at the white and glinting little stone in the palm of my hand, caught now by the candle and winking quite ferociously: gleaming piercing shards of orange and blue.

'It's . . . beautiful. It's . . . lovely. Is it a . . .?'

'Yes. It is. A diamond – a flawless diamond. Quite unlike those very terrible zirconias – do you remember, Clifford? Those little fragments of anthracite on that nasty little ring your father gave to me? This is the real thing. And it's for you. And now look what *I've* got . . .'

Her palm was outstretched – she moved her hand towards mine, until our fingertips were touching. The stone that lay there was a rich and magnificent, an even dangerous green.

'Diamond,' she said. 'And Emerald. That's what we are, now. That's what we must call ourselves, Clifford – because that's what we are, now. I am Emerald. And you, my love – you are Diamond.'

I do not know why, but my eyes became warm, and then a tear was forming, though I just held it back. There was uneasiness within me, and a hint of excitement overlaid by an utter fascination; a thick complicity too was all around us. I looked up and was pierced by just the flecks of fire in the dark and lit-up intensity of her eyes. My mother was gone now, and all that lay open to me in the future was just this blackly glittering lady.

I rather think he liked that: I'm sure of it, no I'm certain that he did. Because it's not every day, is it, that a mother gives her one and only son so special and flawless a jewel. I do so hope he takes good care of it, though – not just plonks it down any old where like he always did with his satchel and those blessed little Matchbox cars of his (always getting under your feet). Edgar, he told me he had dealings with this little man who trades in Hatton Garden: apparently they were a bargain, the diamond and the emerald, and there are some things, aren't there, that you just, I suppose, must take on trust. They're beautiful, I said to Edgar: how much do I owe you? Nothing, he said: forget it. Well that's terribly *sweet* of you, Edgar, and I do so hope you won't think me ungrateful, but there is no way at all, I'm afraid, that I could possibly, could I, 'forget it'. Now no more shilly-shally: how much? The emerald, he said: it's a gift. For you. I want you to have it. And honestly, you know, when he holds me so tightly in those big strong manly arms of his, it's so blissfully difficult to resist. Well then I thank you, Edgar – truly I do – but you must then let me pay for Clifford's diamond: I insist. Yeh yeh – whatever, he went, in his big man gruff voice (he's just like a fluffy giant teddy bear, you know: he really is, when you get to know him).

But I do so love to give him things (Clifford, I'm talking about – with Edgar it's more of a problem: though I knitted him a balaclava, and that seemed to please him – Edgar, I mean). Because it reminds me of when he was little (and I'm back now with Clifford, of course) and when I was the only person in the whole wide world who would shield him from all the bad and frightening things out there. Ah me – him and his sweets and his soldiers and his Airfix kits! So sweet, so terribly sweet. And tucking him in at night-time, and there he'd be always babbling away to me thirteen to the dozen about every sort of nonsense under the sun. I was looking over the old photo albums just the other evening (I do that more and more) and you know you can still see the little boy in him: he's changed really barely at all. I'll always look after him: I think he understands that. Oh and the girls, you know – some of the girls have taken to calling me Mummy, and I do so appreciate the gesture. I try to see they have all they need. I'm always on hand for a bit of advice and any little sewing jobs they might want doing (because you should just see the young girls these days with a needle and thread! Honestly – not the first idea: they're all at sixes and sevens). I buy them things in town if they're too busy working to get out themselves. But they know not to take advantage, I think: firm but fair would be my own summing up, and I imagine they'd agree. All but one of them, anyway. That Lucinda – she really was so terribly naughty. Threatening me, like that. Actually telling me to my face that if I didn't agree to giving her, oh – some quite preposterous sum of money, can't even remember, that she'd be talking to, oh what is it . . .? That dreadful little newspaper that's all about celebrities and scandal. Well I had to be quite firm with her: I don't bow to blackmail, I told her. No but you don't mind *practising* it, she says to me, bold as you like. Terribly rude, and so thoroughly ungrateful, after all we've done for her. Well – there's always a rotten apple, I suppose: you just have to expect it. But one or two of the other girls, you know, I'm really rather closer to, I think, than I ever was to Annette. Isn't that funny? Isn't that odd? She was always so headstrong, you see – well she still is, of course, isn't she? A lot of it is bluster, I do know that much. But where can she go for comfort, the poor little thing? To Clifford? I don't really think he could help her, you know: he'd be blind to the predicament. She could always come to me, of course, but she wouldn't, she wouldn't ever. And I can't, can I? *Say* anything . . . So there it lies. I have to accept it. Along with, ooh – just so very much else. Because despite what people might think, I am not really at all overjoyed, you know, about the person I have seemingly become. And how I am so suddenly *responsible*. But I just had to become . . . well, after so very many years when I had so totally, well – lost all sight of myself, really – I just had to, didn't I, become *something* . . .? And this is all that presented itself. So we make do and mend, and be grateful for small mercies. We all of us can only play (it was Edgar who told me this, and I think it's rather good) – we can only play the cards we are dealt (with so little resort to skill and wisdom, I have decided, and an endless reliance upon the brazen bluff). But I do so hope that my apparent self-confidence is not just persuasive but founded in reality (I hear myself sometimes, and I am practically convinced). Heaven help us all if I am doing it wrong, though: then there could be wigs on the green. And often I do need a support of my own:

'It will, won't it Edgar? All come out right in the end . . .?'

He just grunted, poor love (I think I had woken him); he rolled over then to my side of the bed and he clasped me close, and not too gently.

451

♠

The coming weeks and months, I cannot say that they were easy. A lot of it I tried to – well, distance myself, I suppose. From it. Annette, she was obviously aware, far more aware than I, of everything that was occurring. Well obviously. Change was all around. Amanda, she left us, you know: said she was horrified, when Annette tried to talk to her about . . . all of it. She wasn't even going to listen, she said; and then she left us. Annette, she trusts Amanda, so I think it will be all right (God – hope so, anyway). And Mummy, well . . . (or Emerald, am I really meant to say now? I mean am I *really*? She gets into the most awful state, you know, these days, if I don't) . . . well anyway, whatever you want to call her, she too is – aware. Aware is not quite right. Well actually it's not even remotely close, let's face it: she makes it happen. I mean, Annette, I think, would not like to hear that (and she won't – not from me) but the bare truth of it is that the rules now – you just have to ask Tumulty if you won't accept it from me – they come directly from the top – and the top now, rather bizarrely, is, um . . . Emerald. Which is a silly and rather wrong name, I know – but in these new and strange circumstances, it maybe sounds rather less silly and wrong than, um . . . Mummy. It's quite extraordinary. I'm sorry if I'm sounding slow, or appear to be slack-mouthed and hick about this (forever and annoyingly amazed) but I really do find it all so laughable, really, and difficult to accept. No: not laughable; it's not funny, you know. And no not accept either: I accept anything, this has to be recognised. It's just that when I think of the *source* of all this . . . I mean, I don't think about it that much (I try, as I say, with varying degrees of success, to distance myself as far as I possibly can) but then I

452

catch myself remembering the origin, the deviser of the scheme, and I just tremble, quite frankly. Shudder. I mean, one moment she'll be quizzing me over the detail of my latest abduction, and then she'll be passing to me a toy from a cereal packet – quizzing me with an equal intensity as to whether or not we've already got this thing, and how far are we now ('Diamond'!) from completing the set . . .? I don't think she's going mad . . . Annette does, Annette thinks she's losing it – while not arguing too much, however, with the implementation or course of her particular derangement, if such it may be. What I believe is that the process is over: she's not going mad, it's all in the past now, whatever was the trigger, that's long gone. But if we continue to employ this big little word 'mad', then I think she went it, oh – a good long while ago now, in silence and alone. It was maybe true what she said that time, you know – we shouldn't have left her to fester in those terrible two rooms for nearly so long. Although had that not happened, then in all likelihood she might not have, as it were, um . . . found herself. Been reborn. In the way she clearly has. But alternatively, of course – and I know, I know it's irritating, but I just have to (it's in my nature) at least glance over to the other side of things – her renaissance, if we may call it that, might have assumed a more usual progression: it might well have been a good deal less wicked. Which is a terrible thing, really, isn't it? To say about one's mother. And it has to make you wonder whether it is just the information that I shy away from, and not the spreading bruise, the blemish, the creeping taint of blame. Because for all of us now, black sin is our constant companion, our willing accomplice, a dark and corrupting ally in the waging of a seemingly effortless campaign to ensure that evil will trounce and trample over goodness – annihilate even the sweet lingering scent of it: we all have to be immune now to the mingled stenches of our own exudations.

I attempted, rather wetly, to distil the vital essence of even just

453

the guts of this – tried to be at least passingly articulate – in order to make Annette aware of the first breath of fog, to maybe make her twitch at this first stale trailing of a bad and corrosive air, heralding the coming of if not a storm so ferocious as to smash us all to atoms (and merely in passing) then an enveloping miasma so thoroughly dense as to blind us to our actions. I wanted her to make it stop. She didn't want to, though. I didn't actually ask her, and so she didn't refuse. But she didn't want to anyway. And nor, I have to recognise, would she have been remotely able to: the thunder and momentum of a tumbling boulder – you can only stare in stricken wonder and not even think to outrun or hinder its gathering volition. We can only step aside. Which was more or less the gist of all she had to tell me. Her shoulders were warm against mine in the deep white rumple of bed; her fingers were cool, though, as she tenderly stroked me in the way I like best.

'Will you do it to me now, Cliff?'

'You've never asked me before . . .'

'I've wanted to. You don't have to do it hard, or anything. Not if you don't want to. Let me lie across you. Yes?'

'But Annette – why do you want me to hit you? Why can't I just – caress you, like I always do?'

'It's just a game, Cliff. It's only a little game. It's spanking – it's not "hitting". But you can if you want. Hit me. Hard, if you like. I don't mind. Want you to. Don't want anyone else to. Just you. Because I love you.'

She likes to watch, she'd been telling me, if ever there is what it pleases her to call 'discipline' to be administered. But according to Mummy (Emerald!) – and I do so wish I didn't know this – Annette, she likes to do very much more than just watch. Emerald says that her source was Tumulty – that Tumulty told her, and then she told me; and I wish she hadn't. Sometimes one of our newer girls – Varuschka, most recently: one of my own acquisitions, as it happens (beautiful girl – beautiful bones; I do so hope she's sixteen) – sometimes one of them, the girls, will become over-assertive, or even greedy: they need to be gently reminded, according to Annette, exactly who it is who wields the power. Who has the whip hand, if you like. And did I use the term 'gently'? Well – not that gently, I regret to say. At first I had thought that all she was doing was simply trying out another new word on me, the way she ever more frequently does, these days (and she catches me out, you know, more often than not; I just don't seem able to find the time any more – and I can't imagine why – to diligently comb and fillet my Chambers). Bastinado. Is what she said. And I didn't know: hadn't a clue – hazarded the orphans' home, knew it wasn't that. I was guessing though – after the 'tribady' thing – that it might have something or other to do with sex. But of course it doesn't: it has everything to do with violence. These twin poles, as I see them, for Annette, of course, are generally perceived to be one and the same. You see, she explained (and why do they, these women? Tell me such things?), if you cane the girl on the soles of her feet, you sidestep the inconvenience of any visible damage. Her words. And also it is, she assured me, quite excruciatingly painful: the girl, you see, will remember. Not to step out of line. Again. None of any of it ever seems to faze her. It was just the police, I think – it was only the fear of arrest that alarmed her. Apparently unfounded, as it transpired; the aberrant policeman – so far – he has done as he was told. (How did she know all this? Emerald. Our mother. That it would work. How did she *know* all this . . .?) Anyway. But with Annette, you see – until this day – the violence had always been outwardly directed. Annette, she was always the great inflictor. But now . . . she wants me to hit her. Hard, if I like. Which seems rather strange.

'OK, Cliff? Is that comfortable for you? I'm not too heavy, am I?'

'No no. It's fine. You're fine as you are.'

455

'Do I look beautiful, Cliff . . .?'

'Always. Always you do, Annette. To me.'

'And is my bottom pretty? Do you think it looks pretty, Cliff?'

'It's, um – lovely. A treat.'

'Well . . . go on then, Cliff. Go on.'

'You're absolutely sure about this, are you Annette?'

'Oh God's sake go *on*, Cliff. Go on. Do it.'

'Right. OK, then. If you're sure. There. And there. That all right? Not hurting you too much, am I?'

'I can barely – even *feel* it, Cliff. Oh go *on*. Do it.'

'Right. OK, then. There! How about that then, Annette . . .?'

'Oh Christ. *Hit* me, Cliff. Christ's sake *hit* me. What's wrong with you? I'm not going to *break*, am I?'

'Hope not, Annette. OK, then. Right. What about *that*, then?'

'Mm. Good, Cliff. Good. Go on. Go on. Mm. Mmm. Ow. Oh ow. Oh *please* stop spanking me, sir . . .!'

'Hm? Oh OK. Sorry. Thought you wanted me to.'

'I *do* want you to. Go *on*. Go *on* . . .!'

'But you just said . . .!'

'Oh Jeeeesus, Cliff! Hit me. Yes. Oh yes. Good. Good. Mmm. Mm. Oh *please* stop spanking me, sir . . .!'

'Um . . . that means go on, right?'

'Mm. Right. Well *do* it, can't you? Go *on* . . .!'

'This is all very complicated . . .'

'Oh God. OK – OK, Cliff. It's not working. Just stop. Stop, OK? Right. Let's just touch one another.'

'Right. OK, then. Great. That's what I said in the first place . . .'

Later – I'd come, she'd come, so we were both of us feeling quite mellow, sitting in the drawing room and sipping champagne – Tumulty was suddenly there, knocking belatedly on the door he'd just walked through. He said to Annette that it was OK: he'd got rid of it. And then he strolled away again.

'Got rid of what, Annette? What was he talking about?'

456

'Oh. Nothing.'

'Nothing? Well obviously it's *not* nothing, is it Annette? Or else he wouldn't have said it, would he? What he did.'

'Oh . . . it was just something that, you know: had to be got rid of.'

'Yes. I'm with you so far. But *what*, Annette, is what I'm asking you, you see.'

'You don't want to know, Cliff.'

'Ah – wrong, Annette, you see. Quite wrong. I think it's very obvious that I *do*, in fact, want to know, Annette. Hence my asking, you see.'

'You're bloody annoying when you go on like this, you know Cliff. Don't you have a bar to go to? Isn't that what you said? That you're going to get us another girl?'

'Yes – that is what I said. And that's exactly what I'm going to do. But there remains unresolved, you see, this little matter of—'

'Oh God do you *really* want to know, Cliff?'

'Apparently, Annette. It would rather seem so, wouldn't it?'

'Oh OK, Cliff. Right. Body.'

'Body?'

'You asked: I told you.'

'What – body as in . . . dead body, do you mean?'

'You don't talk of live ones, do you? If it's alive, it's a person. If it's dead, it's a body.'

'Jesus. Who? What happened?'

'Oh please let's leave it, Cliff.'

'Leave it? What do you mean – *leave* it?'

'It's done, isn't it? It's done.'

'What's done? Who's done what? What's *happened*, Christ's sake? Who's died?'

'Oh . . . it's nobody.'

'The body is nobody? Try harder, Annette. Was it one of the punters, or something?'

'Yes. No.'

'Yes? No? Not a punter . . .?'

'I *said* not, didn't I?'

'Well what, then?'

'What do you mean what then? What what?'

'What was it? The body.'

'Oh Jesus.'

'Well? What? Who died, for the love of God?'

'Girl. It was one of the girls. OK?'

'Oh no. Oh no. Jesus. Who? Which one?'

'Oh . . . you don't know her.'

'What do you mean I don't know her? I know all of the girls, what are you talking about?'

'Lucinda. OK? Lucinda.'

'Really . . .? Lucinda? Oh God. Oh dear. Oh dear oh dear. How? Why?'

'She just . . . died. She was a cokehead. You know that.'

'She was? I didn't know that, actually. I had no idea. So it was a – what? Overdose? Is that what you're saying?'

'If you like.'

'What do you mean 'if I like'? Was it or wasn't it?'

'Look, Cliff – it's no good shouting at *me*, is it?'

'I'm not shouting.'

'You bloody are shouting!'

'I just want to *know*, that's all.'

'You want to know? Well ask your bloody mother, if you bloody want to know. Ask your bloody mother.'

'*Our* mother, Annette. She's *our* mother. Remember?'

'She's more your mother than she ever was mine . . .'

'You think so?'

'I know so. She told me. When we were kids. She said to me that you, Cliff – you took after her, and I took after my father.'

'Our father.'

458

'Who aren't in heaven. Yes.'

'I see. The father you killed, you mean?'

'Leave it, Cliff.'

'OK. I will. I'll leave it. I'm going now.'

'Good. Go.'

'Not very friendly, Annette.'

'Oh just fuck off, Cliff. OK?'

'OK. Right then. I will.'

And I did. And all the way to the bar, all I could think was this: the blackly glittering lady, she thinks I take after her.

♠

He says he wants the truth, but he doesn't. Not really. He won't, of course, even mention it to her: won't say a word. He shouts his head off at me all right, but he knows his bloody mother is the one with all the answers – yet he won't, he won't even so much as mention it to her. And he still has this idea, you know – even at the age he is now – that if it is one of your parents who is behaving in a certain way . . . well then it just has to be all right then, doesn't it? Because it is they, after all, who make all the rules. No? He would scoff, of course, Clifford, at so simplistic an exposition, but at base it is the truth of the matter, however much he would argue. Well I've never had any truck whatever with that way of thinking: I knew that what my father did was wrong – that he had to pay the price. But Clifford, I think he could justify his turning any number of blind eyes, really, simply because his mother is the source of the unforgiving sight. Even all he does to get these girls – his own mother told him to, so it's really quite all right. And even I find it sickening, I have to confess – I who can see no wrong in the boy, and God knows the depth of my love for him; I am maybe being quite shockingly hypocritical, in the light of my history, but there – that is all I am feeling. Why, I think, I will always admire Amanda for leaving when she did: she was far from pure, Amanda, but she saw quite plainly where a line is to be drawn, and she did not hesitate and nor would she be cajoled into a reconsideration by all of my disingenuous banter. But I'm quite easy about all that our mother has become: I like it that she's taking care of business, and taking care of me: she never did before. I would love to be a child again . . . up till the moment my father and then the nuns despoiled me. I told this to my doll, Belinda, and I think I saw her smile, as if in welcome. And even that, it made me cry.

It might sound rather terrible, you know – it didn't, maybe strangely, feel it at the time, but looking back now I can see so clearly how very, um – shall we say misguided, I was . . . and so it must sound very terrible, then, if I say that I came to regard these occasional trips to bars and clubs as really quite normal, just a humdrum little bit of business that had simply to be done.

I was terrified the first time, of course – covered in guilt, self-conscious to the point of explosion, but frightened more than anything – but at base, though, I was still very pleased and proud, you know, that this key and fundamental activity had been entrusted to me. Because it was true: I had imagined, my God – for how long? That the simple fact of the day-to-day running of the organisation had been completely outside of me; that Annette – because she loved me, I suppose – continued to ensure that I always enjoyed whatever I wanted, without my having really to ever contribute. And Emerald, I think she would have gone along with that too – because she loved me, I suppose – but she must have divined that if I were actually to be given a serious role . . . then I would maybe grow to fill it? Come to enjoy it, even . . . and certainly feel a whole lot, um – I was going to say *cleaner*, I don't at all know why; but no – I don't think any one of us will ever feel that again . . . but it was good to know that I was no longer just a taker, a hanger-on: a parasite, let's be quite clear about it. And of course her instinct had been as sound as ever (she's still teaching me, really – rearing me – though with rather less emphasis upon the simple difference between right and wrong). I came to be very good at what I did, I'm afraid to say. Yes. And Tumulty, I've noticed, is regarding me with a new and very welcome . . . well, I hesitate to say 'respect', you know, but the bare fact that he regards me at all – it's never in words, of course; it's seldom more than just the set of his shoulders . . . well, let us just say that it does no harm at all to my self-esteem (and then let's just leave it like that).

There were two quite distinct approaches to these little sorties – trawling the bars, never drinking, always sipping, and forever on the alert for a winning potential. Some of these places I went to . . . well, some of them were among the very best-known bars and clubs in London: the ones everyone's heard of – the places that are hard to get into, where books and records and films are elaborately launched. One would make friends with the front-of-house people, that was the first thing. The head barman, his collaboration was nearly always essential. Before I would give them any money, however, I had to be as sure as ever one can be when nefarious dealings are the order of the day, that they would not only cooperate, but that they fully understood the, shall we say – nature of the business; any belated cries of ignorance or innocence would be stepped upon, hard: they simply had to know this. In the early days, one or two of Tumulty's people would be standing just a pace behind me; this served well to reinforce the message. Initially, I concentrated upon the sort of working girls who are collectively described as 'high-class', which never fails to raise a smile in me. It's their utter perfection that makes them stand out – but only just enough to get them noticed by a serious player (or, as came to be the way: me). They are centrefold beauties, superbly dressed and accessorised – but always to just that one degree higher than a regular woman: a great deal of time and money has gone into this scented vision of flawlessness, utter and disarming. The defining factor, of course, is that they are never accompanied but always, if approached, awaiting a friend (or, as came to be the way: me). To these women I would simply suggest that they might be better off if they came to work for us. Some needed an upfront cash inducement, and that was perfectly fine. Others would have to see for themselves one or other of Tumulty's people unsmilingly reach into his inside pocket: that, generally, was more than enough.

But all of this, it was merely business. No one was under any illusion, is what I mean to say; the beginnings of corruption, they were lost now to the past. These women were in the business for the long haul (which wouldn't, in truth, be that long at all; if they knew this, they did not say) and as it was clear to me that they were never now going to come to their senses, then maybe instead they would come to an arrangement. It is on deals such as this that I cut my teeth. The other side, though – the alternative approach to another sort of girl in another sort of place – that was altogether different: dark stain, true sin – and I took to it all with so casual a facility. Because there were, apparently – and I had not had even the faintest idea, you know, because I don't actually seem to have the time, these days, to even riffle through a newspaper: just do the crossword – but it seems as if for some time there has been a spate of usually illegal immigrants homing in on London, with no idea of our language, no money, no plan and often not even anywhere to stay. The men – and I get all of this from Tumulty, so I presume he knows what he's talking about – they tend, if they're honest and hard-working (how sweet a phrase that is), to go into the building trade, for hire by the day. Others become muscle, of course – either legally, as bouncers, or else not. The girls (and this is where I come in) are really so innocent, so young; you would think it might break my heart. But it doesn't. Because I've rationalised it, you see. Look – it's like I said: they've got nothing, some of these girls, nothing at all. So what I am offering them is, well – more than they ever dreamed of, really. A warm and beautiful room, lovely clothes, good meals, hairdressing, use of a luxury car . . . well, the places a lot of these girls come from, you know, you'd have to be a high-ranking official to have even a chance of living like that. Which is why, quite naturally, so many are so eager. I don't, of course, tell them the whole of it, not straight away (well of course I don't), but these girls, they're not stupid, you know; many of them have a good education, a degree – and some, not many, but some do have a tentative grasp upon at least the fundaments of English. They can be quite ravishingly beautiful – the Slavs, the Estonians in particular: an aristocratic beauty that is irresistible here – high cheekbones, wide eyes, a broad expanse of forehead and the most generous of mouths imaginable. So I bring them back to meet Annette. Often they are in pairs, you know – and that's more than fine, of course: two birds with one stone. After a day or so in Ebury Street (the new ones, we always start them off in Ebury Street) they relax, unwind quite a bit, are so excited by the perfumes and the clothes and the jewellery and so on . . . and then they maybe have to admit to themselves that there has to be a catch. It's explained to them. Some nod, slowly and maybe sadly – sigh quite deeply, and embrace it. Others, well – they can go berserk, you know: very volatile. Threaten us with all sorts of things: make a break for the door. This is where I come in again, I'm afraid. I spike the drink. We have such an array of these drugs, oh – I just can't tell you: God alone knows where they all come from. They are not knocked out, the girls (where would be the profit in that?); more, they become . . . compliant. Rather giggly, rather childish, and wholly amenable. Sometimes, between doses, they appear to rouse themselves – find in themselves again some dragged-out vestige of who they really are – and then they can become quite violent. So we have these chains. And I sit with them. Sometimes for days. They stare at me with venom. And then, in time, they are eager to please me – at first, of course, as a subterfuge, and then simply, I think, because we are, the two of us, confined together: this, at least, we have in common. Well yes it is, I suppose, the Stockholm Syndrome – the jailer and the jailed, in a strange and mutual complicity. It is an uneasy bonding, though, and I think neither party will ever forget it. I never, by the way, touch these girls. This has never occurred. I think it is because I see them as my girls, somewhat perversely; I think it is because I know where they have been.

With some of them, the problems begin in the bar itself. Whether or not they understand a single word that I am saying to them, all they do is shake their heads. I point to the door – they shake their heads. I show them money – they shake their heads. I smile a great deal and pay them wasted compliments, and still all they do is they shake their heads. This is the moment, alas, when a few little drops must be added to their drinks. It is most efficacious. Within so much less than an hour, the two of us are laughing away and tottering into a taxi – two tipsy chums, at the end of a night out. The following morning, they look and feel rather awful, I have to say – and then all the other girls are nice to them; they have been told to be, yes – but I think that it is anyway in their nature. Someone of the right nationality can generally be found, and then the learning process, it begins to take its course. The problem with this strategy – and I am not discussing morals here, you understand: I am simply addressing the practical drawbacks – is that once they are in one of our houses, you see – once they have talked among themselves, seen faces, come to terms with the scenario . . . well of course we simply can't then, can we? Ever let them go. Can't. One tried: to get away. One of my girls, I'm afraid (Annette used to tease me about this one, as a matter of fact; she was very young and from nearer to home – Irish, very pretty. Annette used to say that she could be Mary's daughter – remember Mary, Cliff? Your little wife from long ago? Yes Annette – I do, thank you. Well I think this one's her daughter. Thank you, Annette – in other words, mine too: ho ho). But she was the only one, though: the only one who ever tried it. She threw a chair through the window of the downstairs saloon in Ebury Street – tried to clamber through it, cut herself so badly. Tumulty told me that Emerald had decided she should be given an injection: to calm her down – make her sleep. An injection? I can't give her an injection – don't know the first bloody thing, do I? About injections. I'll give her a dose, if you want: handful of pills – but I'm not going to get involved in injections. And then he handed it to me, Tumulty: it was all prepared. He lightly depressed the syringe's plunger, and a mist hissed away from the gleaming needle. Well, I said . . . if you've got it, Tumulty, then you might as well administer it, hadn't you? But Tumulty, he said to me: she was most insistent that it should be you. Why, I said: why? Because it's one of my girls? Tumulty shrugged, as eventually he generally did. So anyway . . . I did that. Antonia was her name. And the joiner and the glazier came along shortly afterwards (two of our special people, needless to say) and then the window was fixed and the chair was a write-off, of course, and that, then, was the end of it, really: let's move on.

So I went to a bar, as I had promised Annette – not one of my usuals; I mean I'd been there before, but it was hardly a regular: near Holland Park, around that way. And I settled myself into a corner – ordered a glass of champagne for the purposes of dipping my upper lip into it, time to time, and unconcernedly set to surveying the scene with I hope a deceptively professional eye. I wasn't, to be frank with you, at all in the mood. Sometimes, the spirit took me – I relished the prospect of unleashing all of my mustered charm upon a stray and receptive (or otherwise) young woman: see if I could inveigle her without recourse to my portable pharmacy. But this night, well . . . the truth of the matter is that I couldn't, could I (well could *you*?), rid my mind of a huge and growing, malignant, concern: the death of Lucinda, and the ridding of her body. That and the shadow of Hanson, the aberrant policeman – and muzzled for how much longer? I do feel I am in danger. And oh yes of course we were *clever* – Emerald, she runs things so tightly; Annette, she holds the girls in the palm of her hand; Tumulty – he's swift and silent and quite without mercy; and me – I cover my tracks. But all it takes is just one lapse, one infinitesimal error – even an unforeseen act of God: a shard of lightning that could in an instant flash us up into a white and stark and then luminous visibility . . . that's all it will take. It is only a matter of when. Emerald, she would never dream of concession; it is Annette's instinct, I think, to deny – to blindly carry on; Tumulty – he will never break ranks: he'll brazen it out to the literal finish. It is only I, now, who would urge a headlong, rapid and silent withdrawal; and I realise – only now, it is only now I realise it – that my view alone, my actions, my arguments, my plaintive desperation (because it could easily come to that) . . . all of these are on a par with the breeze that would whip and hurl my petty words up into the higher air, and silence. I have to face it: at any moment, my life could be over. I sometimes – I'm that ashamed – I sometimes think it should be. And I do feel I am in danger.

So that is what I was thinking, sitting in the bar. And then I was thinking none of it: not a single atom. Because it was then that I saw her. It was then that my eyes were locked upon the girl. But what I felt, it was altogether different – so different, you see, from my customary dispassionate appraisal. This (is how I put it to myself) would appear to be something else entirely.

'Good evening. Would you think me most terribly rude if I were to ask you to join me . . .?'

She looked up – the greenest eyes you ever did see, coyly apologetic and yet glistening with not just a loitering sparkle of amusement, but even the hint of challenge to a man and woman of a duel. Wide the eyes were too, and deep enough to conceal a vast and spattered galaxy of secrets, each one of them so tantalising. One long finger now eased away the weight of her chestnut fringe from the snagging arch of a tapered eyebrow; the eyes could properly be said to be jade, you know – a thing I have never before seen. (Since I approached her table, it is possible that nearly a second now might well have ticked away.)

'My name is Clifford, by the way. May I then? Sit? Get you a drink?'

She appeared to be contemplating this; contemplating something.

'You have a very beautiful speaking voice, Clifford.'

'And . . . you. You too. Very.'

And yes by God: a perfect modulation – very close to the pace and timbre that I had spent, oh God – how many years trying so hard to perfect. But this woman: she was the real thing.

'So – may I sit? Yes? Get you a drink? I'm drinking champagne.'

'I see you are. Well actually, I'm sort of waiting for someone . . .'

And I was checked, momentarily. Can I have been wrong?

Surely not. Not I. No – I wasn't wrong. She was not that, not one of them: this woman, she was the real thing. And then I realised, with a flush of shame, that I was so far down the route now to wherever it was that I could possibly be headed, that I found it hard to accept even so plain and simple a statement as she had made at its own sweet value.

'. . . but it was only a girlfriend who seems to think nothing at all of standing me up. I should be delighted, Clifford, if you came and sat down with me. And I should love a glass of champagne – thank you. The annoyance is – I seem to be stuck on the top right-hand corner . . .'

I had been looking at her eyes (gazing, I suppose) – and at the curve of her jaw, the heavy swing of her hair; some part of my mind had taken in the sitting down part, the thing about champagne – but now I was jolted and set to concentration. And my God: she had on her knee a copy of *The Times*, folded into quarters, the crossword to the fore, a Montblanc ballpoint swinging now between her fingers. A very deep pink lacquer on her elegant nails; the same shade as the lipstick, it is hardly surprising to say. The mouth – just parted – had a fullness and promise that stirred me in a way . . . well, I would say I could barely recall it, but in truth I had never before known such a thing in my life.

I sat down next to her on the buttoned banquette, flew a hand wildly in the direction of the bar and set to furrowing my brow over the top right-hand corner.

'You see the problem is, I think, that you have put in "notice" – do you see? 9 across: you've got "notice". I think you'll find the answer is in fact "native". Yes? You had the N, the T, the I and the E . . .'

'Yes – and then I sort of guessed. I do that if it isn't going smoothly. Or quickly enough. You obviously know about cryptic crosswords. Are you cryptic, Clifford?'

468

'Mm? Oh God no, I wouldn't say that. But I do, you know –
dabble a bit. I'm quite a keen, um – cruciverbalist.'

'Mm. Which means crossword-doer, right?'

'Um – right. Yes it does. Impressive.'

'Oh no not really. Latin roots, isn't it? Ah – champagne.
Excellent.'

She is quite small, you know – which I rather like. But seemingly very long-limbed and graceful, all at the same time. Some
sort of a bouclé two-piece suit, she has on: coral, shot with cross-
flecks of lime. Her ankles made me weep . . . I had never even
focused on a woman's ankles before; but hers, they made me
sigh, made me yearn to encircle them lightly, the slim and the
cool of them in the coil of my fingers. When she inclines her
head, the hair just moves, and I glimpse a new small patch of her
full white cheek, and the hint of pink beneath; her scent is all
around me, and I feel my eyes half closed in the giddy delight of
it, and behind their reddened vision, my mind is dull and hot
and somehow roaring.

'What else do you do, Clifford? Apart from crosswords.'

'I – oh, not much. I'm a tailor. As a matter of fact.'

'Oh but I think that's *wonderful*. Oh I think that's just so exciting.'

'Do you? You do? Well. And, um – what about you? What do
you do?'

'I paint. Not houses. Pictures.'

'My goodness. I've never met. An artist before.'

'But *you* – you are an artist, Clifford. You cut – you make things.
We are both of us artists. Both of us.'

'Well. Yes. I suppose we are.'

And do I have any idea on earth as to just where all the time
went? I do not. Can I recall in extravagant detail precisely all that
we said? I cannot, of course. I was lost in the trance of her. We
drank champagne – we laughed, we spoke: I touched her hand.
During all those hours, those golden hours, when all the horror

receded – when everything and everyone but we two simply ceased to matter, or even exist – I felt expanded by something so insistent within me. I could not know what it was. And then I had it – and the kick of the truth, it nearly felled me. I held her hand. My face, now, so close to hers as to feel the brush of her hair, and still her scent continued to invade me. I spoke now, very carefully:

'You know – I love you. Do you know that . . .?'

'Mm. I do.'

'And – you? Could you – ?'

'I could. I do. I love you, Clifford. From the moment I saw you.'

My eyes were screwed into sadness, so joyous did I feel now: only tears could be true enough for a moment such as this.

'And . . . you don't think it strange . . .? This love?'

'I don't. I don't, Clifford.'

And I nodded, quite slowly, in time with the looming of something colossal and unstoppable.

'I don't . . . even know your name. I just am in bliss . . .'

And she laughed her laugh and kissed to me the word:

'Melissa . . .'

And that was the night when simple goodness, I can only suppose, came to disagree with me. I left Sonya. I just left her. She wailed and clawed at me as I walked through the door.

My boy, my only son – he is an idiot. I thought he was my Diamond, but now the truth is plain to me: he is no more than an idiot. I mean to say – how long has he known this woman?

Whatever her name is. How long? Weeks. That's all. A matter of no more than weeks – and now he says he is quite determined to marry the stupid girl. Whatever her name is. And I said to Annette – who at least has got some sense, at least you can say that about the girl – well, I says to her, how can he anyway? Get married. What about Sonya? His wife. I mean – has he completely forgotten her entire existence? She was good, Sonya: I approved of Sonya. And Annette, she says to me, well so did I – it is I, isn't it, who found her for him: Sonya, she always knew her place. I mean of course I used to *scorn* her: how could you not? It's quite easy to be harsh with people who are so very accepting, always. And then she says to me, Annette, but of course he *can* marry her, this new woman, whatever her name is, because the truth is I only rigged up a pretend marriage, you know, between Clifford and Sonya. She wanted it – she wanted it to be official; Clifford I don't think minded either way. So I got an actor to do it: I didn't want to tie him down, you see. Also, if I ever saw a real priest again, I'd be sick. Or kill him. But maybe, in the light of this, I should have done it properly. *Yes*, Annette, I says to her, you certainly should (because I had no idea, you know – no idea of all this: she tells me nothing. What on earth could have possessed her to get an *actor* to do it? I'm telling you – this girl: honestly). And then she says well look anyway it's done, isn't it? Too late now . . . Well, I says to her, maybe it is and maybe it isn't. I mean to say what in heaven's name is *wrong* with the boy? Hm? Why can't he see that his mother and his sister . . . we *love* him, for goodness sake. We're *family*, aren't we? Because heaven knows we none of us ever had *friends*, did we? Well there was dear Jean, of course – but even she, she was only taking pity on me: I see that now. Clifford, he had that school chum, didn't he, for a short while back then – what was his name? Anthony. Rather odd, I thought, Anthony, though Clifford, of course, he never saw it. And poor Annette, well – no one at all. So the three of us, you see – we're *made* for each other. So what makes him so suddenly blind to us? Well you don't have to tell me, do you? Perfectly plain for all to see: this *woman*. Whatever her name is.

And the *timing*! Maybe Clifford has forgotten – well, there's no maybe about it, is there really? Everything – but everything has just flown right out of his head since . . . all this business with the woman. So obviously he *has* forgotten – but *we* can't, can we? Annette and myself. And Edgar. We can't. Because we are poised, each one of us – and Clifford as well, if only he had the wit to see it – at the very sensitive centre of what I believe people refer to as a delicate balance. The situation – oh yes, very well, I grant you it has now been, will we say, contained. For the present, at least. But what if another of the girls should step out of line? And how much longer can it be before Hanson – before he passes down the line his information? To his pack of sharks. So many uncertainties, you see: so many uncertainties. To be fair, though, there are other aspects that have been going really rather well. Our better-known clients, for instance, they barely demurred when we requested a, um – surtax, let's say, in return for silence. I think they expect it, you know: they're rather wise. The girls too – they've accepted the lower cut (well how could they not?) in a similar spirit: the golden days, they knew they could not last for ever. I'm not actually sure that it is, you know . . . a *pack* of sharks, is it? Not a herd, though. Swarm? Can't be a swarm. Anyway.

But now, of course – courtesy of young Master Clifford – there's yet another uncertainty to add to the list: Sonya. She doesn't know very much – a combination of carelessness and stupidity – but certainly she has enough information to interest the police. How irresponsible, how terribly selfish of Clifford to set her against us. And she keeps on sending him letters, you see; he doesn't open them, but I do. Sometimes the handwriting is perfectly atrocious – a childlike and possibly drunken scrawl.

She protests her unending love, repeatedly – which I suppose is sincere, although it always struck me as being something closer to addiction, the helpless reliance upon his simple presence, and her somewhat pitiable eagerness to please. And she hints at consequences. Never threatens, exactly – never is specific (so not quite so stupid, then) – but she says that she will never divorce him (so the poor little lamb, you see – she of course has no idea, has she, that it was a jobbing actor who blessed their union) and that if he doesn't take her back, she will 'rock the boat' or 'make life inconvenient'. You see? Nothing one can really latch on to. Annette, she says to me, She's a loose cannon, we can't take the risk: she has to be dealt with. Oh good heavens *no* Annette, I says to her – you have to put all such ideas right out of your head. She's – too close. You can't order that sort of thing for someone who is *known* to you. That would be wicked. That would be a sin. And she just snorted, of course, Annette – well she always does, you see, whenever you say the word 'sin' to her, she just openly jeers at you. I sometimes do wonder, quite frankly, where I went wrong with her. And also, I says to her, were we to instruct Edgar to do any such thing, well I think he well might lose respect for us, you know. I mean they don't come any more loyal, as I do not have to tell you – he would do it, have it done, oh yes of course he would: but I think he might then regard us, oh – I don't know, through different eyes, maybe. The cure in this case, I think it could in the long run prove to be far more dangerous than the threat of the disease. And if we are to fix upon anything during these rather troubled times, then the long run must surely be it. Annette, she just says to me: You don't have to, you wouldn't have to even involve him, Tumulty: I'll do it. I'll do it myself. (Honestly – where does she get it all from? What has she become?) Oh no you will do nothing of the sort, my girl, and I don't want to hear another word about it. So there, for the present, it lies; the situation will require monitoring, of course: constant attention. Should one of Sonya's future letters actually contain the word 'police', then I fear we might be forced into thinking again. Which would be a terrible shame, because Sonya at base is so thoroughly blameless: so let us for now just hope that she continues to know her place.

What has always been a mystery to me – because one must remember that I have, of course, until quite latterly, led a very sheltered life – is why they do it: men, I mean. Not the act of congress itself, no no no – or its shabby and deviant offshoots – but why they seem to mind so terribly whether it is with one particular woman or another. I mean to say, assuming that the woman you are with is not quite utterly repellent, what on earth can be the point of risking so much, hurting so many, simply in order to do the very same sort of thing, well – elsewhere? That is why I hated Arthur, I suppose. I didn't know at the time that I hated him, of course; I knew that I wasn't meant to, because he was my husband. And so I did all the wifely things as an expression of love, and blithely assumed that he loved me back. Which he maybe did, in some sort of a way. But I knew all about his very seedy carryings-on. Well of course I did – wives do, you know: you don't need a Mrs Farlow to tell you, because you already know and you don't at all want to confront it. But towards the end, he was giving a whore the family's money, and from time to time unsmilingly raping his wife; which isn't very loving at all, is it really? And then there was Annette; we have never spoken of it, you know, but I am aware that there is always Annette. You would have thought that by killing the man, her anger and need for vengeance would have been long ago sated, but no, not a bit: it fuels her still. That, of course, and the nuns. Clifford, well – he had the slavish adoration of Sonya. He has Annette (which I think is rather sweet: it reminds me of when they were little). And she gives him the run of the girls. Enough, wouldn't you

474

say? For any man. But not, it seems, enough for my Clifford (and I have to remember to tell him that they've stopped doing them now, the Rice Krispies band – they're not giving them out any more, and we never did get a Snap; not a blue one, anyway. Rather sad. They've got Disney transfers now, which are not nearly so exciting). So as I say, he's turned his back on all of us, and all for the sake of a new bag of bones. Almost wilfully silly, isn't it? He barely visits me any more, you know; can't remember the last time we had together one of our lovely lunches. And nor, Annette tells me, is he bringing in any new girls any longer (and we need them, you know – we need them constantly: they are the lifeblood). Ah me. Well – we must keep a grip. Mustn't dwell, you see: have to keep a tight rein. Because if you start to fret, well – before you know where you are, you'll all be at sixes and sevens, and where, please tell me, can be the future in that? Because even at my age, I think I deserve one. A future. If only to make up for the fact that my past, it is so very recent. Life is maybe not, you know, for the young – not just, anyway. It is also for me.

But as to this wedding . . . Wedding! I can barely believe it. Stupid boy. I tried to forbid. I threatened to boycott the entire affair. All to no avail. Annette has arranged it – very small, registry office sort of a thing (well it had to be, really, in view of our black and collective state of sin, not to say Annette's aversion to priests), and I suppose I must go along with it then, must I? I'm not at all happy. I'm not sure I can do it. I think that this – this could be the thing that will break me. Maybe . . . I ought to have a little word with Edgar, you know. It's a school . . . ! That's the word – I'm sure it is: it's a *school* of sharks, not a pack. There. Isn't it funny? When things just come to you like that. No but wait . . . what was I . . .? Oh yes – I have it. Yes. Maybe I should. Have a quiet word with Edgar, over tea. About this woman. Whatever her name is. Maybe something here can be salvaged. Because Clifford: I need him to be my Diamond again. Because if he's with anyone, then it should be me. It should be me, you see.

♠

Look – I do well understand (I can hardly be blind to this) that up till now my so-called adult life has been far from, shall we say . . . conventional, though in some strange and other way it has nonetheless been so very highly ordered, you know – thoroughly compartmentalised, and yes, really quite empty. There was my childhood – fairly regular, I should have said, up until the point, maybe, when my sister killed my father – and this was followed by . . . do you know, I can barely remember it. A period in the gloaming – a time of nothing much at all, really, is about as high as I can rate it – and then . . . all of the rest. But to say now that my life has changed is so ramshackle and weak as to be incapable of fingering even the fringe – shadowing so much as the nature of the bubbling upheaval within and without me. It is rather as if – bear with me – this gleaming row of upright cylinders of quite distinct pigments – test tubes, say – have each been plucked from their rack and hurtled about wildly. I delight in the fluid and so very languid marbling, the heady luxury of so much gorgeous and idle, swimming colour: I am bright-eyed and dancing, caught up in its swirl and made giddy by its ceaselessly luscious and lazy stirrings (its undulating dazzle). Tracing the source of this light and fantastic cascade that carries me away with it – this is altogether more simple: Melissa. There. It is quite as easy as that.

From the evening of our first encounter, the two of us, we have been . . . well, you could almost quite literally term it inseparable. That very first night, we kissed so easily, and tried to depart. I think we were yearning for such sweet sorrow. Any tugging pang, though, was melted by heat. It had to be discarded in favour of a passion that was quite near fearfully uncontainable. We were gasping through the night, exhausted and in a kind of blank and childlike, joyful amazement. The thud of my heart seemed loud and unnatural, like a separate and quite mad being, kicking within me. The shock of her blood-heat, it made me cry out. And when yet again I gave myself wholly to the once more hurly-burly of so astonishing a rapture, it was as if she was most eagerly milking out of me all that I had to give, as I was urging all that was within me to liquefy and course on up and into her quite endlessly so that we might bond together in the ultimate fusion. And then we would just lie there together, adrift on a raft of our own – abstractedly stroking the other's damp and straying hair, our shoulders just stickily kissing. And then, for hours, I could watch her cheek and gaze at her neck and stare with fascination at the way in which each of her fingers would operate when she was stirring tea or smoothing back the counterpane. Each of her words – and then their inflexion – was to be treasured for so very much longer than it took her to say them. When we were, perforce, away from one another, I would lose the time in a gentle welter of just thinking and thinking of her: recalling each word, the cheek I had watched, her neck I had gazed at – see again with fascination the way in which each of her fingers would operate. I had a coral-coloured chiffon scarf, drenched in her, that I wrapped around my face and inhaled so deeply it made me spin. And then the minutes, the slow and aching minutes before we were to meet again – the light in her eyes and that briefest squeal when we did so. All was then lost in the physical impact, that coming together that annihilated the universe. And then, so pleased with each other as well as ourselves, we would settle back down again to frittering away yet another afternoon in that so sweet and blissful way that is only known to lovers.

'Shall I make us something to eat . . .?'

'But then you would have to leave me.'

'Oh Clifford . . .! Kiss me. I do so love you. But shall I? Are you hungry? I'm not. Not really. Never am.'

'Nor I. Don't need it. Just need you.'

'What time is it . . .?'

'Don't know. Don't mind. Are you painting today? Do you want to?'

'I should. I suppose. I do in a way, want to. I want to have painted. But I don't want to . . . *do* anything. Do you know?'

'Mm. I do. I don't, Melissa, ever want to do anything at all, not ever, except to be with you. I love you. I so much love you.'

'Oh Clifford . . . But we *are*, aren't we? Together all the time. We don't do anything. We don't do anything else.'

'I know. And it's wonderful. But I'm so pleased we're going to do it . . . properly. Silly word – but you know what I mean. I want it all to be . . . well: clean. Just the two of us. Broken away from all of the rest. Children. I want to be married to you, Melissa, and be a father. I've never even thought of that before. But I do.'

'Oh I'm so happy, Clifford. I've never been married before. Have you? I've never asked.'

'Me? No. Married? No. There's only you. I don't need anyone else in the entire world. I don't actually remember the last time I was with anyone but you. I can't imagine why I ever was . . .'

'But Clifford . . . I don't – want anyone hurt. I don't quite know what it is I'm saying – it's just maybe a feeling. But I won't ever hurt anyone. You do know, Clifford, that I have no limit? For love – for you – I would happily do anything. But, my

478

Clifford . . . Clifford of mine . . . you must know too I won't ever do that.'

'You have no idea how wonderful it is to hear that. I love you, Melissa.'

'I know. And I love you too.'

And then the spike of desire would blind us to talk, and I would hurl myself into this new and latest rush of our gorgeous selfishness: I fed on it, as if starved and deserving. True love, you know . . . it is the strangest of them all.

♠

I suppose I'm glad . . . yes, yes I am glad, I am . . . that I've arranged the whole of this for dear Clifford – for Cliff, and this new and sudden, vibrant big love of his. I've only met her the once, this Melissa (which sounds, I couldn't help thinking – didn't say it to Clifford – rather like the sort of name that one of my girls might have chosen). I'd organised a little tea party, just a short while back – I thought it might be a good way of bring-ing together Cliff, myself, our mother . . . and that's about all, really; to call it a family would be maybe stretching things. We could, I suppose, include Tumulty – he is, after all, so much in love with me (and I do so wish that he wouldn't be). But our mother, our 'Mummy', who used to be so very sweet and unas-suming, it amazes me to remember – her face became blotched and spattered with crimson and she was screaming at me when I mentioned the proposal. And all my protestations that it was only a *tea* party, for heaven's sake, were met with a fury that is never far from her, these days. It is *not*, Annette, she seethed –

when she had later calmed down sufficiently to at least be coherent – it is *not* just a tea party, it is a *permission*, it is a *licence* for this woman, whatever her name is, to coolly and smilingly steal from me my *diamond*. And I blinked at her and said, Um – excuse me? Your *what*, did you say? Your *diamond*? What in hell does that mean? And she just brushed all that away: Oh, Annette – you wouldn't understand: it's just something between Clifford and myself. And I did not say that it would not be the first time for there to have been something between the two of them; there had never, of course, been anything between the two of *us*, however: my mother, she never had time for me. She scorned me, I imagine, because I took after my father. But I *killed* the man for the sake of all of us: what more did she want from me? I thought she might be grateful, but she never did seem so. I think that's why she sought out and executed that ancient and evil old nun, the swine Joanna: it was not, as she suggested at the time, merely a demonstration of capability. It was not even a gift. Here was simply the settling of a score – a means to the resumption of the status quo, before she deftly set about becoming for the very first time in her life, in control. Well: all history. Anyway, she would not hear of the tea party – was, at the time, determined to boycott the wedding itself, but I hope she might relent. Now that the day has come, I don't think she'll find it within her to stay away: she could not bear it if Clifford came to even slightly not liking her. I did warn her, though – and it takes a steely nerve these days, you know, to warn my mother of anything – but I made it plain to her that there was to be no bad action. Is, I believe, how I put it (because I well know now just how much she is capable of) and I made Tumulty swear to me that he had accepted no instruction from her for any sort of drastic undertaking. He was, at first, evasive – but eventually he grunted out his agreement: I think I can trust him. I used never to have any doubt upon the matter, but my power over Tumulty, that too has been usurped, or maybe rendered. I like to think that he went to my mother because he could, after all, be going nowhere with me. No. No no. That's wrong: I do not like to think it at all.

So anyway – I met her, Melissa: we three took tea. I do not know which of us was the more nervous. She is good-looking enough, I suppose; she clearly loves him – in a way that is maybe more true, if I can put it like that – more true, yes – than the ways in which Clifford has ever been loved before; because unlike all the rest of us, he has never in his life been without it, love, in one form or another. And of course I was jealous. For the very first time. Clifford and I, we have not lain together for so many weeks; he says we will again. I say When; he says Soon. I wonder. Anyway – I decided to be large. I would arrange and pay for the entire shenanigan (and Christ it's expensive; never mind – I love him). And look – quite apart from any other aspect of this, how could he, Clifford, arrange anything at all? He wouldn't have the first idea of even where to begin. Well would he? He's never had to, you see: the golden boy, in many ways. A diamond, if you like. So I have organised this rather spacious suite in the Savoy, overlooking the river, for the sort of reception afterwards; I've just been to look it over – very nice, very nice indeed. Shades of cream, including all the flowers and napery. The wedding itself is in a very pretty building quite nearby, all decked out with the palest pink roses and generous swags of greenery and ribbon. Afterwards, the two of them are going to Venice (*Excellent*, said our mother, when I told her: maybe she'll drown in the street, this woman, whatever her name is). And the registrar, he's real: the least I could do, the second time around – well third, really, if you count that girl, that fellow refugee of mine, from all those years ago. What was her name again? Because Cliff, he told me later about all that nonsense on the ferry – his fevered desperation for the hit of first sex: we laughed about it, it was all so absurd. Mary. That was her name. Who I imagine by now either is driven mad by nine poor Irish children and a forgotten trail of unsuitable men, or else she is dead: long dead. She was never a survivor, Mary. I used to tease Cliff that one of the girls he brought back – pretty thing, Irish – that she might be his daughter from all those years ago. He laughed, but he was rattled, I think.

Poor Cliff, he was stunned when I asked him who, on this day of days, was to be his best man. Well God, Annette – I just don't know . . . anyone. Will *you*, Annette? Will *you* be my best man? I just laughed. Later, he told me he had tracked down his old school friend Anthony Hirsch – the rag trade boy – and had been amazed to find that Anthony, richer than ever now, apparently, was living in Brighton with a designer called Trevor. Well of course I could have told Cliff about Anthony's tendencies from pretty much the day I first met him: his enthusiasm for girls, it clearly was masking so profound a terror. Cliff, fairly interestingly, was at first appalled and then quite openly disgusted by this new revelation ('I knew we weren't blood brothers', he kept on muttering: God knows what that meant). Eventually he decided that Tumulty would serve – that he would be the best man. It concentrates the mind, though, doesn't it? An event such as this. When members of a family begin to think about guests, and so on, and discover that there can in fact be none, none at all, because not one of us ever really knew anyone else . . . ever. Maybe why Cliff is so determined to change all that; maybe why I decided to help him. So there'll just be Tumulty, a few of his men, a few of my girls (all of Clifford's favourites; whether he uses them again or not is entirely his own affair) . . . myself . . . and maybe our mother: we shall have to see. I asked Melissa whether her family might attend, and she said she didn't yet know; perhaps another orphan, literally or otherwise. Maybe why between herself and Clifford there has been such immediate impact.

So. The time has come. Cliff, he's at the Savoy, thinking his thoughts, whatever they be. Tumulty's there with him. They'll be leaving in, oh – ten, fifteen minutes, I should have said. Melissa, she's with me – just downstairs. Oh look I know it's only a registry wedding and everything, but I don't know . . . I thought it would have looked somehow rather crass, if she and Clifford had arrived together. This way, there can be at least a modicum of ceremony. She is wearing a cream two-piece silk suit, Melissa; sort of a hat thing. Quite nice, I suppose. At the reception afterwards there is a distinct danger of her vanishing into the surrounding decor, but there: never mind. Myself, I am wearing red. Rather predictable, and maybe vulgar, but there it is. (I had the shoes dyed specially to match.) Well: everything is set. So let's just get on with it, shall we? See what happens.

Clifford had never before sat in the back of the Bentley. It was, he adjudged – as he fooled with the purple orchid aslant in his buttonhole (Annette sent it over) – roomy enough, though not maybe too satisfactory for a very long journey. This journey, however, was to be only minutes. In total – he had computed this while sipping a glass of calming champagne in the suite at the Savoy – he was less than an hour away from a brand-new and so much purer and more hopeful way of life. He did so hope that Emerald, his mother, would lay aside her fury and attend this wedding. He had had to stop visiting her, so frightening were her eyes as she screamed and screamed at him that it should be *her* – it was *she* who should have her Diamond, and not this stupid other woman, whatever her name was. She could be so very frankly terrifying, these days; when last he saw her, all he had felt was fear.

He resettled himself now into the Bentley's cushions and gazed at the back of Tumulty's head as he swung the nose of the car now into a driveway; the thick roll of muscle that bulged out over his collar, already quite livid, was forced into crimson as he strained his neck both this way and that, the better to negotiate the twin brick gateposts, and then the final sweep and curl to the portico. The gentle grumble of the engine was cut now, and Tumulty was easing himself sideways and out of the driving seat and then he opened the rear door and just stood there in silence. Clifford stepped out – his stomach and guts all balled up into a tender mass of fluttering shyness and keen anticipation, undercut though it was by the stabbing urge to run and duck (a feeling he well knew from when he had ever stood poised upon the verge of committing himself to just anything at all, no matter how welcome).

The heels of his shoes were rhythmically clacking on the black and white chequerboard as he doggedly shadowed the bulk of Tumulty down the length of a corridor. Then it was just the soles he was hearing, lightly slapping the stone and shallow treads of a curving stairway; Clifford was just two steps behind Tumulty, glancing downwards and marvelling, he didn't know why, at the gleaming and distorted floor tiles as they spiralled away from him and seemed quite suddenly so very far below. As Tumulty stood waiting for him at the balustraded gallery, Clifford noticed briefly a seemingly stunted old woman limping across the black and white floor beneath him like an animated pawn, bearing before her a stack of files and oblivious of the small and white and quite egg-like little patch of her scalp, so rudely unconcealed amid its teased and slickly spittled bird's-nest. She was gone now.

Tumulty opened wide a heavy door and stood then with his

484

back against the jamb to prevent it from sighing and springing back shut again; it was all Clifford could do to squeeze himself around and past the sheer and immutable size of the man, forcing himself to hunch and shrivel so that he might just about insinuate himself further into the large and light-filled room beyond. He glanced up at Tumulty, and saw in his face only the usual absence of expression; it had often seemed to Clifford that the huge and looming Tumulty, behind dead eyes, was willing himself into a state of invisibility. He was assailed by the scent of the roses that were all around him, before he had even time to set eyes upon the startling swags and bundles and tightly clustered bursts of them. And then he saw a dazzle of shimmering red – Annette, smiling in a way, and beckoning him on. She looked, Clifford was thinking, really quite wonderful; and what was it? That way she was smiling? Alluring – it was alluring, yes it was, and very much so. She was flanked by the girls – Dolores, Anastasia, Marilyn (lovely Marilyn) and one or two others. They each of them looked like any man's fantasy; they were smiling and softly giggling and were waving their greetings to Clifford with a flurried succession of fingers, the tips of all of them   scarlet and gleaming, sensationally taloned. A small man – hot and shifty, and presumably the registrar – was glancing at them often, his grin held rigid in a wild delight and an utter disbelief that these girls, they could be smiling right back at him. He looked nervously and often too at the four-square wall of Tumulty's men, all in black, their hands softly crossed before them. No one else was here.

Clifford walked over to Annette – smiling and nodding unnaturally to those either side of her – aware of Tumulty plodding closely behind him.

'All right, Cliff? All ready?'

'Oh God, Annette. Yes, I suppose so. Of course I am. It all

looks so wonderful, Annette. And the Savoy. Wonderful. Thank you so much.'

They were both of them whispering, for one reason or another.

'Oh Christ's *sake*, Cliff! What on earth do you mean "thank you"? I love you, don't I? I love you.'

'I know you do, Annette. And I love you too. What, um – what do we do now?'

'Well we wait, don't we? We wait for the bride-to-be. She is clearly exercising her prerogative to be late. Is she bringing anyone along, do you know Cliff? Mother or something?'

'Don't know. She didn't say. But, um – talking of mothers . . .?'

'Mm, well – your guess is as good as mine, I'm afraid Cliff. I saw her yesterday, and she was still in a state of fulmination.'

'Really? oh dear. Fulmination – that's a very good one . . .'

'I like it. Oh look. Cliff – look who's arrived . . .!'

So Clifford did, he did that – he looked across immediately in the direction of the door . . . and there she was: Melissa. His heart gave a kick, and then it softened and warmed. She looked so very beautiful: he had, he now realised – and just since yesterday – missed her so terribly. His eyes were swimming now quite hopelessly as they locked into hers. She walked towards him so demurely, her face maybe tugging hard in the direction of composure, and yet so overcome by the blaze of delight.

'Hello, Clifford . . .'

'Oh Christ *hello*, Melissa. You look – you just look so—!'

'This is Rebecca.'

And Clifford then noticed a woman beside her.

'Rebecca is my friend. I didn't want to be alone. But I didn't want anyone else to come.'

'Well – welcome, Rebecca.'

And Rebecca, she smiled and looked down.

And then there was a new and reedy voice in the air.

'Um – excuse me, ladies and gentlemen . . .' tried the registrar gently – glancing over again at Tumulty's men and somehow managing with just the tic in his eye to apologise quite fulsomely for having ever been born. 'But are we, um . . . ready to proceed, do we think . . .?'

Clifford now was squeezing hard Melissa's hand; he looked over once and glumly at the still ajar door, and then he nodded his agreement. It was Annette's quite sudden intake of breath that made him quickly look back there, and his face now melted into relief: she had come. She had come after all. The deep and vivid green of her costume, it winked and sparkled as she came towards him.

'Oh *thank* you, Mummy – so much for being here . . .!'

Her eyes were red and rimmed; she had been recently crying – Clifford could see that, in his helplessness.

'Emerald . . .' she cautioned, so softly.

'Yes!' Clifford laughingly agreed. 'Emerald. Of course. Look, um . . . Annette – tell the registrar, will you? We won't be long – we can start in just a minute, all right? Look, um – this is Melissa. Melissa – this is my mother.'

Emerald was trying on her kindest smile; Annette looked on in amusement, and Clifford just stood there and held his breath. And then, very slowly, Emerald extended her hand – which was grasped by a tearful Melissa, so very eagerly. Everyone, now – save Tumulty and his men – seemed suddenly so terribly *pleased*; even the registrar – agog again at the girls – appeared to be not quite so much in fear of his life. So the short and immediate scream was so thoroughly unexpected as to rattle just everyone badly, and Tumulty strode forward now towards Emerald as she just stood there and whimpered badly, now her scream was over, the one quivering finger extended in shock, the pain and surprise in her eyes giving way now to a blackly glittering fury as Clifford just jabbered and was wild-eyed and was pleading alternately with Annette and with his mother for just any one of

487

them to please will you tell him what on earth was *wrong* – why did you scream, Mummy? Are you sick? What is wrong? *Tell* me . . .?! And all he could do – as Tumulty held on protectively to each of Emerald's shoulders – was dumbly follow the trajectory of her wavering finger, follow it down to the tremble of Melissa's two juddering hands, as her frightened face was imploring Clifford for immediate help and just any sort of clarification here. And the very next instant, Emerald was shrieking – wildly and uncontrollably.

'How dare you! How dare you! How *dare* you . . .'

And Tumulty was having trouble even holding her now as her face became contorted and she clawed at the air in her frantic attempts to get up close to Melissa. The girls were gasping in unease and incredulity, and Tumulty's men were poised and alert in a taut state of readiness, though sure that the boss for the moment could handle it. The registrar – and no one had noticed – had already scuttled out of the room. Rebecca had backed against the wall.

'That *ring* . . .!' Emerald continued to rave – and Clifford now was helping Tumulty restrain her. 'That was for my *Diamond*! Not for you! Oh Clifford how could you ever *dream* of it . . .?!'

'But it's only a *diamond*, Mummy – I had it made up. I think it looks beautiful! I didn't think you'd—'

And then she somehow broke free – shrugged away from a startled Tumulty – and was tugging hard at Melissa's so stiff and frozen fingers as Melissa stood wide-eyed and yelping at Clifford, and he was now so near hysterical in his muffed and useless efforts to prise away his mother's clawing hands from the jangle of fingers of his bride-to-be – and so when the door of the room was hurtled open and it crashed against the wall, how could anyone be aware amid all the uproar as Tumulty, huddled around Emerald and trying to just ease her away while causing no harm, grunted out once as he was shouldered away and more

488

mad hands now were yanking at Clifford and gouging at his face. The men, as one, moved in – but too late to stop a fire-eyed and maddened Sonya from swinging her fists quite wildly at his face and Clifford – just seeing that blaze in her eyes – he stumbled to the door and she dragged at him as he did this and he was staggering quite badly and thought then that he had lost it but he righted himself somehow and fell out of the room as he pushed away at Sonya as Tumulty, now he had her – but still her arms were windmilling about him and the sullen ache in Clifford's hip as he was rammed now and hard against the railing of the gallery made him sick and more scared and his head now set itself to floating away as all the visions before him were screwed around into a dizzied distortion and his body was swung so swiftly over the parapet and he heard his screams and those of all the others and now it was only Sonya who was holding him back by his two sloppy wrists as his feet were kicking out madly as he dangled in the void and he was roaring in amazement and then sheer horror as one of the men now got a hold of Sonya's hair and punched her hard and in the face and as she folded and collapsed, the man just grabbed a hold of Clifford's shoulder and now it was his mother above him and her tear-soaked and quite contorted lips were making brief and ugly noises as she scrabbled around wildly and held on to his arm – and Clifford was sobbing and spinning quite helplessly as so far below him the cluster of dwarves was gasping, and cowed. He was choking – he was belching for breath – and he bellowed now as Annette and Melissa, he knew that they had him, they were hauling him up alongside of Tumulty as his mother stood quivering, her hands like paper. Sonya, she struck out hard now with her legs and feet and Annette skittered over and brought Melissa with her and Tumulty was kicking out grimly as Clifford's mother gave out the one shriek as she made a frenzied lunge for him and gripped at only nothing as the imploring and so terrified eyes of her son fell away into the air amid a chorus of screaming and he was jarred and stunned as he thumped on to the jutting of the ledge and tried so hard to hang there – but feebly now and faint, amid a twisting of giddiness. Annette was tilting down the stairs and kneeling forward now at the level of the ledge, her face so bent and flattened against the iron of the banister as her taut and aching arms were flailing and plucking at clothes, and now they had the warmth of Clifford's hand – and then the hot slip of it as her terrified eyes were shocked into locking into his final supplication as he spun away and outward to fly in silence, and then he crumped down on to the ground below.

Annette was glazedly staring, strung up into a smothering deafness as the screeching all about her was splintered and shrill. She was breathless as she stumbled her way up the stairs, and she saw then that Tumulty's men, they had the bitch, they had her now, and then she attacked the fastly pinioned Sonya with so pitiless a ferocity that might never again have been unleashed, and as she battered and kicked and slammed her way into Sonya she screamed into her face that she was the committer of a mortal *sin*, did she see?! And that she had broken now the ultimate commandment and that in vengeance for this, for killing before my very eyes the one and only love of my life, the Lord God will have you burn in Hell fire and torment for ever and ever and ever and *ever* . . .! Annette fell back then, quite overcome by this paroxysm of so visceral an agony and lay sprawling on her back, rigid and then convulsive, kicking and striking out fiercely at any frenzied person who should be stooping down to help her. Then she elbowed away any touch or restraint and tumbled her way down the endless stairs, falling over the last of them in her terrible keenness to just get close. And now she hauled herself over to where Clifford was lying so still, and found her mother already kneeling and crouched low above him, and Melissa, she was weeping and seemingly deranged and stroking so hard at his outflung arm, as if in its inertia it was in some way to blame for all of this. The tears of the three of them were falling down now on to his averted face, crushed and askew against the ground. His skull was empurpling and seemed so distended, his hair hot-wet and matted up into spikes. Annette saw the perfectly delineated rivulets of blood snaking their way down so gracefully from this embedded crown of thorns; and now the women, they each of them just clung on to his body.

THE BEGINNING

But. Not a body. Not dead yet. Of at least this much, then, I remain aware, as I continue to lie here quite uselessly. So that is what brought me to this – and maybe it could have been, what? Merely a few hours ago, who can say? Not I. But not years, as first I had believed. Had my memory failed to force me back to the very beginning, had it not then imperiously propelled me forward, I might never have known.

Those people who were clustered all about me, they seem to have gone. I am aware now only of a dim and humming room, with a faint and green glimmering light just somewhere over there, look – I don't know how distant, and maybe to the left or right of me. All, then – everything I not just had but hoped for – just everything has been snatched away from me now, and so very brutally. And of all the people to have done it: Sonya. I mean to say – of all of them, how strange that it had to be her. Because no matter how many years I was with her, you know, she was never anything that could be said to be approaching *pivotal* – no no, not Sonya. Sonya, well – she was just *there*, that's all. And then she wasn't. And then she was again – though very briefly; I fully expect that she's dead, now: she won't have come out of it. Whether she loved me or not. Those people all around me . . . I think they must have been the others: the survivors. The woman and the wedding to me that never quite took place . . . in common, then, with the other two. Because I do see now, of course – and how very strange it is – that far from having been a trigamist, I was never married at all: not once in my life. So I was wrong about that: my memory has shown to me the error.

And Annette. She must be so aware of the enormity of what has befallen us all. And she will know, Annette, that this word, it has nothing to do with scale, and all to do with the darkest extreme of evil: Annette will know this. And she and Melissa, they are both lost to me now. It can be no secret as to which of them, at the end, was the love of my life. And then there is my Mummy – the blackly glittering lady, my gleaming Emerald: the only other woman who ever truly mattered. Well. There it is. Now I am alone. On my own. A maverick. With only God left to me, if I could only just believe in any such fabulous being. Then at least it could be the two of us: the jailer and the jailed. Because I am seeing other things now, and I shrink back, believe me: I try to deny them. I was concerned by my lack of anger at all that has brought me down; I wondered why sadness had yet to take me, in the light of the loves that have all been stolen. But I am beginning to see now that all my fear and despair, they are to be channelled elsewhere. Because I am not dying. My body – all of it – that is gone, long gone. That thing, it might as well still be lying abandoned on the floor, where I last lay stunned (no part of it will move, despite my urgent bidding; I should be hot or cold, though I find I am neither thing). But this mind of mine, it is not even fading. I want the end, but it is not coming; I try to kill panic as I yearn for the end – for where else (at the beginning) can I run to for shelter? It will always be the beginning, now – and I am doomed to go back and back, until so much memory heaves me forward to where I find myself now, just lying here, quite uselessly. And then I shall return once more. My memories – which I am destined to plunder, again and again, and into eternity – are all that's left me. I am locked into me. And I have to recall that my father – diabolically, and by one who newly loathed him – was precipitated into the blink of space before crashing, and instantly welcomed into the bliss of oblivion; so he must have been, then, more deserving than I. And all that is left is the rising terror, while still I beg the dark for the mercy of derangement, that of course will be denied me. For I am not old. The decades, all those tens and tens of years, they are yet to come. The past is to be lived and relived, for all of my future. I know now that this is not the closing: these are not the very last moments of my life. Here is simply the beginning of the rest of it. Simply the beginning.

Not the end.